HOLLYWOOD CONFIDENTIAL

An Inside Look at the Public Careers and
Private Lives of Hollywood's Rich and Famous

Coral Amende

A PLUME BOOK

PLUME
Published by the Penguin Group
Penguin Books USA Inc., 375 Hudson Street, New York, New York 10014, U.S.A.
Penguin Books Ltd, 27 Wrights Lane, London W8 5TZ, England
Penguin Books Australia Ltd, Ringwood, Victoria, Australia
Penguin Books Canada Ltd, 10 Alcorn Avenue, Toronto, Ontario, Canada M4V 3B2
Penguin Books (N.Z.) Ltd, 182–190 Wairau Road, Auckland 10, New Zealand

Penguin Books Ltd, Registered Offices: Harmondsworth, Middlesex, England

Published by Plume, an imprint of Dutton Signet,
a division of Penguin Books USA Inc.

First Printing, March, 1997
10 9 8 7 6 5 4 3 2 1

 REGISTERED TRADEMARK—MARCA REGISTRADA

LIBRARY OF CONGRESS CATALOGING-IN-PUBLICATION DATA
Amende, Coral.
Hollywood confidential : an inside look at the public careers and
private lives of Hollywood's rich and famous / Coral Amende.
p.   cm.
Includes index.
ISBN 0-452-27791-4
1. Motion picture actors and actresses—United States—
Miscellanea.   2. Television actors and actresses—United States—
Miscellanea.   3. Celebrities—United States—Miscellanea.
I. Title.
PN1998.2.A44   1997
791.43'028'092273—dc21   96–39770
                                                         CIP

Printed in the United States of America
Set in Souvienne
Designed by Coral Amende

BOOKS ARE AVAILABLE AT QUANTITY DISCOUNTS WHEN USED TO PROMOTE PRODUCTS OR SERVICES.
FOR INFORMATION PLEASE WRITE TO PREMIUM MARKETING DIVISION, PENGUIN BOOKS USA INC.,
375 HUDSON STREET, NEW YORK, NEW YORK 10014.

(The following page constitutes an extension of this copyright page.)

Muchas gracias, amigos
Jim and Norma Amende, Janet Herrin, Malcolm Knight, Michael Rees, Teressa Rowell, Thomas White, Nancy Yost

Clip art courtesy of:
Aris Entertainment
Art Parts
Broderbund
CD Titles
Corel Corporation
Image Club Graphics
Imsi Corporation
New Vision Technologies Inc.
T/Maker Company
Visual Software, Inc.

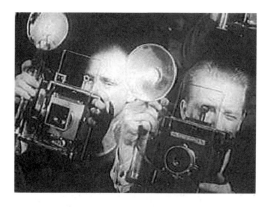

Courtesy of **Celebrity Photo**:
Heather Locklear (title page): John Paschal
Demi Moore (page 16): Janet Gough
Sharon Stone (page 28): Scott Downie
Tori Spelling (page 32): John Paschal
Pamela Anderson Lee (page 34): Kevin Winter
Melanie Griffith and Antonio Banderas (page 39): John Paschal
Arnold Schwarzenegger (page 40): John Paschal
Drew Barrymore (page 48): Scott Downie
Keanu Reeves (page 68): Janet Gough
Tori spelling (page 75): John Paschal
Halle Berry (page 80): Celebrity Photo
Planet Hollywood opening (page 93): Janet Gough
Bruce Willis and Anna Nicole Smith (page 109): Janet Gough
Elizabeth Berkley (page 118): Scott Downie
Jim Carrey and Clint Eastwood (page 131): John Paschal
Barbra Streisand (page 144): John Paschal
Sharon Stone (page 158): John Paschal
Oprah Winfrey and Stedman Graham (page 161): Miranda Shen
Brad Pitt and Gwyneth Paltrow (page 191): John Paschal
Kevin Costner (page 193): Janet Gough
Dennis Rodman (page 209): Steve Trupp
Pamela Anderson Lee (page 243): Miranda Shen
Tom Hanks (page 285): Kevin Winter
Heather Locklear (page 322): Scott Downie

To the Cardiac Department at St. Vincent's Hospital,
New York City

Contents

1 Babes in the 'Wood

2 Here's Looking at You

3 This Business We Call Show

4 Certifiable Proof of Inanity

Lifestyles of the Nouveau Riche and Frivolous

6 Risqué Business

7 Naughty by Nature

8 Sick and Tired

HOLLYWOOD
CONFIDENTIAL

1

Babes in the 'Wood

When a child abruptly quadruples her family's income, some changes may be expected.
— Shirley Temple

"Hey, Drew, you want to get me an autograph too?" [my father] said. "How about putting it on a check?"
—Drew Barrymore

hollywood:

one heck of a tough town. It's difficult enough to break into showbiz for grown-ups, who have at least a few of their wits about them. But for child performers, fame can be a long, grueling ride where the outcome is often unhappy. Like **Jodie Foster** and **Winona Ryder**, many young actors have a stable support system—mom, dad, and other family members—to steer them through the capricious twists and turns of early stardom. But driven, overly ambitious stage parents seem to be the rule in Lotusland, and this attitude can't help but rub off on their children, whose evident precociousness can be chalked up to a combination of growing up too fast, excessive professional and financial responsibilities placed upon too-small shoulders, and the lavish pampering and exorbitant praise heaped upon the successful. Ill-prepared for the pressures of stardom and the inevitable decline in their cuteness and popularity over time, many pint-size performers end up with drug habits or even behind bars once the limelight stops shining on them.

Go away, little GRRRL

I'd scare her, I'd bribe her, I screamed at her. . . . I had to feed her her lines one at a time. I couldn't believe it when she won the Oscar.
—Peter Bogdanovich, on directing Tatum O'Neal in *Paper Moon*

SON OF A BITCH PART

Thrusting one's child into the biz is one way of making up for a parent's own unrealized aspirations. The mothers of **Stefanie Powers, Carol Burnett, Bob Hope, Sally Field, Bing Crosby, Teri Garr,** and **Billy Dee Williams** nursed ambitions of becoming superstars, as did lovely **Anna** (mother of George) **Hamilton**. Norma Desmond wannabe **Jacqueline Stallone** is another who capitalized on her son's (Sylvester's, not Frank's) success and realized at least a modicum of her earlier ambition, becoming a "celebrity astrologer" and all-around crank. (When asked about her origins, Stallone slyly cracked she was "half French and half Martian.")

Notoriously bossy stage parents shaped the lives and careers of **Judy Garland, Betty Grable, Fay Wray, Bing Crosby, Bette Davis, Natalie Wood,** and **Liz Taylor,** whose manipulative mom would stand behind the cameras and cue the young girl like an animal trainer with hand signals. **Shirley Temple**'s mother was convinced she was owed the lion's share of credit for her darling daughter's dazzling deeds, going so far as to assert that, "Long before she was born I tried to influence her future life by association with music, art, and natural beauty. Perhaps this prenatal preparation helped make Shirley what she is today." ꞪꞦL-LO! **Jolie Gabor,** sister of better-known sibs **Zsa Zsa** and **Eva,** claims if they hadn't been pretty girls, their mother would have "drowned [us] like little dogs." And the much disliked duo of **Robin Givens** and mother **Ruth Roper** had a close

WORKS

BREAST

In her seventies, my mother decided to have her breasts lifted. I tried to dissuade her. I said, "It's ridiculous at your age." She said, "If I meet a man, he'll certainly want me to have attractive breasts." I said, "I suppose he would." And she said, "Everyone's doing it—why can't I?" Then the doctor told her she could die on the operating table. She said, "Don't worry about that. If the worst happens, you'll bury me topless."
                                                                            —George Hamilton

M⊙MMY NEAREST

All I knew was that my mother was away
and she was in front of the mirror a lot.
—Melanie Griffith, on growing up as
the daughter of actress Tippi Hedren

symbiosis that lasted well into—and out of—Givens' marriage to barbarous boxer **Mike Tyson**, who, post-divorce, bitterly said they'd only been after his money all along (in fact, Roper once announced, "If I'm not involved Michael doesn't fight").

After child star **Lauren** (*Father Knows Best*) **Chapin** gave up acting, her mother disowned her, though not before taking her to court for—and winning—a share of her residuals. Similarly, **Mary Astor** was sued for nonsupport by her parents, as were **Gene Tierney**, **Paulette Goddard**, and **Veronica Lake**. And **River Phoenix**, whose hippie-dippie parents raised their brood in the money-hungry Children of God religious cult, paid a heavy price for being his family's chief breadwinner. Best buddy and fellow actor **Ethan Hawke** remembers "the really heavy trip his family laid on him. To them, he was the Second Coming, the man of the house at age fourteen. Maybe that's why River always took himself so seriously."

In the pantheon of psycho stage parents, however, no one can top terrifying **Teri Shields**, mother of "Nothing comes between me and my Calvins" **Brooke**. A chronic alcoholic, fractious Teri's heavy boozing and bestial behavior resulted in scrapes with the law, embarrassing blowups on the sets of her daughter's movies, and even a punch to little Brookie's face. Her "career management" was dubious at best, leading to starring roles for Brooke in dogs like *Tilt* and *Just You and Me, Kid* and questionable "modeling" assignments like "Sugar and Spice," a *Playboy* pictorial for which Brooke posed at age ten. (Fee? $45.) Terrible Teri also got herself hired as a "producer" on the pathetic desert epic *Sahara* ("Any resemblance to a good movie is just a mirage," sniped film critic Leonard Maltin), for which she was well compensated: a quarter million dollars' worth, to

NECESSITY IS THE M⊙THER ⊙F INVENTION

I actually did a commercial with my mother when I was
six months old—her first audition back after she had had
me. They wanted me. She said, "You don't get the baby
without me."
—Samantha (*Pump Up the Volume*) Mathis

be exact. Brooke has since grown up (physically, anyway) but remains firmly in mama's thrall. "I'm very impressionable as far as my mom is concerned," she was once heard to say. "If we're sharing something to eat, she can say, 'This doesn't taste very good,' and I'll be like, 'Blecch, blecch, you're right.' Even if I liked it just a second before."

Though Brooke has emerged relatively unscathed from her bout with child stardom, the same cannot be said of *Home Alone* hero **Macaulay Culkin**. Even at a very early age, the celebritot appeared to have star behavior down pat: "I'm not crazy about the stuff," he murmured disdainfully after inking a lucrative endorsement deal with Sprite, "but money is money."

The apple doesn't fall far from the tree, as they say: Culkin's dad, **Christopher**, known as **Kit**, seems to have much to do with his superstar son's attitude problem. Himself a failed child thesp (a string of youthful performances—including a turn with Laurence Olivier in *Becket* on Broadway—led to exactly nothing in terms of an acting career), Kit worked diligently to promote his celebrated progeny—Mac and his less adorable siblings, sister **Quinn** and little brother **Kieran**—and in the process earned the undying enmity of nearly every player in Hollywood. A notorious case in point was Kit's abrupt decision that Mac should star as the bad seed in *The Good Son,* despite the fact that the film had already been cast and was due to begin shooting three weeks later. At the studio's behest, director **Michael Lehmann** tested Macaulay several times but found him wanting; Kit, of course, ultimately got his way by threatening to pull Mac from the sequel to *Home Alone.* This power play cost the studio $4 million to reschedule the *Son* shoot and resulted in the firing of both a promising young actor, **Jesse Bradford**, and Lehmann. (Fox chairman **Joe Roth**, according to Lehmann, told him, "This is the kind of thing I hate to have to say, but my job requires it: if you don't cast Macaulay Culkin you won't make the movie.") Lehmann walked out rather than be forced to direct the untalented lad. "I went to Kit Culkin's house, pleading with him for two hours," he recalled. "We'd hired sixty people; they'd be out of work by Christmastime. I had at

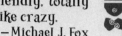

If you went to a Hollywood audition, you would see these kids who are superfriendly, totally insincere, and dropping names like crazy.
—Michael J. Fox

least eight or nine months of my creative life invested. I felt it was cruel and out of place to call his son a powerful movie star and take advantage of it."

The churlish Culkin's twenty-year live-in relationship with **Patricia Brentrup**, mother to their brood of seven, also suffered. In June of 1995, Brentrup plunked down an affidavit in a New York court, claiming that Kit had major problems, specifically "excessive drinking, physical abuse and unfaithful behavior," including one incident in which he "punched me in the head and about the body, causing me substantial injury, and dragged me out to the balcony threatening to push me over the railing. Several of the children witnessed this. . . ." But more important to Brentrup was the damage he was doing to their progeny's chances in Tinseltown. The coup de grâce came when "agents from William Morris informed me in no uncertain terms that if he deliberately botches up this deal [Kieran's star turn in *Amanda*], no one in Hollywood will want to work with our children again." Sadly, the bitter custody battle ensuing from Culkin and Brentrup's very public bust-up seemed to be less about wanting the children than wanting control over their incomes.

Perhaps in response to the ongoing imbroglios at home, coupled with the fact that he was too old to play cutesy-kid roles anymore and couldn't get a job, big Mac began showing signs of a nascent rebellious side. Early in 1995, he dyed his hair shocking pink; in September of the same year, he and his underage siblings threw an un-supervised, noisy beer bash in the family's swank Manhattan digs, prompting neighbors to complain and the press to pounce. And now he's quit acting altogether as his purportedly penniless parents continue their bitter battles over money. Whether he'll be able to overcome his troubles is anyone's guess—if not, he may have to learn life's lessons the hard way, as the following child television actors did.

PROBLEM CHILD

> My advice to young actors?
> Stay out of jail.
> —Alfred Hitchcock

*T*he *Brady Bunch*: **Susan** "little, lisping Cindy" **Olsen** has been arrested twice (in 1991 and 1993) for drunk driving.

Diff'rent Strokes: **Todd** "Willis" **Bridges**, who played cute-as-a-button Gary Coleman's big bro, was stopped for traffic violations in 1983; after a quick search, police found a loaded gun concealed in the car. (Bridges lamely explained he was just trying to protect himself from marauding KKK crazies.) In 1986 the onetime actor was in deep doo-doo again after threatening to blow up autos belonging to garage owner Greg Tyree, who'd done a less-than-perfect job detailing Bridges' car. The following day, Tyree's Mercedes was indeed bombed, and Bridges was sentenced to three years' probation together with three hundred hours of community service, a $2,500 fine and $6,000 in restitution. Three short years down the line (and in the throes of a fourteen-grams-per-day coke habit), he pumped eight slugs into an L.A. drug dealer; however, Bridges was acquitted after claiming he couldn't remember the shooting because he was at the tail end of a four-day binge. (Will anyone be surprised to learn that Bridges' attorney was **Johnnie Cochran**?) And in 1991 he was again nabbed on drug charges (when apprehended, he and a buddy were in possession of forty-eight grams of cocaine between them).

Dana "Kimberly" **Plato** couldn't get arrested as an actress after leaving the series in 1984, but she landed in the slammer in 1991 after undertaking an ill-advised (and ill-disguised) video store robbery in Las Vegas. Plato ran off with $164, but was easily apprehended when she returned to the scene of the crime for the floppy hat and pair of sunglasses she'd left behind. In 1992 she was nailed again for forging a

Valium prescription, followed the next year by a stint in rehab.

Eight Is Enough: **Adam** "Nicholas" **Rich** was pinched in 1983 for possession of marijuana, in 1990 for drunk driving, and in 1991, his busiest year, for burglary, shoplifting (broke into a drugstore to steal morphine, but inexplicably ended up only with some socks and sunglasses), and drug possession (pilfered Demerol from a hospital emergency room).

Father Knows Best: **Lauren** "Kitten" **Chapin** turned to drugs and then turned tricks to support her habit. "No one had ever told me about prostitution—that it was immoral or illegal," Chapin later explained. But "I was valuable because I could help men unwind and forget about their troubles. I saw myself as a kind of psychologist." Chapin ultimately "found God."

Lassie: **Tommy Rettig**, who played the comely collie's original boy companion, was apprehended for growing marijuana and smuggling cocaine.

The Munsters: **Butch** "Eddie" **Patrick** spent eleven weekends in jail in 1979 after being arrested for possession of Quaaludes, and was busted again in 1991 for robbing a limo driver of $130 and beating him senseless.

One Day at a Time: **Mackenzie** "Julie" **Phillips** was arrested in 1977 for possession of cocaine and public intoxication, having passed out on a Hollywood sidewalk.

The Partridge Family: **Danny** "the funny-looking one" **Bonaduce**, before landing a career as a surprisingly well-reviewed talk show host, was nabbed for possession of cocaine (four grams) in 1985, in 1990 for attempting to purchase crack, and in 1991 for the robbery and beating of a transvestite prostitute. Attempting to explain the latter incident, Bonaduce protested it was "Not, as everyone thinks, because I discovered she was a he! Big deal—I grew up in Hollywood, where half the girls I knew had dicks. No, this guy was crazy; he'd been done for assault before, but I was better at fisticuffs. Then he found out who I was and pressed charges. He got $4,500 to have his nose fixed; I got seven hundred fifty hours of community service, cleaning highways." Sometimes life just ain't fair.

REALITY CHECK

Most child actors were lucky enough to get the part in the first place. They cry and complain that now they are no longer little and cute Hollywood has no use for them. What we often fail to appreciate is that being little and cute may have been our only skill. Now that we are not so little anymore, and certainly not cute, some of us may have to face reality, stop whining, and get real jobs.

—Danny Bonaduce

SON OF A BITCH, PART 2

Fame can have a curious side effect: parents who wanted nothing to do with their offspring before they became famous begin crawling out of the woodwork to claim their (un)fair share of the glory. **Meg Ryan**'s mother, for one. **Susan Jordan**, who left her husband and children to pursue an acting career when Meg was fifteen, has made a cottage industry out of whining to women's magazines about her daughter's coldness. Jordan never misses a photo op, either, posing for the articles' accompanying cheesecake shots in form-fitting T-shirts and bun-hugging hot pants (sagging skin, leathery tan, bunion-o-rama—you get the idea). At this writing, Ryan was not interested in patching things up—and who could blame her? Likewise **Demi Moore**, whose embarrassingly uncouth, alcoholic mother posed in the altogether for a sordid spread in a sleazebag men's magazine in 1993 (the layout even included a shot of the blowsy babe working a pottery wheel à la Demi in *Ghost*). This, believe it or not, was the *pinnacle* of the lowlife barfly's attention-grabbing antics: she'd also "tried" suicide and been arrested on several occasions for drunk driving. And in 1994 she was charged with arson after feuding with a female bartender, whose house was burned to the ground soon after the tiff.

Celebrity parents who have attempted to cash in on their prominent progeny's success with literary endeavors include **Jim Carrey**'s dad, who tried unsuccessfully to hawk an "unauthorized" biography of funny sonny; **Jaid** (mother of Drew) **Barrymore**, who penned a how-to book, *Secrets of World-Class Lovers: Erotic Tips and Sensual Stories for a Lifetime of Sexual Fulfillment* (this after posing for *Playboy* at age forty-nine!); and celebutante **Georgia Holt**, mother of **Cher**, whose smarmy, ear-licking tome *Star Mothers* was as close as she ever came to celebrityhood. A cursory flip through its

DIFFERENCE BETWEEN US

THE I did an interview where I described her as a teacher, and she called me up and said I shouldn't have said she was a teacher—I should have called her an "educator"! You know why we don't get along? Because I'm famous and she's not!

—Laurence Fishburne, on dear old mom

COMMIE MOMMY

It was hard growing up seeing all this press against your mother. I'd be sitting next to a girl in chemistry [class] and she'd say, "Your mother's a Commie." —Natasha Richardson, on mom Vanessa Redgrave

pages, however, reveals the real star of the family: "Of all the thrills Cher's stardom has brought me, a very special one was watching her perform at the Hollywood Bowl—was it *really* twenty years ago?—in a concert to aid the blind. I remember my father gripping my arm tightly and saying, 'That's you up there. That's you up there made over!'" Holt also claims to have been "considered quite beautiful as a young woman and a 'blonde,' and that was hard on Cher though I didn't realize it then (not that I could have done anything about it if I had)." Living in the shadow of such a powerhouse must have been rough on Holt's ugly-duckling daughter!

Cher is like her ultraglam mom in one way, though: her romantic track record is *almost* as varied as Holt's, who has been married *nine times*. Three of these blissful unions were to Cher's father, **John Sarkisian**, who, when she was eight, was sent to the slammer for possession of heroin. **Keanu Reeves**'s biological father, **Sam** (the actor was raised by a California family after being given up for adoption as a baby), a native Hawaiian, also landed in the hole for drug-related crimes: in 1994 he was sentenced to ten years for cocaine possession. **Woody Harrelson**'s papa is incarcerated too, albeit for a much more serious offense: the assassination of a federal judge.

Parental boozing contributed to the traumatic childhoods of many well-known stars: **Steve McQueen, Warren Beatty** and **Shirley MacLaine, Carol Burnett, Elizabeth Taylor**, and **Cary Grant**, among others. **Sir Alec Guinness** was victimized by his hooch-hound mother, who once broke into his house and stole some of his possessions to pawn for more booze. **Marlon Brando** attributes his general lack of emotion to his alcoholic upbringing: "My mother was *everything* to me, a whole world. I used to come home from school but she wouldn't be there and there'd be nothing in the icebox. Then the telephone would ring and it would be somebody calling from a bar to pick her up. Then one day I didn't care anymore. She was there in a room holding on to me and I let her fall. I couldn't take it anymore, watching her break apart like a piece of porcelain. I stepped right over her. I was indifferent. Since then I've been indifferent."

Robert Blake, James Garner, Marvin Gaye, Joan Crawford, the Beach Boys' Wilson brothers, and Rock Hudson (reportedly born some nine months after his mother had an affair) were physically abused by parents. Tony Curtis remembers his mother "beat me unmercifully for no reason. She used to slap my face because I was such a good-looking boy." YEAH RIGHT. Delta Burke, Roseanne, Traci Lords, and Oprah Winfrey all claim to have suffered sexual molestation as children. Peter O'Toole said he was brought up as a girl for the first twelve years of his life, Jack Nicholson grew up believing his grandmother was his mother and his mother was his sister, and Anthony Quinn's father told him the family had adopted him after finding him in a pig sty! The granddaddy of all childhood horror stories, however, belongs to Richard Pryor. Both his parents, Gertrude and Buck, were involved in the family business, a bordello run by Pryor's grandmother. They were also lifelong boozers who frequently engaged in violent fights, Gertrude having once nearly made Buck into a eunuch using only her fingernails. The young Pryor was molested at six by a neighborhood teen, beginning a cycle of erratic and often violent behavior culminating in his discharge from the army in 1960 for slashing a fellow enlistee with a switchblade—and leading to Pryor's serious drug addiction and other acts of self-destruction.

Lest we paint too bleak a picture, it's important to point out that many celebrities did have happy childhoods. Steven Spielberg (then called "the Retard" by school chums) at an early age began showing some of the characteristics that would later make him famous. Mom Leah Adler describes his relationship with three younger sisters: "He used to stand outside their windows at night howling, 'I am the moon. I am the moon.' They're still scared of the moon. And he cut off the head of one of Nancy's dolls and served it to her on a bed of lettuce."

The Name of the Rose
Stars named after
famous people/things

🍀 Brett Butler: Lady Brett Ashley
in Hemingway's
The Sun Also Rises
🍀 Dean Cain (*Lois & Clark*):
Dean Martin
🍀 Michael Caine (born Maurice
Micklewhite): *The Caine Mutiny*
🍀 Macaulay Culkin: historian
Thomas Babington Macaulay
🍀 Doris Day:
silents star Doris Kenyon
🍀 Leonardo DiCaprio: parents
were standing in front of a da
Vinci painting when little Leo first
began stirring in mama's womb
🍀 Mariel Hemingway:
a Cuban bay
🍀 Dustin Hoffman:
silents star Dustin Farnum
🍀 Shirley MacLaine:
Shirley Temple
🍀 Marilyn Monroe (born Norma
Jean Mortenson): Norma
Talmadge and Jean Harlow
🍀 River Jude Phoenix:
Siddhartha's River of Life and the
Beatles' "Hey Jude"
🍀 Uma Thurman: a Hindu
goddess. Uma, according to dad
Bob, "means 'the Middle Way' in
Tibetan and is the name of the
mother goddess in Indian
mythology. It's actually UmA."
🍀 Sigourney Weaver (born
Susan Weaver): a character in *The
Great Gatsby*
🍀 Debra Winger: Debra Paget

HITCH YOUR WAGON TO A STAR

If it's your goal to get ahead in Tinseltown, it helps to have a famous relative or two. Nepotism is one of Hollywood's most time-honored traditions, going as far back as the dawn of the movie era and continuing into the days of the "studio system," when **Ogden Nash** wrote this couplet about the founder of Universal Pictures:

Uncle Carl Laemmle
Has a very large faemmle.

(The rhyme served another purpose as well: no one knew how to pronounce his name until it came out.) And comic columnist **Robert Benchley** dubbed Columbia "the pine tree studio" because of all the **Cohns** there.

Sister ACT

Actors whose famous siblings paved the way for their own careers

William Baldwin: "I can honestly say that if Alec had never gone into the business, I wouldn't be an actor."

Jim Belushi: even brother John's sterling comedic rep couldn't save Jim from a string of flops—mainly due to the fact that no one in their right mind would look at this guy and think leading man

Kieran and Quinn Culkin: Quinn was cast in *The Good Son* and Kieran in *Amanda* as conditions of Macaulay's continuing to work

Mariel Hemingway: debuted in 1976's *Lipstick* starring big sis Margaux

Dee Dee Pfeiffer: has sort of gotten her career off the ground (with a recurring role on TV's *Cybill*), perhaps because she's related to one of Hollywood's most stunning stars, sister Michelle

Leaf (a/k/a Joaquin) Phoenix (Nicole Kidman's dimwitted lover in *To Die For*): not as charismatic or attractive as his more talented brother River

Julia Roberts: debuted in *Blood Red* (1986) starring brother Eric

George Savalas: was paid $10,000 per week to appear with brother Telly on *Kojak*

Frank Stallone: has failed at both singing and acting careers despite his brother's megawatt star power

Most of **Francis Ford Coppola**'s family works in showbiz in one capacity or another: nephew **Nicolas Cage** and sister **Talia Shire** are actors, wife **Eleanor** shot much of the footage used in *Hearts of Darkness* (a documentary about the problem-plagued shoot of his own *Apocalypse Now*) and—when **Winona Ryder** backed out at the eleventh hour—one hundred percent talent-free daughter **Sofia** was cast opposite **Andy Garcia** as the tragic young *femmina fatale* in *The Godfather, Part III*. (And people say Garcia isn't a great actor.) Other filial favors include **Jenny Lumet**'s appearance in father **Sidney**'s *Q&A*; **Sage Moonblood Stallone** (nice name, babe) in *Rocky V* and *Daylight*; **Melanie Griffith** in *The Harrad Experiment* (starring both her mother, Hitchcock fantasy doll **Tippi Hedren**, and Griffith's future on-again, off-again lover/husband/abuser, **Don Johnson**); **Tori** (daughter of **Aaron**) **Spelling** in TV's trashy teen melodrama *Beverly Hills, 90210*; and seven-year-old **Rumer Willis** in *Striptease*, about which mom **Demi Moore** said: "I felt it was something that was really going to give her the opportunity to understand what I do." (Like take your clothes off?) And then there's the sad saga of **Chris** (*Batman Forever*) **O'Donnell**, who as a young aspiring actor was given a big break. He was cast as **Barbra Streisand**'s son in *The Prince of Tides*, only to be replaced at the very last minute by the inexperienced but well-connected **Jason Gould**—Streisand's son. "Your mother will understand," cooed La Streisand to crestfallen Chris.

Marrying Hollywood royalty can be just as good as being born into it. Domestic helper **Marcia Garces** married big-shot boss **Robin Williams** and has been elevated to full-fledged Hollywood honchette status, having earned a producer's credit on hubby's star vehicle *Mrs. Doubtfire*. But this form of career opportunism can backfire, as great Dane **Brigitte Nielsen** found out when her movie career fizzled along with her marriage to **Sylvester Stallone**. Not so for **Tom Arnold**, the flabbergastingly unfunny comedian whose baffling rise to TV and movie stardom began right about the time he married **Roseanne**. "She's my partner," he proudly proclaimed. "I don't control her any more than she controls me. If she tells me to do something professionally, I do it."

KID GLOVES, ANYONE?

She was coddled and babied at the time because she had a boyfriend—a guy named Spielberg—who was a friend of the director, Brian De Palma.
—Andrew Stevens, who co-starred with Amy Irving in *The Fury*

"Here, Rumer, let mommy
show you how it's done."

SKOOL DAZE

Speaking of stupidity, how many young celebs put any kind of emphasis on education? Not many, apparently. The following stars didn't quite make it through high school:

Danny Aiello
Brigitte Bardot
Drew Barrymore
Robert Blake
Sonny Bono
Ellen Burstyn
Nicolas Cage
Michael Caine
George Carlin
Jim Carrey
Cher
Jackie Collins
Sean Connery
Tom Cruise
Johnny Depp
Bo Derek
(you're surprised?)
Robert Downey Jr.
Lola Falana
Laurence Fishburne
Carrie Fisher

Michael J. Fox
Redd Foxx
James Garner
Cary Grant
Gene Hackman
Eartha Kitt
Jerry Lewis
Courtney Love
Rob Lowe
Dean Martin
Lee Marvin
Elaine May
Steve McQueen
Melina Mercouri
Robert Mitchum
Demi Moore
Roger Moore
Olivia Newton-John
Peter O'Toole
Al Pacino
Joe Pesci

Lisa Marie Presley*
The Ass Formerly
Known as Prince
Richard Pryor
Anthony Quinn
Keanu Reeves
Roseanne
Rene Russo
Charlie Sheen
Frank Sinatra
Anna Nicole Smith
Ringo Starr
Rod Steiger
Quentin Tarantino
Danny Thomas
Uma Thurman
John Travolta
Mike Tyson
Peter Ustinov
Robert Wagner
Flip Wilson

*According to the authors of *Elvis, My Dad: The Lisa Marie Presley Story*, "Both **Elvis** and **Priscilla** graduated from high school. Lisa couldn't manage that. She's not particularly alert." Oh, but she married well.

And the truly education-ally challenged:

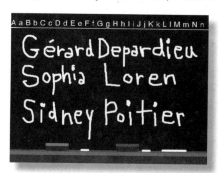

AaBbCcDdEeFfGgHhIiJjKkLlMmNn
Gérard Depardieu
Sophia Loren
Sidney Poitier

Grammar school dropouts

WHERE in the World...?

I was asked to come to Chicago because Chicago is one of our fifty~two states.
—Raquel Welch

Every city I go to is an opportunity to paint, whether it's Omaha or Hawaii.
—Tony Bennett

New Jersey?
—Tori Spelling, when asked by Howard Stern to name the capital of New York

ODD JOBS

It's comforting to know our favorite stars have useful skills to fall back on in case their careers ever hit a stall. "I started in movies by doing small student films in New York and waitressing," says screen sweetie **Sandra Bullock**, "two very important talents to have as an actor." White trash wild child **Courtney Love** was a groupie and a stripper (at Jumbo's Clown Room in Hollywood, among other such venues) beginning at age fourteen, giving her the opportunity to develop and hone the skills she would later need as the wife of a rock star.

Jon Bon Jovi flipped patties at Burger King, Lorenzo Lamas was a fry cook at McDonald's, supermodel/nonactress **Jerry Hall** worked as a cashier at the local Dairy Queen (someone else presumably did the counting), **Sharon Stone** worked the counter at McDonald's, and **Anna Nicole Smith** earned her wings at Jim's Krispy Fried Chicken in Mexia, Texas. Best of all, though, is the picture of überhunk **Brad Pitt** working in a rubber suit as an El Pollo Loco fowl. BR-KA WK!

STAND AND DELIVER

[I was] the worst postman in the history of the post office. . . . I used to start my route at daybreak and I would finish long after dark. I'd stop for doughnuts, I'd play with animals, I'd go home with my bag of mail and just lay around the house.
—Dennis (*NYPD Blue*) Franz

They loved the nightlife: Big, beefy nightclub bouncers included **Tom Arnold**, **Alec Baldwin**, **John Goodman**, **Chazz Palminteri**, **Burt Reynolds**, and **Jean-Claude Van Damme**. **Carol Burnett** was a hatcheck girl, and on the wrong side of the bar serving up drinks were **Tom Arnold**, **Linda Fiorentino**, **Jon Stewart**, and **Mike Ovitz**. And New York clubbies must be having a tough time forgetting Bruno himself, **Bruce Willis**: "I was a much bigger star as a bartender than I ever have been as a movie star. I was quite popular."

Other Hollywood hopefuls found employment opportunities in the theater: **Sylvester Stallone**, **Lauren Bacall**, and **Barbara** (as she was then known, prior to deleting the extraneous **a** for sleekness' sake) **Streisand** worked as ushers, while one of **Gary Cooper**'s earliest gigs was selling advertising space on theater curtains. **Jon Peters** and **Danny DeVito** (then known by the clever *nom de groom* "Mr. Danny") were employed as hairdressers; **Sandra Bernhard** gave manicures (a great way to meet women); and **Richard Chamberlain**, **Lorenzo Lamas**, and **Bill Paxton** all worked with fine automobiles—as chauffeurs and parking lot attendants.

WAITING ON FAME

In Hollywood, the words "waiter" and "actor" are well nigh interchangeable. A representative sampling of those who labored in the food service industry (giving new meaning to the term "soda jerk"):

Alec Baldwin
Antonio Banderas
Ellen Barkin
Kathy Bates
Sandra Bullock
David Caruso
Geena Davis
Ellen DeGeneres
Dana Delany
Robert Downey Jr.
Patrick Duffy
John Forsythe
Andy Garcia
James Garner
Gene Hackman

Woody Harrelson
Dustin Hoffman
Burt Lancaster
Jessica Lange
Jon Lovitz
Rob Morrow
Julia Ormond
Anne Rice
Roseanne
Mary Steenburgen
Meryl Streep
Barbra Streisand
Kathleen Turner
Raquel Welch

DISCOURAGING WORDS

She can't talk. She can't act. She's terrific.
—Louis B. Mayer, on Ava Gardner

So you work at your calling—you sign up for Method classes, spend hours perfecting your tan, tone your physique at a trendy gym on a daily basis, brave the endless round of open auditions and cattle calls—and it finally pays off. Your agent calls and says he's lined up a screen test . . . hooray! Bye-bye poverty, hello bigtime, right? Think again. Here's what the experts had to say about some of Hollywood's best and brightest:

Fred Astaire was dismissed with three short phrases: "Can't act. Slightly bald. Can dance a little." Producer **Sam Goldwyn**, after viewing **Bette Davis**'s first screen test, yelled, *"Who did this to me?"* (Upon seeing it herself, Miss Davis was equally appalled: in her own words, she "ran from the projection room screaming.") A Universal Pictures executive told the young **Clint Eastwood**, "You have a chip on your tooth, your Adam's apple sticks out too far, and you talk too slow." (The same man also told **Burt Reynolds** he couldn't act—guess he was half right.) And **Peter**

CALL US, WE'LL CALL YOU

DON'T

I don't know what we can use you for, but if we ever do need you we'll need you real bad.
—The director of Jack Nicholson's
first screen test

BR⊙THERLY ADVICE

I told him if he became a lawyer I wouldn't have nothing to do with him. Hot damn, who likes a lawyer? That and ever having an earring in his ear.

—Rooster McConaughey, brother of
media sensation Matthew McConaughey

Falk, who has a glass eye, was fobbed off thusly by Columbia Pictures head **Harry Cohn** in 1958: "For the same price I can get an actor with two eyes."

Clark Gable was initially thought too unattractive to be in pictures. "Look at his big, batlike ears!" exclaimed producer **Irving Thalberg** upon first sighting; likewise, studio founder/producer **Jack Warner** chastised director **Mervyn Le Roy** for commissioning a screen test for the homely hunk: "Why do you throw away five hundred dollars of our money on a test for that big ape?" **Robert Montgomery** and **Robert Taylor** were thought to be too skinny to be successful, and **Cary Grant**'s looks, unbelievably, were also judged subpar. "You're bowlegged and your neck is far too thick," a Paramount executive smugly informed the young actor.

The screen's top sirens didn't escape unscathed, either: after a screening in Berlin of *Gösta Berling* (1924) starring a young **Greta Garbo**, **Louis B. Mayer** turned her down because "We don't like fat girls in my country." The cameraman who first shot **Sophia Loren** complained, "She is quite impossible to photograph: too tall, too big-boned, too heavy all around. The face is too short, the mouth is too wide, the nose is too long. What do you want of me, miracles?" **Jane Russell** was "unphotogenic" as well as having "no energy," "no spark." And a prescient casting agent once said of the nine-year-old **Elizabeth Taylor**, "The kid has nothing. Her eyes are too old."

KITTEN WITH A WHIP

Classy Elizabeth Hurley began her career in entertainment by fronting a punk band called the Vestal Virgins, part of whose shtick was flicking whips at the audience.

WORKING STIFFS

There's something odd about the official bios of certain stars: what's listed as their debut wasn't their first film at all. This is usually because they've appeared in an embarrassing or disastrous film that would be unwise to fess up to. For example, **Sylvester Stallone** claims to have made his debut in Woody Allen's *Bananas* (1971), but his initiation into film actually happened a year earlier when he played one of the title characters in a soft-core porno flick called *A Party at Kitty and Stud's* (later retitled *The Italian Stallion* to cash in on Stallone's burgeoning popularity), which featured full southern exposure **(THE HORROR, THE HORROR!)**. "They told me there'd be some nudity," he later remembered, "but when they said they'd give me $200 . . . I did it. . . . I'm ashamed of that film." **Madonna**, paving the way for her subsequent shenanigans, starred in *A Certain Sacrifice,* a truly dreadful student film in which she appeared nude and French-smooched both guys and gals. No one will be surprised to hear that **Bo Derek** (then sweet seventeen and billed as Kathleen Collins, her given name) first appeared in John Derek's soft-core flop *Fantasies* (1973), but **Spalding** (*Monster in a Box*) **Gray** fans may be shocked to learn that his first screen appearance was as the star of a hard-core porn effort entitled *The Farmer's Daughter.*

Jamie Lee Curtis began her career as queen of the screamers in *Halloween* (1978) and its sequel (1981), *The Fog, Prom Night,* and *Terror Train* (all released in 1980) before going on to tantalize some of Hollywood's biggest names in A-list movies. **Pia Zadora,** slathered in icky green body makeup, played one of the alien tots in 1964's *Santa Claus Conquers the Martians;* **Robert Vaughn** grunted his way through 1958's *Teenage Caveman;* **Demi Moore** was a tragic victim of *Parasite* (1982); **Clint Eastwood** played a lowly lab employee in the 1955 screecher *Revenge of the Creature;* and—in drag, yet!—**Donald Sutherland** played a witch in *Castle of the Living Dead* (1964), in which he also had a role as a soldier. Talent will out!

5 MINUTES OF SHAME

Then there are those in the celebrity firmament that are famous for . . . what exactly? As a service to future generations, here is a mini *Who's Who* of the inexplicably eminent:

John Wayne Bobbitt: was so mean and nasty to his wife, Lorena, an uneducated South American immigrant, that she cut off the family jewel and tossed it in a field. With her help the police were able to retrieve it, and Bobbitt's subsequent somewhat successful surgery made him a new man—one who was in demand for tasteless porno films, the first of which was *John Wayne Bobbitt: Uncut.* (Groan.) "He can't act," announced his erstwhile agent, Hollywood has-been Ruth Webb. "I saw the film. Eight orgasms and his expression never changes. Like milking a cow." Other activities in which Bobbitt and his micropenis participated were a transvestite Lorena look-alike contest and a short stint strip-teasing customers at a gay nightclub in Fort Lauderdale.

Divine Brown: twenty-dollar hooker who's made a cottage industry out of being caught flagrante delicto with mincing English actor **Hugh Grant** in a car on her seedy Sunset Strip beat (carriage-trade Hugh actually paid $60). So sensational was the charge against the supposedly straitlaced star that the Divine one's "story" became the subject of an international bidding war between competing periodicals, who tacked up Wanted posters along the boulevard of broken dreams. ("Divine Brown sold her story to the highest-bidding tabloid," remarked **Bill Maher**. "What a whore!") Brown went on to pose for South American lingerie ads and to film a television commercial for L.A.'s KXEZ (the radio station she claimed the cuddlesome couple were listening to when corraled by the coppers), proving her mettle as an actress by delivering this howler with a straight face: "Easy 100.3 is the perfect radio station to listen to while you work." Despite the spot's obvious appeal, listener complaints forced the station to yank the offending ad and issue a

SIMPLY DIVINE

My British movie star, he wanted a beautiful black woman. The blacker the berry, the sweeter the juice, right?
—Divine Brown

public apology. No fear, though—the starstruck streetwalker will be in video stores any minute now with *Taken for Granted*, a reenactment of the night she blew it.

Joey Buttafuoco: ill-bred, overfed cokehead auto mechanic who cheated on his wife, **Mary Jo**, with homicidal nymphet **Amy Fisher**, dubbed the "Long Island Lolita" after she shot her inamorato's better half. Each accused the other of masterminding the dirty deed, but it was Amy who ended up doing real time in the slammer, where she spent her time engaged in deep thought and writing a book. Meanwhile, Joey and Mary Jo (confined to a wheelchair with Fisher's bullet permanently lodged between her brows) became instant celebrities, so in demand that they had no trouble snaring invitations to such high-profile events as the 1994 Academy Awards ceremony, where Mr. Goodwrench regaled reporters with evidence of his newfound fame: "I think we're going to **Elton John**'s house next," he gushed. "This is a fabulous industry. *Fabulous.*" Buttafuoco has since been arrested several times, but the plucky mechanic still dreams of becoming a rock star and actor. FABULOUS.

Heidi Fleiss: succeeded **Madame Alex** as Hollywood's pre-eminent pander, serving up hot call girls to the biggest names in the biz. Surprisingly, most of her high-flown celebrity friends deserted her when it came time to go on record, leaving her bereft save for a very red-faced **Charlie Sheen**. Fleiss plans to come out with a book, which she says will be "very introspective. It's going to be about how things came to be, the camaraderie, the sorority-type feeling." Can't wait.

Jessica Hahn: easily swayed church secretary who had cheap sex in a Florida motel room with televangelist/tax-evader/embezzler **Jim Bakker**. Asserted the whey-faced minister at the time: "When you help the shepherd, you're helping the sheep"—a line dim-bulb Hahn apparently had no trouble swallowing. Her titillating tabloid testimony began the mawkish minister's long slide into ill repute—and, as a completely unexpected bonus, also paved the way for Hahn's lustrous career as entertainment industry plaything. (Unfortunately, things didn't work out as well for Bakker, who, drenched in tears, blubbered about his misdeeds on national television and lost his beautiful wife, **Tammy Faye**, to a rival preacher/

criminal while he was in stir.) A series of plastic surgeries helped the now-mostly-silicone tart net a spread in *Playboy* magazine, as well as appearances in raunchy rock videos and at scummy wrestling matches.

Tonya Harding: trailer trash tomboy whose small-town dreams of making it big as a super-star skater resulted in a shattering blow to the knee of rink rival **Nancy Kerrigan**. The big-boned blonde plea-bargained her way out of doing hard time, but didn't have an easy time attempting to jump-start a career in showbiz. Though she picked and chose her work carefully, turning down big-money offers to wrestle in Japan (too trashy) and to appear in a Woody Allen movie (didn't approve of his morals), Harding was never able to cut much ice with the public. The gallant gal did manage one starring appearance, however: the unauthorized straight-to-video release of frolicsome footage from her and hubby **Jeff Gillooly**'s XXX-rated wedding-night shenanigans, which the fun couple had recorded for posterity.

Kato Kaelin: slacker/celebrity house-guest ("I was just there in the guesthouse. I never asked for attention") who never did quite make up his mind whether he was for or against his notorious former landlord/murderer (oops, *acquitted accused murderer*) **O.J. Simpson**. Kato's wit, charm, and disarming personality inspired such admiring comments as "He's just a professional houseguest with bad hair" (**James Garner**) and "There is a rumor now that there may soon be a Kato Kaelin doll on the market . . . you wind it up and it crashes at Barbie's Malibu Dream House" (**Jay Leno**). As for Kato's own ambitions: "My daydream was to go to Hollywood, to be discovered," he mused. "I saw it as me hanging out with the cool people. That sounds so shallow, though."

Menendez brothers (Lyle and Eric): couple of spoiled rich kids who wrote a script about deliberately, premeditatedly offing their parents, then actually carried out the scenario and were forced by a mountain of evidence to confess. Fortunately, the jury didn't believe them—the first time, anyway. After a second trial, the Beverly Hills bad boys were slammed behind bars where they belong.

2 Here's Looking at You

Looks play a crucial role in an aspiring actor's chances of success. With rare exception, we want our icons to be the most physically awesome specimens of humanity on the planet, and unless this is the case they're usually relegated to character-actor status. Is it any wonder, then, that public figures spend *mucho* time and money ensuring they look better than the rest of us?

> If I have to diet, I'm gonna diet. If I have to work out, I'm gonna work out. If I have to sleep upside-down like a bat so I don't look like a basset hound, that's what I'm gonna do. Because *I'm not leaving!*
>
> —Sharon Stone

A lucky few were born with perfect proportions, dewy skin, and even features—and the rest of them want us to think they were. But it's not difficult to spot them: the over-the-hill Lothario whose ears are too far back on his head, the antediluvian diva whose facial skin is stretched into a fright mask, the flat-chested starlet who suddenly takes on a marked resemblance to **Dolly Parton**. Yes, welcome to the wonderful, wacky world of cosmetic enhancement.

Stars' reps are routinely instructed to deny their clients have had anything done. For example, in a press release sent out by **Michael Jackson**'s manager, the self-morphing singer was "quoted" attempting to pooh-pooh some of the rumors that have come down the pike regarding his rather . . . drastic physical transformation: "**NO!** I've never taken hormones to maintain my high voice. **NO!** I've never had my cheekbones altered in any way. **NO!** I've never had cosmetic surgery on my eyes. **YES!** One day in the future I plan to get married and have a family. Any statements to the contrary are simply untrue." Phew! Glad we got that cleared up.

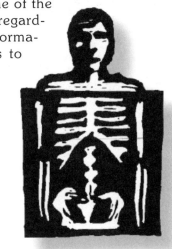

Other celebs subscribe to the "don't ask, don't tell" credo—like **Cher** ("If I want to put my tits on my back,

Hell no, she won't go

that's my business"). **Jane Fonda**, who is rumored to have had a boob job, an eyelid lift, and other facial alterations, along with a procedure said to create a wasp waist via the removal of lower ribs, says, "I may have and I may not have. I think, what's the big deal? I never said I would never have plastic surgery. I said you have to make friends with the aging process and with your wrinkles and you have to do everything you can." (And she did.)

Unless a would-be actress is at least a C-cup by the time she's seventeen, breast implants are de rigueur—although admitting she's gotten them is not. Vapid vixen **Anna Nicole Smith**, whose early photos show a sweet-faced but flat-as-a-board young woman, claims that giving birth to her son resulted in her current set of torpedoes, and Minnie Mouse–soundalike **Jennifer Tilly** says she took a role calling for topless scenes *simply to convince everyone that her* large chest *was entirely natural!* 👁👁👁. But makeup artist **George Masters** spilled the beans on **Raquel Welch** ("She's silicone from the knees up"), and **Pamela Anderson Lee** admits her basketball-size bodice-fillers aren't God-given: "I had implants. But so has *every* single person in Los Angeles. These are things that people don't realize. . . ." (We're beginning to, Pammy.) And silicone-enhanced Amazon **Brigitte Nielsen** (who, reportedly given a choice between a Mercedes and a boob job from then-husband **Sylvester Stallone** [who, according to onetime datemate **Janice Dickinson**, offers boob jobs as gifts to many of his floozies], chose the latter), says, "I'll use science to help nature if that's what I feel like." (And she did.)

Many stars have a love-hate relationship with plastic surgery. **Robert Blake**, who's been in showbiz most of his life (and who recently got a facelift), decries the pressure of having to look good: "It sucks, what's happening to society. Every chick's got a chest full of styrofoam, and we all encourage each other to do it . . . so [I did] it too. I'm sorry I gave in to that shit." Rebel actress **Martha Plimpton** agrees with Blake's point of view: "This whole plastic surgery thing as moral dilemma makes me nauseous," she says. "Anyone who says it is a moral dilemma is so fucking deluded that they should have their head examined. It's a question of, do I mutilate myself for the sake of people making money off me or not?" And, as we've seen, the results aren't always as expected. Robert Blake again: "All of the guys I went to acting class with who became movie stars look the same way they did back in acting class, except they have mouths like lizards . . . now I look like them." Still, an actor's face is his fortune, and no expense is spared (although discounts are probably available if you marry your plastic surgeon, as **Victoria Principal** did). But too much surgery can backfire on the recipient—**Robert Mitchum** actually lost the lead in *Atlantic City* to **Burt Lancaster** because, due to a facelift, he suddenly looked too youthful for the role!

HOLDING BACK THE YEARS

So who's really had what done? We all know it's impossible to put together a definitive collection of all the plastic surgeries performed in Hollywood—the list would fill a book by itself. But the rumor mill, together with physical evidence and confessions by celebrities themselves, yields some interesting results.

facelift

Bea Arthur		**Dean Martin**
Lauren Bacall		Robert Mitchum
Lucille Ball		**Mary Tyler Moore**
Mr. Blackwell		Paul Newman
Robert Blake		**Nick Nolte**
Carol Burnett		Al Pacino
Dyan Cannon		**Mary Pickford**
Cher		Elvis Presley
Gary Cooper		**Victoria Principal**
Joan Crawford		Juliet Prowse
Bette Davis		**Burt Reynolds**
Marlene Dietrich		Debbie Reynolds
Phyllis Diller		**Joan Rivers**
Kirk Douglas		Roseanne
Michael Douglas		**Mickey Rourke**
Faye Dunaway		Frank Sinatra
Barbara Eden	**George Hamilton**	**Liz Smith**
Cristina Ferrare	Rita Hayworth	Barbara Stanwyck
Henry Fonda	**William Holden**	**Gloria Swanson**
Jane Fonda	Michael Landon	Elizabeth Taylor
Zsa Zsa Gabor	**Angela Lansbury**	**Lana Turner**
Jackie Gleason	Sophia Loren	Barbara Walters

CAUTION BODY UNDER CONSTRUCTION

liposuction

Tom Arnold
Joan Rivers
Kenny Rogers
Roseanne

neck

Phyllis Diller
Angela Lansbury
Victoria Principal

eyes

Loni Anderson
Johnny Carson
Cher
Phyllis Diller
Jane Fonda
Melanie Griffith
Goldie Hawn
Katharine Hepburn
William Holden
Rock Hudson
Michael Jackson
Elvis Presley
Victoria Principal
Joan Rivers
Roseanne
Diane Sawyer
Barbara Walters

facial reconstruction

Ann-Margret
Montgomery Clift
Mark Hamill
Van Johnson
Carole Lombard
Melanie Mayron
Merle Oberon
Jack Palance
Jason Robards
Edward G. Robinson

boob job %

Paula Abdul
Brett Butler
Dyan Cannon
Cher
Geena Davis
Bo Derek
Phyllis Diller
Shannen Doherty
Nicole Eggert
Morgan Fairchild
Jane Fonda
Melanie Griffith
Jessica Hahn
Jerry Hall
Mariel Hemingway
Iman
Janet Jackson
La Toya Jackson
Jenny Jones
Pamela Anderson Lee
Heather Locklear
Courtney Love
Liza Minnelli
Demi Moore (denies)
Mary Tyler Moore (denies)
Brigitte Nielsen
Dolly Parton
Juliet Prowse
Joan Rivers
Nancy Sinatra
Anna Nicole Smith
Tori Spelling (denies)
Jennifer Tilly
Raquel Welch
Jackie Zeman

Tori Spelling hasn't had a boob job

ears

Phyllis Diller
Michael Landon
George Raft
Rudolph Valentino

hair implant/ transplant

Tom Arnold
Hugh Downs
Elton John
Michael Keaton
Frank Sinatra

tummy tuck

Phyllis Diller
Joan Rivers
Roseanne

butt lift

Mr. Blackwell
Phyllis Diller
Roseanne

breast reduction

Loni Anderson
Ursula Andress
Drew Barrymore
Soleil Moon Frye
Whoopi Goldberg
Roseanne

chin and jaw

Carol Burnett
Bette Davis
Phyllis Diller
Michael Jackson
Melanie Mayron
Marilyn Monroe
Elizabeth Taylor

teeth fixed

Nicolas Cage
Phyllis Diller
Jessica Hahn
Joan Rivers
Denzel Washington
... and just about
every other celeb
you can think of

collagen lips

Loni Anderson
Melanie Griffith
Barbara Hershey
Madonna
Michelle Pfeiffer
Nancy Sinatra

cheeks

Cher
Phyllis Diller
Melanie Griffith
Michael Jackson

KNEE-JERK REACTION

Some guys look at themselves in the mirror for
twenty years, then decide to get a nose job or
an ear lift or something. I don't know. I just
couldn't see myself getting my knees stretched.
—Danny DeVito

Pamela shows off her unnatural resources

Paula Abdul
Rona Barrett
Milton Berle
Sonny Bono
Nicolas Cage
Cher
Bo Derek
Phyllis Diller
Barbara Eden
Nanette Fabray
Connie Francis
Annette Funicello
Eva Gabor
Zsa Zsa Gabor
Mitzi Gaynor
David Geffen
Melissa Gilbert
Lee Grant
Juliette Greco
Jennifer Grey
Joel Grey

Steve Guttenberg
Joan Hackett
Jessica Hahn
George Hamilton
Lisa Hartman Black
Janet, La Toya, and
Michael Jackson
Al Jolson
Carolyn Jones
Alan King
Cheryl Ladd
Carole Landis
Dean Martin
Melanie Mayron
Cameron Mitchell
Marilyn Monroe

Rita Moreno
Laraine Newman
Peter O'Toole
Michelle Pfeiffer
Suzanne Pleshette
Stefanie Powers
Joan Rivers
Roseanne
Diana Ross
Jill St. John
Talia Shire
Dinah Shore
Nancy Sinatra
Sissy Spacek
Candy Spelling
Tori Spelling
Sting
Marlo Thomas
Johnny Weismuller
Raquel Welch
Tina Yothers

HEDY LAMARR'S BEAUTY SECRET

All you have to do is stand still and look stupid.

the THIGHS have it

When I wake up and look in the mirror I realize one of the reasons I don't own a handgun: I would have shot my thighs off years ago.
—Oprah Winfrey

HAIR APPARENT

In Hollywood, the men are just as vain as the women—sometimes more so, particularly when it comes to their crowning glory. Full follicular foliage was considered so vital to **Sean Connery**'s swashbuckling image as James Bond that Warner Bros. shelled out $52,000 for the great Scot's toupee in *Never Say Never Again*. But touchy **William Shatner** gets highly indignant if anyone dares to imply that the suspiciously dark and luxuriant thatch atop his dome isn't all his own, and even stomped out of one interview when the subject was so much as raised.

Another option for less than ideally hirsute men comes in the form of hair transplants—a most painful procedure, according to **Tom Arnold**: "They open you up ear to ear, cut off a piece of your scalp, show it to you, then sew that up, take out donor hair from the back of your head, where hair always grows, punch three hundred to four hundred holes in the top of your head and put in one, two, sometimes four little hairs in each of the holes. I've had this done five times." We always knew he was a glutton for punishment. (Can they do anything about sweat glands, Tom?)

A star is shorn: a less messy solution for a thinning pate is simply to shave it, à la **Bruce Willis**. ("He's got one of the finest bald heads I've ever seen. It's a monument to cranial architecture," says **Terry Gilliam**, who directed Willis in *12 Monkeys*.) Or, if you have the clout, you can have your locks drawn in frame by frame by computer in your movies, as **Kevin Costner** reportedly did for *Waterworld* (an allegation he vehemently denies).

HELL Toupee

Steve Allen
Fred Astaire
Jack Benny
George Burns
Humphrey Bogart
Lee J. Cobb
Sean Connery
Gary Cooper
Bing Crosby
Sam Donaldson
Brian Donlevy
Henry Fonda

Rex Harrison
Charlton Heston
Gene Kelly
Liberace
Fred MacMurray
Fredric March
Ray Milland
Robert Montgomery
David Niven

Laurence Olivier
Jack Paar
George Raft
Charles Nelson Reilly
Carl Reiner
Rob Reiner
Burt Reynolds
Peter Sellers
Paul Simon
Frank Sinatra
Rod Steiger
James Stewart
Andy Warhol
John Wayne

Celeb rug-wearers

TOO BIG FOR YOUR BRITCHES

> You never see a
> woman who is
> a normal
> weight in
> the movies
> nowadays, or
> very rarely . . . The
> striving for perfection—it's what brought
> down the Roman empire.
> It's about seeking this perfection
> that's totally unattainable.
> —Kyra Sedgwick

A major stumbling block for many would-be stars is Hollywood's unspoken requirement that celebrities be at least ten pounds underweight. **Tiffani-Amber Thiessen**, who replaced bad-girl **Shannen Doherty** on the teen soaper *Beverly Hills, 90210*, is a sterling example of someone who would be considered svelte and sexy anywhere but in Tinseltown. "People expect me to be thin and perfect and I'm not," she said in an interview with *TV Guide*. "I've had to struggle with my weight since I was seventeen, and it's been an ongoing battle. There's a lot of added pressure because I work with so many beautiful, thin people, and I've been asked to lose weight by producers. It really hurts, but that's part of what this business is about."

Sure, there are those who've made a career out of packing on the poundage, like **Roseanne**—but even she tries to disclaim responsibility for her porcine physique: "I turned my life over to a higher power. . . . See, like ninety-eight percent of overeaters—particularly women—had a problem with sexual abuse as a child." Yup, uh-huh . . . she always did have a teensy tendency toward exaggeration. Her teevee hubby, suet-swaddled **John Goodman**, is less coy when chatting about his flab: "It's pretty sad when a person has to lose weight to play **Babe Ruth**."

Livin' LARGE

Paula Abdul
Kirstie Alley
Alec Baldwin
Linda Blair
Yasmine Bleeth
Marlon Brando
Delta Burke
Cher
Tyne Daly
Robert De Niro
Emilio Estevez
Melanie Griffith

Tom Hanks
Grace Kelly
Joan Lunden
Kelly McGillis
Roger Moore
Jack Nicholson
Nick Nolte
Ryan O'Neal
Dolly Parton
Lynn Redgrave

Stars who've ballooned

Isabella Rossellini
Steven Seagal
Brooke Shields
Alicia Silverstone
Sally Struthers
Charlene Tilton
John Travolta
Kathleen Turner
Brenda Vaccaro
Denzel Washington
Carnie Wilson
Shelley Winters

Ready-to-ERR

The most deplorable celeb fashion trends of late

"Vamp" and "Hard Candy" nail polish
the return of bell-bottoms
nonprescription nonsunglasses
baby barrettes (especially on men)
satin dresses on less-than-perfect bodies (are you listening, Melanie Griffith?)
gargantuan jeans and tees
underwear peeking over the tops of jeans

lingerie as evening wear
haystack perms
platform shoes
ponytails on men
visible lip liner
thrift-store chic
skunk-striped hair
grunge
heroin chic
'60s revival
go-go boots
ripped jeans

red ribbons
rubber dresses
urban cowboys
Caesar haircuts
blond hair/black roots
bandage dresses
pattern-mixing
combat boots

Big satin doll with tiny Spanish sex toy

Real men wear red ribbons

DOUBLE EXPOSURE

Sometimes what you see isn't what you get. Because of actor insecurity and/or no-nudity clauses, that naked body writhing on the screen is more likely to be a no-name hardbody double than the star you paid to see. **Julia Roberts** (in *Pretty Woman*) and **Kim Basinger** (in both *My Stepmother Is an Alien* and *Final Analysis*) were doubled by **Shelley Michelle**, who claims she's also subbed on-screen for **Anne Archer** (who took all the credit for her "great body" on a talk show appearance), **Catherine Oxenberg**, **Barbra Streisand**, and **Madonna**. Others who've used the somatic services of doubles include **Demi Moore** (*Ghost*), **Meg Ryan** (*When a Man Loves a Woman*), **Barbara Hershey** (*A Dangerous Woman*), and **Brooke Shields** (*Endless Love*). (Conversely, when asked if she'd used one in *Ready to Wear*, **Tracey Ullman** screeched with laughter. "No! With that big cellulite ass rolling across the screen, it had to be me. I don't know where you'd find buttocks like mine, dear.")

On the other hand, some celebs just can't get enough exposure. **Pamela Anderson Lee** has posed several times for *Playboy*, both before and after breast-implant surgery. "I hadn't read *Playboy*," the dark-of-tan, light-of-intellect bombshell claims, perhaps a trifle disingenuously. "When I looked at it I thought, 'This is beautiful. I can't believe they want me.'" This was obviously a good move for the bleached-blond beach babe, whose career skyrocketed after her first frock-free pictorial; ditto for **Sharon Stone**, whose *Playboy* spread jump-started a lackluster career. But personal gain is not on the agenda for some high-minded stars. **Joan Collins**, who appeared in the magazine in 1983, claimed she was actually performing a service to society by posing in the buff: "In doing so I felt I was breaking the ageism taboo that so many women feared and dreaded." Thanks, Joan—the world is a more liberated and empowered place now.

It can be embarrassing when pre-stardom starkers shots suddenly turn up for all the world to see, but they aren't necessarily career-breakers. "Artsy" photos of a hirsute **Madonna** were featured in both *Playboy* and *Penthouse* in 1985, with no visible effect on her popularity. **Arnold Schwarzenegger** threatened to sue *Spy* magazine when they published a photograph of the bulbous bodybuilder in the buff (the March 1992 issue), along with an explanation: during Arnie's early days pumping iron in Europe, it was apparently quite common for the athletes to supplement their incomes by posing in the altogether for the coterie of gay men who follow the sport. Though a few eyebrows were lifted at the time, the incident hasn't affected Schwarzenegger's good-guy, he-man image one whit.

PUBLIC FIGURES

Others who've taken it all off:

Pamela Anderson Lee: *Playboy*
(February 1990; February 1991; July 1992)
Ursula Andress: *Playboy* (July 1965)
Ann-Margret: *Playboy* (August 1966)
Paula Barbieri: *Playboy* (October 1994)
*The fact that her boyfriend was in jail, having been accused of a
sensationally gruesome double murder, wouldn't have anything
to do with why she was picked, would it?*
Brigitte Bardot: *Playboy* (March 1958)
Drew Barrymore: *Interview* (1992); *Playboy* (January 1995)
Kim Basinger: *Penthouse; Playboy* (February 1983)
Marisa Berenson: *Playboy* (c. 1976)
Sonia Braga: *Playboy* (October 1984)
Rae Dawn Chong: *Playboy* (May 1982)
Joan Collins: *Playboy* (March 1969; 1983)
Cindy Crawford: *Playboy* (July 1988)
Bo Derek: *Playboy* (March 1980)
Shannen Doherty: *Playboy* (March 1994)
Erika (*Baywatch*) Eleniak: *Playboy* (July 1989)
Linda Evans: *Playboy* (July 1971)
Morgan Fairchild: *Playboy* (August 1986)
Farrah Fawcett: *Playboy* (December 1978; November 1995)
*For the latter appearance, Fawcett received a payment of
$1 million plus a royalty on each copy sold.*
Sherilyn Fenn: *Playboy* (December 1990)
Jane Fonda: *Playboy* (August 1966)
Zsa Zsa Gabor: *Playboy* (March 1957)
Robin Givens: *Playboy* (September 1994)
Melanie Griffith: *Playboy* (October 1976)
Funny, they haven't asked her back.
Jessica Hahn: *Playboy* (November 1987)
Margaux Hemingway: *Playboy* (June 1978)
Mariel Hemingway: *Playboy* (April 1982)
Barbara Hershey: *Playboy* (August 1972)
Charlton Heston was a nude model in pre-fame days.
La Toya Jackson: *Playboy* (March 1989, November 1991)
Margot Kidder: *Playboy* (March 1975)

Nastassja Kinski: *Playboy* (August 1979)
Sophia Loren: *Playboy* (November 1957)
Tina Louise: *Playboy* (May 1958)
Elle Macpherson: *Playboy* (May 1994, November 1994)
Madonna: *Playboy* and *Penthouse* (September 1985)
Jayne Mansfield: *Playboy* (February 1956)
Pamela Sue Martin: *Playboy* (July 1978)
Jenny McCarthy: *Playboy* (October 1993; December 1996)
Donna Mills: *Playboy* (October 1987)
Marilyn Monroe: *Playboy* (first issue, December 1953)
Demi Moore: *High Society* (1986); *Oui* (1982); *Vanity Fair* covers, pregnant (1991) and not (1992)
Julie Newmar: *Playboy* (May 1957)
Brigitte Nielsen: *Playboy* (September 1985)
Kim Novak: *Playboy* (October 1959)
Dian Parkinson: *Playboy* (December 1991)
Bernadette Peters: *Playboy* (December 1981)
Dana Plato: *Playboy* (June 1989)
Paulina Porizkova: *Playboy* (November 1986)
Victoria Principal: *Playboy* (September 1973)
Vanessa Redgrave: *Playboy* (April 1969)
Burt Reynolds: *Cosmopolitan* (April 1972)
Mimi Rogers: *Playboy* (March 1993)
Arnold Schwarzenegger: *After Dark* (early 1970s)
Jane Seymour: *Playboy* (July 1973)
Nancy Sinatra (ugh!): *Playboy* (March 1995)
Anna Nicole Smith: *Playboy*
(May 1992; June 1993; February 1994)
Suzanne Somers: *Playboy* (February 1980)
Elke Sommer: *Playboy* (September 1964)
Sharon Stone: *Playboy* (July 1990)
Elizabeth Taylor: *Playboy* (January 1963)
Mamie Van Doren: *Playboy* (February 1964)
Raquel Welch: *Playboy* (February 1977)
Vanna White: *Playboy* (July 1986)

NO STONE UNTURNED

Sharon Stone, despite her seeming love of showing skin, in 1995 vowed to do no more nude scenes. "Sharon Stone said she won't take her clothes off in any more movies," commented Conan O'Brien. "So in her next movie she'll be naked the entire time."

NO NUDES IS GOOD NUDES

Some stars, for our sake, should have mandatory no-nudity clauses in their contracts. Those we'd like to see less (or none) of: saggy-butted, multichinned **Michael Douglas**; droopy, imploding **Clint Eastwood**; tub-o'-lard **Dennis Franz** (love your acting, though, babe); and stubby, troll-like **Harvey Keitel**. On the distaff side: micro-bosomed, saggy **Sonia Braga**; cellulite-ridden, potbellied **Melanie Griffith**; the increasingly rotund **Bette Midler** (too much cleavage is not always a good thing, Miss M—a caveat **Susan Sarandon**, **Elizabeth Taylor**, **Roseanne**, **Glenn Close**, **Marlee Matlin**, and **Zsa Zsa** should also heed); silicone-fortified **Mamie Van Doren**, whose missile-shaped mammaries stand at attention twenty-four hours a day and don't match her heavily pancaked, craggy kisser; and, of course, the ultra-exhibitionistic, perpetually Lycra-wrapped never-was **Sally Kirkland**.

Those who should never under any circumstances appear in public without long pants, high collars, and full-length sleeves: gone-to-seed **Joan Collins** (you're not twenty-five anymore, no matter what your sycophants tell you), saggy-legged **Tony Curtis**, and frog-faced **Frances Fisher** (still dresses like she's a mere slip of a girl). Last but not least, the "you look great but we've seen enough already!" category: **Madonna** (bo-o-oring), **Sharon Stone** (*must* she appear naked in every movie she does?), **Drew Barrymore** (at least until she gets those god-awful tattoos removed and washes her hair), **Demi Moore** (an Australian reporter once remarked quite accurately that "her thighs are just hilarious"), and **Heather Locklear** (admits she's bowlegged, so why does her *Melrose Place* costumery consist entirely of six-inch miniskirts?). And no more cleavage-revealing outfits for **Tori Spelling**, *please*, until she gets that bad boob job fixed!

THE HEIGHT OF STUPIDITY

F or reasons unknown, there are more short people concentrated in entertainment than in any other profession. Could be the "short person complex" had something to do with these folks' drive to succeed . . . but that wouldn't explain all of them, would it?

4'11"
Estelle Getty
Gloria Swanson
Charlene Tilton
Nancy Walker

5'
Patty Duke
Janet Gaynor
Helen Hayes
Dolly Parton
Pia Zadora

5'1"
Geraldine Chaplin
Ruby Dee
Sheena Easton
Carrie Fisher
Bette Midler
Debbie Reynolds

5'1½"
Sally Struthers

5'2"
Paula Abdul
Linda Blair
Sally Field
Eva Gabor
Carol Kane
Veronica Lake
Priscilla Presley
Joan Rivers
Natalie Wood

5'6"
Woody Allen
Paul Anka
Peter Falk
Dustin Hoffman

5'5"
Jason (*Seinfeld*) Alexander
Peter Lorre
Rod Serling

5'4½"
Alan Ladd

5'4"
Robert Blake
Mel Brooks
Michael J. Fox
Arte Johnson
Roman Polanski

5'3"
Sammy Davis Jr.
Mickey Rooney

5'2½"
Prince

5'2"
Dudley Moore
Paul Simon

5'
Danny DeVito

4'7"
Gary Coleman

3'11"
Hervé (*Fantasy Island*) Villechaize

34"
Emmanuel Lewis

THE SHORT REPORT

I wish I had a dime for every time I've been called "diminutive." I'm not—I'm just damn short.
—Michael J. Fox

BODY LANGUAGE

It's now official: once you've "arrived" in Tinseltown, you *must* get a tattoo. The wholesale slapping-on of indelible body art has attained Hollywood-rite status, whether it's to immortalize a beautiful relationship (**Johnny Depp, Roseanne, Tom Arnold**), a career milestone (**Pamela Anderson Lee**), or just some stupid totem sacred to its wearer (**Julia Roberts**). Over time, we've also seen the emergence of a tattoo truism, which celebs contemplating emblazoning themselves with the name and/or likeness of a lover would be wise to heed: the second that moniker is drawn on, the relationship will go KABLOOIE!

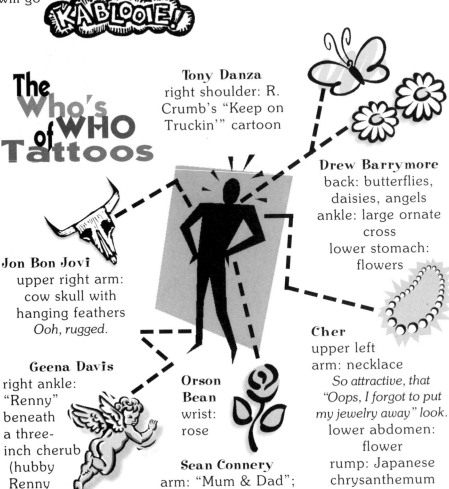

The Who's of WHO of Tattoos

Tony Danza
right shoulder: R. Crumb's "Keep on Truckin'" cartoon

Drew Barrymore
back: butterflies, daisies, angels
ankle: large ornate cross
lower stomach: flowers

Jon Bon Jovi
upper right arm: cow skull with hanging feathers
Ooh, rugged.

Cher
upper left arm: necklace
So attractive, that "Oops, I forgot to put my jewelry away" look.
lower abdomen: flower
rump: Japanese chrysanthemum
left ankle: flower

Geena Davis
right ankle: "Renny" beneath a three-inch cherub (hubby Renny Harlin)

Orson Bean
wrist: rose

Sean Connery
arm: "Mum & Dad"; "Scotland Forever"

Robert Mitchum
arm: unnamed obscenity

Brigitte Nielsen
rump: Sylvester Stallone's name
rump: Mark Gastineau's name
And hers on his . . . they've since split up, of course.

Whoopi Goldberg
left breast: Charles Schulz's bird Woodstock
I don't even <u>wanna</u> know the reason.

Melanie Griffith
left buttock: yellow pear
She called Don Johnson "Pear."

Lorenzo Lamas
right shoulder: Harley emblem
He's so darn <u>manly</u>!

Roseanne
back: "Tom"
left breast: "Tom"
thigh: tiny garter and pair of stockings
rump: "Tom"
upper right thigh: "Property of Tom Arnold"*
Now covered by flowers and a flying fairy.

Courtney Love
left ankle: ankle bracelet

Sylvester Stallone
rump: Brigitte Nielsen's name

Peter Fonda
shoulder: dolphins
inner forearm: three stars

Pamela Anderson Lee
left ring finger: "Tommy's" in the shape of a wedding ring (marriage to Tommy Lee)
upper arm: circlet of barbed wire (movie role: *Barb Wire*)
Clever, eh?

Tommy Lee
body almost entirely covered
highlights: "Pamela" on penis (now, that's devotion!) . . . according to Anderson Lee herself, "When he gets excited it says, 'I love Pamela very, very much. She's a wonderful wife and I enjoy her company to the . . . uh . . . to the *tenth* degree!'"; Mayhem" across stomach above belly button; "Bobbie" (for former lover Bobbie Brown) in script on side of neck
Too bad she dumped him after claiming he beat her up.

Traci Lords
left ankle: crucifix
'Cuz she's so . . . pious.

Tom Arnold
right arm: "Roseanne" with rose in scroll
back: "Roseanne"
over heart: portrait head of Roseanne*
Do we sense a theme here?

*Removal/obfuscation attempted

Tattoos are like stories—they're symbolic of the important moments in your life. Sitting down, talking about where you got each tattoo and what it symbolizes, is really beautiful. Body piercing, too, I think is beautiful.
—Pamela Anderson Lee, who is pierced in a place she refuses to name

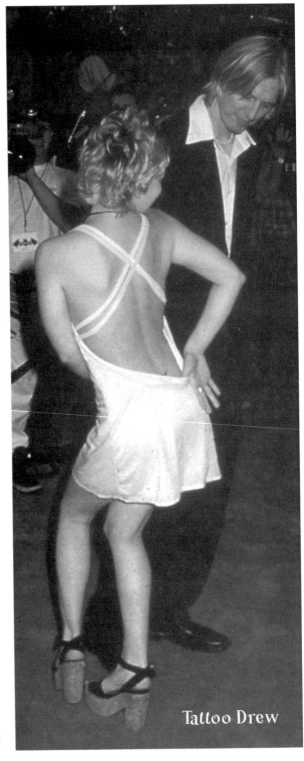

Tattoo Drew

Sean Penn
right arm:
"Madonna"
When asked if he and his ex-wife kept in touch, Penn smirked, "Not exactly."

Johnny Depp
arms: Indian chief head; "Betty Sue"; "Winona Forever"*
"I was thrilled when he got the tattoo. Wouldn't any woman be?" (Winona Ryder); tattoo now reads "Wino Forever" due to removal attempts after breakup.

Flip Wilson
upper forearm: winged "13"; cross

David Bowie
left ankle/calf: Japanese love ode
In honor of wife Iman.

Janeane Garofalo
arm: THINK
Maybe she can't read.

Carré Otis
left wrist: bracelet

Ringo Starr
arm: half-moon; shooting q star
Cosmic, man.

Iman
ankle: "David" with Bowie knife

Julia Roberts
left shoulder: red heart ringed by Chinese word-picture meaning "strength"
Gift from fizzled flame Kiefer Sutherland . . .

Kennedy (MTV "personality")
groin: pink elephant
So no prospective lover will ever mistake her for a Democrat?

Michael Madsen
bicep: wife Jeannine Bisigano's name
They've gone their separate ways.

*Removal/obfuscation attempted

Along with their love of subdermal ink, modern primitives insist on piercing as many body parts as are visible to the naked eye (and, in the most gruesome examples, some that aren't). Models like **Christy Turlington** and **Naomi Campbell** are on the cutting edge of this flipped-out fad, together with celebs like **Lisa Bonet** and **Tommy Lee** (nostril), **Daphne** (*Melrose Place*) **Zuniga** and **Cher** (navel), and **Janet Jackson** and **Madonna** (nostril and navel). What are they missing? Only a bone through the nose (could be next). And let's make sure to look these people up when they're seventy to see what those oh-so-trendy gaping holes look like then, shall we?

TINY LITTLE FLAWS

They add character, right?

Hey, nobody's born perfect—but some celebs have more to over come than others. A forceps delivery resulted in paralysis of the left side of **Sylvester Stallone**'s face (including his mouth, which may be why he speaks so . . . mellifluously); for this reason he will only be photographed from the right. Stallone may also be Hollywood's only leading man to have had only *one side* of his face lifted: when he was preparing to make *Rocky*, he lost a significant amount of weight, causing the left (dead) side of his face to sag, so he had it raised to match the no-less-dead-looking right. **Martin Sheen** is another whose forceps delivery left him with a small imperfection: his left arm is three inches shorter than the right. **Dudley Moore** was born with a club foot, **Demi Moore** with crossed eyes, and **Julie Andrews** bowlegged.

Elizabeth Taylor came into the world looking like a miniature monkey, according to her mother: "Her ears were covered with thick black fuzz—and inlaid into the sides of her head. . . ." Excess hair is a persnickety problem for many male stars, as well: **Hugh Grant, Tom Cruise, Chris O'Donnell, Christian Slater**, and **Matt Dillon**, to name just a few, are members of the unibrow (one long, caterpillar-like strip above the eyes) club. But **Gene Tierney** was fond of her flaws—so fond that her contracts stipulated her teeth could remain in their natural, semisnaggled state. And due to an early playground accident, **Cary Grant** was left with just one front tooth (check it out next time you see a smiley photo of the dashing star).

Those plagued by bad skin include **Courtney Love** (may be why she smears lipstick all over her face), **Tommy Lee Jones, Christian Slater, Mickey Rourke, James Woods, Ray Liotta, Edward James Olmos**, and **Bill Murray**. And we've all wondered about the big bumps (whatever they are) on **Robert De Niro** and **Robert Redford**'s mugs.

After one too many cosmetic surgeries, **Joan Rivers** was left with an asymmetrical nose, and the tip of **Robert Taylor**'s leaned left. Those with eye problems include **Julie Andrews** (one wayward), **Rita Hayworth** (one smaller than the other), **Shannen Doherty** (one lower), and **Peter Falk** (only *has* one). **James** (*Dangerous*

Game; Bad Girls) **Russo** admits, "I've got a pea head, and I've played a couple of pea heads." Even the near-perfect **Grace Kelly** thought her butt was too large, and **Greta Garbo** wished her feet were smaller.

Top grossers: then there are the truly bizarre birth defects. Sometime actor **Mark "Marky Mark" Wahlberg** has a third nipple, and **Andy Garcia** confessed he was "born with a cyst on my shoulder. My mother told me this story, and she has this tendency to exaggerate, but she said it had little arms and legs and hair and everything. Now, this could be completely medically untrue, but she told me it was a twin that never developed. . . . My mother said it was quite large, the size of a softball. They just snipped it off." EEEEUUW!

PAINT YOUR WAGON

There *are* ways—whether permanent (plastic surgery) or stopgap (read on)—of dealing with even the most severe imperfections. The solution most often seen in Tinseltown, particularly for superannuated sex goddesses, is to apply one's industrial-strength maquillage with a shovel, like wrinkly old fossils **Liz Taylor**, **Carol Channing** (face by Madame Tussaud), **Mamie Van Doren** (years of sun worship have resulted in Van Doren's leatherlike face), and **Joan Collins** (heavily pancaked puss is always several shades lighter than the rest of her). Others who must have attended the Tammy Faye Bakker School of Cosmetics: **Sally Kirkland** (looks like an apple doll under a fright wig), **Peggy Lee** (I'm melting! I'm melting!), Sly's mom/psychic kook **Jackie Stallone** (hideous, headband-bound visage frightens small children—and most adults), **Dolly Parton** (revels in her cheap look), **Pamela Anderson Lee** (overdrawn upper lip line grows ever closer to her nose), **Madonna** (no more collagen, please), and **Loni Anderson** (face is a gooey mess). And then, of course, there are the "men": **Michael Jackson** (uses more eyeliner and lipstick than Lisa Marie and Priscilla combined—perhaps the germ-rebuffing surgical mask he wears everywhere is in reality a clever way of protecting the layers of glop on his much-reworked mug) and the **Absurdity Formerly Known as Prince** (androgyny is one thing, but the Artist Now Known as Freak looks like something agents Mulder and Scully ought to be chasing).

DIRTY LOOKS

Take a bath, why don't you!

Pamela Anderson Lee
Drew Barrymore
Yasmine Bleeth
Gérard Depardieu
Johnny Depp
Leonardo DiCaprio
Nicole Eggert
Whoopi Goldberg
Daryl Hannah*
Ethan Hawke
Goldie Hawn
Don Johnson
Tommy Lee
Courtney Love
Madonna
Mickey Rourke

*"I have seen her on many occasions, and she is quite simply in need of a shower or bath."
—Donald Trump*
When she first arrived in Hollywood, Joan Crawford rarely worried about personal hygiene, causing her wardrobe assistants to get into the habit of picking up her carelessly discarded clothing with sticks! (Later in life, Crawford became a compulsive clean-freak.)

EYE OF THE BEHOLDER

I have to be honest. The first time I saw Cher I thought she was a hooker.
—Ronnie Spector, singer, the Ronettes

She's got this gold tooth in her mouth and all this shit around her eyes. She looked like Beetlejuice or something.
—Mark "Marky Mark" Wahlberg, on Madonna

HOT DISH

Some Hollywood secrets are just too hot to handle. Though the truth may be widely known within showbiz circles, it's a whole different kettle of fish when it comes to speaking out publicly. But stars will be stars, and there will never be a shortage of scandalous stories in Tinseltown. Herewith we present a few of the more sensational examples. For legal reasons, we can't reveal the protagonists' names . . . but their deeds speak for themselves:

This ageless, once-hot star of a steamy soap was an even hotter hooker— with some very famous clients— when she first arrived in Hollywood!

Mrs. Megastar threw a screaming fit at that fancy affair when her hunky hubby was all over one of the (decidedly male) members of the catering staff. This wasn't the first time—or the last—that her famous mate made his predilections known . . . but the last straw came when she caught him in bed with her aspiring-actor brother. Hope the idol's new wife is a bit more tolerant!

A certain movie stud—famous for dating that lovely who loves big men— enrages his same-sex partners with his preference for receiving over giving!

Miss Leading Legend once made a porno film with an unlikely co-star: a soda bottle!

(See also page 217)

3

This Business We Call Show

DOUGH RE ME

Boy, ya gotta wonder if today's studio heads long for ye olde days of yore when actors not only listened to their directors but were also on fixed salaries and made whatever movies the higher-ups assigned them. They could even be loaned out to other studios or traded back and forth like baseball cards. In other words, they were basically treated like the cattle they are. Today, of course, things are much different. Not only are actors paid astronomical per-project fees, but they also insist on stamping their films with their own sometimes peculiar creative vision and throwing hissy fits over trailer size and other amenities.

Historically, **Elizabeth Taylor** and **Marlon Brando** were the first actors to be paid a million dollars to appear (in *Cleopatra* and the odd *Fugitive Kind,* respectively); now salaries are surpassing the $20 million mark—more if you take into account the generous profit participation deals top stars command. (**Goldie Hawn** ended up with more than $10 million from *Private Benjamin* due to her back-end deal, and **Dustin Hoffman** made over $25 million for his appearance in *Tootsie.*) Are they worth it? Is wooden-faced, ponytailed **Steven Seagal** convincing enough to merit a whopping $15 million salary? Slurring **Sylvester Stallone** and one-note wacko **Jim Carrey** $20 million? *Kurt Russell,* for God's sake, *$10 million*? I THINK NOT. Megawatt names do not a hit make (think *The Last Action Hero* with **Arnie** and *Hudson Hawk* with **Brucie**)—yet star salaries continue climbing at an alarming rate. Money doesn't grow on trees . . . except, apparently, in Tinseltown.

HAVING A BALL

On *Batman* [*Forever*] I didn't have to fight for every single idea or dollar . . . you just went to them and said, "I think I should have solid-gold testicles in this scene." And they go, "Call the prop department! Get the testicle masters on the phone!"
—Jim Carrey

THE REEL DEAL

Jason Alexander: $125,000 per episode of *Seinfeld*

Tim Allen: $200,000 plus "executive consultant" fees per episode of *Home Improvement*

Tom Arnold: *turned down* $4 MILLION to star in a big-screen version of *McHale's Navy*

Kevin Bacon: $2.5 MILLION

Alec Baldwin: $5.5 MILLION

Antonio Banderas: $4 MILLION and rising

Angela Bassett: $2.5 MILLION

Warren Beatty: asking $9 MILLION

Marlon Brando: received $3.5 MILLION for two weeks' work on *Superman* (1978)

Jeff Bridges: $5 MILLION

Sandra Bullock: $500,000 for *Speed* (1994)
$2 MILLION for *The Net* (1995)
$6 MILLION for *A Time to Kill* (1996)
$10.5 MILLION for *In Love and War* (1997)
$12.5 MILLION for *Speed* sequel (deal inked in 1996)

Nicolas Cage: asked $9 MILLION, got $6 MILLION for *Face Off* (deal done 1996)

Dean Cain: $75,000 per episode of *Lois & Clark*

RAISING CAIN

When Dean Cain (Superman and his alter ego Clark Kent in TV's *Lois & Clark*) asked the show's producers for a salary increase, they declined, citing their desire to be fair to co-star Teri Hatcher. "But I play two roles," Cain reportedly whined.

Jim Carrey: $25,000 per episode of *In Living Color*
$150,000 for *The Mask* (1994)
$7 MILLION for *Dumb and Dumber* (1994)
(Co-star Jeff Daniels got only $500,000)
$7 MILLION for *Batman Forever* (1994)
$20 MILLION each for *Cable Guy* (1996) and *Liar Liar* (1997)
"Why shouldn't I get $20 million when they [the studio] get half a billion? It's ridiculous, but it's fair."

Chevy Chase: 1992 asking price $6 MILLION (we can assume this has since dropped significantly)

George Clooney: got $10 MILLION for *Batman & Robin* (1997)

CHUMP CHANGE

It's like I blot my lipstick with the paychecks I get.
It's like, "Should I floss my teeth with this or blow
my nose on it?" And I'm not just like being a little
bitchy actress: "Life is so hard, I'm not getting paid
anything." I'm *not* getting paid anything.
—Indie actress Parker Posey

Sean Connery: $10-$13 MILLION
Bill Cosby: $1 MILLION per episode of *Cosby*
(series debuted 1996)
Kevin Costner: $14 MILLION for *Waterworld* (1995)
plus percentage
Tom Cruise: $14-$15 MILLION for
Interview with the Vampire (1994)
raked in about $60 MILLION, including "producer"
fees, for *Mission: Impossible* (1996)
$20 MILLION for *Jerry Maguire* (1997)
Billy Crystal: $7 MILLION
Macaulay Culkin: $100,000 for *Home Alone* (1990)
$5 MILLION plus percentage for
Home Alone 2: Lost in New York (1992)
$8 MILLION each for the 1994 flicks *Richie Rich* and *Getting Even
with Dad* (co-star Ted Danson received only $4 million);
now the poor kid can't get a job (presumably the $50 million he's made
since 1990 will help ease the pain).
Mac is *still* asking $8 MILLION—
or at least he was until he "quit acting."
Ted Danson: made almost $12 MILLION per season on *Cheers*
Geena Davis: $7 MILLION for 1996's $100 million flop
Cutthroat Island (talk about money down the drain!)
Daniel Day-Lewis: $8 MILLION
Robert De Niro: $6 MILLION
Got just $50,000 for *Taxi Driver*.
Johnny Depp: $5 MILLION
Danny DeVito: $5-$6 MILLION
Michael Douglas: $12 MILLION for *Disclosure* (1995)
current fee $18 MILLION
Richard Dreyfuss: asking $5 MILLION
Clint Eastwood: $10-$15 MILLION
David Duchovny: $100,000 per *X-Files* episode
Emilio Estevez: asking $5 MILLION

Chris Farley: $6 MILLION
Harrison Ford: received a paltry $1 MILLION for *Clear and Present Danger* (1994);
now commands $20 MILLION (got it in 1996 for *The Devil's Own*)
Jodie Foster: $9 MILLION for *Contact* (deal inked 1996)
Morgan Freeman: got $5 MILLION for *Kiss the Girls* (1997), while co-star Ashley Judd received only $450,000
The *Friends* cast (**Jennifer Aniston, Courteney Cox, Lisa Kudrow, Matt LeBlanc, Matthew Perry,** and **David Schwimmer**: $75,000 per episode in 1996 (up from a measly $22,500 1995 salary)

A FRIEND INDEED

The cast of *Friends* say they want $100,000 an episode. You know what I say? It's time to make new friends.
—Rosie O'Donnell

Andy Garcia: $3–$5 MILLION
Richard Gere: $7–$8 MILLION
Mel Gibson: received $10 MILLION for *Lethal Weapon 3* (1992)
$20 MILLION for *The Conspiracy Theory* (deal inked 1996)
Danny Glover: $2 MILLION
Whoopi Goldberg: $8 MILLION for *Sister Act II* (1993)
now up to $10 MILLION
Kelsey Grammer: $250,000 per episode of *Frasier*
Hugh Grant: $7–$8 MILLION
Melanie Griffith: asking $1 MILLION in 1992;
now significantly higher
Gene Hackman: $6 MILLION
Larry Hagman: $75,000 per episode of *Dallas*
Tom Hanks: $15–$20 MILLION
Woody Harrelson: $5.5 MILLION
David Hasselhoff: miniscule $60,000-per-episode *Baywatch* acting fee supplemented by producer's fees
(plus he's a part-owner of both *Baywatch* and *Baywatch Nights*)
Teri Hatcher: $75,000 per episode of *Lois & Clark*
Goldie Hawn: $5 MILLION asking price
after 1996's *First Wives Club*
Dustin Hoffman: $7 MILLION
Anthony Hopkins: $3–$4 MILLION
Holly Hunter: $2.5 MILLION
Samuel L. Jackson: $4.5 MILLION

There was a certain change when I was halfway through the shooting of *A Time to Kill*. A script came to me and they said, "We'll let you play this part and we'll pay you a million dollars." And I was going, "How? Why? What's this about?"
—Matthew McConaughey

Don Johnson: $150,000 per *Nash Bridges* episode plus "producer" fees

Tommy Lee Jones: $7.5 MILLION

Michael Keaton: His $5 MILLION salary for *Batman* was doubled for its sequel; it was reportedly his $15 MILLION demand for the third installment that nixed another turn as the Caped Crusader. Obviously, the man behind the mask is irrelevant, as shown by the success of both Val Kilmer and George Clooney in the hit flicks.

Nicole Kidman: $3.5-$4 MILLION

Val Kilmer: $6 MILLION

Ricki Lake: $4-$5 MILLION (films)

Jessica Lange: $2.5 MILLION

Pamela Anderson Lee: $60,000 per *Baywatch* episode

Jennifer Jason Leigh: $1 MILLION

Jay Leno: over $10 MILLION annually

David Letterman: $14 MILLION annually

John Lithgow: $75,000 per episode of *3rd Rock from the Sun*

Heather Locklear: $100,000 per episode of *Melrose Place*

Julia Louis-Dreyfus: $125,000 per episode of *Seinfeld*

Andie MacDowell: $5-$6 MILLION

Madonna: asking $1 MILLION (worth every penny!)

Cheech Marin: $75,000 per episode of *Nash Bridges*

Steve Martin: $7 MILLION for *Sgt. Bilko* (1996)

Matthew McConaughey: price skyrocketed from $200,000 to $2 MILLION per project in 1996

Demi Moore: unless you were wandering the frozen tundra during '95 and '96, you know that Ms. Moore became the highest-paid actress in the history of the universe for the spectacularly awful *Striptease* (1996), for which she received **$12.5 MILLION**

Eddie Murphy: **$8 MILLION** for *Beverly Hills Cop II* (1987) **$16 MILLION** for *The Nutty Professor* (1996)

MONEY TALKS

He once came to me and said, "Jeez, I'd love to do some of those small films you do." I told him, "We make those films for less than your salary," and he said, "Oh, well, I can't cut my salary."
—Nick Nolte, on Eddie Murphy

Bill Murray: **$10 MILLION** for *Groundhog Day* (1993)

Liam Neeson: **$3 MILLION**

Paul Newman: **$5 MILLION** for *Blaze* (1989)

Jack Nicholson: **$10 MILLION** for *Hoffa* (1992) **$7 MILLION** for two weeks' work on *A Few Good Men* (also 1992)

Chris O'Donnell: **$4 MILLION** for *The Chamber* (1996)

Rosie O'Donnell: **$8 MILLION** annually

Al Pacino: **$9 MILLION**

Jason Patric: **$6 MILLION**-plus for *Speed 2* (1997) Keanu would've gotten almost double that

Michelle Pfeiffer: **$9–$10 MILLION**

Brad Pitt: got **$17.5 MILLION** in 1996 for *Meet Joe Black* (1997)

Annie Potts: **$50,000** per episode of *Dangerous Minds*

Bill Pullman: **$5–$7 MILLION**

Robert Redford: asking **$10 MILLION**

Keanu Reeves: asking **$11 MILLION**

Burt Reynolds: received **$5 MILLION** for *Cannonball Run* in 1980; now, of course, much lower

Michael Richards: **$125,000** per episode of *Seinfeld*

Tim Robbins: **$3.5–$4 MILLION** per film

Julia Roberts: **$12 MILLION** for *My Best Friend's Wedding* (1997) asked **$12 MILLION** for *In Love and War* (1997) but the studio decided on Sandra Bullock instead (for a paltry $10.5 million)

Roseanne: **$600,000** per episode plus a big back end. (A big back-end *deal*.)

Kurt Russell: **$10 MILLION** for the 1996 bomb *Escape from L.A.* "You know, I feel when an audience sees my name attached to a film, they think it'll probably be a good movie."

a rumored **$13 MILLION** for *Breakdown* (1997)
$15 MILLION for *Soldier* (deal inked 1996)
"If they're willing to pay me that much, I must be worth it."
Yeah—and Elizabeth Taylor has aged well.
Rene Russo: **$2.5 MILLION**
Meg Ryan: **$8.9 MILLION**
Winona Ryder: **$2.5 MILLION**
Adam Sandler: **$2.5 MILLION** for the inaptly named *Bulletproof*
(1996); **$5 MILLION** for *The Wedding Band* (1997)
Susan Sarandon: **$3 MILLION**
Arnold Schwarzenegger: **$15 MILLION** for both *True Lies* (1994)
and *The Last Action Hero* (1993)
$20 MILLION for *Batman and Robin* (1997)
Steven Seagal: **$15 MILLION**
Jerry Seinfeld: **$300,000–$400,000** per episode inclusive of
"executive producer" fees
Charlie Sheen: **$5.2 MILLION** for *Terminal Velocity* (1994)
Alicia Silverstone: after *Clueless* (1995), signed a
$10 MILLION, two-picture deal with Columbia
Christian Slater: **$5–$6 MILLION**
Wesley Snipes: **$10 MILLION**
Sly Stallone: **$12 MILLION** each for *Rocky IV* (1985)
and *The Specialist* (1994)
In 1995, inked a three-picture deal worth
$60 MILLION with Universal
Howard Stern: **$12.5 MILLION** annually
Patrick Stewart: **$5 MILLION**
Sharon Stone: **$7 MILLION** plus
(received **$6 MILLION** for *Last Dance* [1996])
Meryl Streep: **$4–$5 MILLION**
Babs Streisand: **$5 MILLION**
You mean she gets more than Meryl Streep . . . ?
John Tesh: made almost **$7 MILLION** *just from touring* in 1996.
YIKES!

WORTH-LESS!

Money doesn't mean anything to me
except as an affirmation of the music.
—John Tesh

Emma Thompson: $3 MILLION
John Travolta: did *Pulp Fiction* for a measly $140,000
$5 MILLION for *Get Shorty* (1995)
$8 MILLION for *Phenomenon* (1996)
$17 MILLION for *Primary Colors* (1997)
perhaps in an attempt to one-up Jim Carrey and Sylvester Stallone, asking
price skyrocketed in '95 and '96 to $21 MILLION
got $60 MILLION for three pictures in 1996
Jean-Claude Van Damme: $7.5 MILLION
Barbara "Shoot me through a nylon stocking" **Walters**:
$10 MILLION annually
Denzel Washington: $10 MILLION for *Courage Under Fire* (1996)
Sigourney Weaver: $30,000 for *Alien* (1979)
$5 MILLION for *Alien 3* (1992)
$11.25 MILLION for *Alien Resurrection* (1997)
Robin Williams: $15 MILLION
Bruce Willis: $5 MILLION for *Die Hard* (1988)
$15 MILLION for the threequel *Die Hard with a Vengeance* (1995)
$16.5 MILLION for the film version of the poorly written
Dean Koontz novel *Mr. Murder* (1997)
$35 MILLION expected take for the fourth,
badly needed installment of *Die Hard*
Oprah Winfrey: made $75 MILLION in 1995
1996 income estimated at nearly $100 MILLION

WHAT IT'S REALLY ALL ABOUT

I'm deeply grateful for the opportunity to work.
—Al Pacino

The work is its own reward—that's what I like to say. Mostly because I've heard it's a good thing to say.
—Conan O'Brien

I just try to do the work on a daily basis and try to hit it pure.
—Matthew McConaughey

My honor is my work—there is none greater.
—William Hurt

To me, the work is the important thing.
—Sally Field

STAR TREATMENT

Keeping the talent happy is always a high priority, especially to the talent themselves. For this reason, elaborate contracts, stipulating *exactly* what a star requires in the way of amenities, are handed in to the powers that be. Food and drink are among the items most often demanded; for example, **Madonna** has required bubble gum and Hot Tamales candies, **Steven Seagal**, organic food, and **Claudia Schiffer**, mineral water and Skittles candies—with all the purple ones removed. (She may have gotten this idea from rock raunchsters **Van Halen**, whose insistence upon the removal of brown M&Ms from *their* candy dishes is legendary in the rock world.) Similarly, woe betide the caterer who substitutes turkey roll for the real bird in Aerosmith's dressing room: **Steven Tyler** has been known to overturn the entire table upon spying such affronts.) This taste for life's finer things can sometimes backfire, however. On the set of *Silverado,* actor/citrus connoisseur **Scott Glenn** continually chastised the film's food-service personnel for serving concentrated orange juice instead of far superior fresh-squeezed. Their solution? They mixed some pulp into the concentrate, sprayed a bit of the mixture on the counters to make it look like they'd been slaving over fresh fruit, then proudly presented the result to Glenn. "Now that's orange juice!" he cried, and downed it with gusto. They later fessed up. ("He's still bitter about that," snickers the caterer.)

Hotels must also be up to snuff, even down to interior decoration. **Babs Streisand** requires peach-colored toilet paper and towels (goes so well with her creamy complexion); and **the Artist Still Known as Prince** wants his rooms draped with flowing fabrics and filled with the scent of his favorite incense (likewise **Eddie Murphy**, who requires peach potpourri). **Joan Crawford** wouldn't walk into a room unless toasted French bread and seven packages of cigarettes (three opened) were waiting for her—and she also made sure she was told in advance

the exact number of steps from her room to the elevator. Los Angeles Lakers fanatics **Danny DeVito** and **Jack Nicholson** had their hotel put up a satellite dish during the filming of *Hoffa* so they wouldn't miss any games, and tango student **Robert Duvall** had a dance floor installed in his hotel. ("I practice about two hours a day," he explained. "I think you should approach your hobby with the same ferociousness you bring to your work.")

Arnold Schwarzenegger will not fly commercially; he insists on private planes—as does **Madonna**, who also keeps a fleet of limos on standby at all times. **William Hurt** was supplied with a private jet while filming *Until the End of the World* in the wilds of outback Australia because he insisted he needed to be near a church. **Suzanne Somers** demanded *green* jets, and **Clark Gable** would only fly in airplanes with more than two engines—and he also had to be informed of the plane's make in advance. **Bill Cosby** must have a white Jaguar available for his personal use, and **Eddie Murphy**'s limo bills on the set of *Coming to America* set producers back to the tune of $5,000 a week (this in addition to his $5,000 weekly "living allowance")!

Personal trainers are required by both Murphy and **Joe Piscopo**, but not **Roseanne**—she gets foot massages instead. **Farrah Fawcett** must have a personal sauna within a hundred yards of her dressing room or trailer. *The Hard Way* must've been an expensive project: **James Woods**'s personal hairdresser was paid $6,000 per week (presumably to camouflage his thinning thatch) and **Michael J. Fox** had an assistant whose sole function was to insert the tiny thespian's contact lenses each day. **Jane Seymour** is another who is rumored to be pampered to the nth degree; her television show, *Dr. Quinn, Medicine Woman*, reportedly employs assistants to scurry around with a square of red carpet for the actress to stand on. The show is also responsible for supplying Seymour's weekly delivery of London rainwater (to the tune of $1,200 per shipment), with which she washes her lengthy locks!

A METHOD TO MY MADNESS

I've been planted here to be a vessel for acting, you know what I mean?
—Leonardo DiCaprio

Any actor worth his or her salt (and many who aren't) studies "the Method," a school of acting that teaches the student to reach deep inside himself and dredge up emotion through exercises like pretending to be an animal or a tree. It's so popular that most of the people we see on the big screen—even those who look like they couldn't act their way out of a paper bag—have studied it at one time or another, resulting in earnest discussions of topics like one's *craft*, one's *instrument*, *being in the moment*, *sensory circles*, and *imaginative personalization*. It also results in actors doing things no rational human being would do, all by way of getting into a role.

Marlon Brando, who had signed up to play a paralyzed character in *The Men*, lived at the Van Nuys Hospital for Paraplegics for a month and spent all his time in a wheelchair. **Sean Penn** stubbed a cigarette out on his hand to "find" his character, doped-up surfer Jeff Spicoli, in that famous art film *Fast Times at Ridgemont High*. **Mariel Hemingway** got breast implants after landing the role of murdered Playmate Dorothy Stratten in *Star 80*, and **Nicolas Cage** had two of his teeth pulled—without novocaine! OUCHIE!—to look more like *Birdy* (and who can forget his casual consumption of a live cockroach in *Vampire's Kiss*?).

ACTING

I don't understand this Method stuff. I remember Laurence Olivier asking Dustin Hoffman why he stayed up all night [for his role in *Marathon Man*]. Dustin, looking really beat, really bad, said it was to get into the scene being filmed that day, in which he was supposed to have been up all night. Olivier said, "My boy, if you'd learn how to act you wouldn't have to stay up all night."
—Robert Mitchum

Stars who've drastically altered their appearance for a role include **Robert De Niro**, who gained sixty pounds to play boorish boxer Jake La Motta in *Raging Bull* (it's also worth noting that he turned down the title role in *The Last Temptation of Christ* because, he said, there was no way he could research it), **Ralph Fiennes** (twenty-five pounds for his role as the vicious camp commandant in *Schindler's List*, 1993), **Lynn Redgrave** (fifty pounds for *Georgy Girl*, 1966), **Shirley MacLaine** (thirty pounds to play *Madame Sousatzka* in 1988), **Anthony Hopkins** (thirty pounds for *Nixon*, 1995), and for 1995's *The Perez Family*, **Marisa Tomei**, who fatuously remarked, "I wanted to enhance my voluptuousness, so after I got the part I just started eating." On the other end of the scale, so to speak, is **Gary Oldman**, who starved himself to look like pathetic punkster Sid Vicious in *Sid and Nancy*— his efforts were so successful that he ended up in the hospital being treated for malnutrition. **Jennifer Jason Leigh** slimmed down to an ultra-svelte eighty-six pounds for her role as an anorexic teenager in *The Best Little Girl in the World*; she also pens a full diary for each of her characters prior to actually playing the parts. And **Dustin Hoffman** put so much energy into Ratso Rizzo's coughing fits for *Midnight Cowboy* that he actually vomited. YUCK! ICKO!

N◎ STRETCH MARKS, EITHER

AND

I feel cheated, never being able to know what it's like to get pregnant, carry a child, and breast-feed.
—Dustin Hoffman

"Research" is an integral part of "the process," necessary for total immersion in one's role. **Charlie Sheen** spent two grueling weeks in boot camp for his role in *Platoon,* and for their roles as male prostitutes in *My Own Private Idaho,* **River Phoenix** and **Keanu Reeves** hung out (and reportedly took drugs) with real street hustlers while staying with director **Gus Van Sant** in Washington State. Reeves, perhaps utilizing this early training, delved deep into himself during a stint on stage in Canada as *Hamlet,*

Keanu Reeves *Is* Johnny Mnemonic

TAKING SHAPE

I got to do some stuff in it that was . . . that was bitchin'. Like, the physical aspect of the character and its portrayal. I was doing really precise, straight lines. Investigating that shape with emotion. I was doing a whole thing of, like, mother equals round. Anger equals straight. I saw the heart as a round notion. The journey of this character starts out very angular and straight. By breaking him down, compassion is born. And he gains responsibility and compassion and a warming. Then he's open for an embrace.

—Keanu Reeves

and produced a remarkable insight into Shakespeare's philosophical prince: "He speaks fairly often about the nature of living. And the nature of conduct. I mean, one of his soliloquies begins, 'To be or not to be . . . ', which, um, some people ask themselves." (Reviewer Vit Wagner of the *Toronto Star* had this to say about the actor's subtle, moving performance: "Reeves said all the words in the right order.") After hiring a psychiatrist to psychoanalyze the Fletcher Christian character in *The Bounty* (1984), **Mel Gibson** said, "I'll be playing him as the manic-depressive paranoid schizophrenic he really was." (Takes one to know one, Mel.) But **Julianne Moore**, who played a pregnant woman in *Nine Months,* recalls her attendance at Lamaze classes, "which was fun but embarrassing because I was the only one not pregnant." And finally, there's supersensitive **Ron Silver**—who almost got axed from the TV movie *Kissinger and Nixon* (1995) because of his insistence on meeting with **Henry Kissinger** even though he'd been warned the sour Kraut was not at all pleased with the book (a 1992 Walter Isaacson bio) upon which the film was based. The sly statesman, during a lunch arranged by the star-struck but thick-as-a-plank thespian, said he'd help by supplying classified documents— but needed a copy of the script to learn which might be most helpful. Silver happily handed it over, and the film's producers soon received a lengthy letter from Kissinger's attorneys threatening to shut the production down.

But first prize for ultimate Method Madness rightfully belongs to **Daniel Day-Lewis.** For *In the Name of the Father,* the 1994 film about a wrongfully imprisoned IRA supporter, Day-Lewis lost thirty pounds on a diet of nothing but prison food; to look suitably haggard, he spent sleep-deprived nights in a phony jail cell on the film's Dublin set, where he had crew members lock him in and pelt him

The face of young Hollywood

with water and abuse. For *The Last of the Mohicans* (1992), the actor went to survival camp, where he learned to roll his own cigarettes; track, kill, and skin animals; make fire; and hollow out tree trunks to make canoes. After all that, he's still a wimp!

Another thing about the Method: the characters become real people in the "minds" of actors, leading to ever-so-earnest remarks like these:

Patricia Arquette, on her role as a murderess in *True Romance*: "I just wanted to protect Alabama. I didn't want anyone to hurt her, so I lashed out . . . I loved Alabama. What a terrible childhood she had—always saying, 'I've got to get noticed, I'll put on a pretty dress.' Of course I wanted to protect her."

Elizabeth Berkley on her *Showgirls* role: "It's not like it's just 'Here's another breast scene.' At its heart, it's about moral choices. What you give up for love. How far would you go to get what you want? What would you give up for your dream? These are the questions she's faced with along the way. I just hope that people really care about my character and go on that journey with her." [Note: The film received a universal critical drubbing, reviewers paying particular attention to Berkley's "performance": one said she resembled an elongated meat puppet; another, that her emotional range ran the gamut from hot to bothered.]

Glenn Close, on playing Norma Desmond in Andrew Lloyd Webber's stage version of *Sunset Blvd.*: "I keep thinking: embrace the diva. You're playing one, be one! It seems to me that real divas demand total worship from those around them. And they're not terribly subtle. I'm more subtle about how I demand to be worshiped."

Patrick Swayze, to a reporter on the set of *City of Joy* (1992): "I'm deep into Max's anger now. . . . It was scary. I mean, sometimes I would be throwing up in my room just from the emotion, you know."

Sigourney Weaver: "Since I've been playing victims I've taken up karate. I did it every night after shooting to help lift the depression of these characters."

EVENING STAR

It's hard to act in the morning. The muse isn't even awake.
—Keanu Reeves

METHOD-OLOGY

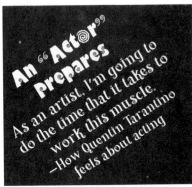

An "Actor" Prepares

As an artist, I'm going to do the time that it takes to work this muscle.

—How Quentin Tarantino feels about acting

Smelly!

Before I play a character I always choose a scent for her to wear. Then whenever I put that fragrance on I feel like I'm inside the character's skin.

—Irene Jacob (*Othello*)

Hard Work

To play a good bimbo, it is not so easy.

—Izabella Scorupo, *Goldeneye* Bond babe

A World of Hurt

I want to encourage others not to be ashamed to have a human condition called *pain*.

—Rod Steiger

Part and Parcel

Regarding *Terms of Endearment*, 1983:

For three months I walked around with pregnancy pads. Every two weeks I added weights. I slept with the pads. My back was killing me. I never gave in.

—Debra Winger

Debra insisted that I and her parents call her by her character's name, Emma.

—co-star Shirley MacLaine

Dead-on Delivery

Before I played Napoleon I called the AMA to get his autopsy. He had several diseases when he died, and learning about them helped me play him. It made him human to me.

—Rod Steiger

Keep in Touch

To get my resources, I have to hang. I have to know and be in touch with and keep the pulse of every walk of life, man.

—Matthew McConaughey

"Art" and "Craft"

If I ever start talking to you about my "craft," my "instrument," you have permission to shoot me point-blank.

—Drew Barrymore

THE STORY OF MY LIFE

Who should've starred in
these Hollywood hits

Altered States: Robert Downey Jr.

The Bad and the Beautiful: Tommy and Pammy Lee

The Bad Seed: Drew Barrymore

Carnal Knowledge: Warren Beatty

The Crying Game: Kathie Lee Gifford and Tom Hanks

Dazed and Confused: Robert Downey Jr.

The Deer Hunter: Kurt Russell

Diamonds Are Forever: Zsa Zsa Gabor

The Elephant Man: Marlon Brando

Enter the Dragon: Barbra Streisand

Fatal Attraction: Sean Young

The Goodbye Girl: Sharon Stone

Good Morning, Vietnam: Jane Fonda

It Happened One Night: Hugh Grant

Hook: Divine Brown

The Hunger: Marlon Brando and Liz Taylor

The Man Who Knew Too Much: Robert Kardashian

Married to the Mob: Frank Sinatra

Menace II Society: O.J. Simpson

Misery: Val Kilmer

Mister Roberts: Lyle Lovett

Much Ado About Nothing: Sandra Bullock

Pee~Wee's Big Adventure: Hugh Grant

A Place in the Sun: George Hamilton

Pulp Fiction: Joan Collins

Reversal of Fortune: Mickey Rooney

The Rocky Horror Picture Show: Sly Stallone

Save the Tiger: Brigitte Bardot

sex, lies and videotape: Rob Lowe

Sunset Blvd.: Hugh Grant

Suspicion: Oliver Stone

Unforgiven: Roman Polanski

The Verdict: O.J. Simpson

What's Love Got to Do with It: Tom Cruise and Nicole Kidman

White Palace: Aaron Spelling

The Year of Living Dangerously: Robert Downey Jr.

Young Frankenstein: Judd Nelson

TIP

Don't do something,
just stand there.
—Clint Eastwood

Ham 'n' CHEESE

Special Mention

Faye Dunaway, *Mommie Dearest* (1981)
Dennis Quaid, *Great Balls of Fire!* (1989)
Robert Downey Jr., *Natural Born Killers* (1994)
Dianne Wiest, *Bullets Over Broadway* (1994)
Mel Gibson, *Maverick* (1994)
Brad Pitt, *12 Monkeys* (1995)
and *Seven* (1996)

Lifetime Achievement Awards

Jim Carrey
William Shatner
Richard Harris
Richard Burton
Dennis Hopper
Al Pacino
Elizabeth Taylor
Jack Lemmon
The Barrymore family (except
Drew, who can't act at all)

The Hamola Hall of Fame: celebrating scenery-chewing as a way of life

BLACK-LISTED!

One part I campaigned for and didn't get was
Hannibal Lecter in *The Silence of the Lambs*.
It turned out that they didn't want a black
man to play a cannibal. I had never thought
about it that way, but now I understand.
—Louis Gossett Jr.

COMING APART AT THE SCENES

It might just be the *lack* of a Method (coupled with outsize egos) that lead other actors to take roles which seem . . . well, ill-advised at best. How else to explain the casting of mindless mantrap **Nicollette Sheridan** as an M.D. in the TV movie *Virus* (1995), or **Barbra Streisand** as an irresistibly seductive temptress in just about *every* movie she's made? This kind of casting seems specially designed to stretch our suspension of disbelief to the breaking point—and it works. Other egregious examples:

Bridget Fonda as a hardened hit-woman (1993's *Point of No Return*) delicately clenching her glass jaw every time she pulls the trigger.

Heather Locklear and **Sarah Jessica Parker** as skimpily clad crime-fighters, in TV's *T.J. Hooker* and the 1993 film *Striking Distance,* respectively.

Going Locklear and Parker one better: seventies supermodel **Rene Russo** as an FBI agent (*In the Line of Fire*, 1993) and big-boned bimbo **Anna Nicole Smith** as a CIA agent (*To the Limit*, 1995).

Cher (*Suspect*, 1987) and **Cindy Crawford** (*Fair Game*, 1995) as attorneys?!?

Obviously, many casting decisions are made on the basis of name alone, studios hoping audiences will flock to theaters just for the pleasure of seeing a favorite star. But the results can be deadly, as in **Melanie Griffith**'s stinkeroo star turn as a sexy young (now there's a stretch) bilingual spy in *Shining Through* (1992). (That squeaky voice! That ingenuous demeanor! That bad acting!) Likewise, audiences didn't seem to buy all-American icon **John Wayne** as Genghis Khan in *The Conqueror* (1956) or, more recently, **Sharon Stone** as a feminist gunslinger (sure, there were plenty of 'em in the Old West) in 1995's *The Quick and the Dead*. Other films that would have benefited from a spot of role-reversal: think slick-haired, whining **Woody Harrelson** and dimpled, dashing **Robert Redford** in *Indecent Proposal* (1993);

anemic, badly bewigged **Tom Cruise** and Spanish sex bomb **Antonio Banderas** in *Interview with the Vampire* (1994).

Then there are movies where the actor seems a tad, er . . . overextended, like **Jane March** in *The Color of Night* (1994)—she played three separate roles and wasn't convincing in any of them. How on earth did **Michael Douglas** get into character as a reluctant lover in *Disclosure* (1995)?

Or **Sharon Stone** her role as the dutiful, understanding wife in *Intersection* (1994)? **Tori Spelling** as a perennial virgin in television's *Beverly Hills, 90210*? Must be the Method!

TALKING TURKEYS

Beginning with **Tony** "Yondah lies da castle of my foddah" **Curtis**, Hollywood has a long-standing tradition of using actors whose accents fade in and out faster than speeding bullets. Even the most talented sometimes have problems wrapping their mouths around a foreign ethnicity: witness **Laurence Olivier** in *The Jazz Singer* as the Orthodox Jewish father of prodigal prodigy **Neil Diamond**. In one of the film's most dramatic—and unintentionally, hilariously surreal—scenes, Olivier screams, "I hef no son!" Or **Ralph Fiennes** as the scion of an Old-American family in *Quiz Show* (1994). (Perhaps his parents educated him in England? Though of course technically inaccurate, his erudite English elocution was somehow easier to take watching Fiennes play a nasty Nazi in *Schindler's List* [1993].) **Winona Ryder** and **Keanu Reeves** had teddible trouble with the King's English in *Bram Stoker's Dracula* (1992), putting their performances at the level of a high school play—still far superior to **Tori Spelling** (clearly hired solely for her brilliance as an actress) in a reeky episode of *90210*. In a televised "tribute" (read: ripoff) of MTV's *The Real World*, Spelling pretends to be a teddibly upper-crusty English girl (or maybe she was pretending to be an actress pretending to be an English girl). Don't miss this episode—a true classic of its kind—in reruns.

Aaron's
beautiful,
rich,
talented,
and rich
daughter

TALKING TURKEYS, PART DEUX

British
Kevin Costner, *Robin Hood: Prince of Thieves* (1990)
(an American in Sherwood Forest)
Marlon Brando, *Mutiny on the Bounty* (1962)

Irish
Jeff Bridges and Tommy Lee Jones, *Blown Away* (1994)

Hispanic
Marisa Tomei, *The Perez Family* (1995)
Robbie Benson, *Walk Proud* (1979)

Upper-Crust East Coast
Jennifer Jason Leigh, *Mrs. Parker and the Vicious Circle* (1994)
(technique borrowed from lockjaw victims)

Lower-Class Brooklyn
Geena Davis, *Angie* (1994)
Sandra Bullock, *Two If By Sea* (1996)

Southern
Demi Moore, *The Butcher's Wife* (1991)

WRONG TURNS

Deciding which parts to take and which to turn down is never an easy task. Actors aren't exactly renowned for their mental prowess (one reason agents and managers are able to make a living)—but it's still kinda hard to believe the following roles, many of which earned Oscars for their portrayers, were deemed inferior:

Alfie (1966)
Played by: **Michael Caine** (Best Actor nominee)
Rejected by: **Anthony Newley, James Booth, Terence Stamp, Laurence Harvey**

All in the Family (TV series)
Role: **Archie Bunker**
Played by: **Carroll O'Connor**
Spurned by: **Mickey Rooney**

Ben-Hur (1959)
Played by: **Charlton Heston** (Best Actor winner)
Ix-nayed by: **Burt Lancaster**

Bonnie and Clyde (1967)
Role: Bonnie Parker
Played by: **Faye Dunaway** (Best Actress nominee)
Kissed off by: **Tuesday Weld, Jane Fonda**

Butch Cassidy and the Sundance Kid (1969)
Played by: **Robert Redford** and **Paul Newman**
Both roles disdained by: **Warren Beatty**

Casablanca (1943)
Role: Rick Blaine
Played by: **Humphrey Bogart** (Best Actor nominee)
Declined by: **George Raft** ("Whoever heard of Casablanca? [And] I don't want to star opposite an unknown Swedish broad.")

Cat Ballou (1965)
Twin drunken desperadoes played by: **Lee Marvin** (Best Actor winner)
Vetoed by: **Kirk Douglas**

The Country Girl (1954)
Played by: **Grace Kelly** (Best Actress winner)
Passed up by: **Jennifer Jones, Greta Garbo**

Dynasty (TV series)
Role: Krystle Carrington
Played by: **Linda Evans**
Scorned by: **Angie Dickinson**

Gone With the Wind (1939)
Role: Rhett Butler
Played by: **Clark Gable** (Best Actor nominee)
Sloughed off by: **Gary Cooper** ("*Gone With the Wind* is going to be the biggest flop in Hollywood history. I'm just glad it'll be Clark Gable who's falling flat on his face and not Gary Cooper.")

Kramer vs. Kramer (1979)
Played by: **Dustin Hoffman** (Best Actor winner)
Shunned by: **James Caan** ("middle-class bourgeois bullshit")

Network (1976)
Role: Howard Beale
Played by: **Peter Finch** (Best Actor winner)
Given the cold shoulder by: **Henry Fonda**

One Flew Over the Cuckoo's Nest (1975)
Role: Nurse Mildred Ratched
Played by: **Louise Fletcher** (Best Actress winner)
Turned down by: **Anne Bancroft, Colleen Dewhurst, Angela
Lansbury, Geraldine Page, Jane Fonda, Ellen Burstyn**
Role: Randle Patrick McMurphy
Played by: **Jack Nicholson** (Best Actor winner)
Brushed off by: **James Caan**

Patton (1970)
Played by: **George C. Scott** (Best Actor winner)
Dismissed by: **Rod Steiger**

Perry Mason (TV series)
Played by: **Raymond Burr**
Scoffed at by: **Fred MacMurray**

Sunset Blvd. (1950)
Role: Joe Gillis (narrator/protagonist)
Played by: **William Holden** (Best Actor nominee)
Eschewed by: **Montgomery Clift**

Superman (1978)
Played by: **Christopher Reeve**
Pooh-poohed by: **James Caan** (as evidenced herein, the Caan man
has a history of turning down only the best roles)

Terms of Endearment (1983)
Role: Emma Horton
Played by: **Debra Winger** (Best
Actress nominee)
Written off by: **Sissy Spacek**

The Three Faces of Eve (1957)
Played by: **Joanne Woodward** (Best
Actress winner)
Given thumbs-down by: **Eva Marie
Saint**

HOLLYWOOD HOT FLASHES

Temper tantrums, prima donna behavior, capricious demands . . . today's stars are able to indulge in all sorts of bad behavior and still keep their jobs. **Kim Basinger** and **Alec Baldwin**, for example: together they starred in Disney's *The Marrying Man* (1991), where their on-set conduct was so outrageous that they became the subjects of a legendary lambasting in *Premiere*. The bickersome Bs disdainfully declined repeated requests for rehearsals, demanded ever bigger and better on-location digs, and generally annoyed the hell out of cast and crew with their boorish behavior. One fed-up crew member snidely whiplashed Basinger: "You can have diva behavior, but you've got to back it up with more than *hair*." The script was also a problem, not meeting the tip-top

standards we've come to expect from a Kim Basinger movie. "Whoever wrote this doesn't understand comedy," sneered the actress, perhaps unaware that the screenwriter was **Neil Simon**. When confronted about her bad rep, Basinger claimed it was a bad rap: "I write scripts constantly. I run my own production company. I'm also a very determined businesswoman. I've a town to deal with. I've got a lot of things to do, and I don't have time to be classified as difficult, and I don't have time to care."

Notorious perfectionist **Barbra Streisand** refused to call it quits on *The Mirror Has Two Faces* until everything was *exactly* the way she wanted it—and if a few people (including **Dudley Moore**) had to be let go in the process, so be it. By the time the flick wrapped, in March of 1996, about fifteen crew members had either quit or been axed, and the budget had soared to $46 million.

Halle Berry, another undeniable beauty who's undeniably temperamental, felt she was absolutely justified in throwing her weight around on the set of *Losing Isaiah* (1995). She explained, "We were doing reshoots and the assistant director was supposed to phone me with the call time to show up for shooting. I felt like these assistant

Work it, girl!
Halle Berry shows part
of what allows *big,
big stars* to get away
with temper tantrums

directors didn't know what the hell they were doing and anyway, when I didn't get a phone call, I thought, 'It's not *my* job to call you, it's your job to call me.' So I went to sleep. . . ." **Jim Carrey** refused to communicate with the outside world until he got his way, locking himself in his trailer on the set of *Ace Ventura: When Nature Calls* until the original director was replaced with his handpicked successor. **Paul Muni** was in the habit of posting his wife outside his dressing room door to warn all comers that "Mr. Muni does not communicate with anyone."

Kelsey (*Frasier*) **Grammer** conveniently took sick when he decided the show's producers weren't paying him enough. Paramount execs were so enraged by his power play that they actually sent a doctor to his house and had a Grammer-free *Frasier* script written. He was back to work three days later. Grammer may have gotten this bright idea from dim-bulb **Suzanne Somers**, who pulled a similar stunt with the producers of *Three's Company*—asking, nay *demanding*, a raise from $30,000 to $150,000 per episode plus ten percent of the back end. . . . Bye-bye, Suzanne.

Walking off the set has proven to be a popular tactic with small-screen stars who feel they deserve a bigger piece of the pie— but as in Grammer and Somers' cases, it doesn't always result in the desired effect. **Rob Morrow** (*Northern Exposure*) and **Michael Chiklis** (*The Commish*) attempted to sweeten their deals in this manner, as did **David Alan Grier** and **Jim Carrey** on the show *In Living Color* (compromises were reached in the aforementioned cases, the settlement figures reportedly being much less than the stars had been asking for). **Malik Yoba** and **Michael De Lorenzo** of *New York Undercover* asked for pay hikes from $20,000 to $75,000 per episode, along with better trailers, better gyms, and better food. (Better forget it.) Yoba insisted greed wasn't the motive: "You can pay me all the money in the world but you can't disrespect me. It had nothing to do with money. It's about respect." Then why did he go scurrying back to the set, tail between legs, when the show's executive producer began auditioning replacements?

Eddie Murphy's habitual lateness cost the producers of *Boomerang* more than a million smackers, and **Laurence Olivier** once castigated **Marilyn Monroe** for the same vexing vice: "Why can't you be on time, for fuck's sake?" he fumed. Monroe blithely replied, "Oh, do you have that word in England too?" The late **Louis Malle**, who directed *Atlantic City*, recalled that star **Burt Lancaster** "was difficult. I mean, he wasn't extremely easy to deal with. He would become . . . Irish, very Irish. He'd start drinking around 5:00, like a lot of people do, especially old people, like when the night falls. . . . Night shooting with Burt was always a problem." And **Faye Dunaway** became so irritated with **Roman Polanski** during the filming of *Chinatown* that she doused the diminutive director with a cup of urine.

Movie stars' megalomaniacal demands now include creative decision-making; script, co-star, and director approval; and liberal rewrites according to whim. **Claude Kerven**, who'd been hired to direct the **Demi Moore/Bruce Willis** project *Mortal Thoughts,* was fired at Moore's insistence because "what he was getting was not what I was wanting." *Ghost* was also apparently a stressful shoot: whenever Moore wanted to discuss a scene with director **Jerry Zucker** (who says her incessant inquiries became "difficult and frustrating"), she'd have the entire set cleared. **Kevin Costner** ousted original *Waterworld* (aka *Fishtar* and *Kevin's Gate*) helmsman **Kevin Reynolds**, who later bitterly remarked, "In the future Costner should only appear in pictures he directs himself. That way he can always be working with his favorite actor and his favorite director."

"**Dustin Hoffman**'s perfectionism?" says the actor's *Tootsie* co-star, **Teri Garr**, "If you argue with him on something, he wants his point and he wants his way. Finally, if you say, 'All right, we'll do it *your* way,' he'll say, 'No, I don't want to do it my way until you *like* doing it my way.' It's not enough to *give in* to him, you have to *like* what he wants too!" **Anthony Hopkins** calls **Shirley MacLaine** "the most obnoxious actress I've ever worked with," and **Norman Jewison** says **Steve McQueen** was "the most difficult actor" he ever had the displeasure of directing. Director **Peter Bogdanovich** likened working with **Cher** in *Mask* to "being in a blender with an alligator." **John Travolta** was a little more diplomatic when dishing the dirt on *Urban Cowboy* co-star **Debra Winger** who, he said, "can cause, how shall I put it, consternation among her co-workers." But **Danny Cannon**, director of the **Sylvester Stallone** actioner *Judge Dredd*, is more forthright: "I'd rather stick needles in my eyes" than do a sequel, he said after filming was completed. This isn't Stallone's first creative clash with a director: after hiring **Don Zimmerman** to direct *Rhinestone*, Stallone wrested control of the picture away from him and made major changes to the script to give himself more screen time (at the expense of uncomplaining co-star **Dolly Parton**), by most accounts making a charming potential hit into an unmitigated flop.

It should be noted that actors aren't the only ones who behave like spoiled brats, to wit:

Producer **Stanley Jaffe** once suffered a nosebleed after yelling too loudly at his employees.

Dawn Steel screened a prospective employee by asking, "The last [assistant] left because I called her a cunt. Would that be a problem for you?"

Producer **Scott Rudin** (*The Firm*), who went through thirty assistants in a little over a year (and who was the inspiration for the tyrannical boss in *Swimming with Sharks*), had the phone in his office customized so that at the touch of a button he could send a message instantaneously to his subordinate of the moment: "String cheese *now!*" Rudin also reportedly cracked his car windshield when in a fit of pique he threw his cellular phone at it.

Producer **Jon Peters** allegedly tore an associate's shirt to rags in one of his trademark binges o' rage.

Mutiny on De Bont-y: On the set of *Twister* (1996), action-flick director **Jan De Bont** threw a cameraman bodily into a ditch, whereupon his entire crew walked out.

"As you know, I have a reputation for being difficult. But only with stupid people." (Val on himself, according to original *Tombstone* director Kevin Jarre, who was fired a month into shooting)

Kilmer once touched a lit ciggie to a camera operator's hair, thereby ruining his co-star's closeup. Hey, accidents *do* happen!

On the set of *The Doors*, Kilmer insisted everyone call him "Jim" (as in Morrison, his role); he also had mail delivered to his character on the set of *The Ghost and the Darkness* (1996). **"Val would arrive [on the set], and an argument would happen,"** said Richard Stanley, director—until he was fired, three days into shooting—of *The Island of Dr. Moreau* (1996). His replacement, John Frankenheimer, said, **"I don't like Val Kilmer, I don't like his work ethic, and I don't want to be associated with him ever again"** and, after filming the final scene, **"Cut! Now get that bastard off of my set."**

"We would all butt heads when we couldn't define a motivation for his character. He wanted to know who Nick Rivers was and why he would say things, and in the context of a parody, you think, `Is it really so important?' There's always a point when I work with him when I vow not to work with him again."
— Jim Abrahams, director of *Top Secret*, 1984

"Childish and impossible."
— Joel Schumacher, director, *Batman Forever*

While shooting *The Island of Dr. Moreau*, Kilmer refused to rehearse, insisted on wearing a blue armband while filming, and felt he was entitled to use cue cards because co-star Marlon Brando was. **"You're confusing the size of your paycheck with the size of your talent,"** commented Brando.

✳ONLY

WOMYN BLEED

You know what the word difficult means? It means I'm a woman and I can't be controlled.
—Kim Basinger

If I was a petite, brunette, ethnic lawyer, then my behavior would be totally acceptable. But we Barbie dolls are not supposed to behave the way I do.
—Sharon Stone

In Hollywood, a woman can be an actress, a singer, a dancer—but don't let her be too much more.
—Babs Streisand, who *isn't*

The producers of *90210*, according to Shannen Doherty, "felt they had no control over me. I think it bothered them that a woman could speak her mind so strongly and not care what they did to her."

I've never had a problem standing up for myself, but it was like what Bette Davis says—a man does that and he's admired, a woman does that and she's a bitch.
—Cybill Shepherd

The fact is, a man can be difficult and people applaud him . . . a woman can try to get it right and she's a pain in the ass.
—Faye Dunaway

THE DIFFICULT LIST

movies

tee-vee

Fred Astaire
Alec Baldwin
Kim Basinger
Warren Beatty
Wallace Beery
Marlon Brando
Yul Brynner
Gary Busey
Jim Carrey
Cher
Kevin Costner
Bobby Darin
James Dean
Speed director Jan
De Bont ("Fucking
hell shit!" is a favor-
ite expression)
Brian Donlevy
Kirk Douglas
Richard Dreyfuss
Whoopi Goldberg
("Do your fucking
job" is a favorite
line)
Cary Grant
Richard Harris
Dustin Hoffman
Whitney Houston
(hey, the habitu-
ally late diva had
to be on *some*
difficult list)
Sally Kellerman
Val Kilmer
Hedy Lamarr
Burt Lancaster

Charles Laughton
Jerry Lewis
Patti LuPone
Shirley MacLaine
Marilyn Monroe
Demi Moore
Eddie Murphy
Kim Novak
Luise Rainer
Julia Roberts
Mickey Rourke
Peter Sellers
Sharon Stone
Barbra Streisand
Rod Taylor
Spencer Tracy
John Travolta
Raquel Welch
Bruce Willis
Debra Winger
James Woods
Loretta Young
Sean Young

Jason Bateman
Valerie Bertinelli
Lisa Bonet
Genevieve Bujold
Gary (*M*A*S*H*)
Burghoff
Delta Burke
Brett Butler
David Caruso
Ellen DeGeneres
Johnny Depp
Shannen Doherty
Fred (*Hunter*)
Dryer
Faye Dunaway
Redd Foxx
Robin Givens
Bryant Gumbel
Kate Jackson
Don Johnson
Brian Keith
Shelley Long
Kristy McNichol
Dan Rather
Roseanne
Jane Seymour
Cybill Shepherd
Suzanne Somers
Philip Michael
(*Miami Vice*)
Thomas
Charlene Tilton
Robert Urich
Ken Wahl
Raquel Welch
Bruce Willis

It's hard to deal with the criticism.
~Rene Russo

I think nothing diminishes a work of art more than criticism.
~Kevin Spacey

Everyone's a CRITIC!

I really try not to read too much about what people think of me.
~Laura San Giacomo

I'm getting better at divorcing myself from what's written about me.
~Hugh Grant

I tend to get bad reviews and I don't know exactly why.
~Chevy Chase

I don't read reviews much.
~James Garner

I don't really read reviews.
~Tim Robbins

I don't read the reviews.
~Val Kilmer

I never read my reviews.
~John Malkovich

I now realize that critics' opinions don't mean shit to me.
~Emilio Estevez

I don't think I'm ever going to read reviews again.
~Bridget Fonda

I don't read reviews unless somebody plants it on my forehead and I can't escape it.
~Paul Newman

What's in a nickname?

Claudette Colbert: the Fretting Frog
Demi Moore: Gimme Moore
Loretta Young (born Gretchen Young): Gretch the wretch
Julia Roberts, while filming *Peter Pan*: Tinkerhell
Wendy Finerman (producer): Wendy Whinerman;
Whiner Finerman
Sharon Stones
Jodie Foster, director/star of *Little Man Tate*: BLT (Bossy Little Thing)
Patty Duke, during *The Patty Duke Show*: the Little Shit
Macaulay Culkin: MacMonster
Kristy McNichol, during *Family*: Snippy
Cybill Shepherd, during *Moonlighting*: Snivel

Stars whose bad behavior has earned them appropriately acid appellations

QUALITY CONTROL

There comes a time in some careers when the powers that be decide enough's enough and the other shoe drops—at last. Beauty queen turned tart-tongued ensemble player **Delta Burke** was fired from *Designing Women* due to frequent flare-ups with her co-stars and the show's producers, **Harry** and **Linda Bloodworth-Thomason**, who said, "We are all mentally exhausted from the daily trials and tribulations of Delta Burke." Adding to the combustible mix was Burke's burgeoning girth (her weight reportedly soared as high as 210 pounds), and huffy hubby **Gerald McRaney**, who ran interference with the show's staff on behalf of his belligerent better half. Fighting with the hands that feed is never a good idea, as both Burke and **Harvey Keitel**—who was replaced by **Martin Sheen** after battling with *Apocalypse Now* helmsman **Francis Ford Coppola**—now know.

    Shannen Doherty, axed from *Beverly Hills, 90210* because of habitual lateness, diva behavior, and tantrums, excused her less-than-sterling rep by blaming all the people who "aren't separating Shannen from Brenda Walsh. They hate the character so they automatically hate me." Later, she added, "If [**Aaron Spelling**] fired me because I was late, then he'd have to fire his daughter **Tori**. And he'd have to fire **Luke** [**Perry**] and **Jason** [**Priestley**] and some of the others." Funny, they're all still on the show. But now that she's had some time to think about it, the cockeyed minx waxes philosophical: "Reflecting on it now, I wonder where all that press came from. I don't know how much *90210* thrived on it. If you think about it, that press did quite a bit for the show. . . . Who knows? It benefits everyone but the actor. Everybody else makes out fine, everybody else gets out without a wound, and meanwhile I come out crippled." POOR BABY.

    "That's what happens when you're ahead of your time," whined **Geraldo Rivera** when he was axed by ABC in October 1985, adding, "When I die people will understand." **Connie Chung** took it a step further in 1995, charging her ex-bosses with sexism when she was cut from her co-anchor position (alongside **Dan Rather**) on the *CBS Evening News*. It's hard to know exactly why Chung was fired— probably a combination of her "soft" reporting style and the fact that on national television she conned **Newt Gingrich**'s mom into admitting her son thought first lady **Hillary Clinton** was a bitch—but *60 Minutes* producer **Don Hewitt** pooh-poohs her blame-shifting: "I told Connie to get off the sexist thing; it doesn't fly. This may have been mismanaged from the start, but it's not because she's a woman." Low ratings were to blame for the termination of **Joan Rivers**' late-night gabfest, which probably made time-slot competitor and bitter rival **Johnny Carson**—on whose *Tonight Show* Joan learned her chops—very happy. But **Raquel Welch** turned the tables on her executioners: she won a breach-of-contract/defamation suit against MGM, who'd fired her during the 1982 *Cannery Row* shoot and were eventually forced to fork over a $10 million settlement— still probably a better bargain for the studio than having her in the movie.

Drug use and abuse can adversely affect one's employment history, as **Mackenzie Phillips** learned when she was let go from television's *One Day at a Time* in 1980 due to her erratic behavior. She's since cleaned up her act, but has never been able to resume her position in the Hollywood hierarchy. Not so **Demi Moore** (as of this writing, the highest-paid actress ever), who was fired for similar reasons by *St. Elmo's Fire* director **Joel Schumacher**. Party girl Moore's solution was to check herself into rehab, whence she called Schumacher the same night, pleading for a second chance—which she got.

MISERY LOVES COMPANY

During the shoot of *Sleeping With the Enemy* (1991), star Julia Roberts became *muy* irritated at having to do reshoots of a lake scene in which she was repeatedly doused and dried. Her solution? To force the entire crew to strip down to their skivvies. Many of them simply walked off the set rather than submit. Director Joseph Ruben later said, "I was at a low ebb, and Julia was so cold and having such a hard time, and somehow her request did not seem so unreasonable. . . . With the benefit of hindsight, I think it was *very* unreasonable."

DON'T GIVE UP YOUR DAY JOB
GROSS NATIONAL PRODUCTS

Some celebrities are so talented that one creative outlet just isn't enough. **Fabio**, for example: not content with his niche as a romance-novel cover model, the squinty-eyed, swollen superstud shilled a butter substitute in a national ad campaign, as well as Frosted Cheerios ("I eat Cheerios. I really eat it."), and has "written" a book and recorded an "album" (*Fabio After Dark*). If that wasn't sufficient, fans could also dial a 900 number and have passionate words of lahf crooned into their eager ears for a mere $1.99 per minute. **Al Cowlings** parlayed his notorious friendship with **O.J. Simpson** into $2.99 a minute from people who called in to hear taped messages about the "framed" former football star. **La Toya Jackson** gets $3.99 a minute for her Psychic Network, but she gives you a generous dollar-a-minute discount for using a credit card. "Time to RePsychle yourself!" trumpets the ad for **Dionne Warwick**'s Psychic Friends Network. At $3.99 a minute it's obviously a steal, but for doubters Warwick offers this testimonial: "'It's not enough to have a friend who understands and is willing to listen,' says a legal assistant from Florida. 'I want answers.' And that's just what they get, from the nations [sic] top mediums rather than from psychics—or pretend psychics—who just happen to man a phone bank."

"Dollywood" is a ninety-three-acre Tennessee shrine to the pneumatic **Ms. Parton**; for unknown reasons, millions of tourists pass through its portals every year. **The Pygmy Formerly Known as Prince** owns a chain of New Power Generation shops which sell the minuscule musician's overpriced line of seduction tools—clothing, jewelry, candles, perfume (ooh, "Insatiable"), and oils—as well as concert memorabilia, records, and videos. **Annette Funicello** has a line of teddy bears, **Morgan Brittany** sells dolls (with cutesy-pie names like "Earth Angel" and "Cuddling Love"), and **Cher** sank a couple of million into Sanctuary, a mail-order business hawking gothic furniture and accessories, including ugly, pricey clothing. Ugly, cheap clothing is sold by **Jaclyn Smith** for Kmart, and **Kathie Lee Gifford** has a similar line with Wal-Mart (some stores have all the luck). Called on the carpet by the media for unwittingly using contractors that employ sweatshop laborers, Gifford, teary-eyed as usual, has turned this unfortunate faux pas into a national campaign to fight the same sort of injustice. (A side effect, of course, is lots of free publicity for the line. Just an observation.) **Sofia Coppola** turned her back on a potentially lucrative career in nepotistic acting assignments to churn out clothing—skimpy minidresses, belly-baring T-shirts and so on—under her own Milk Fed label, and **Jada Pinkett** (*Menace II Society; Jason's Lyric*) makes "T-shirts and T-shirt dresses that have things like **SISTER POWER** and **IT'S HARD TO LOVE A SOLDIER WHEN HE CAN'T LOVE YOU BACK** on them. Basically statements for young women, things I wanted to say." YOU GO, GIRL!

Forget about Armani, Chanel, and Dior: If you want to dress like a star, you can wear ties by **Frank Sinatra**, sunglasses by **Sophia Loren**, and safari-inspired togs by **Stefanie Powers**, together with **Vanna**'s Comfort Pumps for those long, hard days standing in front of a game board. And to smell like a celeb, try **Cher**'s "Uninhibited," **Babs Streisand**'s "Memories," **Vanna White**'s "Perfection" (four vowels, six consonants), or even "Bridges" (*The Bridges of Madison County* movie tie-in: "When there is nowhere else to go, except towards love") by **Warner Bros.**, a company renowned for their fine *parfums*.

If you need to shed a few pesky pounds, look no farther than Cybergenics, whose pitchwoman **Morgan Fairchild** ("television and film star and one of the world's most beautiful women," according to florid ad copy) exclaims pertly, "The results I reviewed are impressive!" Or you can go to Manhattan's Fashion Cafe, mostly owned by **Claudia Schiffer**, **Naomi Campbell**, **Elle Macpherson**, and **Christy Turlington** ("OK, I admit it, a tacky theme restaurant for tourists is not what I'm typically associated with. Then I said to myself, 'Wait a minute, how is it possible for a model to sell out?'"), where, according to **Dennis Miller**, "The entire menu is specially prepared to taste as good on the way up as it does on the way down."

Speaking of tacky theme restaurants for tourists, **Steven Spielberg** and **Jeffrey Katzenberg** are among the owners of Dive! restaurants in Los Angeles and Las Vegas, and coming soon are *Baywatch* restaurants, courtesy of the show's spindly-legged star, **David Hasselhoff**. Other eateries and drinkeries that celebs put their names on include Miami's Bar None bar (**Oliver Stone**), Bash nightclub (**Sean Penn**), and the Blue Door restaurant (**Madonna**); Manhattan's Mulholland Drive Cafe (**Patrick Swayze**), Nobu restaurant and the Tribeca Grill (**Robert De Niro**), and Twins restaurant (**Tom Berenger**); and in Los Angeles, Eclipse (**Whoopi Goldberg**, **Steven Seagal**, and **Joe Pesci** . . . if any of these people have had their hands in any of the food, I don't want it), Mulberry Street Cafe (**Cathy Moriarty**), Rubirosa (**Christina Applegate**), Schatzi (**Arnold Schwarzenegger**), Sanctuary (**Pamela Anderson Lee**), and the increasingly ubiquitous Planet Hollywood (**Bruce Willis** and **the missus, Arnold Schwarzenegger**, and **Sly Stallone**). And you can boogie down in L.A.'s nightclubs of the notable—the House of Blues (**Dan Aykroyd**, **Jim Belushi**, and **Aerosmith**) and the Viper Room (**Johnny Depp**) being perhaps the most well known.

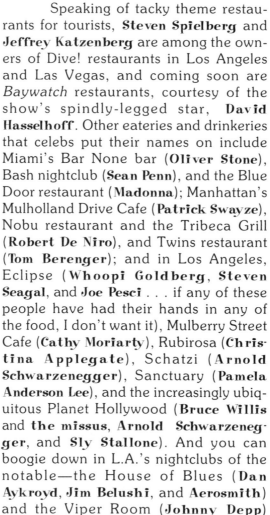

 WATCH

David Hasselhoff is opening up a chain of *Baywatch* restaurants. In fact, the sign on the door says, "No shoes, no silicone, no service."
　　　　　　　　　　　　　　—Jay Leno

Planet Hollywood: coming soon to every town near you

FACE THE MUSIC

Celebs like **Willis** and **Depp** aren't satisfied merely owning happenin' nightspots. No, they must also share their gifts by *performing as musicians* for the multitudes who frequent their clubs. Along with too many other actors, they seem to nurse delusions that they're rock stars in addition to being successful screen idols. Thus we get **Clint Eastwood**'s recording of "I Talk to the Trees" and **William Shatner**'s way *way* over-the-top rendition of "Lucy in the Sky with Diamonds" (not to mention *Trek*mate **Leonard Nimoy**'s hapless hipster version of "Proud Mary"). These days we've got **David Hasselhoff** (really, really, really big, nay *huge* in Germany), oddly overgrown, shockingly successful *Entertainment Tonight* sap **John Tesh**, whose substance-free, bombastic orchestral pap he labels "Teshmusic," and the fleetingly famous **Tonya Harding**, who was booed off the stage and pelted with refuse at a Portland music festival in 1995 when she tried to show off her pipes. Her *vocal* pipes.

With celebrity vanity projects, you can tell a lot about the singers from the titles they choose for their albums. We can learn all we need to know about **Cybill Shepherd**, for example, just by perusing her 1979 album: *Vanilla*. **Michael Jackson**: *Bad* and *Dangerous*. **Joan Crawford**: *The Devil's Sister*. **Polly Bergen**: *All Alone by the Telephone*—well, you get the idea. A cursory glance at other albums churned out by actors through the years produces several additional obvious categories:

Punny Business

Genuine Dud: **Dudley Moore**, 1966
Barbi Doll: **Barbi Benton**, 1975
A Twist of Lemmon: **Jack Lemmon**, 1958
By George: **George Hamilton**, 1966
Rock Gently: **Rock Hudson**, 1971

Groovy, Man

Kinetic Voyage: **Barbi Benton**, 1989
Songs for a Swingin' Sellers: **Peter Sellers**, 1959
Harp in Hi-Fi: **Harpo Marx**, 1957

People So Famous They Only Need One Name

Lola Wants You: [Albright], 1957
Chad [Everett], 1976
Marty [Feldman], 1968
Annette [Funicello], 1959
Marjoe [Gortner], 1970
Goldie [Hawn], 1972
Hello, Jerry! [Herman], 1965
Sal [Mineo], 1958
Telly [Savalas], 1974
Stephanie [Princess of Monaco], 1991

What Time Is It?

It's Time for Tina: Tina Louise, 1958
It's Time for Regis: Regis Philbin, 1968
It's Ann Sothern Time: 1961

Thanks, but No Thanks

Sweet 'n' Gritty: **Michael Moriarty**, 1992
Disco Bill: **Bill Cosby**, 1971
My Favorite Songs from 'Mary Poppins': **Ray Walston**, 1965

Excuse Me?

The Color of Sex: **Kim Basinger**
Music to Listen to Records By: **Edie Adams**, 1959
David Hemmings Happens: 1967

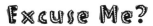

If an Hour or Two Just Isn't Enough

An Evening with **Hugh Downs** (1959)
An Evening with **Jerry Herman** (1972)
An Evening with **Carol Lawrence** (1964)
An Evening with **Danny Thomas** (1954)
An Evening with **Edward Woodward** (1974)

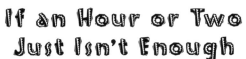

Scary Thoughts

Tinkling Piano: **Merv Griffin**, 1966
I'm Your Woman: **Sandra Bernhard**, 1988
Jayne Mansfield Busts Up Las Vegas: 1962

Celebrity Poetry Korner

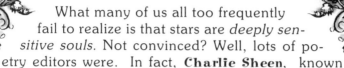

What many of us all too frequently fail to realize is that stars are *deeply sensitive souls*. Not convinced? Well, lots of poetry editors were. In fact, **Charlie Sheen**, known for his delicate sensibilities, published an entire collection in 1990 (*A Peace of My Mind*). Sheen's style is strict rhyme: "Cryin' and yellin' from daylight till night, One giant shit sandwich 'Fuck you' take a bite." We've certainly all been *there* before. Career choices were a matter of concern to the young man as well—in another selection, he asks "Teacher" if he should "play guitar and join the band? Or head to the beach and walk in the sand?" Note the subtle subtext here.

Another of Sheen's generation who has explored life's darker subcontinents is **Ally Sheedy**, whose "insides slosh about like a nauseous ocean," perhaps because she's been drinking "Diet Cherry Coke to quiet the sound." **Woody Harrelson** also dwells on themes of liquid, albeit with a politically correct environmental twist ("We're drinking bottled water, we'll soon be drinking bottled air . . .") and warns his "patriotic generation" that "Hey you, we've got a lot of thinking to do." **Sean Penn** wonders what's on his chin ("It's fucking shit, man") and even makes up his own words, calling one night "so bloody unchristmas." HOO-AH.

Traci Lords, princess of porn, has hitherto untapped depths that so far have only come out through her poetry: she has, she sighs, "so much to say" because she's "lost in today, But all my friends, they're so far away." Too bad, so sad. **Justine Bateman**, vapid Mallory on *Family Ties*, walks "through the sky" and with just one set of eyes, is able to "surmise all the things I can see." And **Keanu Reeves** uses some of his deeper thoughts for a more commercial purpose—they turn into lyrics for his band, Dogstar: "Isabelle is a girl, Isabelle loves her world," begins one sonnet. "You can tell by the way she smiles, Cutest girl by a country mile." Burt Bacharach could learn a thing or two here.

NAOMI CAMPBELL, RENAISSANCE WOMAN

In addition to her stunning good looks and undeniable charm, Miss Campbell possesses the kind of keen insight and self-assurance usually reserved for world leaders. Additionally, she has enough talent for at least three or four people, allowing her to move beyond the rather limited (if ultraglam) confines of the catwalk. Sometimes it just doesn't seem fair that one person is blessed with *all these gifts.*

As TRAILBLAZER: "[In 1989] I saw my face on the cover of American *Vogue,* and I felt that it was a true victory. I was the first black model to make the cover of a big American fashion magazine. I cried!" [Actually, that honor belongs to Beverly Johnson, who appeared on the cover of American *Vogue* in 1974.]

As ALTRUIST: "I look at [modeling] as something I'm doing for black people in general."

As ENTREPRENEUR: Naomi is part-owner of New York's Fashion Cafe.

As ROCK STAR: the nonappearance of Campbell's eagerly awaited album *Babywoman* in the U.S. isn't just a question of a fashionably late release. Though it's out in the U.K. (Naomi's homeland, after all), it's reportedly so bad that an American release is now out of the question.

As PERFORMANCE ARTIST: Naomi once did a spur-of-the-moment bump 'n' grind stripdown for the lucky patrons of a Manhattan dyke bar.

AS OBJECT OF PERFECTION: "Everyone always says I have the perfect body. I don't have big tits. I don't have wide hips. I fit *every* outfit that's put on me." And, "[My best features are] my legs and butt. I like my shoulders. My waist is twenty-two; my hips are thirty-three or thirty-four. My face is very animated. I have a little button nose. My lips are full but not huge." (*The same could be said about her brain. . . .*)

AS BEST-SELLING AUTHOR: Naomi got a book deal resulting in the release of *Swan* in 1994. The volume is a bodice ripper set in the dazzling world of fashion modeling (a milieu in which Naomi—and, presumably, uncredited co-author Caroline Upchur—feels right at home. . . . Write what you know). The risible *roman à clef* is not strictly autobiographical: Campbell's title character is cleverly disguised as a *white* supermodel who offers tantalizing glimpses into the glamorous world of the runway: "They'd sent a chauffeur-driven Mercedes to collect me and I scampered through the rain wearing nothing underneath my raincoat but a toweling robe over my bare skin. I decided years ago that it was crazy to get dressed since the whole day is spent running from one designer's show to another, being whisked in and out of clothes by the dressers. 'I might just as well arrive naked,' I explained to the press when I did it for the first time, giving them yet another opportunity to print a story about how outrageous I am." The book was remaindered almost as soon as it was printed.

AS COURTESAN TO THE STARS: Naomi's famous dates have included Mike Tyson, Sylvester Stallone, Robert De Niro, Adam Clayton (U2), and Eric Clapton.

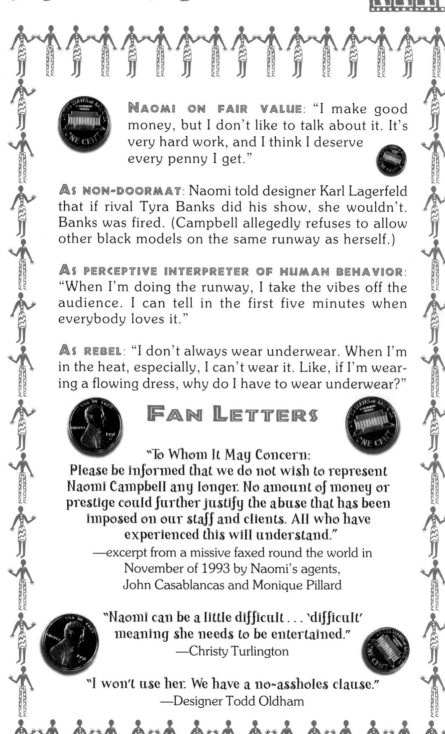

NAOMI ON FAIR VALUE: "I make good money, but I don't like to talk about it. It's very hard work, and I think I deserve every penny I get."

AS NON-DOORMAT: Naomi told designer Karl Lagerfeld that if rival Tyra Banks did his show, she wouldn't. Banks was fired. (Campbell allegedly refuses to allow other black models on the same runway as herself.)

AS PERCEPTIVE INTERPRETER OF HUMAN BEHAVIOR: "When I'm doing the runway, I take the vibes off the audience. I can tell in the first five minutes when everybody loves it."

AS REBEL: "I don't always wear underwear. When I'm in the heat, especially, I can't wear it. Like, if I'm wearing a flowing dress, why do I have to wear underwear?"

FAN LETTERS

"To Whom It May Concern:
Please be informed that we do not wish to represent Naomi Campbell any longer. No amount of money or prestige could further justify the abuse that has been imposed on our staff and clients. All who have experienced this will understand."
—excerpt from a missive faxed round the world in November of 1993 by Naomi's agents, John Casablancas and Monique Pillard

"Naomi can be a little difficult . . . 'difficult' meaning she needs to be entertained."
—Christy Turlington

"I won't use her. We have a no-assholes clause."
—Designer Todd Oldham

ALTERNATE

mta/maw*

Maude Adams
Stephen Baldwin
William Baldwin
Antonio Banderas
Kim Basinger
Marisa Berenson
Candice Bergen
Halle Berry
Josie Bissett
Susan Blakely
Naomi Campbell
Joanna Cassidy
Courteney Cox
Cindy Crawford
Geena Davis
Cameron Diaz
James Garner
Linda Gray
Melanie Griffith
Patti Hansen
Margaux
Hemingway
Mariel
Hemingway
Natasha (*Species*)
Henstridge
Whitney Houston
Elizabeth Hurley

Lauren Hutton
Iman
Jessica Lange
Kelly Lynch
Andie MacDowell
Ali MacGraw
Elle Macpherson
Demi Moore
Patrick (*Melrose Place*) Muldoon
Chris O'Donnell
Michelle Pfeiffer
Paulina
Porizkova
Priscilla Presley
Rene Russo
Susan Sarandon
Cybill Shepherd
Brooke Shields
Anna Nicole
Smith
Sharon Stone
Uma Thurman
Twiggy
Liv Tyler
Sela Ward
Vanna White
Elijah Wood

atm**

Halle Berry
Revlon

Josie Bissett
Giorgio Beverly
Hills

Jon Bon Jovi
Versace

Mel Brooks
Neiman Marcus

Gabriel Byrne
Donna Karan

Willem Dafoe
Prada

Bo Derek
Bijan

David Duchovny
Saks Fifth Avenue

* model-turned-actress/ model-actress-whatever
** actor-turned-model

VOCATIONS

band wagon
celeb band members

Melanie Griffith
ironically enough, for Revlon's "Age-Defying" product line

Kadeem Hardison
Saks Fifth Avenue

Mariel Hemingway
J. Crew

Dennis Hopper
Hugo Boss

Elizabeth Hurley
Estée Lauder

Matt LeBlanc
Saks Fifth Avenue

Jerry Lewis
Saks Fifth Avenue

Madonna
Versace

John Malkovich
Prada

Demi Moore and Bruce Willis
Donna Karan

Baywatch's
Gina Lee Nolin
Sasson

Natalie Portman
Isaac Mizrahi

Lisa Marie Presley
Versace

Molly Ringwald
Tweeds, and others

Joan Rivers
No Excuses jeans

Tim Roth
Prada

Antonio Sabato Jr.
Calvin Klein underwear

Fisher Stevens
Saks Fifth Avenue

Sharon Stone
signed with the Marilyn agency

Tina Turner
Hanes hosiery

Jack Wagner
Saks Fifth Avenue

Mark "Marky Mark" Wahlberg
Calvin Klein underwear

Kevin Bacon
The Bacon Brothers (vocals)

Kevin Costner
Roving Boy (vocals)

Johnny Depp
P (bass, vocals)

Dermot Mulroney
Sweet & Low Orchestra (cello, mandolin)

Lou Diamond Phillips
The Pipefitters (vocals)

River Phoenix
Aleka's Attic (guitar, vocals)

Keanu Reeves
Dogstar (bass)

Frank Whaley
The Niagaras (drums)

Bruce "Bruno" Willis
The Accelerators (vocals, harmonica)

ROCK STARS' REVENGE

musicians-turned-actors

Tony Bennett: *The Oscar* (1966)
Michael Bolton: *Meet Wally Sparks* (1996)
Jon Bon Jovi: *Moonlight and Valentino* (1995)
David Bowie: *The Man Who Fell to Earth* (1976)
Labyrinth (1986)
The Linguini Incident (1992)
Basquiat (1996)
Harry Connick Jr.: *Copycat* (1995)
Independence Day (1996)
Rita Coolidge: *Pat Garrett and Billy the Kid* (1973)
Roger Daltrey (The Who): *Lisztomania* (1975)
McVicar (1980)
Evan Dando (The Lemonheads): *Reality Bites* (1994)
Heavy (1996)
Neil Diamond: *The Jazz Singer* (1980)
John Doe (X): *Georgia* (1995)
Bob Dylan: *Pat Garrett and Billy the Kid* (1973)
Art Garfunkel: *Carnal Knowledge* (1971)
Bad Timing: A Sensual Obsession (1980)
Whitney Houston: *The Bodyguard* (1992)
Waiting to Exhale (1995)
Ice Cube: *Boyz N the* Hood (1991)
Trespass (1992)
Friday (1995)
Ice T: *New Jack* City (1991); *Trespass* (1992)
Tank Girl (1995)
Chris Isaak: *The Silence of the Lambs* (1991)
Little Buddha (1993)
Janet Jackson: *Poetic Justice* (1993)
Mick Jagger: *Ned Kelly* and
Performance (both 1970)
Freejack (1992)

FOLKS

We were in Milwaukee playing the Metalfest . . . we're a
folk band—we should not have been there. They threw
beer at us and told us to fuck off. It was beautiful.
　　　　　　—Keanu Reeves, on playing with Dogstar

REMARKABLE C◎INCIDENCE

John Tesh used to
play in Yanni's band.

David Johansen (New York Dolls): *Freejack* (1992)
Grace Jones: *Boomerang* (1992)
Kris Kristofferson: *A Star Is Born* (1976)
Lone Star (1996)
Lyle Lovett: *The Player* (1992)
Madonna: *Desperately Seeking Susan* (1985)
Shanghai Surprise (1986)
Who's that Girl? (1987)
Body of Evidence (1993)
Four Rooms (1995) and *Evita* (1996)
Ricky Nelson: *Rio Bravo* (1959)
Queen Latifah: *Jungle Fever* (1991); *Set It Off* (1996)
Lou Reed: *Blue in the Face* (1995)
Robbie Robertson (The Band): *The Crossing Guard* (1995)
Henry Rollins: *Johnny Mnemonic* (1995)
Diana Ross: *Lady Sings the Blues* (1972)
The Wiz (1978)
Tupac Shakur: *Juice* (1992); *Poetic Justice* (1993); *Gridlock* (1997)
Ringo Starr: *Candy* (1968); *Caveman* (1981)
Sting: *Quadrophenia* (1979); *Brimstone & Treacle* (1982);
Dune (1984); *The Bride* (1985)
Mark "Marky Mark" Wahlberg: *The Basketball
Diaries* (1995); *Fear* (1996)
Dwight Yoakam: *Sling Blade* (1996)
Frank Zappa: *Baby Snakes* (1980)

[Michael Jackson] wanted to be a movie star very badly ... You
take that face and blow it up on a screen and it looks silly.
—Screenwriter Howard Rodman

CHAIRMAN ◎F THE

A new study shows that one out of every four drivers
has fallen asleep at the wheel while on the road. And
for half of those, the last thing they remember hearing
is "And now here's a new one from John Tesh."
—Dennis Miller

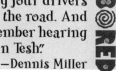

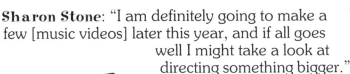

BLAND AMBITION

D o people who've had it all still have ambition? Why, of course they do!

Madonna: "Eventually I would like to direct."

Ten-year-old **Tina Majorino**, star of *Waterworld* and *When a Man Loves a Woman*: "I really want to direct. I know it's not easy, but I've always wanted to make my own movie."

Isabella Rossellini: "One day I'd like to direct because I like to have more control over my destiny."

Tom Cruise: "When I first started as an actor, I always knew one day that I wanted to produce my own movies, and direct."

Burt Reynolds: "I want to live a quiet, pseudointellectual life and go out and direct a picture two times a year."

Sharon Stone: "I am definitely going to make a few [music videos] later this year, and if all goes well I might take a look at directing something bigger."

Sage (son of Sly) **Stallone**: "In the future, when I get out of school, I'll probably be starring in a couple of films, and I'll be directing some films, and maybe writing or producing some films."

Ed Harris: "I think that as the years go by I might want to direct."

Demi Moore: "I feel like I have a lot of growing and learning to do before I take on directing."

Diane Keaton: "Now that I'm actually doing it, I wonder why everyone wants to in the first place. You have to think of *everything*."

Rosie Perez: "I just love power, and that's why I'm producing now."

Anna Nicole Smith: "I really want to be a serious actress."

Supermodel **Bridget Hall**: "I'm focused on acting classes, and I want to get into abstract painting."

Paula Abdul: "I've really got the acting bug now. I feel in my soul that it's the right direction for me."

Liv Tyler: "I want to study aromatherapy, massage and art. I want to be a jack-of-all-trades."

Anne Rice: "I'd love to write country music someday."
Hey, why not—Robert James Waller did.

Yoko Ono: "I'd like to be a more forward person. A person who isn't a doormat."

Judd Nelson: "This career might be a stepping stone to the governorship of California and then to the presidency. There's a precedent, and it's been done by lesser men."
There is no lesser man than you, Judd.

Michael Moriarty, announcing his intention to run for President: "This country is in such desperate need for an honest man, they're gonna go looking for me 'cause I'm right out of a Frank Capra film."
Yeah—You Can't Take It With You.

Ted Turner: "I've got a pocketful of big plans. But I'm not going to show my hand. I mean, you didn't see Eisenhower faxing Hitler the plans for the invasion of Europe."
No, and you didn't see Mamie hawking workout tapes in skimpy unitards, either.

4

Certifiable Proof of Inanity

Fame is a perversion of the natural human instinct for attention.
—Al Pacino

Anybody who tells you he doesn't want to be famous is full of crap.
—Jon Lovitz

THE EGO HAS LANDED

Once I was walking down the street and dogs were barking at me. I said, "Ah, I must have made it. Even animals recognize me!"
—Jon Lovitz

I'm not going to be modest anymore. I'm a movie star, and it's lovely.
—Anthony Hopkins

Ah, egotism. Without it you don't stand a chance in Tinseltown. And it's expected of stars, particularly the older ones (think **Gloria Swanson** in *Sunset Blvd.*)—after all, these people are *artistes*, and a touch of the high-strung goes with the territory. But the smart ones know not to reveal their true, I-am-the-center-of-the-universe sentiments publicly (not good for one's image) except with a tinge of irony: "One thing I hope I'll never be is drunk with my own power. And anybody who says I am will never work in this town again" (**Jim Carrey**).

REALITY BITES

I think when I was younger I wanted to tell everybody everything because I thought I was so damn interesting. Then I heard the snoring.
—David Duchovny

I hired, fired, cast, produced, directed, wrote, acted, hyped the show in the media. I spent all my time trying to bring lousy scripts to life, trying to bring mannequins with suits on to life.

—Robert (*Baretta*) Blake

Let's correct the impression that [the producers of *Starsky & Hutch*] made *me* a star. It wasn't that way at all. You see, I'm an artist . . . so they called *me* in. The public applauded and gave *me* fame. All of the above had nothing to do with the producers. It was *me* who made it a success.

—Paul Michael Glaser

I see myself hot for the next seven years at least. I've analyzed everyone around, and I just don't see anyone who has what I do.

—Richard Grieco

Of course *The Magnificent Seven* would have been nothing without *me*.

—Yul Brynner

When I'm working well, I like to think I'm doing God's work.

—Faye Dunaway

Success and fame and all of its rewards, that is what you want. That is what everybody probably wants. In short, you want what I got.

—Jason (*Seinfeld*) Alexander, addressing graduates of Boston University's School for the Arts

You tell *me* if I'm wrong about this, but I guess I don't have the fame of a director in America. I have the fame of a movie star.

—Quentin Tarantino

I am known in parts of the world by people who have never heard of Jesus Christ.
—Charlie Chaplin

There's nothing better than to know I can be taking a bath at home and at the same time someone is watching *me* in Brazil.
—Babs Streisand

A select group of my classmates thought I was more interesting than anything in the classroom.
—Bruce Willis

I learned to act on the big screen. **I** was never a spear-carrier. **I** was always the star. Always.

—Rob Lowe

RuPaul is a boundless energy that can pour **itself** into whatever shape **it** wants.

—RuPaul
At least ol' Ru got the gender right.

I've got taste. It's inbred in **me**.

—David Hasselhoff

If you're really funny, you're really funny. **I**'ve been funny since **I** was four.

—Bob Saget (host of America's Funniest Home Videos)

When you have as much critical mass, so to speak, as **I** have, even if you do nothing it makes a gigantic amount of money.

—David Geffen

A Top Gun instructor once told me there are only four occupations worthy of a man: actor, rock star, jet fighter pilot, or president of the United States.

—Tom Cruise *(Didn't he leave out 'Scientologist'?)*

We've all had hypothermia at times on [*Baywatch*]. David Charvet almost had to be hospitalized. But it's easier for **me** to endure the cold because **I**'m an owner of the show and **I**'m the highest-paid guy.

—David Hasselhoff

This is an actual bloody *legend* in front of you.

—Ringo Starr

I'M TOO SEXY

Why do people treat me with fun just because I am the biggest, strongest, and most beautiful man in the world?
—Arnold Schwarzenegger

I'm wicked. I'm sexy. I'm heaven.

A guy like me, like Mel Gibson, like Tom Cruise, like Stallone, they can walk on the street and twenty girls, thirty, forty, they want those guys.
—Jean-Claude Van Damme

I built my body to carry my brain around.
—Sylvester Stallone
Well, he is sorta stunted-looking. . . .

—Matthew McConaughey, during a photo shoot

Macho guys might feel threatened by me.
—Michael Bolton

Any man in Hollywood will meet me if I want that.

As a teenager I crept around on eggshells because people kept telling me I could destroy men.
—Cybill Shepherd

I was [in Hollywood] with no money, and all these people saying they wanted to do this and that for me. People wanted to marry me. People wanted to put me in the movies.
—Pamela Anderson Lee

I'm magnificent! I'm five feet eleven inches and I weigh one hundred thirty-five pounds, and I look like a racehorse.
—Julie Newmar

I've always looked older and sounded older. When I'm forty and everyone else is starting to age, I'll always look the same.
—Cathy Moriarty

I look fabulous for my age.
—Jane Fonda

Men think I'm beautiful and terrific. They take me to dinner and tell me how wonderful I am. . . . It's fun.
—Alana "The Piranha" Hamilton Stewart

Pregnancy is hard, and trying to come back from it [physically] is scary. But I've had two kids and look at me now.
—Rachel Hunter

—Sharon Stone

No, make that any man *anywhere*.

Steven Spielberg, Back-Patter to the STARS

I hate tooting my own horn, but after Steven saw *Yentl*, he said, "I wish I could tell you how to fix your picture, but I can't. It's the best film I have seen since *Citizen Kane*."

—Barbra Streisand

I remember talking to Spielberg and he said, "I don't want to see you lose that—there's a spontaneity to what you did in *Sleep With Me*. I had never seen it before. It was a special thing."

—Quentin Tarantino

AW, SHUCKS

You've just gotta wonder when people who've spent their entire lives clawing their way to the top suddenly turn their backs on fame and become ingratiatingly, cloyingly humble.

Acting has destroyed my ego. I have very little self-respect now. I don't particularly admire actors, and so to be one is something I don't particularly admire.

—Hugh Grant

I'm much prouder of being a father than being an actor.

—Bruce Willis

I don't want to be super-famous, man. That would be awful.

—Keanu Reeves

I watch other actors and think, "That's a proper actor—I'm a plumber, really."

—Jeremy Irons

Yale actually invited me—little smog-ridden me—to sink my blond teeth into its dusty brick and ivy. Just coat me with some eastern tsuris, grease up my hair for luck, and watch me dive into the depths of academia.

—Jodie Foster

I've never found myself sexy at all.

—Liv Tyler

I'm not an active feminist, but being on *Baywatch* was against everything I am morally.

—Nicole Eggert

Eggert presumably isn't against earning huge piles of moolah.

Bobby De Niro and I are close friends. And Chris Walken. I have a lot of superstar friends. Like Mikhail Baryshnikov and Liza Minnelli. I'm lucky to have a group of such talented friends.

—Joe Pesci

I don't want followers. I don't want any fucking guru stuff.

—Jim Carrey

I have an open invitation to have dinner with Arnold Schwarzenegger, I've met Warren Beatty and I really like Warren Beatty and I'd like to hang out with Warren Beatty. But the bottom line is I'm busy. . . .

—Quentin Tarantino

Apparently not.

I'm nowhere near as sexy as I come off on camera.

Film just loves me. — David Caruso

THE SMART SET

Everything on the show's revolutionary. And people aren't gonna get half of it for fifty years.

—Roseanne

[An] existential action film . . . screenplay by Sartre. Dialogue by Camus.

—*Sylvester Stallone, on his movie* Assassins

I'd walk out of offices with my fingers in my ears so I wouldn't hear someone who didn't know as much as I did telling me what to do.

—**Kevin Costner, describing his days as a struggling actor**

If I was just normally intelligent I could probably get away with it—but I'm *fiercely* intelligent, and that's threatening.

—Sharon Stone

I very often think I'm brilliant, still.

—Matthew Broderick

I was a straight-A student in high school and I never did anything but show up. . . . I took the Stanford-Binet IQ test, and I guess 180 is the highest it will go, and I got them all right. I didn't miss one. My score was 180 plus.

—*James Woods*

I'm almost rational to a fault.

—**Robin Givens**

She's a lot of other things to a fault too.

I'm just an independent thinker.

—Oliver Stone

SPIRIT
of Survival

I was leaving *No Escape*, shot in the wilds of Australia, for two weeks, and a helicopter was going to pick me up and drop me off where a car would take me to the airport. The helicopter pilot—an Aussie with tattoos, not someone you fuck with—dropped me off in the middle of the jungle. I said, "This doesn't look right," but he left me there, alone, in the fucking rain forest. I'd heard stories about python snakes; after an hour I started going crazy. Someone at the base camp figured it out, but I was there for *two hours*!
—**Michael Lerner**

The physical labors actors have to do wouldn't tax an embryo.
—Neil Simon

I wasn't afraid for my safety. I'd rather take a bullet in the head than not make a movie.
—Lara Flynn Boyle, on shooting *The Big Squeeze* in gangland L.A. in 1996

GOOD AT MY JOB

I'm an actor, not a star.
Stars are people who live in Hollywood
and have heart-shaped swimming pools.
—Al Pacino

I'm not an expert on anything but laughs. I just know how to make people feel good.
—Jim Carrey

If I've made it a little easier for artists . . . to work in violence—

I'm really proud I was able to embody a police officer with *NYPD Blue*. I believe in the cop that John Kelly was.
—David Caruso

My only regret in the theater is that I could never sit out front and watch me.
—John Barrymore

I already knew tap dancing and ballet. Now I know lap dancing too.
—*Showgirls* star Elizabeth Berkley (Adds "writer" Joe Eszterhas about the movie's stunningly stinky script: "It's a spiritual message. And forgive me, but I think it's almost a deeply religious message on a very personal level." [This may be why the hirsute hack beseeched teenagers to use fake IDs to get in to see it.]

The guy I was reading with got lost because he was so busy watching me.
—Samuel L. Jackson, on his audition for *Pulp Fiction*

I've made some great ones. *Risky Business* still stands up. It's timeless. They study that film in film school.
—Rebecca De Mornay

Yeah, I've made stupid movies. But you know, I like my work in every film I've done.
—Bruce Willis

—Quentin Tarantino

great, I've accomplished something.

Elizabeth Berkley
shows off her
talent

WAAAAAH!

Scratch an actor and you'll find an actress.
—Dorothy Parker

Or why life is tough when you're a celebrity. Hey, cry me a river.

During the filming of *Gunfight at the O.K. Corral,* fans surrounded Burt Lancaster and asked for his autograph. "Why don't you ask [co-star Kirk] Douglas for his?" Lancaster said. "Great performer. Of course, you don't recognize him without his built-up shoes." At which Douglas began to cry.

I always believe I can handle everything and keep all those balls in the air—and then I can't understand why I'm crying hysterically at the end of the day and I feel overloaded and can't sleep.

—Michelle Pfeiffer

I don't need another thing to worry about. Why add more to my angst?

—Al Pacino

Sometimes I go nights without sleeping because I'm up doing my homework because I had a premiere to go to the night before. It's the price you have to pay.

—Natalie Portman, child star

I've sold too many books to get good reviews anymore.

—John "Überhack" Grisham

If I'm such a legend, then why am I so lonely?

—Judy Garland

Just standing around looking beautiful is so boring, really boring, so boring.

—Michelle Pfeiffer

Being a sex symbol is a heavy load to carry, especially when one is tired, hurt, and bewildered.

—Marilyn Monroe

It's not as easy as it looks, being on all the time. I mean, what happens if I'm in a bad mood?

—Vanna White

Vanna, you're not deep enough to have moods.

I'm still doing that thing you do when you're a kid, when you're eleven and a half and you tell everybody you're twelve. It's because of my appearance—this pituitary nightmare that is my life.

—Michael J. Fox

I mean, from the moment some of my girlfriends laid eyes on him, they *hated* him. One used to say that I had Patty Hearst syndrome—that I was like a kidnap victim. He was constantly working on me psychologically to make me feel like I was always in danger and weak and that without him constantly there I was vulnerable.

—**Sharon Stone, after the inevitable breakup with Bill MacDonald (who, she once daffily declared, had been her lover in a past life), the married producer with whom she had an affair on the set of *Sliver* (and whose divine union was busted up in the process)**

I don't even get an allowance.   —**Macaulay Culkin**

As I lay on the floor in my dark, empty room, Tuppins, my puppy, licked at the tears running down my face. "Oh, Tuppins," I sobbed, "why has God forsaken me?"

—**Tammy Faye Bakker, describing her last night in the house from which she was evicted by Jerry Falwell in 1988**

I feel like a hard hat a lot of the time. I feel like I'm sixty floors up and people are dropping rivets on my head.

—**Sylvester Stallone**

I'm down, I'm scared, I don't know what the answers are. Hold me.

—**Paul Michael Glaser, to David Soul on the set of *Starsky & Hutch***
Glaser was also reportedly in the habit of going off by himself until his "karma cleared."

I was part of one of the biggest movies of the year, but all I've gotten from being in *The Flintstones* is a lot of five-year-olds running after me in Thrifty drugstores.   —**Halle Berry**

I'm working on a project where I'm making a CD of Shakespearean sonnets, and in doing research I've found that whoever wrote them— there is some debate as to whether it's Shakespeare—I'm a lot like the author. They show someone who is passionate, intense, ironic, and who very much enjoys being in love. And like the author, I'm very susceptible to being hurt.

—**Patrick Stewart**
Immediately after uttering the preceding statement, Stewart realized it would probably "haunt me for the rest of my life."

I'm  .   —**David Caruso**

TALKIN' TRASH

In an industry dominated by oversize but ever-so-delicate egos, it's inevitable that friction will occur—and talking trash *is* Tinseltown's fave pastime.

Some take the high road (if gossip has a high road) by restricting their commentary to "professional" opinions of other celebrities' work . . .

I wondered, what motivated Michelle Pfeiffer to do [*Wolf*]? It was a completely nothing role. It's the kind of movie I'd have to do because I needed the job. —*Mimi Rogers*

The worst thing I saw not only this year but in my lifetime was Sunset Blvd. *in Los Angeles with Glenn Close.*
—Tony Randall

The Specialist. It was horrible. [Sly Stallone] has to take it to another level—it's called acting class. The action thing just ain't working for him. —LL Cool J

If I were [Jim] Carrey's manager I would have said, "Jesus Christ, didn't somebody read this [Dumb and Dumber]*? All those toilet jokes? What is this?" If Carrey would like a shortcut to career suicide, get dirty, get sleazy. His longevity will be cut by twenty years.* —Jerry Lewis

It's amazing what a broad will do for a buck.
—*Frank Sinatra, on Shirley MacLaine's 1995 tell-all autobiography, in which she wasn't particularly flattering to her ol' buddy*

I think I would rather drink latex paint than be in a movie with Steven Seagal. —Henry Rollins

The Bridges of Madison County by Robert James Waller was a pathetic, poorly written, pseudointellectual, pseudospiritual, pseudodocument of schmaltz. —*David Duchovny*
Couldn't have said it better myself.

I always thought that Chevy Chase was the luckiest man in Hollywood. I don't dislike him. It's just that even after his talk show bombed they were still giving him movie deals. When he signed a film deal a few years ago, the joke was that his lawyers were looking it over to see if it conflicts with the deal he's already made with the devil.

—*Bill Maher, host,* Politically Incorrect

. . . while others get, shall we say, a little more personal:

If you look at [Jerry] Seinfeld, here is this creepy Scientologist guy porking teenage girls. . . . —Bobcat Goldthwait

Whoopi Goldberg—a nation decides not to hurt somebody's feelings. —*Sam Kinison*

Jodie Foster. I hate everything she stands for and everyone gathered around her to help her stand for it. It's a big fat fuckin' lie. Let's not be who we are. Let's hide behind our art. Let's oppress everybody who is exactly like us. In her fuckin' Armani with her tits hangin' out. And constantly rewarded and rewarded. And by who? The power structure that she totally speaks for. —Roseanne

I wish James Dean would never have died. Then he'd be fat and acting on *Dynasty* or something. There wouldn't be this whiny-boy act that's so prevalent everywhere.

—*Jane* (Frasier) *Leeves*

Rosie Perez? I don't think I could spend eight or ten weeks on a movie set with her. Her voice would drive me back to heroin. —Charlie Sheen

Jill St. John . . . what a sack of shit. —*Tony Curtis*

STAR WARS

Some tiffs degenerate into all-out feuds worse than the Hatfields and McCoys ever *dreamed* of—played out for all the world to see. . . .

Klaus Kinski and Werner Herzog

Kinski on Herzog: This much idiot no one has ever been in the world!
Herzog on Kinski: He's not aging well. The best thing to happen to his career is for him to die immediately.

Michael Caine and Richard Harris

Caine on Harris (and Peter O'Toole and Richard Burton): Drunks.
Harris on Caine: An overfat, flatulent, sixty-two-year-old windbag, a master of inconsequence now masquerading as a guru, passing off his vast limitations as pious virtues.

Drew Barrymore and Chris O'Donnell

Barrymore on O'Donnell: When we first met, I was like, "Fucking frat boy, get out of my face," and he was like, "Hollywood chick, go fuck yourself." *[Before becoming friends, according to Barrymore.]*
O'Donnell on Barrymore: It's funny, because we're polar opposites as far as taste and upbringing. I shop retail. She's Miss Thrift Shop.

Woody Harrelson and Courtney Love, co-stars of *The People vs. Larry Flynt* (1996)

Harrelson: The day before we read [the script] together, she called [director] Milos Forman and he handed me the phone. "So you're the freaky rock-star drug-addict," and she said, "And you're that guy who's fucked every woman in Hollywood."

Isaac Bashevis Singer (author of *Yentl*) and Barbra Streisand

Singer on Streisand: My Yentl wanted to study the Torah—she didn't want to be a singer.
Streisand on Singer: If a writer doesn't want his work changed, he shouldn't sell it.
Singer on Streisand: I must say that Miss Streisand was exceedingly kind to herself [in the film]. The result is that Miss Streisand is always present, while Yentl is absent.

Charlie Sheen and Eric Stoltz

Sheen admitted to *Movieline* magazine he wanted to "jam" **Stoltz**'s girlfriend, **Bridget Fonda**. Stoltz's outraged reply was given to the magazine in the form of a fax, excerpted herewith: I think he obviously has some need to be perceived as a shocking, in-your-face predator. A lot of actors are like this. I find there are two kinds of actors (or actresses) that you work with constantly: (1) The Respectful Actor. This person is kind and giving and talented and fun to work with and respectful of your relationship. (2) The Predatory Actor. This person is kind and giving and talented and fun to work with but feels that because they are famous they don't have to function within society's rules, i.e., if they are hungry, they eat; if they are attracted to their co-star, they act on it, married or not, no matter what destruction may ensue. These people obviously should be in therapy.

Jennifer Lee and Deboragh Pryor,
ex-wives of comedian Richard Pryor

Lee on Pryor: The last time Deboragh stopped by [Richard's house] the first words out of her mouth were, "Make me a martini and give me a thousand dollars."

Pryor on Lee: Here's a woman who went on *Geraldo* saying, "[Richard]'s the worst human being I've ever met. I'll never speak to him again." I resent being pushed aside. If I call she never gives him my messages. When I was Richard's caretaker I always passed along her messages, even when she was faxing him pictures of her breasts.

Cybill Shepherd and Bruce Willis, whose fights and
tantrums on the set of *Moonlighting* were the stuff of legend

Shepherd on Willis: You know, I became a success when I was twenty. But on *Moonlighting* Bruce was going through that first success and I had to pay for it.

Willis on Shepherd: Sometimes I figure if the first *Die Hard* movie had failed I'd still be saying, "Cybill, would you come on?"

Joan Rivers (and Spike, Joan's little doggie)
and the *60 Minutes* staff

60 Minutes to Rivers: It has been brought to my attention from a number of women at *60 Minutes* that your employees are allowing Spike to urinate over the toilet bowls of the ninth-floor bathroom. We would appreciate it if your employees could walk your dog outside. I thank you.

Rivers fired back: This is absolutely impossible, as everyone knows Spike urinates over the toilet bowls on the eighth floor.

Joe Eszterhas and Mike Ovitz

Eszterhas, the hack screenwriter who's showered with monumental mountains of money for churning out ludicrous, repetitively plotted, sex-and-violence-laced epics like *Basic Instinct* and *Jade,* decided in 1989 to leave **Ovitz**'s Creative Artists Agency for International Creative Management "because Guy McElwaine was back in the agency business and Guy was my oldest friend in town." What followed was a blood feud, with vituperative accusations and recriminations bandied about in letter after venomous letter between the dueling duo.

from Eszterhas's October 3, 1989 letter to Ovitz: You told me that if I left—"my foot soldiers who go up and down Wilshire Boulevard each day will blow your brains out." You said that you would sue me. "I don't care if I win or lose," you said, "but I'm going to tie you up with depositions and court dates so that you won't be able to spend any time at your typewriter." You said: "If you make me eat shit, I'm going to make you eat shit." When I said to you that I had no interest in being involved in a public spectacle, you said: "I don't care if everybody in town knows. I want them to know. I'm not worried about the press. All those guys want to write screenplays for Robert Redford." You said: "If somebody came into the building and took my Lichtenstein off the wall, I'd go after them. I'm going to go after you the same way. You're one of this agency's biggest assets." You said: "This town is like a chess game. ICM isn't going after a pawn or a knight, they're going after a king. If the king goes, the knights and pawns will follow." . . . That night at dinner at Jimmy's, [CAA agent] Rand Holston was friendly, too, but he described the situation more specifically. Rand said you were the best friend anyone could have and the worst enemy. What would happen, I asked Rand, if I left CAA? "Mike's going to put you into the fucking ground," Rand said.

from Ovitz's response of the same day: When I received your letter this morning I was totally shocked since my recollection of our conversation bore no relationship to your recollection. Truly this appears to be one of those Rashomon situations, and your letter simply makes little or no sense to me. . . . Best wishes and continued success.

Katharine Hepburn and John Barrymore

Hepburn: Thank goodness I don't have to act with you anymore.
Barrymore: I didn't know you ever had, darling.

ABOUT FACE!

Some decisions just aren't made to last.

While she was a struggling actress, **Vanna White** posed for a series of revealingly risqué lingerie shots, which she pleaded with pal **Hugh Hefner** to run in *Playboy*; now that she's America's sweetheart, she feels the photos were clearly exploitative.

Sharon Stone's pantyless interrogation scene in *Basic Instinct* was one of the most controversial ever in a movie. Stone claimed to have been "tricked" into shedding her undergarments, saying director **Paul Verhoeven** told her they "reflected too much light." "Sharon Stone's a fucking liar," vents Verhoeven. "Right before the shot, she gave me her panties and said, 'These are a present for you. I don't need them.' Then she shot the scene and afterward she checked it out on video and said, 'Looks good.' We left and never talked about it until she saw it in the movie. Then she got upset because we were sitting there with her manager and her agent and everybody was saying, 'What?! What did you do?!' Then she came after me and the rest is media history." It's interesting to note that when positive feedback about the scene began rolling in, Stone changed her tune and smugly claimed it had been her idea all along.

Vacuous perennial virgin (and proud of it) **Brooke Shields** gave an interview to *Details* magazine in 1995, when the following exchange took place:

Q: Perhaps we could say that you intended your pledge as a guideline, not an inviolable rule.

A: Well, I do think people should wait—definitely. But that's, uh, safe to say—what you just said before.

(Shields actually "lost it" in college—some say to fellow student **Dean Cain**.)

Shamelessly self-absorbed, neo-Gothic hag **Anne Rice** had a lot to say about the casting of boy-next-door **Tom Cruise** as the sinister, sexy, bloodsucking freak of her turgid series of magniloquent melodramas (Cruise is "no more Lestat than Edward G. Robinson is Rhett Butler"). After months of deriding the studio and everyone connected with the film, Rice evidently had a sudden epiphany after viewing the finished product. In a late-1994 "open letter" she paid to have published in *Variety,* the overwrought ink-slinger did a complete 180 from her previous position. Some highlights:

This was for me an event of indescribable excitement. Living in a dramatic clutter of laserdiscs and videotapes, I am nourished daily by movies, loving them as much as books. . . . I loved the film. I simply loved it. I loved it from start to finish, and I found myself deeply impressed with every aspect of its making, including its heartfelt and often daring performances by all the actors and actresses, its exquisite set design and cinematography, and its masterly direction. But most personally, I was honored and stunned to discover how faithful this film was to the spirit, the content and the ambiance of the novel, *Interview With the Vampire,* and of the script for it which I wrote. I was shocked to discover that **Neil Jordan** had given this work a new and distinctive incarnation in film without destroying the aspects of it which I hold so dear. I never dreamed it would turn out this way. . . . When you see this film, I think you will marvel, along with me, as to how something that developed with so many difficulties and so much controversy could turn out to give so many people what they want.

A postscript added, "Be prepared to give the studio, the producers, stars and everybody else just as much advice and help with the sequel as you did with this first film! By this time, perhaps they will be used to us." FAT CHANCE.

As if the letter weren't enough, the risible Rice also taped a message inserted at the front of the film as released on videocassette. The vampire Lestat, she dramatically declared, is "my devil, my dark lover, my alter ego. . . . Sometimes I think he's my conscience and, um, this could be the last book that I ever write with him—I don't know. I do know that when I go out on the road for this book this summer, I want to hear from you. I want to see you and I want to talk to you and I want to find out how *you* feel about the film and how *you* feel about the books."

(Dear Anne: like Lestat, they suck.)

THEY'RE OUT TO GET ME

The [Hollywood] hills are alive . . . with the sound of paranoia, conspiracy theories, and crank statements.

Patricia Arquette, during an interview with *Us* magazine soon after her marriage to actor **Nicolas Cage**, pulled out a twenty-dollar bill, tore off a corner, and showed a reporter the bill's threads. "This is so the United States government can scan you," she explained. "They can tell if you're carrying too much currency. When I showed this to my husband it really wowed him. When I pulled out this little spy trick, he knew how well he'd done with me."

John Cusack (he's a rebel): "Given the things I said about Reagan—that he's a criminal who used the Constitution as toilet paper—it wouldn't surprise me if my phone was tapped."

When the Fox network canceled the sitcom *Roc* (because of poor ratings), sore loser **Charles S. Dutton** cried racism. They "wanted monkey shows," he opined. "Whenever you hear white executives in Hollywood saying a black show is not funny enough, I interpret that as saying, 'You niggers ain't being nigger enough for us.'"

Spike Lee, despite the critical lauding of most of his films, has his own theories about why he's not doing *even better*: he speculated that ticket sales for *Malcolm X* were being credited by computer to white-produced movies like Disney's *Aladdin,* and that the Cannes Film Festival's Palme d'Or prize went to *sex, lies and videotape* in 1989 because its director, **Steven Soderbergh**, is a honky.

When **Jerry Lewis** made an appearance on *Donahue* in 1981, a female caller told the washed-up comic that she found telethons repulsive. Lewis's subsequent tirade included charges of anti-Semitism, capped off with this brutal blow: "I've got to get you an autographed photo of Eva Braun." Lewis also reportedly has each room in his house bugged so he can view the goings-on with equipment set up in his private bathroom.

"The American public really does have a death wish for me," cried cantankerous **Courtney Love**. "They want me to die. I'm not going to die." Aw, come on . . . please?

Michael Moriarty, after a very public spat with **Janet Reno** on the subject of television programming, puled about his plight in "An Open Letter to My Country," published in *Variety:* "I am now a blacklisted actor because of my vehement opposition to Janet Reno."

Edward James Olmos claimed he was being stalked by the "Mexican Mafia" after the 1992 release of his gang flick *American Me.*

Steven Seagal (which he pompously pronounces Sea-GAL rather than SEA-gull, the way the rest of his tribe does) says he's worked for the CIA, claims to have made a mob "hit" to earn money when he was broke, and carries a loaded, cocked revolver in his belt. Seagal's former partner, **Gary Goldman**, says the actor takes sensational stories he's heard and ascribes them to himself. In an apologetic letter to a reporter who'd interviewed them both, Goldman wrote, "The plain truth of the matter is that Seagal was and is a gutless coward who is trying to convert the heroic deeds of those brave men into a personal history for himself."

After the United States attacked Libya in 1986, macho **Sylvester Stallone** decided not to attend the Cannes Film Festival, fearful of becoming a victim of terrorism.

Oliver Stone, the Caucasian equivalent of Spike Lee, whimpered, "There's 1,001 vultures out there crouched on their rocks saying, 'Ah, here comes Stone.'" Maybe this is because "We have a fascist security state running this country. . . . Orwell did happen. But it's so subtle that no one noticed." Despite these threats to his well-being, Stone has proven himself a canny career opportunist. Even in the face of grave, imminent danger, the paranoid publicity-hound always has his priorities straight: veteran Hollywood scribe **Army Archerd** reported that as the *difficile* director was entering the 1991 Academy Awards ceremony (held on March 30, 1992), he was set upon by militant gay protesters yelling, "Shame! Shame!" (They objected to Stone's insinuation in his movie *JFK* that Kennedy's assassination was planned by gays.) Nervously, Stone whispered, "It would be something if I was assassinated by some CIA man disguised as a homosexual."

Melvin and **Mario Van Peebles**, the paranoid pair who made the historically suspect 1995 film *Panther* (about the Black Panther organization), believe J. Edgar Hoover and the Mafia conspired to get inner-city residents hooked on drugs to stop the burgeoning black power movement. "Isn't it strange that the rise of drugs corresponds to the rise of militancy in the ghetto?" wondered Melvin. "You're not going to get the FBI to hand you documentation, but you can look statistically at when drugs accelerated into the black community." Added Mario, "It couldn't have happened without the authorities' cooperation."

I don't know if it's neurotic or just true," says director **Gus Van Sant**, "but some friends told me all the hotel rooms in New York have cameras in them because they saw a show where Donald Trump found a camera in his hotel-room lamp. So I was looking for this camera. . . . Never found it. I figured it was behind the mirror."

AN EMBARRASSMENT OF RICHES
MY MOST EMBARRASSING MOMENT

Nicolas Cage, in front of his high school prom date, vomited all over the front of his tuxedo.

Jim Carrey, on meeting **Jimmy Stewart**, his lifelong idol: "What I learned from it was don't honor false gods. You know, nobody in this business is a god. But I was just goo-goo over him, and he got embarrassed and got red and walked away."

Joan Collins: before *Dynasty* catapulted her back into the limelight, the washed-up actress was so broke that she decided to tool on down to her local unemployment office, where, humiliatingly, she was recognized by other deadbeats while waiting on line.

Ted Danson: his 1993 blackface roast of then-girlfriend **Whoopi Goldberg** at a Friars Club dinner included graphically scatological personal references as well as this charming tidbit: "The tabloids

First impressions are
important when
meeting one's heroes.

say that our life together is scandalous. I mean this sincerely: a lot of our life is very ordinary. I'll never forget the time I took Whoopi to meet my parents. And I know that the tabloids have said things about us that wasn't [sic] true. And I was worried about how my parents would react when I brought Whoopi home, because they're so stuffy and out of touch. But Whoopi fit right in. After she did the laundry and washed the dishes and dusted and generally tidied up the place, my father—my dear, sweet father—offered to give her a ride to the bus stop. . . . "

Janeane Garofalo: the sometime MTV personality cornered **Mel Gibson** at the 1996 MTV Movie Awards with mic in hand. Apparently a bit flustered, Janeane was only able to fire off a few stupid questions (like "Do you think I look fat in this dress?") before Mel stormed off in a huff.

Hugh Grant: backstage at the 1994 Academy Awards ceremony, "I saw **Clint Eastwood** and the only thing I thought of saying was, 'Hey, are you presenting an award?' It was my biggest show business blunder to date." (Prior to Grant's public peccadillo with the Sunset streetwalker, that is.)

Robin Leach: it's a tough call to pick the stupidest question ever asked by the lardy *Lifestyles* host, but one standout was, "Liberace, are you a gentle man living in a crazy world?"

Shirley MacLaine: "Someone handed me cocaine at a party in a dish with a gold spoon. I thought it was Sweet'n Low and put it in my coffee."

Nancy Reagan: in the midst of a thank-you speech by hubby Ronald to **Vladimir Horowitz**, who had just performed at the White House, the featherweight first lady fell ass-over-teakettle off the stage into a planter of chrysanthemums. "Honey, I told you to do that only if I didn't get any applause," quipped the playful prez.

Ronald Reagan: during a high-level meeting with Arab leaders, Reagan offhandedly remarked to the Lebanese foreign minister, "You know, your nose looks just like Danny Thomas's."

Burt Reynolds: scrawling his way into immortality in the concrete in front of Mann's (formerly Grauman's) Chinese Theater, Reynolds misspelled his own name.

Geraldo Rivera: has had so many embarrassing moments (Geraldo attacked by neo-Nazis, Geraldo in face bandages, Geraldo as sex addict . . .) that it's hard to know where to begin, but one little gem was the "adventure you and I will take together," the un-sealing (via explosive) of gang boss Al Capone's under-ground storage chamber. After much fanfare, the bomb went off and the smoke cleared to reveal . . . mounds of dirt and an empty bottle (and an awful lot of egg on Geraldo's face).

Barbara Walters: asked both Lauren Bacall and Katharine Hepburn what kind of trees they'd be—if they were trees.

Vanna White: "My biggest embarrassment was when I fell flat on my face. The guy had just won a brand-new car in a bonus round. I was clapping so hard, I was so excited for him, I missed the last step and fell right on my face. It was terrible. I was so embarrassed. So I picked myself up and dusted myself off and went over to the winner to congratulate him and he said, 'Did you have a nice trip?'"

Sean Young: the obstreperous actress, who desperately wanted to play Catwoman in 1992's *Batman Returns*, crashed the lot where director **Tim Burton**'s production company was located, but was rudely rebuffed. Never one to take no for an answer (witness her behavior after being rejected by on-set fling James Woods), the aggressive actress then appeared—in full Catwoman garb—on **Joan Rivers**' talk show and demanded an audition. (Alas, she didn't get it.)

EMBARRASSMENTS IN PRINT

It's bad enough when a star's meaningless maunderings are broadcast live for the whole world to see . . . but at least there's some consolation in the fact that most viewers aren't recording these unfortunate lapses in judgment for posterity. It's a whole different kettle of fish, however, when celebrities commit themselves in print.

Megalomaniacal moviemaker **Renny Harlin** was tapped to direct storklike **Geena Davis** (coincidentally, his wife) in the overblown pirate fantasy *Cutthroat Island* and—perhaps fearing that cast and crew weren't as visionary as himself—penned a memo telling them *exactly* what was needed: **"I don't want** big, **I want huge. I don't want** surprising, **I want stunning. I don't want** fast, **I want explosive. I don't want** accidents, **I want disasters. I don't want** dirt, **I want filth. I don't want** a storm, **I want a hurricane. I don't want** hills, **I want mountains. I don't want** groups, **I want crowds. I don't want** fear, **I want panic. I don't want** suspense, **I want terror. I don't want** fights, **I want battles. I don't want** beautiful, **I want awesome. I don't want** humor, **I want hysteria. I don't want** horses, **I want stallions. I don't want** boats, **I want ships. I don't want** events, **I want action. I don't want** good, **I want great. I don't want** interesting, **I want mind boggling** [*sic*]. **And, I don't want** love, **I want passion."**

Adipose actress **Kathy** (*Sister Act*) **Najimy** sent a touching form letter to two hundred of her closest friends, including **Robin Williams, Bette Midler, Gloria Steinem, Katie Couric, Whoopi Goldberg,** and—though she misspelled their names, they are near and dear nonetheless—**Greg Kinnear, Mercedes Ruehl,** and **Dianne Wiest:**

For the New Year, I took some time to think about the amazing **(mostly) glorious past five years I've experienced in "show bizness." I thought of those of you who have directly inspired, supported, employed, cared for, motivated, encouraged or guided my artistic endeavors. I honor and thank you.**

Love, Kathy Najimy

n 1993, a trio of Tinseltown's finest young thespians sent a memo printed by *Harper's* magazine under the headline "When Actors Think Really, Really Hard") to Hollywood talent agencies:

To: All the people capable of change

From: Eric Stoltz, Bridget Fonda, and Matthew Modine

In this economically difficult and environmentally important time we live in, it is important to always look for opportunities and ways to save.

May I humbly suggest to the powers that be at Creative Artists Agency to take the opportunity to lead our industry in a new direction.

The scripts that are sent to clients and brought home by agents could surely be printed on both sides of the page. Whatever inconvenience that the reader might have (none that I can think of) would be alleviated by the realization that less paper, therefore less resources, are being consumed.

Every night scripts are sent back and forth across the United States via Federal Express. If you send more than two scripts to a client, you would be forced to use the larger Fed Ex packaging and pay more. Just think of the savings if the scripts were double-sided! I have spoken to the kind gentlemen in your mailroom and the manufacturers of the copiers used in our mailroom. All have said that the most difficult thing about copying a script *duplex* or *duplexing* is, NOTHING: "With the machines we got all ya have to do is push a button."

Or consider the fact that instead of schlepping ten pounds of scripts home you carry five!

Or consider the trees that won't be cut down.

Or consider how many gallons of deadly dioxin won't end up in our nation's rivers from bleaching the script paper white.

Or consider that books are printed on both sides. People read books all the time without any malfunction to their nervous systems. One simply adjusts their eyes, head, or wrist.

Let's have the world-famous Creative Artists Agency be the leader in this very simple, yet necessary, move.

Thank you for your time.

Eric Stoltz, Bridget Fonda, and Matthew Modine

IF I ONLY HAD A BRAIN

I used to think the human brain was the most fascinating part of the body. Then I realized, well, look what's telling me that.
—Comedian Emo Phillips

Why *do* we hang on their every word, anyway?

My favorite thing to tell the press about what my aunt [Jane] has said to me is, "Oh, don't pay too much attention to the press."
—Bridget Fonda

[As a child,] I thought I'd either be an actor, a baseball player, or a fire engine, according to my parents.
—Robert Downey Jr.

Even if she [Brooke Shields] weren't an actress, it would still be very important for me to have her in my life.
—Andre Agassi
Huh?

If you use these words in every possible combination, you'll start every day with the right attitude. Love life. Live to love. Love to live. Try it—you'll see.
—Robin Leach, on the words *life, live,* and *love*

What you make of your life is what you make of the random moments in your life.
—**Geraldo Rivera**

What would happen if you melted? You know, you never really hear this talked about that much, but—spontaneous combustion? It exists! It's documented. It happens. . . . [People] burn. From within. And yet sometimes they'll be in a wooden chair and the chair won't burn, but there'll be nothing left of the person. Except sometimes the teeth. Or the heart. No one speaks about this—but it's for real.

—Keanu Reeves

EARTH TO

KEANU

You look at him and you can see the wheels are turning but you can't figure him out—if he's happy, if he's sad. . . . You just want to say, "What's happening in there?"

—Dina Meyer (Reeves's *Johnny Mnemonic* co-star)

I'd rather be called sleazy than to be identified as intelligent.

—**Phil Donahue**
You got it.

By the time I was thirteen I realized I'd be more successful at something physical rather than mental.

—Arnold Schwarzenegger

Good-looking people turn me off. Myself included.

—Patrick Swayze

There are two types of people: mopers and copers. I'm a coper.

—*Nancy Glass*, American Journal *host*

J.K. livin'.

—*Matthew McConaughey (McConaughey's life philosophy, it was a line uttered by his character in Dazed and Confused. It means "Just keep livin'.")*

Pi is pi. It's a formula. But it's been a while since I've used it.

—**Nicollette Sheridan,** when asked by a reporter if she remembered what "pi" was

If you live through the initial stages of fame and get past it . . . then you have a hope of maybe learning how to spell the word *artist*.

—Patrick Swayze

I remember the 1992 vice presidential debate when Ross Perot's running mate, Admiral Stockdale, wondered aloud, "Who am I? Why am I here?" . . . I still ask the same question: "Who am I and why am I here?"

—Andrew Shue
We're wondering too, Andrew.

I need someone I have verbal and spiritual collateral with, where I can go to the bank and withdraw some of her feelings and knowledge.

—Sly Stallone
Must be why he dates so many models.

It is always difficult to be meaningful and relevant, because there's just not enough time.

—Oprah Winfrey

Dirty Dancing was a sweet little film, but I had a very specific point I wanted to bring off about class structure and social prejudice.

—Patrick Swayze
Wonder who taught him those three-syllable words?

I will never do Pulp [Fiction] 2, but having said that I could very well do other movies with these characters.

—Quentin Tarantino

We won't make a sequel [to Batman], but we may well make a second episode.

—Producer Jon Peters
Well, what do you expect from a Barbra Streisand protégé?

PHONEY business

She says things like, "Uh, what did you think about my last phone call?"
—Liz Smith, on Raquel Welch

Literary
LOTUSLAND

I wouldn't have filmed *The Color Purple* if the Alice Walker book had been a big fat novel ... the reason I read it is because it's thin.

—Steven Spielberg

I've seen [Kenneth Branagh's *Much Ado About Nothing*] three times. It's a great play that's full of humor ... I'm not used to that kind of culture and style.

—Pamela Anderson Lee

I'm astounded by people who take eighteen years to write something. That's how long it took that guy to write *Madame Bovary*, and was that ever on the best-seller list?

—Sylvester Stallone

Not many people have read the book.

—Demi Moore, explaining why her film version of *The Scarlet Letter* has a happy ending

I mean, [*Hamlet* is] a great story. It's got some great things in it. I mean, there's something like eight violent deaths.

—Mel Gibson

Why should I read all those words that I'm not going to get to say?

Laurence Fishburne, when asked if he'd read the original after acting in a contemporary version of *Othello*, from which two-thirds of Shakespeare's dialogue was excised

I read biographies of the greats, and they were so messed up that I thought I'd better mess myself up. But I couldn't. I'm too small.

—Winona Ryder

When I see these guys write all this macho stuff I want to smash their heads.

—John Turturro

MODELS AREN'T ~~STOOPID~~ ~~STUPID~~ DUM

I believe that mink are raised for being turned into fur coats and if we didn't wear fur coats those little animals would never have been born. So is it better not to have been born or to have lived for a year or two to have been turned into a fur coat? I don't know.

—Barbi Benton

I don't think I was born beautiful. I just think I was born me.

—Naomi Campbell

*W*e don't "vogue." We are "vogue."

And, *I* don't diet. I just don't eat as much as I'd like to.

And, *P*eople think modeling's mindless, that you just stand there and pose, but it doesn't have to be that way. I like to have a lot of input. I know how to wear a dress, whether it should be shot with me standing up or sitting. And I'm not scared to say what I think.

—Linda Evangelista

I've always been a bit more maturer than what I am.

—Samantha Fox
And more literater too.

*I*t's just my same normal life, but now I get to go to movie premieres and to parties.

And, *S*ometimes I wish I didn't drop out of school.

—Bridget Hall

I never bothered with exercise. I just had a good time. If it meant drinking three bottles of wine every night, then I did.

—Yasmin LeBon (married to simple Simon LeBon of Duran Duran)

I don't have to *fake* dumb. I *am* dumb.

—Jerry Hall
. . . and blond

CLEARLY BRILLIANT

I'm the guy who did—what's Mick Jagger's girlfriend's name? I'm the guy who did four parts with her. You try that sometime. It's like talking to a window.

—Bryant Gumbel

*W*hat truly surprised and satisfied me when I did my first show for John Galliano is how he explains every moment of the event. He comes to each of us individually to tell us about the part we're supposed to play when we show his beautiful creations. Just like for a play. For example, for a dress that was inspired by a storm or by anger, I have to imagine I'm playing the part of Scarlett O'Hara in *Gone With the Wind*.

—Kate Moss

I'm so naive about finances. Once when my mother mentioned an amount and I realized I didn't understand, she had to explain: "That's like three Mercedes." Then I understood.

And, *S*moking kills. If you're killed, you've lost a very important part of your life.

—Brooke Shields

the BIG Picture

Learn to act like someone else, but also be yourself.

Advice to models from famed fashion photog Arthur Elgort

Don't be tense.

Don't talk on the phone too long.

Look at yourself in the mirror once in a while.

Look at the clothes. Lots of times you won't like them. How can you make them work? Sit, stand, jump, laugh, cry, runaway [sic].

Don't bite your nails.

Line up some nice vacations that you look forward to. Late December and August are good times.

—from *Arthur Elgort's Models Manual*

WHAT I AM

A little self-revelation is good for the soul, right? Here, some of Tinseltown's most introspective thinkers offer up their inner-most essences:

I'm such a ham.
—**Bob Hope**

I'm a meathead.
—*Keanu Reeves*

I'm so pretentious—
I love it!
—**Julie Delpy**

I am the Jackie Robinson of Shakespeare.
—*Laurence Fishburne*

I'm a very shy woman, very sensitive, very emotional, very volatile, with quite a sense of humor.
—Joan Collins

I'm old.
I'm young.
I'm intelligent.
I'm stupid.
—**Warren Beatty**

I'm just a hair away from being a serial killer.
—*Dennis Hopper*

I am simple, complex, generous, selfish, unattractive, beautiful, lazy, and driven.
—*Babs Streisand*

I'm an alcoholic. I'm a drug addict. I'm a homosexual. I'm a genius.
—**Truman Capote**

When the camera's rolling, I'm a desperate motherfucker.
Or, alternatively, I'm a spew machine.
—**Jim Carrey**

I'm a sensitive person.
—*David Hasselhoff*

I'm everything.
—**Madonna**

I'm an instant star. Just add water and stir.
—David Bowie

I'm a highly, highly, highly creative human being.
—**Kim Basinger**

I'm a multifaceted, talented, wealthy, internationally famous genius.
—Jerry Lewis

I'm a whore, all actors are whores.
—*William Holden*

I am a fellow with an exceptional talent.
—Jackie Gleason

Deep inside I'm so . . . I mean, I'm so sensitive.
—*Jean-Claude Van Damme*

I like trash. I am trash.
—*Producer Don Simpson*

I will just say that Ving Rhames is like a mixed salad.
—Ving Rhames (actor, *Pulp Fiction, Mission Impossible*)

I am just too much.
—Bette Davis

I don't know, people say I'm a sex symbol but I think I'm an actress.
—Pia Zadora

I was a twerp if ever there was one.
—Laurence Olivier

I am the incurable ham and Hollywood is a ham's paradise.
—Charles Laughton

the BABS Babble box

Why should an actor give up his role as citizen just because he's in show business?

With no special interest and serving no personal or financial agenda, artists make moral commitments to many issues that plague our society.

Well, most artists turn up on the humanist, compassionate side of public debate, because this is consistent with the work we do.

So much of what the artist needs to flourish and survive is at risk now.

The persistent drumbeat of cynicism on the talk shows and in the new Congress reeks of disrespect for arts and artists.

What can I say? I have opinions. No one has to agree. I just like being involved.

Sorry, Rush, Newt, and Jesse, but the artist as citizen is here to stay.

From Barbra's landmark "Artist as Citizen" oratory, foisted on students at Harvard in February of 1995.

Babs enlightens
the world

WHAT I AM NOT

I'm not a snob. Ask anybody. Well, anybody who matters.
—Simon LeBon

I'm no alcoholic, I'm a drunkard. The difference is, drunkards don't go to meetings. —Jackie Gleason

I am not the archetypal leading man. This is mainly for one reason: as you may have noticed, I have no hair. —Patrick Stewart

So I'm not the world's greatest actress. —Madonna

I'm no actor and never have been. —Clark Gable

I'm no actor and I have sixty-four pictures to prove it. —Victor Mature

I'm a versa-tile actress. —Greta Garbo

I'm not perky. —Kathie Lee Gifford

I am not a bimbo. —Jessica Hahn

I'm not a bimbo. —Anna Nicole Smith

I am not a slut. —Vanessa Williams

I was not a Ritalin kid. —Jim Carrey

CAUSE CELEBRITE

Touching, isn't it?

I don't care about the Oscars. I make movies to support the causes I believe in.
—Jane Fonda
Yeah, like Barbarella

I happen to dig being able to use whatever mystique I have to further the idea of peace.
—Garrett Morris

I never think about what I want. It's about what you want to give to other people.
—Oprah Winfrey

Sometimes [poor people] don't smell too good, so love can have no nose.
—Bighearted Tammy Faye Bakker

They hunted for seven days, and the meat . . . was chopped up and put into stews. . . . From that we got forty thousand meals that fed the homeless in Hawaii for almost six months. A guy came to me one day and said that I was being considered for a Nobel Prize.
—Kurt Russell, about his "shoot-outs" where hunters pony up big bucks to kill animals in the company of celebrities

A nation is only as strong as it treats its animals.
—Kim Basinger

People don't know about the human part of me that really cares about the world. For instance, I don't know what I feel about wearing my furs anymore. I worked so hard to have a fur coat and I don't want to wear it anymore because I'm so wrapped up in the animals. I have real deep thoughts about it because I care about the world and nature.

—Diana Ross

People can be cynical when actors take stands, but the hemp movement's something I'm very passionate about.

—Woody Harrelson (Harrelson was arrested on June 1, 1996, for planting four hemp seeds at a legalization rally in Lexington, Kentucky.)

[Hollywood] should continue their efforts—and I applaud them—to eliminate rain-forest lumber from set building. . . . They should really have an aggressive bike-riding program.

And on celebrity garbage: Throw this away? Where is *away?* One person's *away* is another person's backyard.

Ed Begley Jr., who lives in a solar-powered house and drives an electric car

When I got on [*Melrose Place*] I thought, "Here's a real opportunity to utilize all the different contacts I have to inspire young people all over the country."

—Andrew Shue

I don't feel we did wrong in taking this great country away from [the Indians]. There were great numbers of people who needed new land, and the Indians were selfishly trying to keep it for themselves.

—John Wayne

How many actresses can say they've built toilets in Mexico?

—Michele (*L.A. Law*) Green, who went south of the border to work on a philanthropic sanitation project
. . . and how many would want *to?*

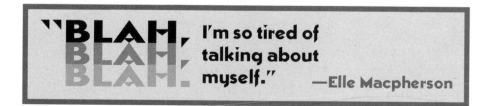

"BLAH, BLAH, BLAH. I'm so tired of talking about myself." —Elle Macpherson

5

Lifestyles of the Nouveau Riche and Frivolous

HOLIER THAN THOU

It will come as no great shock to those of you who've read this far to learn that actors are the most emotionally needy people on the face of the earth. Hitting the big time brings fame, adulation, money, and power, of course, but also paradoxically seems to create the burning desire to prove one is a worthwhile person. Thus freshly minted movie star **Jim Carrey** cleans out the self-help shelves at his local bookstore, **Barbra Streisand** becomes goofy guru **Marianne Williamson**'s best buddy, and **Ted Danson** consults astrologers, psychics, and palm readers (and "loves them all"). The undisputed king of kookiness, however, is **Patrick Swayze**, whose lack of mental acuity leads him down ever-stranger paths of soul-searching. (*GQ* mag called the thickheaded thespian an "insecure, chain-smoking, crystal-carrying, mantra-chanting, new-age actor." Sounds right to me.) Swayze has drifted dreamily through Scientology, Buddhism, Transcendental Meditation (TM), tai chi, and Zen archery, and now carries a magic stick with which he "blesses" his movie sets (*see* "Lucky Charms," ahead).

MOON-STRUCK

I live by full moons. I vibrate with emotion and can never figure out what's wrong with me. Then I go, "Oh, it's the full moon!"
—Patrick Swayze

Swayze is far from the only cracked actor to jump on the bliss bandwagon. Most seem to follow a fairly consistent two-stage pattern: supreme self-indulgence succeeded by a precipitate plunge into a messy morass of guilt. To meet the constant need for redemption and salvation, Hollywood is full of gurus-to-the-stars, each promising more health, happiness, forgiveness, enlightenment, and wisdom than the last. And—like most everything and everyone else in L.A.—each has his or her fifteen minutes of fame when Tinseltown trendoids proclaim they've found the secrets of the universe (after which the enlightened ones are likely to be thrown over for the next faddish faith promising exactly the same thing—but in a slightly different way). This prevailing piety is perhaps best summed up by an ancient Eastern adage: "When the student is ready, the teacher appears." Looks like it's not such a *new* age after all.

THE NEED FOR CREED

Now that the '80s are really over, we are all like repentant sinners. No one prays to God like someone with a severe hangover.
— Writer/director Michael Tolkin
(*The Rapture; The New Age*)

Astrology, under star-sign stars like the late **Linda Goodman**, is a spiritual staple that never goes completely out of style. Among the major-league multitudes that let the stars be their guide: **Nancy** and **Ronald Reagan, Ed Asner** (wanted to know "Will I make it?"), **Burt Reynolds, Jonathan Winters, Karen Valentine, Valerie Bertinelli, Rose Marie, John Barrymore, Mary Pickford** and **Douglas Fairbanks** (had their charts done each morning), **Ida Lupino, Marilyn Monroe, Barbara Eden, Tommy Smothers, Morey Amsterdam, Marlene Dietrich, Cary Grant, Steve McQueen, Sonny and Cher, Grace Kelly, Ronald Colman, Tyrone Power, Robert Cummings, Susan Hayward,** and **Brigitte Nielsen**, who needs all the help she can get.

CHEAPER BY THE DOZEN

I've gone through est and LifeSpring and A Course in Miracles and so many things that helped me deal with my demons and dark voices.
— David Geffen

Astroyoga, as practiced by ever-so-enlightened **Siri Dharma** ("Princess on the Path to Infinity") **Galliano**, seems to be a personalized yoga-based "metaphysical fitness" regimen directed by (and at) the stars. "The first thing I do is look at a person's sign," explains Galliano. "Then I check the astrological aspects of the Earth, new moon, full moon, solstice and equinox. I find out when the planets are lined up in favorable or unfavorable aspects." Admirers: **Jessica Lange, Linda Gray, Glenn Close, Louis Gossett Jr., Christopher Reeve, Susan Sarandon, LeVar Burton, Shelley Long, Daryl Hannah,** and **Richard Gere.**

WANT TIBET?

Hopefully, through a chain reaction of positive energy we'll be able to make a difference.
—Goldie Hawn, at the 1996 Tibetan Freedom Concert

Buddhism (Hello, Dalai). This ancient practice and other forms of Eastern mysticism are popular among celebrities, who seem to think a religion's value is based upon its provenance (the farther away, the better). Practicing Buddhists include lama-lover **Richard Gere** ("All our daily lives . . . the thing we call reality is just an expression of the spirit"), **Harrison Ford** and wife **Melissa Mathison** (a screenwriter who wrote a biopic of the Dalai), model-of-serenity **Courtney Love, Christy Turlington, Spalding Gray, Patrick Swayze, Uma Thurman** (her father was the Dalai Lama's first American Buddhist monk), **Tina Turner, Jean-Claude Van Damme, Oliver Stone** (Buddhist name "Mindok" [probably translates as "paranoid"]), and **Carré Otis**. (Otis also practices "Vision Quest": "It's a rite of passage. You go 'up on the hill'—that's the Native American slang for it—directed by a guide or elder. You spend four days and nights up there with no food and water, praying for a vision.") And **Sharon Stone** had chanting monks—poolside, yet!—helping to celebrate her thirty-eighth birthday.

SETTING THE RECORD STRAIGHT

I'm not particularly religious. I'm more of a cultural intriguist.
—Uma Thurman
I'll say—check out her September 1996 Playboy spread!

Channeling is performed by "channelers" or "channels" who can go into a trance and act as conduits for bygone beings who yearn to impart earth-shattering wisdom. Failed entrepreneur **J.Z. Knight** was the first to ~~make this up~~ bring this ancient wisdom to light—by dredging up a thirty-thousand-year-old apparition from Atlantis, who goes by the name Ramtha. Among her converts: loopy **Linda**

Evans (who lives but a short distance from the guru-ette in Washington State but denies she moved there to be close to Knight), **Richard Chamberlain**, and **Shirley MacLaine**. (MacLaine, of course, is famous for having written about her mystical experiences and beliefs—among which are (a) that a UFO constantly hovers above her head, and (b) that she's lived many, many distinguished lives—in several books.) Knight, who charges outrageously for her "services," says she never really *wanted* the money: "I had some difficulty for a time with Ramtha's saying that these teachings must be paid for. That went against *everything* I thought was important. . . . But Ramtha made a statement that has been constant: 'People do not appreciate in binary thinking what they get for free.'" Right on, O capitalistic Spirit of Atlantis! Life isn't just a bowl of cherries for Knight, though: sadly, her soulmate and husband, a horse trainer, recently flew the coop after coming out of the closet.

Sharon Gless and **Michael York** are devotees of a similar "nonphysical entity"/"spark of consciousness" channeled by **Jach Pursel**, a Florida businessman; others who believe are **Ted Danson, Joe Bologna, Barry Manilow**, and **Lesley Ann Warren**.

THE CAT'S ME⊚W

The last time I felt really loved was two days ago when a friend brought over a tape of a channeler. . . . The guy was saying that animals are put on earth to show human beings how to love. While I was listening, my two cats jumped up on the chair and snuggled me—they *never* do that. I was projecting love and they felt it and gave it back.

—Elizabeth Perkins

Jowly publishing sensation **Deepak** "Health is a higher state of awareness" **Chopra**, with his "something old, something new, something borrowed" blend of the mystical and the medical, seems to have supplanted Marianne Williamson in the (granted, easily transferable) affections of Hollywood spiritualists. Some of his Tinseltown truth-seekers: **Demi Moore, Michael Jackson, Sandy Gallin, Olivia Newton-John** ("Because he's a doctor, he anchors his thoughts in scientific background"), **George Hamilton, Oprah Winfrey**, and **Liz Taylor**. Despite the fact that he's co-written a script he's hoping to have produced (lucky us), he insists he's not all that taken with Tinseltown. "Less than one percent of the attention is from Hollywood," protests Chopra. "Ninety-nine percent is from the general populace." Ah, those little people.

JOY SHTICK

The instant you think, "I'm happy," your brain produces a chemical that relays the news of your happiness to all fifty-two trillion of your body cells—who rejoice and join in.
—Deepak Chopra

Christian Scientists past and present include **Carols Burnett** and **Channing**, **Doris Day**, **Paul Newman**, **Ginger Rogers**, and **Jean Stapleton**.

Crystals provide energy and have healing powers, according to those who carry, sleep with, and proudly display them. The formerly almost value-less quartz fragments can be quite costly these days—but no price is too great for peace of mind, right? **Tina Turner**, **Burt Bacharach**, **LeVar Burton**, **Jane Fonda**, **Sharon Stone**, **Richard Gere**, **George Hamilton**, **Liz Taylor**, **Lisa Bonet**, **Bianca Jagger**, and **Bruce Willis** are believers—as is **Cybill Shepherd**, who has them custom-channeled (perhaps mixing metaphysical metaphors) for members of her family. *Dynasty* vixen **Stephanie Beacham**'s parents "live on Dartmoor [in England] and I visit them whenever I can. I particularly love that area because there's a lot of quartz in the ground and it's very energizing."

THE RITE STUFF

Firewalking is part of my process. Rebirthing is part of my process. I follow the medicine path and I attend sweat lodges, an ancient Native American ceremony of purification.
—LeVar Burton

est, ubiquitous "feel-good" movement of the '70s, counted among its fans **Raul Julia**, **Valerie Harper**, **Ted Danson**, and **John Denver**.

Ghosts and poltergeists have been spotted by **Donald Pleasence**, **Susan** (*Brady Bunch*) **Olsen**, **JoBeth Williams**, **Joan Rivers**, **Lar Park Lincoln** (*Knots Landing*), **Susannah York**, **Robin Givens** (whose house, she claims, contains the ectoplasmic essence of former tenant **John Lennon**), and **Mitzi Gaynor** (has a ghostly maid who helps dust the chandeliers). **Charlene Tilton** describes an

incident in which a neighbor asked her to turn down her radio and she refused: "Things began to happen. The plug jerked out of the wall without anyone being near it. When I pushed it back into the socket, it was jerked out again so violently that sparks flew. The neighbor stood there frozen with terror." **OOH, SCARY!** **Steven Spielberg** says he's "always wanted to see a UFO and I never have. But ghosts—that's another story." **Mickey Rooney** claims to have been the only one to see a ghostly, golden-haired busboy in a crowded restaurant, and says the apparition advised him to clean up his act and become a Christian. And **Christina** *Mommie Dearest* **Crawford** insists that fires broke out spontaneously on the walls of the home in which she was raised (that tempestuous Joan!).

LIGHT UP MY LIFE

I've never seen a full apparition, but I once saw what could be termed ectoplasmic light, and that scared the hell out of me.
—Dan Aykroyd

Crybaby **John Bradshaw** promises Inner Child Liberation (bound to be a hit in a town where tantrums are so popular) through use of "nonshaming" therapy and workshops (during which participants cradle each other while listening to lullabies) with weighty monikers like "Homecoming: Reclaiming and Championing Your Inner Child." Followers of the onetime schoolyard-bully victim include **Carol Burnett** and daughter **Carrie Hamilton, Cher, Quincy Jones, Nick Nolte, Roseanne** (hasn't her inner child been liberated for quite some time now?), **Babs Streisand, Oprah Winfrey,** and **Steven Spielberg**. As silly as it all sounds, Bradshaw has sold a frightening number of copies of his 1992 tome entitled *Homecoming: Reclaiming and Championing Your Inner Child.*

John-Roger (born Roger Hinkins) is known to devotees as the "Mystical Traveler" who runs the "Movement of Spiritual Inner Awareness," or MSIA (one guess how it's pronounced: yes, *messiah*). Begun about 1970 (after a "divine spirit" called John the Beloved, aka the Mystical Traveler Consciousness, entered Roger Hinkins' body during routine kidney-stone surgery), the religion offers its three thousand members "aura balancing" (at $75 a pop) and "individual soul progression." Some male adherents are lucky enough to be selected to "receive the seed of the Traveler"; i.e., to have sex with the sensuous swami. Silly **Sally Kirkland** is a fan (*quelle* surprise!), as is addlepated **Arianna Huffington** (wife of failed California political hopeful **Michael Huffington**), who is one of J-R's "ministers of light" (probably means she does a lot of fund-raising). And self-help-book author **Pete McWilliams**, who actually believed J-R's 1988 edict that the author's supposedly AIDS- and TB-ridden aura could be cured only by splitting bylines and income with the greedy guru, was sued by J-R and MSIA in 1994 for breach of contract and back royalties.

TABLE TALK

My brother invited a medium—a nice, ordinary-looking Jewish lady with blond hair—to his house. We sat around the table with all the lights on and put our hands on it. And then it began. The table started to spell out letters with its legs. It sounds crazy, but I know it was my father who was telling me to be brave, to have the courage of my convictions, to sing proud!

—Barbra Streisand

Arizona-based W. Brugh Joy is a former medical doctor who turned to spiritual matters after a serious illness and now helps famous folks like **Barbra Streisand, Richard Chamberlain**, and **Michael Crichton** "reopen the forces of nature." The Joy boy also recommends that his followers eat a "'vibrationally balanced' life-essence diet, which would . . . include plants and plant products, minerals, and even insects."

Pint-size performer **Hervé Villechaize** claimed to have psychic powers, and **Kim Basinger** once took an emergency leave from the set of *The Marrying Man* to consult with her personal psychic—who happened to reside in Brazil! Others who have sought help from savvy seers include **Peter Sellers, Lee Marvin, Susan Strasberg, John Travolta, Linda Evans, Elke Sommer, Clint Walker,** and **Lindsay Wagner.**

CALL GIRL

I would be so embarrassed to have one of those [psychic hotline] numbers appear on my phone bill, because I don't know how I would explain it to my business manager. It would almost be like saying, "Okay, I'm white trash."
—Jennifer Tilly

For some, belief in reincarnation seems to be a natural outgrowth of the fear of dying. **Sly Stallone, Ernest Borgnine, Loretta Lynn, Juliette Greco, Tina Turner, David Carradine, John Travolta, Glenn Ford, Rose Marie, Ann Miller,** and **Willie Nelson** all believe they've lived before. One well-known "past-life regression" expert is **Patricia Rochelle Diegel,** who claims to be so highly competent that she's able to determine the past-life identities of certain stars just by viewing their visages up on the big screen. Her conclusions:

Tom Cruise: a French fighter pilot during World War I [role-playing for *Top Gun* . . . ?]

Jane Fonda: Angeline Grimke, sister of abolitionist/suffragette Sarah (who is—yep, you guessed it—**Gloria Steinem**)

Mel Gibson: Mike Fink, "the rugged riverboat man"

William Holden: explorer David Livingstone

Stacy Keach: (a) the earl of Kensington, a rich gambler and womanizer; and (b) a high-ranking soldier under Alexander the Great

Stephen King: Bram (*Dracula*) Stoker

Vincent Price: Edmund, an actor-pal of Shakespeare

The Rat Pack (Sinatra, Bishop, Martin, Davis, Lawford): a gang of

Old West outlaws [makes sense to me].
  Spencer Tracy and **Katharine Hepburn**:
Count and Madame Francois de La Fayette
  (seventeenth-century French nobles)
         The Kennedy Klan:
     Bobby Kennedy: Octavius
  John F. Kennedy: Marcus Aurelius
  Joseph Kennedy Sr.: Julius Caesar
    Teddy Kennedy: Tiberius
Peter Lawford: one of Caesar's generals
Jacqueline Onassis: Calpurnia, Caesar's last
        wife

LIFE IN THE PAST LANE

Our old friend Shirley MacLaine
has a birthday today. Sixty-one
years old. And also 185; 496; 1,278.
—David Letterman

"It just contains the secrets of the universe. That may be hard for people to handle sometimes, hearing that," says comeback kid **John Travolta** about sci-fi writer **L. Ron Hubbard**'s sci-fi religion, Scientology. One of the most controversial (and downright scary) organizations in the world, Scientology has managed to chalk up an impressive roster of acclaimed adherents including **Kirstie Alley, Anne Archer, Karen Black, Nancy Cartwright** (the voice of cartoon character Bart Simpson on TV), **Tom Cruise** ("It's helped me be more me") and wife **Nicole Kidman** and ex-wife **Mimi Rogers, Isaac Hayes** (who lives at the group's Celebrity Centre [sic] in Hollywood), film composer **Mark Isham, Al Jarreau, Juliette Lewis** (onetime boyfriend **Brad Pitt** also tried it briefly), **Judy** (*The Waltons*) **Norton Taylor**, Travolta's wife **Kelly Preston** (coincidence? I think not), **Priscilla** and **Lisa Marie Presley**, and rock musician **Edgar Winter**. Dabblers include **Jerry Seinfeld** (the courses he took, he says, were "fabulous"), **Patrick Swayze**, producer **Don Simpson, Demi Moore,** and **Emilio Estevez** (who refuses to discuss it, explaining, "I don't

DENY-ANETICS!

Yes, he has taken some courses in Scientology and
read some of the books. He is always trying to gain
more information from a wide range of sources,
and that does not identify him as a Scientologist.
—Sonny Bono's publicist

YOU'VE GOT TO HAVE FAITH

Sharon Stone once claimed to have cured herself of lymph cancer with "a lot of positive thinking and a lot of holistic healing."

want my phones tapped").

Siddha yoga (whatever that is) practitioners include **Lisa Bonet, John Denver, Isabella Rossellini, Melanie Griffith** and **Don Johnson, Phylicia Rashad, Marlo Thomas,** and **Rosanna Arquette.**

G⚇D IS MY ⚇-PILOT

The only agent I need, baby, is God. I know what I want to say. I know what I want to do. I'm a positive, strong black man. I don't need nobody to feed it to me.
—Martin Lawrence
Lawrence certainly needs something—check out Chapter 7.

The spirit world offers a copious cornucopia of guides and teachers (guardian angels) for those who will but listen. **Rudolph Valentino** and wife **Natasha Rambova** were among Hollywood's first organizers of séances, and believers in spiritual advisers (one of Rudy's was an "old Egyptian" named Meselope; another, an American Indian named Black Feather) and Ouija boards. **Mae West** claimed she wrote her scripts "directed by spirit control" in a trance; **Sigourney Weaver** believes she was protected during the African shoot of *Gorillas in the Mist* by the spirit of anthropologist **Dian Fossey**; and **Gary Busey**, laid up in the hospital following a near-fatal motorcycle crash in 1988, had a vision of a supernatural spirit who informed the actor he *couldn't* die because he "still had gifts that he must share." Hmm . . . wonder what they are. **Peter Sellers** believed he'd "been" each of his roles in past lives, and that his spirit guide was a comic who died around the turn of the century. "I want a spirit to take charge of me so that I can produce what I hope to produce," Sellers said. "I think that in there somewhere is the beginning of the advanced form of mediumship, although I must think at that point that you must start thinking in terms of spirit guides because if you didn't know your way around in that area you could get taken over by all kinds of wrong things." (Sellers was also in the habit of discussing his problems with a trusted feline "familiar.") **Stephanie Beacham**, who played kindly *Sister Kate* on her short-lived TV show, is guided by a nun: "Sister Cyrill became my spirit guide . . . while I was recovering from routine surgery. I decided to consult some psychic healers to assist the conventional medicine. All three psychics told me that I had a nun watching over me and that her name was Sister Cyrill."

GOTTA HAND IT TO HIM

If I come back in another life I want
to be Warren Beatty's fingertips.
—Woody Allen

Messianic Marianne Williamson, a failed torch singer, is the self-styled "bitch for God" who, in the words of *People* magazine, preaches a "trendy amalgam of Christianity, Buddhism, pop psychology and twelve-step recovery wisdom." Williamson worked at one time for biographer **Albert Goldman**, who remembers her as "very, very profoundly confused and had no conception of what to do with herself. She was a woman of emotion, like an actress in an Italian movie." Williamson has become a celebrity herself after penning best-selling books and creating a religious organization that seemingly caters specifically to movie stars like **Liz Taylor** (for whom she acted as minister when the tubby actress wedded social inferior **Larry Fortensky**), **Kim Basinger**, and **Cher**. Other devotees: corpulent comedian **Louie Anderson, Rosanna Arquette, Linda Blair**, both **Clintons, Laura Dern**, entertainment impresario **Sandy Gallin**, psycho **Cyndy Garvey, David Geffen, Daryl Hannah, Anjelica Huston, Norman Lear, Garry Marshall, Anthony Perkins, Theresa Russell, Roy Scheider,** film exec **Dawn Steel, Barbra Streisand, Lesley Ann Warren, Raquel Welch**, and **Oprah Winfrey** (who told her talk show audience she'd experienced a whopping 157 miracles after reading Williamson's book *A*

SEX SYMBOLISM

I have to straighten out my karma. I've become a
sex symbol, which is an absurd thing for me.
—Sharon Stone
It's absurd for some of us too, Sharon.

She believes
in miracles

I'M HENRY VIII, I AM

(*Return to Love*).

Past lives of current stars. (Yep, this is what they believe.)

Tori Amos: "I have vivid memories of being a prostitute in another life." (*Some might say . . . oh, never mind.*)

Ernest Borgnine: a centurion in the Roman legions

Sean Connery: an alcoholic railroad builder in Africa who lived with two native women, both of whom bore him sons, and who died of alcohol poisoning

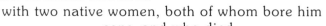

Mac Davis: a Mexican *bandido* who spent *mucho* time behind bars during the early twentieth century

Phyllis Diller: a German *hausfrau* who had seven children with her husband, a teacher/choirmaster

Lola Falana: a man married to a beautiful but evil woman who murdered the couple's little girl

Glenn Ford: 1. Launvaux, a cavalryman serving under Louis XIV in the seventeenth century
2. Charles Stewart, a Scottish music teacher (late 1700s)

Juliette Greco (French singer/actress, *The Sun Also Rises*): "Four hundred years ago I was burned at the stake as a witch . . . I am glad that my kind of sorcery goes by a different name today. Perhaps this time it can do me more good than the last memory I have of it."

George Hamilton: an unscrupulous, womanizing *(hey, I thought you were supposed to learn from your past lives)* rubber-plantation owner in South America who was shot and killed by a field hand

Loretta Lynn—the Coal Miner's Daughter claims to have been:
1. a Cherokee maiden ("I was an Indian princess once. My name was Little Flower.")
2. the long-suffering wife of a bedridden old coot
3. a rural American housewife

4. a restaurant worker during the 1920s

5. a serving wench in the household of an English monarch, with whom she had a torrid dalliance. ("The king's best friend kept grabbing me behind the king's back and I was afraid to tell the king about it because they were such buddies. The king died before I did, and his best friend choked me to death.")

Shirley MacLaine, who seems to be testing the limits of how many different new-age creeds one person can believe in at one time:

1. a Mongolian nomad

2. a poverty-stricken wretch in the streets of India

3. a Parisian dance-hall girl

4. "I was definitely a prostitute in some lifetimes. It's no accident that I played all those hookers in the movies."

5. MacLaine's daughter was her mother in one past life and her sister in another

6. an "actor-oracle" in ancient Greece

7. MacLaine "recalls" being a court jester for Louis XV. Apparently a little too smart-alecky for her own good, she was decapitated by the king himself: "I watched my head rolling on the floor. It landed face up and a big tear came out of one eye." The incident, traumatic though it was, *did* serve a higher purpose: MacLaine claims it somehow cured her of stage fright. (Of late, MacLaine has changed her metaphysical tune. "I'm not interested in that anymore," she told one journo. "I think the life we lead now is most important.")

Lee Majors: a French orphan who moved to America and became a Union army officer during the Civil War

Ann Miller: a resident of Atlantis (maybe she knew Ramtha)

Willie Nelson: Nelson's most recent past life was as an Indian living somewhere in Texas. To those who doubt the nasal crooner has lived before, he offers "proof": the fact that he was writing poetry at "four or five."

("What does a four-year-old know about love triangles? Yet I was writing about them and they were my own ideas.")

Stefanie Powers: King Tut's wife, Ankhesenanmun

Katey (*Married . . . with Children*) **Sagal**: a Chinese boy—which is why, she says,

she has "strong masculine energy"

Sly Stallone:

1. "I was once an American Indian."
2. "Another time I was a wolf."
3. "I was also part of a well-to-do South American family."
4. a victim of beheading by the Jacobins during the French Revolution

John Travolta: In addition to believing he lived as **Rudolph Valentino**, Travolta says, "I have the distinct feeling that I chose my family. . . . In the next [lifetime] I may be even more causative." (And I'd always heard you *couldn't* choose your family.)

Tina Turner: a Parisian cabaret dancer

Robin Williams: "While I haven't really examined my past lives, I have a feeling that one of them had to be as a Shakespearean actor in the time of Shakespeare." (Because he's done so well as a

 # SPACE Oddities

Ed Asner
Kaye Ballard
Fran Drescher
DeForest "Bones McCoy" Kelley
Shirley MacLaine
Olivia Newton ~ John
Cliff Robertson

Celeb UFO-sightings

We partied all the time, and quite a few of us saw a UFO. During a cookout, a craft appeared, hovered for a few seconds, then disappeared at warp speed.
—Patti D'Arbanville, describing the shoot of *Big Wednesday* with Gary Busey and Jan~Michael Vincent

KNOCK WOOD!

serious dramatic actor in *this* lifetime.) Celeb superstitions.

Dick Cavett touches every eighth parking meter while walking down the street.

Mitzi Gaynor forces folks who whisper in her dressing room to walk out, spin, spit, and swear before she'll let them back in.

Lena Horne believes a hat on a bed equals death.

Michael Lerner wore his "lucky" pair of green boating gloves with his tuxedo to the 1991 Academy Awards ceremony. (They didn't work—he lost.)

Charlene Tilton will only trim her hair during a full moon and behind closed shades so she won't become a "dumb blond." (Hey Charlene: something's not working here.)

LUCKY CHARMS

They don't leave home without 'em.

Danny Aiello: a coin "my friend Carmine had blessed by the pope"

Karen Black: scarab

John Garfield: an old pair of shoes, which had to appear in each of his films

Jerry Lewis: carries family pictures onstage in his wallet

Claude Rains: intaglio ring

Edward G. Robinson: an old silver dollar

Barbara Stanwyck: gold medallion

Patrick Swayze: a gem-studded scepter ("It's my magic wand. It's been in the hands of holy men in India and Japan and all over the world. I put it into each person's hand and say that this is to bless the production and create an atmosphere of mutual goal devoid of ego.")

Sean Young: a large Bible (Young also seems to sincerely believe she can heal people simply by touching them)

CITIZEN CANINE

The lifestyle of a celebrity pet is often every bit as lavish as that of its celebrated owner. **Stallone**'s dogs, for example, follow their muscular master everywhere—via first-class airline seats; **Liberace**'s pampered poodle dined with his mincing master each evening at the same table and in his own chair; **Halle Berry** takes her two pooches along to the grocery store, where they ride in the cart and presumably help her shop wisely; and **Madonna**'s Chihuahua Chiquita was the lucky recipient of a $7,500 diamond choker from Tiffany's.

Pet names reflect the tastes of their owners, and while some use the monikers as narcissistic celebrations of their own careers (*Terminator 2: Judgment Day* star **Eddie Furlong** has a cat named T2; co-star **Arnold Schwarzenegger** a Labrador named Conan; and **Mel Gibson** an Australian cattle dog named Maverick), others show striking similarities (obviously a case of great minds thinking alike):

Celebrities

Steve Allen: springer spaniel Mr. T
Kirstie Alley: black chicken Billy Idol; cat Elvis
Tallulah Bankhead: lion Winston Churchill;
Sealyham terrier Hitchcock
Bonnie Bedelia: cat Brando
Bo Derek: horse Tanya Tucker
Erik Estrada: Persian cat Gucci
Eva Gabor: cat Zsa Zsa
Kathie Lee Gifford: dog Regis
Victoria Jackson: cat Jolson
Ricki Lake: dog Zsa Zsa Gabor
Courtney Love: dog Bob Dylan
Ed McMahon: cat W. C. Fields
Luke Perry: potbellied pig Jerry Lee
Dennis Quaid: golden retriever Fawn Hall
(because she shreds everything)
Geraldo Rivera: dog Connie Chu; canary Maury
Chirp (*"That's funny. Maury and I have a snake
we call Geraldo."*—Connie Chung)
Jaclyn Smith: poodle Vivien Leigh
Sally Struthers: cat Joan Pawford
Jack Wagner: golden retriever Elvis

Fictional/Historical Figures

June Allyson and Dick Powell: cocker spaniel Heathcliff
Tallulah Bankhead: monkey King Kong
Orson Bean: cat Pussy Galore *(Bond babe)*
Dirk Bogarde: Mastiff Candida
Kim Cattrall: Siamese Nellie Bly
Doris Day: dog Barney Miller
Bo Derek: horse Tarzan
Douglas Fairbanks: Mastiff Marco Polo; terrier Zorro
Valerie Harper: dog Billy the Kid
Tippi Hedren: leopard Cleopatra;
cheetah Rhett Butler
Charlton Heston: Saint Bernard Portia
Michael Jackson: ram Mr. Tibbs
Shirley Jones: dog Cyrano
Matthew McConaughey: Miss Hud
Catherine Oxenberg: cats Tristan *und* Isolde
Tiffani-Amber Thiessen:
golden retrievers Bonnie and Clyde
Vanna White: cats Rhett Butler and Ashley

SADDLE SOAR

The beauty is in not squelching their spirit but
to keep it alive—finding out how to keep the
little bird alive, not beat it into submission.
—Patrick Swayze, on working with horses

Self-Explanatory

Lauren Bacall: cocker spaniel Puddle
Catherine Bach: Persian cat Kitty
Lucille Ball: toy poodle Tinker Toy
Candice Bergen: cat Furball
Susan Dey: parakeet Tweetie
Roger Ebert: Orange Cat
Eva Gabor: cat Miss Puss Puss
Brian Austin Green: boa constrictor Bo
Merv Griffin: Irish setter Poochie
David Hasselhoff: Kitty Kat
Kelly LeBrock: cat Scratch
Victoria Principal: cat Terra Catta
Daniel J. Travanti *(Hill Street Blues)*: Kitty

Booze Hounds

Don Adams: poodle Brandy
Anne Archer: dog Bordeaux
Brigitte Bardot: dog Gin
Drew Barrymore:
horse Mocha Bailey
Linda Blair: terrier Pilsner
Doris Day: dog Heineken
Frank and Kathie Lee Gifford: bichons
frises Chablis and Chardonnay
Ronald Reagan and Jane Wyman:
Scottish terriers Scotch and Soda

RECYCLING HOLLYWOOD-STYLE

When complimented on a pair of boots
she was wearing, actress Sarah Miles
said they were "Gladys, my late Skye
terrier."

Baked Goods

Johnny and Joanna Carson: Yorkshire terrier Muffin
James Dean: dachsund Strudel
Corey Feldman: dog Twinky *(all right, so he can't spell)*
Meredith MacRae: cat Crumpet
Vincent Price: dog Brownie
Victoria Principal: Burmese cat Buns
Ronald Reagan: cockapoo Muffin
Tanya Roberts: Siamese cat Buns
Arnold Schwarzenegger:
Labrador Streudel
Aaron Spelling: poodle Muffin
Loretta Swit: dog Croissant
Janine Turner: poodle Eclair

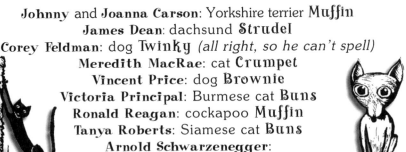

ER heartthrob George Clooney tells what happened to himself and his pet potbellied pig, Max, during the 1994 Los Angeles earthquake: "Max was in the bed with me and woke up minutes before it happened. And I was yelling at him for waking me up—when everything just exploded. So I'm naked, with Max, and running . . . 'cause I'm in a house on a hill, and if it's going down I want to be up on the street, dodging the next house. My buddy, who lives in the downstairs guest house, comes running up. And he's naked. With a gun, because he thought someone was breaking in. And I'm trying to write a note to my folks, trying to explain to them in case we die that it's not what it seems: two naked men, a gun, and a pig."

BABY GRAND

Pets aren't the only ones given oddball appellations by celebs. Get a load of these noteworthy nipper names:

Literate Lads and Lasses

Harry (*Night Court*) **Anderson**: Dashiell
Bruce Willis and **Demi Moore**: Rumer Glenn (*after author Rumer Godden*); Scout LaRue
(*"The first one, Rumer, we got in a bookstore on Madison Avenue when my wife was four months pregnant. Scout is from* To Kill a Mockingbird." [Bruce Willis])

Cosmic Kids

Robbie Benson: Lyric
Marisa Berenson: Starlite Melody
David Carradine and Barbara Hershey: Free Seagull
Mia Farrow and Andre Previn: Lark Song and Summer Song
The Phoenix Phamily: River, Leaf, Summer, Rain, and Liberty
Susan St. James: Harmony and Sunshine

Geographical Juniors

Alec Baldwin and Kim Basinger: Ireland Eliesse
Robert De Niro and Diahnne Abbott: Raphael
(Named after the hotel in Rome in which he was conceived. "I'm just glad they weren't staying at the Hilton," quipped Shelley Winters.)
Olivia Hussey: India Joy
Nastassja Kinski and Quincy Jones: Kenya
Kurt Russell and Season Hubley: Boston
David Soul: China
Sean Young: Rio

Children of the West

Laurence Fishburne: Montana
Frank and Kathie Lee Gifford: Cody
Melissa Gilbert: Dakota
Melanie Griffith and Don Johnson: Dakota
Woody Harrelson: Denni Montana
Judd Hirsch: Montana
Roseanne and Ben Thomas: Buck
Kurt Russell and Goldie Hawn: Wyatt
Robin Williams: Cody

Come Again?

Kevin Bacon and Kyra Sedgwick: Sosie
David Brenner: Slade Lucas Moby
Lou Gossett Jr.: Satie
Phil Hartman: Birgen
Mariel Hemingway: Dree
Eddie Murphy: Bria
Linda Purl: Lucius Jackson Arthur Plantagenet Cary
Ahmad and Phylicia Rashad: Condola
Geraldo Rivera: Simone Cruickshank
Nicolas Roeg and Theresa Russell: Statten
Sam Shepard: Jesse Mojo
Sylvester Stallone: Sage Moonblood

RICH AND STRANGE

What good is being wealthy if you can't buy a few overpriced baubles now and then?

WHEELS OF FORTUNE

Cars of the stars.

Fatty Arbuckle's capacious Pierce-Arrow was large enough to house a bar, a toilet, and of course the elephantine Arbuckle himself.

"It" girl **Clara Bow** owned a Kissel convertible painted the same not-found-in-nature shade as her red hair.

'20s superstar **Francis X. Bushman** not only smoked lavender cigars, but also tooled around town in a lavender Rolls replete with lavender-liveried servants.

For a mere $150,000, **Bobby Darin** got himself an ostentatious showboat of an auto partially painted in diamond dust.

Stepin Fetchit had a pink Rolls with his name on the trunk—in neon!

Funny fellow **Buster Keaton** had a thirty-foot land cruiser custom-built with bunks that slept six, a gallery, an observation deck, and a pair of drawing rooms.

Oater star **Tom Mix** owned an auto with a tooled leather saddle and a set of steer horns on its elongated hood.

Shaquille O'Neal drives a Ford he calls the "Van of Def," which boasts a three-thousand-watt stereo system with more than thirty speakers and a dozen bass boosters. Not surprisingly, he (and it) once got a ticket for disturbing the peace.

Arnold Schwarzenegger started a Tinseltown trend when he purchased a $57,000 Hummer (Humvee), the seven-foot-wide all-terrain vehicle that ferried soldiers about during the Gulf War. The extravagant Austrian now owns six.

Gloria Swanson drove a leopard-upholstered Lancia.

PRESENTS OF MIND

John Barrymore's fifty-fifth birthday was celebrated with a most spectacular gift from the actor's best buddies: a naked woman, wrapped in cellophane and crowned with a silver bow.

On the occasion of Warner Bros. exec **Mark Canton**'s birthday one year, a guest asked the burning question, "What do you give to a man who *wants* everything?"

Michael Jackson sent a very personal gift to **Elizabeth Taylor** one year: a life-size doll of himself! Gee, now everybody's gonna want one.

Sometimes it's the humble-yet-heartfelt gift that says the most. **Carole Lombard** presented inamorato **Clark Gable** with a hand-knitted penis warmer one year!

On the last day of shooting the film *Always*, generous guy **Steven Spielberg** gifted each of the film's four stars—**John Goodman, Richard Dreyfuss, Holly Hunter**, and **Brad Johnson**—with a red Mazda Miata.

After filming of *The Truth About Cats and Dogs* was completed in 1995, star **Uma Thurman** bestowed upon each of her three assistants a replica of the pricey necklace her character wore in the movie.

CONSPICUOUS CONSUMPTION

How celebrities spend their hard-earned moolah . . .

$45 MILLION Unreal estate: "The Manor," a sixty-five-thousand-square-foot mansion built to house **Aaron Spelling**, frog-faced wife **Candy**, and daughter **Tori**. The compound includes a doll museum, eight two-car garages, four bars, three kitchens, a gym, a theater, an Olympic-size swimming pool, a large room set aside just for wrapping gifts, a bowling alley, six formal gardens, and twelve fountains. "It has very high ceilings because Candy and I both get claustrophobia," Spelling revealed in his 1996 autobiography. "It's been described as the largest single-family dwelling in Los Angeles County, a home with an indoor bowling alley, skating rink, and outdoor zoo. . . . We do have a bowling alley but we certainly don't have a skating rink or zoo."

$30 MILLION John Travolta's Gulf Stream II jet. (He owns four other planes as well, along with three Rolls Royces. . . . This guy is going places.)

$20 MILLION Cost of Braselton, the Georgia town purchased by kooky **Kim Basinger** in the hopes of turning it into a tourist attraction (?). Now that she's declared bankruptcy, she's dropped the project.

$15 MILLION Ferret-faced **Donald Trump**'s Manhattan digs. "One of the important things is [that] I've used all onyx," the intemperate entrepreneur said in an *InStyle* puff piece. "Onyx is a precious stone, many times more expensive than marble. And everyone agrees it is more beautiful. I don't believe there is an apartment like this anywhere in the world. The view, the solid bronze window frames, the fountain all brand-new and carved. Did you see the way the window shades go up and down, all remote? And they're bulletproof. They're incredible. They're soft stuff and yet they catch bullets. Pffft!" Added **The Marla**: "The spectacular thing about this home are the views. They're so empowering." (Her heart's in the right place, even if her syntax isn't.)

$4.9 MILLION Price paid by **Madonna** for a Florida manse (officially appraised at only $1.5 million) she saw and fell in love with while being photographed for her embarrassing pseudoliterary vanity project *Sex*.

$2 MILLION The "Honey Fitz," a yacht on which JFK purportedly trysted, recently purchased by magician **David Copperfield** for fiancée **Claudia Schiffer**.

$1 MILLION Sum offered to the London Hospital Medical College by **Michael Jackson** for the Elephant Man's bones (unfortunately, they're not for sale).

$153,000 Aston Martin Lagonda purchased by **Liz Taylor** on a whim.

MATERIAL

I am one of the most romantic men you will ever meet. I form deep attachments to people, to places, to pants. I was attached recently to a pair of pants. I just loved them. And I know I have my closet full and that I have to throw something away. But I can't! I am tormented by this. You see, I can love even objects. I get very passionate about everything. *Everything.*

—Antonio Banderas

$80,000 Cost of the Versace wedding finery worn by **Sting** and **Trudie Styler**; after the ceremony, the once-donned duds were donated to a "Save the Rainforests" campaign.

$75,000 Monthly upkeep on "The Manor" (see above). This may go up each December, when **Spelling** hires a snow-making machine.

$50,000 Price of putting in a pond next to **Michael J. Fox**'s Connecticut home so he could teach his son to fish.

$22,000 **Evel Knievel**'s good-luck charm: a gem-encrusted, bourbon-filled cane.

$21,000 Cost of the caviar with which **Madonna** stocks her private plane while on tour.

$10,000 Price of the custom-made thirty-inch doll in the likeness of **La Streisand**, ordered by fervid fan **Richard Simmons**; the mannequin is accurate down to its talons of death.

$3,000 Monthly cost of the Arkansas mountain water used by **Bruce Willis** and **Demi Moore** for cooking, bathing, and drinking.

$150 Weekly cost of the French shampoo with which **William Shatner** has his guard-dogs bathed.

You can't TAKE it with YOU

Because of her lavish spending habits, Pamela Lee is said to be having financial troubles—which is strange because her two largest assets are liquid.
—Conan O'Brien

Kim Basinger
Steven (*Scarface*) Bauer
Morton Downey Jr.
Redd Foxx
Zsa Zsa Gabor
Hammer
La Toya Jackson
Cheryl Ladd

Jerry Lee Lewis
Wayne Newton
Olivia Newton-John
Susan Powter
Burt Reynolds
Mickey Rooney

Stars who've declared bankruptcy

MAD MONEY

Part of the loot went for gambling and part for women. The rest I spent foolishly.
—How George Raft went through $10 million

HOLLY-WEIRD

Tom Arnold, reports *Details* magazine, is in the habit of barking commands like this to his hapless assistants: "Mrs. Fields cookies! I want it right away. And I want ice cream. Super Fudge Chunk. With nuts in it. And a bunch of Mrs. Fields cookies. Three dozen of them. Good ones! Well, git in the car and git going. It's just over in fucking Brentwood!"

Patricia Arquette has "a slight case of Imelda Marcos—I have about a hundred fifty pairs of shoes."

David Copperfield is fond of sucking women's hair.

Joan Crawford was a clean freak. She'd only take showers (feeling that sitting in one's begrimed bathwater was revolting) and followed guests around her house cleaning all they touched, with particular attention paid to doorknobs.

A nine-foot rooster graces the driveway in front of **Johnny Depp**'s house.

Hugh Grant admits, "I've always had a crush on cheerleaders. Catholic cheerleaders— my double favorite."

George Hamilton's socks are tossed out after a single wearing.

Jean Harlow couldn't stand wearing underwear.

Wacky **Woody Harrelson** has a strange way of reducing stress: in a thirty-foot-high tepee at his Malibu abode, he chants and beats a large drum.

Michael Jackson's mansion contains a room decorated in wallpaper the pop star designed himself. Pattern: little Elizabeth Taylor heads. The room also boasts a movie screen which shows the larger-than-life (in more ways than one) Taylor's films twenty-four hours a day.

"I grew up in a house full of women," **Andie MacDowell** reminisces, "and I remember the freedom of being naked because we didn't have guys around. Today, I just walk into the kitchen naked all the time. We're just, like, the Naked Family."

COOKING?

For me a kitchen is like science fiction. I only go there to open the refrigerator and take something out.

—Ann-Margret

Madonna, extravagant though she may be with herself, pinches pennies when it comes to her oversize entourage. She "goes over her hotel bills with a fine-tooth comb," says publicist Liz Rosenberg. "She says, 'Who had this Evian? I didn't.'"

Liam Neeson is a strange one: "Since I was a boy I've had a thing for ice-cold water. I prepared for *Rob Roy* by staying in baths of ice. I've got an industrial-size ice machine. I'm working on trying to do it four times a week for twenty minutes each time."

Al Pacino and galpal **Lyndall Hobbs** had everything—ceiling, walls, floor—in their Manhattan condo's master bedroom painted black.

Dolly Parton lolls about eating cookies while watching exercise videos.

Buzz magazine reported that in 1996 **William Shatner** had his bathroom customized to resemble the bridge of the Starship *Enterprise*, complete with "captain's chair."

Charlie Sheen installed a fireman's pole in his Malibu home.

To safeguard against anyone else showing up at an event in the same clothing, overindulged **Tori Spelling** snaps up every other size of the off-the-rack frocks she purchases.

During his fleeting but passionate marriage to Danish pastry **Brigitte Nielsen**, **Sylvester Stallone** commissioned a twelve-foot statue of the devoted duo. They broke up before it could be finished, however, so Sly changed his order: it was now to be a monument to himself, wearing only a G-string. (Title? *The Age of Steel*. Hmm.) In the marriage's few seconds of happiness, Stallone had a table custom-built with a reproduction of the beauteous Brigitte's face in its center, and even had braces put on her poodle puppy when she whined that its teeth weren't straight.

"It's shocking and disgraceful," says **Patrick Stewart**, "but I'm absolutely obsessed with *Beavis and Butthead*. . . . It is an extraordinary, powerful, and important piece of work. It also makes me laugh like a drain."

Barbra Streisand has always been a model of taste (OK, bad taste). When she first began making real money, she had the kitchen walls in her Manhattan apartment redone—in red patent leather.

Jean-Claude Van Damme has one assistant whose sole function it is to pick the lint from his musclebound master's jackets.

SEC⊚NDHAND SM⊚KE

A guy gave me a cigar that I know was expensive saying, "Here, this is a so-and-so cigar," and I didn't know what to say because I don't know what that means. I thought, "Should I take up cigar smoking? Do I have time to learn to smoke cigars?"

—Tom Arnold

Tipping their HANDS

The Good

Tom Arnold
Brett Butler
George Clooney
Robert De Niro
Goldie Hawn
Julia Louis-Dreyfus
Helen Mirren
Sylvester Stallone
Sharon Stone
Meryl Streep
Mike Tyson

The best and worst tippers in Tinseltown

THE BAD

Lauren Hutton
Eddie Murphy
the *90210* gang
rock stars
Sean Penn
Kato Kaelin

THE DOWNRIGHT UGLY

Notorious tightwads
Sean Connery
Clark Gable
Cary Grant
Steve McQueen
Babs Streisand

6

Risqué Business

WARNING:

TO READ THIS CHAPTER YOU MUST BE 18 OR HAVE YOUR PARENTS' PERMISSION.*

(FOR THOSE OF YOU WHO ARE OVER 18: AT LAST—THE GOOD PART!)

*Sensitive parents, including my own, should also avoid this like the plague.

Every time I get close to Hollywood
I get excited.
—Newt Gingrich

BUSINESS AFFAIRS

"All love scenes shot on the set," pronounced porcine **Alfred Hitchcock**, "are continued in the dressing room after the day's shooting is done. Without exception." How right he was. Being on a movie set—in whatever capacity—may *sound* glamorous, but the reality is that most of the time you just sit around and wait for something to happen. No wonder, then, that the bored and the beautiful turn to each other for a little stimulation when things are slow. But the short attention spans of egocentric entertainers virtually guarantee that the majority of on-set trysts are strictly short-term, as gullible **Gary Cooper** found out after co-starring with **Ingrid**

Bergman in *Saratoga Trunk*: "Ingrid loved me more than any woman in my life loved me. The day after the picture ended, I couldn't get her on the phone." There is, of course, speculation on *every* movie set about pairings that are all in a day's work . . . but some of these rumors are more pervasive than others:

The Accused (1988): **Jodie Foster** and **Kelly McGillis**
All of Me (1984): **Steve Martin** and **Victoria Tennant**
Batman (1989): **Kim Basinger** and **Prince**
Batman Forever: **Val Kilmer** and **Drew Barrymore**
Batman Returns (1992): **Michelle Pfeiffer** and **Michael Keaton**
Beautiful Girls (1995): **Uma Thurman** and **Timothy Hutton**
Blue Velvet (1986): **Laura Dern** and **Kyle MacLachlan**
The Boost (1988): **James Woods** and **Sean Young**
Bugsy (1991): **Warren Beatty** and **Annette Bening**
The Call of the Wild (1935): **Clark Gable** and **Loretta Young**

Carlito's Way (1993): **Al Pacino** and
Penelope Ann Miller
Children of a Lesser God (1986):
William Hurt and **Marlee Matlin**
Cleopatra (1963): **Richard Burton** and
Elizabeth Taylor
Corrina, Corrina (1994): **Whoopi Goldberg**
and **Lyle Trachtenberg**
Dangerous Liaisons (1988):
Michelle Pfeiffer and **John Malkovich**
Dark Victory (1939): **Bette Davis**
and **George Brent**
Destry Rides Again (1939): **Marlene Dietrich**
and **James Stewart**
Dick Tracy (1990):
Warren Beatty and **Madonna**
Eddie (1996): **Whoopi Goldberg** and **Frank Langella**
(Both were married at the time.)
The Eighth Day: **Uma Thurman** and **Ethan Hawke**
Elephant Walk (1954): **Peter Finch** and **Vivien Leigh**
(Leigh was ultimately replaced [in the film] by Liz Taylor.)
Every Which Way but Loose (1978):
Clint Eastwood and **Sondra Locke**
Father of the Bride, Part II (1995):
Steve Martin and **Diane Keaton**
Ferris Bueller's Day Off (1986):
Matthew Broderick and **Jennifer Grey**
Flatliners (1990): **Julia Roberts**
and **Kiefer Sutherland**
Flesh and the Devil (1927): **Greta Garbo**
and **John Gilbert**
The Fly (1986): **Geena Davis** and **Jeff Goldblum**
The Getaway (1972): **Steve McQueen**
and **Ali MacGraw**
Head of the Class TV series: **Brad Pitt**
and **Robin Givens**
Heat (1995): **Ashley Judd** and **Robert De Niro**

 LADY LOVE

I don't worry about [little sister] Ashley professionally, but is she going to fall in love with every guy that she's in a movie with?
—Wynonna Judd

Heathers (1989): **Winona Ryder** and
Christian Slater
Heavy (1996): **Liv Tyler** and **Evan Dando**
Higher Learning (1995): director **John
Singleton** and model/actress **Tyra Banks**
Honeysuckle Rose (1980): **Willie Nelson** and
(still-married-to-Spielberg) **Amy Irving**
In Love and War (1997): **Sandra Bullock**
and **Chris O'Donnell**
Innerspace (1987): **Meg Ryan**
and **Dennis Quaid**
Legends of the Fall (1994):
Brad Pitt and **Julia Ormond**
The Lost Man (1969):
Sidney Poitier and **Joanna Shimkus**
Love in Paris (sequel to *Nine ½ Weeks*; 1997):
Mickey Rourke and **Agatha de la Fontaine**
Love Story (1970): **Ali MacGraw** and **Ryan O'Neal**
The Marrying Man (1991): **Kim Basinger** and **Alec Baldwin**
Melrose Place TV series:
Grant Show and **Laura Leighton**
Daphne Zuniga and **Dan Cortese**
Courtney Thorne-Smith* and **Andrew Shue**
(*"*We were two nice kids under this incredible stress. I don't know
if I could have gotten through it without him.*")
Men in White (1934): **Clark Gable** and **Elizabeth Allen**
Milk Money (1994): **Ed Harris** and **Melanie Griffith**
Morocco (1930): **Marlene Dietrich** and **Gary Cooper**
Project X (1986): **Matthew Broderick** and **Helen Hunt**
Racing With the Moon (1984): **Sean Penn** and **Elizabeth McGovern**
Reckless (1935): **William Powell** and **Jean Harlow**
Risky Business (1983): **Tom Cruise** and **Rebecca De Mornay**
Romeo & Juliet (1997): **Leonardo DiCaprio** and **Claire Danes**
The Saint (1997): **Val Kilmer** and **Elisabeth Shue**
Saratoga Trunk (1945): **Gary Cooper** and **Ingrid Bergman**
Satisfaction (1988): **Julia Roberts** and **Liam Neeson**
Seven* (1995): **Gwyneth Paltrow** and **Brad Pitt**
*"*A serial killer matches wits with Brad Pitt. We're all gonna
die.*"—*Jim* (Entertainment Weekly) *Mullen*
Showgirls (1995): director **Paul Verhoeven** and **Elizabeth Berkley**
Siesta (1987): **Ellen Barkin** and **Gabriel Byrne**
Smilla's Sense of Snow (1997): **Gabriel Byrne** and **Julia Ormond**
Splendor in the Grass (1961): **Warren Beatty** and **Natalie Wood**
State of Grace (1990): **Sean Penn** and **Robin Wright**
Steel Magnolias (1989): **Julia Roberts** and **Dylan McDermott**

Swing Shift (1984): **Goldie Hawn**
and **Kurt Russell**
Thelma & Louise (1991): **Brad Pitt** and
Geena Davis
A Time to Kill (1996):
Matthew McConaughey and **Ashley Judd**
Matthew McConaughey and **Sandra Bullock**
(Busy guy.)
Too Young To Die (1989 TV movie):
Brad Pitt and **Juliette Lewis**
Two Much (1995): **Melanie Griffith** and
Antonio Banderas
("His friends are so relieved. They were
afraid he'd get involved with an actress."
[Jim Mullen, Entertainment Weekly*])*
Viva Las Vegas (1964): **Elvis Presley** and **Ann-Margret**
Project X (1987): **Matthew Broderick** and **Helen Hunt**
Wild at Heart (1990): **Nicolas Cage** and **Laura Dern**
Wild Orchid (1990): **Mickey Rourke** and **Carré Otis**

About that *Wild Orchid* shoot: just how "realistic" were those steamy sex scenes between **Mickey Rourke** and **Carré Otis**? Consensus was that the concupiscent couple really did the dirty deed. Whenever graphic sex is featured in a movie, rampant rumormongering (did they or didn't they?) leads to titillating speculation—and increased box office. Stars are usually coy about such matters, but **Kris Kristofferson** shamefacedly admitted he and *The Sailor Who Fell from Grace with the Sea* co-star **Sarah Miles** did—not during the film's shoot, but afterward, when both were being photographed for a *Playboy* spread. "That was just about the worst thing I've ever done," sighed Kristofferson. "My face where it was for ten million people [to see]. We were acting our roles in the movie and I just, uh, got into it, ya know?"

HUNKA HUNKA BURNIN'

In *Mighty Aphrodite*, Woody Allen "didn't just keep his clothes on under the sheet. He kept his shoes on too. When I asked him why, he said it was in case there was a fire." —Helena Bonham-Carter

ODD COUPLES

BEAUTY AND THE BEAST

Where Partner A is a tad more comely than Partner B.

Pamela Anderson Lee and Tommy Lee
Antonio Banderas and Melanie Griffith (your choice)
Kim Basinger and Prince
Warren Beatty and Madonna
Porn star Danyel Cheeks and Tony Curtis
*"Tony's just a beautiful, beautiful person. He's so mature
and treats me so well. I just love being with him."*
Curtis denies the dalliance.
Tom Cruise and Mimi Rogers
Ted Danson and Whoopi Goldberg
Bo and John Derek
Donna Dixon and Dan Aykroyd
Sheena Easton and Prince
Clint Eastwood and Frances Fisher
Jill Eikenberry and Michael Tucker
Angie Everhart and Sylvester Stallone
Mia Farrow and Woody Allen
Sherilyn Fenn and Prince
Jennifer Flavin and Sylvester Stallone
Larry Fortensky and Elizabeth Taylor
Robin Givens and Mike Tyson
Don Johnson and Barbra Streisand
Ashley Judd and Michael Bolton
Diane Keaton and Woody Allen
Kelly LeBrock and Steven Seagal
actually, anyone *and Steven Seagal*
Heather Locklear and Tommy Lee
Sophia Loren and Carlo Ponti
Brigitte Nielsen and Sylvester Stallone
actually, anyone *and Sylvester Stallone*
Carré Otis and Mickey Rourke
Lisa Marie Presley* and Michael Jackson
* *"Do we have sex? Yes, yes, yes!"*
Julia Roberts and Lyle Lovett
Isabella Rossellini and David Lynch
Claudia Schiffer and David Copperfield
Arnold Schwarzenegger and Maria Shriver
Nicollette Sheridan and Michael Bolton
Brooke Shields and Michael Jackson

GET A GRIP!

...**OR** a cameraman, a production assistant . . . hey, love the ones you're with!

Julie Andrews and scenic designer **Tony Walton**
Kim Basinger and makeup artist **Ron Britton**
Sandra Bullock and grip **Danny Podilla**
Chevy Chase and production assistant **Jayni Luke**
Glenn Close and stage carpenter **Steve Beers**

Geena Davis and bodyguard/security expert **Gavin De Becker**
Tracey Gold and production assistant **Roby Marshall**
Whoopi Goldberg and cinematographer **David Claessen**
Whoopi Goldberg and union organizer **Lyle Trachtenberg**
Holly Hunter and cinematographer **Janusz Kaminski**
John Hurt and production assistant **Jo Dalton**
Victoria Jackson and Florida cop **Paul Wessell**
Buster Keaton and script girl **Natalie Talmadge**
Wayne (*Seinfeld*) **Knight** and makeup artist wife, **Paula Sutor**
Burt Lancaster and film coordinator **Susie Scherer**
Traci Lords and propmaster **Brook Yeaton**
Rob Lowe and makeup artist **Sheryl Berkoff**
Marlee Matlin and L.A. traffic cop **Kevin Grandalski**
Randy Quaid and production assistant **Evi Motolanez**
Roseanne and bodyguard **Ben Thomas**
Sissy Spacek and art director **Jack Fisk**
Sharon Stone and assistant director **Bob Wagner**
Jeanne Tripplehorn and stuntman **David Barrett**

JUNIOR PARTNERS

What can I do? I'm hot.

—Jack Nicholson's response to being confronted by Anjelica Huston over his affairs with younger women

Older Men, Younger Women

Jack Haley Jr. and Liza Minnelli: 12 years
Humphrey Bogart and Lauren Bacall: 16 years
Rod Stewart and Kelly Emberg: 16 years
Kevin Kline and Phoebe Cates: 16 years
Richard Gere and Cindy Crawford: 17 years
Peter Sellers and Britt Ekland: 17 years
Jerry Seinfeld and Shoshanna Lonstein: 21 years
Warren Beatty and Annette Bening: 21 years
Carlo Ponti and Sophia Loren: 21 years
Ed and Victoria McMahon: 22 years
Alan Thicke and wife Gina Tolleson: 22 years
Orson Bean and Alley Mills: 23 years
Frank and Kathie Lee Gifford: 23 years
Mike Todd and Liz Taylor: 23 years
Rod Stewart and Rachel Hunter: 26 years
Johnny and Alex Carson: 26 years
Dudley Moore and wife Nicole Rothschild: 28 years
Robert Duvall and wife Sharon Brophy: over 30 years
Dennis Hopper and wife Victoria Duffy: 31 years
Roy Boulting and Hayley Mills: 32 years
Ed McMahon and Pam Hurn: 32 years
Rod Steiger and wife Paula Ellis: 34 years
Clint Eastwood and wife Dina Ruiz: 35 years
Charlie Chaplin and Oona O'Neill: 36 years
Hugh and Kimberly Conrad Hefner: 36 years
Tony Curtis and wife Lisa Deutsch: 37 years
Woody Allen and Soon-Yi Previn: 39 years
Glenn Ford and wife Jeanne Baus: 40 years

Anthony Quinn and **Kathy Benvin**: 46 years
The aged actor and his former secretary produced a daughter in 1993, at which time Quinn's oldest son was fifty-two!
Tony Curtis and pneumatic popsy **Jill Vanden Berg**: 46 years
"Can you imagine me with a woman old enough to be my wife? No, really, I'm serious. Can you imagine me walking into Spago with a seventy-year-old woman? Forget it. Fuck that! I don't have the spirit. My girlfriend is twenty-five years old perfect."
Tony Randall and wife **Heather Harlan**: 50 years
J. Howard Marshall II and **Anna Nicole Smith**: 63 years
"Well, he's an older gentleman. He's eighty-nine. I love him. He loves me. He asked me to marry him so many times and I just wanted to establish myself first. I didn't want somebody to say, 'Aw, she married for money.' . . . I don't care what people think. I love him, and we're in love and that's it."

Older Women, Younger Men

Sharon Stone and **Dweezil Zappa***: 12 years
**"She is a very talented woman and yes, she is a natural blond."*
Susan Sarandon and **Tim Robbins**: 12 years
Cher and **Val Kilmer**: 13 years
Tutor **Jackie Domac** and **Edward Furlong**: 13 years
Roseanne and **Ben Thomas**: 14 years
Linda Evans and **Yanni**: 15 years
Diana Ross and **Bob Silberstein**: 15 years
Cher and **Tom Cruise**: 16 years
Juliet Mills* and **Maxwell Caulfield**: 18 years
**"He likes a woman to make his house pretty and be pretty for him, and that's the way I like to be."*
Mary Tyler Moore and husband **Robert Levine**: 18 years
Joan Collins and **Peter Holm**: 20 years
Cindy and **Michael Landon**: 20 years
Liz Taylor and **Larry Fortensky**: 20 years
Martha Raye* and husband **Mark Harris****: 35-plus years
**"He makes me feel young and womanly.
I'm really in love this time."*
***"Yes, I'm looking for a boyfriend," the pathetically lonely Harris confessed in an intimate interview with a gay magazine after Raye's death in 1994. "I had a little French boyfriend, but he got married." Harris is attempting to pick up the pieces by marketing his own line of furs, and recently spent $40,000 on plastic surgery, including a scrotum tuck.*

THE LOLITA SYNDROME

ama Mia! **Woody Allen** has been expounding upon the same theme in his films for years now: older man lusts after younger woman at the expense of current relationship. In this case, reality imitates art—when Woody took up with **Soon-Yi Previn**, his long-term relationship with longtime (and long-suffering) love **Mia Farrow**, who'd adopted Soon-Yi years before, exploded like the *Hindenburg*. Allen lamely defended himself by explaining, "The heart wants what it wants."

Frasier star **Kelsey Grammer** was sued by the family of seventeen-year-old Sarah Savage (only *sounds* like a porn star), who'd worked as the Grammer family's baby-sitter. The girl said she'd started having sex with the follicularly challenged actor when she was just fifteen, and her attorneys claimed they had damning evidence—in the form of taped messages allegedly left by Grammer on Savage's answering machine. The contents of the tapes were never made public, the case having been settled out of court. But after Grammer badmouthed the girl's clan in the press, he received another Savage salvo: a $19 million civil suit claiming he'd caused them untold emotional distress and mental anguish by attempting to "depict the family as dysfunctional and driven by avarice and spite."

Shades of **Roman Polanski**: randy rocker **Don Henley** was arrested at his Hollywood Hills home after a hot-tub session with two underage girls nearly turned deadly. The trio had been smoking cocaine, and one of the teens began convulsing. She was rushed to the hospital for treatment (she recovered), and though the incident was splashed all over the tabloids, it was reportedly Henley's powerful connections and willingness to spend huge amounts of dough that got him off the hook.

Hot-blooded twenty-two-year-old **Don Johnson** began dating early-bloomer **Melanie Griffith** when she was just fourteen—the same age at which she moved in with him.

Jerry Lee Lewis married thirteen-year-old cousin Myra Brown in 1957, and the resultant public outcry nearly KO'ed the Killer's career. "I would say that hurt me bad," Lewis later lamented. "It's very stupid for a person to flush $50 billion down the commode, which is probably what I did."

Rob Lowe had similar career problems after a night of carousing in 1988. In Atlanta to attend a political convention, Lowe picked up two underage girls at a nightclub and took them back to his hotel room, where he decided to record their sexcapades for posterity. Unfortunately for the former Brat Packer, who'd gotten up to use the bathroom, the two girls absconded with the videotape, which soon became evidence in a sensational court case. Lowe, one of the girls' mothers charged, used his "celebrity status as an inducement to females to engage in sexual intercourse, sodomy, and multiple-partner sexual activity for his immediate sexual gratification, and for the purpose of making pornographic films of these activities." After settling (out of court, natch), Lowe performed his penance: twenty hours of community service.

Roman Polanski is forbidden to return to the United States because of his criminal conduct with thirteen-year-old Samantha Gailey in 1977. According to the girl's testimony, Polanski lured her to Jack Nicholson's house with promises of meeting the star, who wasn't home when they arrived. Polanski plied her with champagne and Quaaludes, then began photographing her in various states of undress. Drifting in and out of consciousness, she was raped and sodomized for hours. After returning home, Gailey told her mother what had happened, and mom was immediately on the horn to the cops. Polanski was charged with six felonies (including child molestation and furnishing drugs to a minor), but a deal was eventually struck: Polanski pleaded guilty to just one count (of unlawful sexual intercourse), but fled the country prior to sentencing to avoid imprisonment.

The AGE of Innocence

Jerry Seinfeld's girlfriend Shoshanna Lonstein turns twenty-one years old next week. Seinfeld said in honor of the event he'll stop bathing her in the sink.

Jerry Seinfeld proposed to Shoshanna Lonstein on the night of her twenty-first birthday. Apparently he wanted to wait to make sure she wasn't just using him to buy beer.

Conan O'Brien comments on Jer's May-December romance

HOT PURSUITS

Lotusland's immoral majority.

Pamela Anderson Lee confesses, "I can honestly say, hand on heart, that I have dated nineteen guys in my life. And of those nineteen I have slept with fifteen." Now, *that's* something to be proud of.

Roseanne once gave tubby hubby **Tom Arnold** a very special present: "For my third sobriety birthday, Roseanne had me blindfolded and taken to this hotel room. In the room were two of Heidi Fleiss's women, and they were together in front of me, uh, romantically. It was wonderful to watch—fabulous, fucking great! Roseanne was waiting upstairs. I went up. She'd made a cake and jumped out of it in a sexy outfit. Great! But she held it against me, those girls. . . . So you dream about these things—two women was my biggest fantasy—but don't do it if you want to stay married. It makes things incredibly weird. Just say no." The Arnolds, as everyone knows, have since split, the main reason for the bust-up reportedly being Tom's affair with the couple's comely assistant, Kim Silva. Maybe so, sez Tom: "The precipitating factor in our divorce was first Kim and then my career. . . . I never slept with her. . . . Well, nothing happened that did not involve Roseanne. That's all I'm going to say."

Warren Beatty is legendary even in ultra-jaded Tinseltown circles for his sexual appetite and lengthy list of conquests. Actress **Sonia Braga** lays it on the line: "Frankly, who in Hollywood hasn't made love with him? Not having sex with Warren is like going to Rome and not seeing the pope."

Heavenly **Halle Berry** was allegedly "kept" by John Ronan, a Chicago dentist, while she was trying to make it in showbiz. "It became a monthly thing for three years, of me guaranteeing her rent," Ronan told a *Premiere* reporter, and as proof he produced a Western Union document showing $21,500 in monetary transfers to the actress between 1989 and 1991. When Ronan sued for return of the money, Berry showed up in court—and won.

It's the Pitts

Women have no shame. Grown women. Educated women. Famous women. Women with boyfriends. Women with husbands. They're all just shameless. You really wouldn't believe what I have to put up with. Women come right up to him and press their bodies against him from behind. And I'm right there!

—Gwyneth Paltrow, on life as Brad Pitt's girlfriend

Puff-pated **Jon Bon Jovi** admits he was "a little gigolo when I was seventeen. And I had older women picking me up when I was fifteen. So I've been around the block a time or two, you know?"

Plain brown rapper **Bobby Brown**, according to his body-guard, has a thing for blondes and once boasted of having "had **Madonna** in the back of a limo." Wonder if **Whitney** would be surprised to hear that—or care.

THERE, D⊙NE THEM

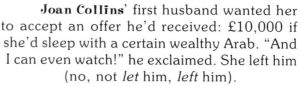

BEEN She says black men aren't romantic. She shouldn't judge everyone by her five or six hundred bad experiences.
—Jim (*Entertainment Weekly*) Mullen, on Madonna

Joan Collins' first husband wanted her to accept an offer he'd received: £10,000 if she'd sleep with a certain wealthy Arab. "And I can even watch!" he exclaimed. She left him (no, not *let* him, *left* him).

"In my young days I used to pick up sluts," says **Kevin Costner**, hastening to add, "I don't mean that nastily. It's more a term of endearment, really, for girls who know how to speak their minds." OKEY-DOKEY.

Director **Michael Curtiz** was once caught flagrante delicto with a makeup girl by cast and crew members on a movie set. "Oh my God!" Curtiz screamed disingenuously. "What are you doing down there? Get off! Get off!"

Supposedly supersensitive **James Dean** was a sexual compulsive and "rough trade" aficionado who frequented Hollywood gay leather bars, where he was known as "the Human Ashtray" because he loved being burned with cigarette butts. (In fact, the coroner noted a literal "constellation" of old scars while autopsying the actor's body.)

Precocious pervert **Gérard Depardieu** admitted to participating in a gang rape (at age nine!), a coming-of-age ritual that continued throughout his teens, he says.

Hunky **Matt Dillon** likes to be tied up, according to *Details* sex columnist Anka.

"Hey, kids, let's go
play with my friend
the hula dancer!"

LAYING IT ⊚N THE LINE

I don't make love. I fuck.
—producer Don Simpson

Famed Hollywood hedonist **Robert Evans** likes women to urinate and defecate on him, according to the authors of *You'll Never Make Love in This Town Again.* G ʌ ꟽ Ɗ!

"In college," says sexy **Linda Fiorentino**, "I slept with a couple of guys, like we all do, and a couple of girls, like we all do. Then I got to New York City and I just blossomed into this sexual creature. My sister Terry and I would just go into a bar and say to some guy, 'I don't know your name, I don't care, let's go.' We couldn't remember which one of us fucked which one . . . We were like guys. It was all a game."

Everyone knows **Clark Gable** had **George Cukor** fired as director of *Gone With the Wind*, ostensibly because he didn't want a "woman's director" at the helm. The real reason? Cukor knew about Gable's early male-to-male casting couch experiences, and Gable couldn't look him in the eye.

Steve Guttenberg got himself into a bit of a jam after tying a beautiful blond fan to a hotel-room bed, then going out for condoms. Problem was, he forgot which hotel he left her at. "She was furious," Steve said shamefacedly. "It took me eight hours to find her again. When I did, she was so angry she wouldn't even let me make love to her."

Screamin' **Sammy Hagar** likes 'em five at a time, dissolute **Don Henley** and **Jack Nicholson** are also fond of multiples, and **Woody Harrelson** is a self-admitted sex addict.

Judy Holliday, when lunged at by a lecherous studio exec, whipped out her falsies and said, "I think this is what you're after." No word on whether she got the job.

WORK MATES

The people we work with are all charming and rich and handsome and talented and beautiful. And often completely amoral.
—Eric Stoltz

WHIPPING BOYS

Sexual sadists...
Wallace Beery
David O. Selznick
Erich von Stroheim

...and masochists
James Dean
Emil Jannings
Charles Laughton

Latin lover **Engelbert Humperdinck** had amassed a total of seventeen paternity suits by 1990. "I now have more paternity suits than leisure suits," he sighed.

Decadent **Don Johnson** threw a little party in his Hong Kong hotel room to celebrate Planet Hollywood's grand opening there in 1994. The guest list? **Patrick Swayze, Charlie Sheen,** and six young Chinese women.

Playing footsie: publicist **Chuck Jones** admitted to the theft of more than two hundred pairs of shoes from former client **Marla Maples Trump**. (What—she didn't notice?)

"Anyone I've ever wanted to be with, I've had," boasts **Calvin Klein**.

Chico Marx, when caught smooching a chorus girl, offered this classic excuse: "I wasn't kissing her. I was whispering in her mouth."

Biographer Penina Spiegel had this to say about **Steve McQueen**: "Steve liked groups. He liked showing off his body and his peepee. The first guy to take off his shirt was Steve, the first guy to drop his pants was Steve."

Marilyn Monroe was all too familiar with the casting couch. Upon signing her first major contract, the budding bombshell breathed a sigh of relief: "Well, at least that's the last cock I have to suck." Monroe also reportedly turned tricks for a while as a struggling actress.

"Anything goes" is the motto of the bad boys of **Mötley Crüe**, who once challenged each other to a crude contest: seeing which member could bonk the most babes without bathing. And the winner was . . . **Nikki Sixx** (17 days, 30 conquests). Sloppy seconds, indeed!

FORWARD THINKER

When Sharon [Stone] was introduced to me she looked straight at my husband, the director; when introduced to him, she declared, "We *know* each other, don't we?"
—Holly Palance, Hollywood columnist and daughter of one-arm-pushup king Jack Palance

"Tony [Perkins] isn't exactly Norman Bates, but he's awfully kinky," remembered fashion designer **Halston**. Added tiny **Truman Capote**, "He pretends not to know if he's really gay or not. Just ask any one of the small army of his ex-lovers! Of which *I* am not one! I don't like blood, and Tony's a sadist. He likes to see blood. I mean, he *is* Norman Bates."

Musician **John Phillips** (The Mamas & The Papas) is into spanking and bondage.

Elvis Presley liked to watch teenage girls, wearing nothing but white panties, wrestle.

"[Muammar] Qaddafi's a drag queen," according to **Heidi Fleiss** predecessor **Madame Alex**. "He dresses in women's clothes."

Actor **Aldo Ray** remembered an early casting-couch experience: "**George Cukor** gave me my big break in this business. He thought I could be a star, and I knew somebody important like him could really help me, so I let him take his pleasure and it didn't compromise me in the least."

the more the MERRIER

Orgies have been part of Hollywood's sexual landscape since the earliest days of movie-making. Valentino was one who threw "parties" on a regular basis, as did Lionel Atwill, whose legendary pileups were frequented by Victor Jory and Josef von Sternberg, among others. Today, clandestine gay-only orgies, attended by young heartthrob actors who can't afford to be seen in public without a beautiful woman in tow for fear of despoiling their carefully crafted images, are the thing. And there's no worry about salacious stories being leaked to the tabs, since each participant has just as much to lose as the next.

Rotund **Roseanne** admitted to lesbian affairs and stints at prostitution during her days as a struggling stand-up comedienne.

Focus is important if you want to be a star. No one knows that better than **Arnold Schwarzenegger**, who confesses, "Many times while I was getting laid, in my head I was doing a business deal."

After watching **Johnny Carson** spill a drink on his desk, considerate guest **Cybill Shepherd** said, "You should have spilled it in your lap—then I could have cleaned it up."

Anna Nicole Smith supplemented her strip-club income with prostitution before she became a star, according to biographers Eric and D'Eve Redding.

Sly Stallone reportedly loooooved the *ménages à trois* he had with on-again, off-again girlfriend **Jennifer Flavin** and model **Naomi Campbell**.

Rudy Valentino was fond of wearing corsets.

"With men," explains vapid vixen **Raquel Welch**, "it's like I'm trying *every* color in the jellybean jar to see what's going to taste good."

VICTIM ⊚F

We are so busy talking about sexual harassment in corporate America, but in Hollywood it's rampant. I have experienced sexual harassment *from a woman*. It didn't have anything to do with the fact that she was attracted to me. It was a power trip.

—Martha Plimpton

Mae West, when asked how she knew so much about men, blithely replied, "Baby, I went to night school."

Vanna White had a little help while struggling to make it: she was reportedly "kept" by a prominent—and very married—Las Vegas entertainer (who, incidentally, also had two other mistresses). He paid for Vanna's Hollywood apartment and acting lessons.

During the filming of *Terms of Endearment,* according to **Shirley MacLaine** in the autobiographical *My Lucky Stars*, she was ambushed by co-star **Debra Winger** under the covers during a bed scene with **Jack Nicholson**. When the cameras started to roll, Winger began licking her way up MacLaine's legs. As soon as she heard the word "Cut!" (and not a moment before), MacLaine kicked Winger off, prompting the younger actress to sneer, "You shouldn't knock it if you haven't tried it." (MacLaine swears she passed.)

Movie mogul **Daryl Zanuck** closed his office each day at 4:00 to indulge in assignations with studio employees. His favorite and most frequent guest was actress **Carole Landis**.

IT'S WHO ☀ YOU BLOW

Casting couch: fact or fiction?

I'll tell you when I came across some awful characters: when I came to Hollywood. Once I was on a big movie and I got called to the director's hotel room. Only he was in bed, and I was like, "No! This is not happening to me!" *So what did she do?* "I'm not fucking getting into bed with you." And I got fired.
—Stacey (*Clueless*) Dash

The casting couch is the name of the game in Hollywood. I know there are stars, especially women, who have made a career from sexual favors.
—Phyllis Diller

There were all these sleazy guys going, "Hey, baby, do you want to be a model?" Giving me cards with naked girls in champagne glasses. They would say, you know, MITCH, PHOTOGRAPHER.
—Cameron Diaz, about a Hollywood shindig she attended when she was just sweet sixteen.

You can't sleep your way into being a star—it takes much, much more—but it helps.
—Marilyn Monroe

You can only fuck your way to the middle.
—Sharon Stone

Natural Endowment of the Arts

Some of Tinseltown's biggest names . . .

Fatty Arbuckle
Scott Bakula
John (*CPW*) Barrowman
Warren Beatty
Milton Berle
Humphrey Bogart
Marlon Brando
James Caan
Jim Carrey
Dick Cavett
Charlie Chaplin
Gary Cooper
Willem Dafoe
John Derek
Matt Dillon
Errol Flynn
Woody Harrelson
Jimi Hendrix
Chris Isaak
Don Johnson
Tommy Lee Jones
Tommy Lee

David Letterman
Huey Lewis
Lyle Lovett
Michael Madsen
Roddy McDowell
Liam Neeson
Jason Patric
Jason Priestley
Aldo Ray
Robert Redford
Christopher Reeve
John Schneider
Arnold Schwarzenegger
David Sheehan
Frank Sinatra
Jimmy Smits
David Soul
Patrick Stewart
Kiefer Sutherland
Bruce Willis
James Woods
Bill Wyman

CHEATERS NEVER PROSPER

"**B**eing a star," **Denzel Washington** told **Barbara Walters** in 1993, "temptation is all around, and I haven't been perfect." Washington is far from the only Hollywood actor who has fooled around—in fact, it wouldn't be much of an exaggeration to say that most showbiz marriages allow a little room for extracurricular activity. **Joan Fontaine** explained that "the main problem in marriage is that for a man sex is a hunger, like eating. And if he can't get to a fancy restaurant he'll make for the hot dog stand." Long-suffering **Cindy Costner** learned this firsthand—throughout her marriage to **Kevin**, her childhood sweetheart, the priapic performer was linked with a bevy of beauties including actresses, models, a publicity agent, a hatcheck girl, and a hula dancer. His constant cheating finally caused the marriage's collapse in 1995. "I try to conduct my life with a certain amount of dignity and discretion," Kev confessed, "but marriage is a hard, hard gig."

AFFAIRS OF HONOR

I don't sleep with married men, but what I mean is that I don't sleep with happily married men.
—Britt Ekland

Another whose marriage foundered under the strain of constant infidelity is limelight-loving **Michael Douglas**, who once confessed to being "your basic flasher. I've always loved exposing myself." Despite seeking professional help, Douglas and wife **Diandra** split up in 1995—though whether they'll actually divorce is anyone's guess. **Sammy Davis Jr.**, according to *Deep Throat* doyenne **Linda Lovelace**, "had his own code of marital fidelity. He explained to me that he could do anything with me except have normal intercourse because that would be cheating on his wife." (She also claimed he asked for lessons on the art of giving oral sex to a man—and practiced on her male manager!) Model **Kelly LeBrock** grew tired of husband **Steven Seagal**'s constant dalliances, saying he was "an inveterate liar who lived in a fantasy world." And in 1994, overpaid hack screenwriter **Joe Eszterhas** left his wife and kids by announcing, "I've fallen in love with **Naomi** [**Baka**, whose husband of five months, *Sliver* producer **Bill MacDonald**, had just been poached by **Sharon Stone**]," then bounding into her adjoining hotel room and crying, "I love you. We're leaving."

Always a WOMAN for me

Womanizing Hall of Famers

Desi Arnaz		
John Barrymore		Sean Penn
Warren Beatty		Joe Pesci
Bobby Brown		Jon Peters
Kevin Costner	Dennis Hopper	George Raft
Tony Curtis	Billy Idol	Dennis Rodman
Michael Douglas	Lorenzo Lamas	Charlie Sheen
Clint Eastwood	the aptly named	Frank Sinatra
Robert Evans	Robin Leach	Harry Dean
Eddie Fisher	Rob Lowe	Stanton
Woody Harrelson*	Steve McQueen	Rod Stewart
David Hasselhoff	Eddie Murphy	Kiefer Sutherland
Don Henley	Jack Nicholson	Alan Thicke
Buck Henry	Ryan O'Neal	Peter Weller

"Maybe it's a mother complex. . . . I was kind of a mama's boy until I was twenty-one. It's just a continuation of the Oedipus complex." And, "I definitely have a sex drive that is kind of beyond my understanding."

THE FEMININE PERSPECTIVE

HIGH INFIDELITY

"Fidelity is possible," says Michelle Pfeiffer, currently married to TV wunderkind David Kelley. "Anything is possible if you're stubborn and strong. But it's not that important. Traditional marriage is very outdated. I don't think people should live together the rest of their lives suppressing frustrations." Susan Sarandon agrees. "If someone is very special to you, is it really that important if every now and then he takes off and has a liaison with someone else? I mean, is it really catastrophic?" Apparently not—not in Hollywood, anyway.

Old Dogs, New Tricks

Famous names linked in the news with "Hollywood Madam" Heidi Fleiss

James Caan
studio execs Mark Canton and Barry Josephson
Shannen Doherty
Robert Evans
Vitas Gerulaitis
Don Henley
Dennis Hopper
Timothy Hutton
Billy Idol
*claims he was "just a friend" and
"never used her professional services"*
Mick Jagger
Madonna and various employees
of her company, Maverick Records
*sued in 1995 by ex~employee Sonji Shepherd, who charged that
"Payola, strippers, gentlemen's clubs and airline tickets
for Heidi Fleiss and her working girls—
these are just a few of the illegal, unethical and
immoral business schemes which permeated
the workplace. . . . "*
Judd Nelson
Jack Nicholson
*"In terms of sexual prowess," sez Heidi, "Jack is a goddamn
great lover."*
record producer Richard Perry
Jon Peters
Arnold Schwarzenegger
*won a libel suit against French magazine Voici in 1995 after
they published an interview with an ex~Fleiss call girl who
claimed he'd used her services*
Charlie Sheen
Pauly Shore
Oliver Stone
Drugstore Cowboy producer Nick Wechsler

GOD SAVE THE QUEENS

An unending source of fascinated showbiz speculation is "are they or aren't they?"—who's gay and who's not. While being homosexual today has nowhere near the stigma it had in the forties or fifties, conventional wisdom still says audiences just won't buy gay men in straight roles. (Not to mention the respect given to gay women: "Hollywood thinks lesbianism is fine as long as the dick prevails," harumphs **Lili Taylor**.) So the Hollywood closet remains packed to the rafters—and probably will for some time to come.

Gay or Bisexual Men

Nick Adams

Peter Allen

Director **Pedro Almodovar**

Horror director/novelist **Clive Barker**

Fashion arbiter **Mr. Blackwell**
Admits to affairs with Tyrone Power, Cary Grant, and Randolph Scott.

Ray (the Scarecrow) **Bolger**

Marlon Brando (at least once)

Lenny Bruce

Raymond Burr

Richard Burton
Blamed a lifelong drinking problem on the fact that he'd once been a homosexual.

Dan (*Frasier*) **Butler**

Truman Capote

Monty Python-er **Graham Chapman**

Maurice Chevalier

Montgomery Clift

James Coco

George Cukor

James Dean

Alain Delon

Former Fox head **Barry Diller**

Robert Downey Jr.

Rupert Everett
Confesses to being a onetime "rent boy."

Director **Rainer Werner Fassbinder**

Is Tom Cruise Gay?

Nicole Kidman: "Honestly, wholeheartedly, looking you straight in the eye—it's *not* true. . . . We don't feel comfortable discussing what we do in bed at midnight—even though it *is* pretty damn good."

Tom Cruise: "All the stuff I've heard about myself: that I'm a misogynist. I'm a homosexual. I'm brainless. How can I be all of these things?"

Well . . .

Entertainer
Harvey Fierstein
*Created a miniscandal
in 1984 when he
thanked his lover
publicly during the
Tony Awards telecast.*
Malcolm Forbes
*The magnate was "outed"
after his death by
Outweek magazine,
which claimed he
was straight in public
but privately hung out
in gay biker bars.*
Will Geer (yes, Grandpa
Walton)

Is Keanu Reeves Gay?

David Geffen: "I hear that I'm supposed to be married to Keanu Reeves. I've never met or laid eyes on [him]." And, "If Keanu Reeves was gay and interested in me, I'd be thrilled to death."

Keanu Reeves, responding to rumors that he had an affair with a Canadian ballet dancer: "I'm not gay and there's no ballet dancer. I love women more than any guy I know. Only ignorant people assume those ballet dudes are gay."

David Geffen
"Cher and Marlo [Thomas] knew everything there was to know about me. I've never kept it a secret. After Marlo and I broke up I thought I really had to pursue seeing who I was as a gay man, and I have done so."
Sometime actor **Jason Gould**
Son of Babs Streisand and Elliott Gould.
Cary Grant
Merv Griffin
Sued in 1991 for nonsupport by Brent Plott, who claimed he and Griffin "lived together, we shared the same bed, the same house."

Nigel Hawthorne
Director (*Safe*) **Todd Haynes**
Rock Hudson
Howard Hughes
Usually impotent with female sexual partners, Hughes once asked **Bette Davis** to perform oral sex on him and swear like a sailor so he could pretend she was a man.
She obliged.
Director **James Ivory**

Is Whitney Houston Gay?

"If I was gay I swear I would say it but I ain't never liked a woman in my bed, I swear to God. And [personal assistant] Robyn is my friend. I've known her since high school. She's my good friend. But no, I ain't gay and never have been gay." And, "Even when we were kids growing up, people thought we were gay. I think it had a lot to do with Robyn's being athletic." [Note: The ongoing speculation about Houston is due in part to her seeming unconcern over Bobby Brown's numerous and constant infidelities.]

Mick Jagger

Says ex-lover **Bebe Buell**: *"I used to get calls from Mick and* **David** [**Bowie**] *at three in the morning inviting me to join them in bed with four gorgeous black women. . . . Sometimes they wanted me to join them with four gorgeous black men. Mick had affairs with several black men that I know of. Nobody famous, just great-looking guys from Long Island."*

WHAT THE POT CALLS THE KETTLE

Fag . . . fag hag.
—Janice Dickinson, on Mick Jagger and Jerry Hall

Elton John

"I went to a psychiatrist recently and he said, 'Were you ever molested as a child?' And I said, 'No, I was dying to be molested, dying for someone to have a fiddle around.'"

Danny Kaye

Child star **Tommy Kirk**

Charles Laughton

According to wife **Elsa Lanchester**, *"It was only after we'd been married about two years that I learned of his homosexuality. One night the police came around and said they were holding a boy who claimed Charles owed him some money. It was then that he broke down and confessed his homosexuality. He cried and admitted he picked up boys from time to time. I told him it was perfectly all right, that I understood, that it didn't matter. But of course it did—particularly his deception. If he had only told me before our marriage."*

CAA agent **Bryan Lourd** (**Carrie Fisher**'s former flame.)

Paul Lynde

George (*Route 66*) **Maharis**

Marcello Mastroianni
(at least once)
Producer **Ismail Merchant**
Sir Ian McKellan
Sal Mineo
Vincente Minnelli
Ramon Novarro
Laurence Olivier

Are Blake Edwards and Wife Julie Andrews Gay?

Blake Edwards: "I'm not gay. I've never had any kind of a homosexual relationship."
Julie Andrews: "I can assure you, I'm not gay."

Director **Pier Paolo Pasolini**
TV personality Charles Perez
Anthony Perkins
Cole Porter
Tyrone Power
Aldo Ray
Rex Reed
Charles Nelson Reilly
Director **Tony Richardson**
Vanessa Redgrave's ex.
Yves Saint Laurent
Dick Sargent
Director John Schlesinger
Randolph Scott
Howard Stern (at least once)
Oliver Stone (at least once)
Robert Taylor
Director **Gus Van Sant**
Conrad Veidt (*Casablanca*'s Nazi commandant)
Gore Vidal
Andy Warhol
Director **John Waters**
Clifton Webb
Rolling Stone publisher **Jann Wenner**
*"Outed" when he left his wife for Calvin Klein employee **Matt Nye**
(Wenner's ex-wife calls Nye "Soon-Yi").*
Tennessee Williams
Franco Zeffirelli

Is Rod Stewart Gay?

One particularly persistent rumor had it that after "servicing" as many as a dozen men in rapid-fire order, Stewart got "fed up," so to speak, and had to be rushed to the hospital. "Oh, the come-in-the-tummy story," Rod said, when asked about it recently. "That one's amazing! I was on my honeymoon with Alana in 1979 in Italy, and it was on the news that I'd been rushed to the hospital and they'd pumped out twelve pints! Can you imagine *that*?"

come out, COME OUT, whoever you are

Kirstie Alley and husband Parker Stevenson
Chastity Bono
Richard Chamberlain
Tom Cruise
Ellen DeGeneres
Dom DeLuise
Malcolm Forbes

Jodie Foster
Richard Gere
Whitney Houston
Rock Hudson
Tab Hunter
Michael Jackson
Kristy McNichol
Jim Nabors
Brigitte Nielsen
Rosie O'Donnell
David Hyde (*Frasier*) **Pierce**

Keanu Reeves
Tom Selleck
Lily Tomlin
John Travolta*
Jann Wenner

*Porn star Paul Barresi claimed he was Travolta's lover for a time, and also says, "Some men in Hollywood . . . find me attractive . . . I've let them use me in the hopes of furthering my acting career."

Celebrities who have been "outed" (rightly or wrongly) by the media

Gay or Bisexual Women

Maude Adams

Dame Judith Anderson

Jean Arthur

Director (*Nana*) Dorothy Arzner

Joan Baez

"Being bisexual, you're very much looked down upon by the uppity members of gay lib. . . . If you swing both ways, you really swing. I just figure, you know, double your pleasure."

PLAY MISTER

I've never had sex with a woman, but I've been on dates with a woman.
—Sharon Stone

Tallulah Bankhead

Drew Barrymore

"Do I like women? I like women. Do I like them sexually? Yeah, I do. Totally. To the extent of how I fool around with them, I think that when I was younger I was with a lot of women. I used to love to be with women. I haven't been with a woman in a long time. It's weird. Women are so much more selective with women than they are with men."

Amanda (*Married . . . With Children*) **Bearse**

Sandra Bernhard

Judy Carne

Claudette Colbert

Joan Crawford

Sandy Dennis

Seventies supermodel **Janice Dickinson**

"Fuck Helmut Newton. Why should I take my clothes off for him? I took my clothes off for his wife."

Marlene Dietrich

Lynn Fontanne

YOUTHFUL EXPERIMENTS

I have had relationships with women—when I was younger. Not a lot of them. It just wasn't something that kept my interest.
—Cher

GLAAD TO MEET Y☉U

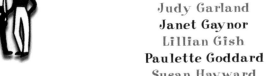

Actress Ming~Na Wen (*The Single Guy*), at the 1996 annual Gay and Lesbian Alliance Against Defamation Media Awards: "This is the only awards show where people show up with their real dates."

Greta Garbo
Judy Garland
Janet Gaynor
Lillian Gish
Paulette Goddard
Susan Hayward
Designer **Edith Head**
Judy Holliday
Nancy (*The Beverly Hillbillies*) **Kulp**
Elsa Lanchester
Gertrude Lawrence
Beatrice Lillie
Courtney Love
Myrna Loy
Madonna (at least once)
Mary Martin
Elsa Maxwell
Kristy McNichol
Marilyn Monroe
Agnes Moorehead
Roseanne (at least a few times)
Margaret Rutherford
Barbara Stanwyck
"I'm with the boys—
I want to go where the boys go."
Lily Tomlin
Mae West

Others are a little more ambiguous—**Madonna**, for example, who never provided a definitive answer as to whether her relationship with comedienne **Sandra Bernhard** was friendship or love . . . but the two parted bitter enemies not long after. And freak-of-nature **Dennis Rodman**, who coincidentally dated Madonna for a time, allowed that "people think I'm gay or bisexual. Well . . . maybe I am." His appearances in drag to promote his book *Bad As I Wanna Be* (not to mention his self-wedding) didn't help.

J. Crew model David . . . oh, sorry!
It's Dennis Rodman.

vicious
RUMORS

Leonardo DiCaprio, on the rumors that dog him: "That I'm gay. I heard a rumor that some guy said I was passed out in front of his home after a party for the whole night after doing too much coke. . . . I heard that I was going out with Ellen Barkin. That I'm an alien. Nothing that odd, I guess."

And Matt (*Friends*) LeBlanc, on the rumors that dog *him*: "One was that I was gay. Another was that I spend all my time in strip bars and I say things to the strippers like—and this is a direct quote from the *National Enquirer*—'My mom would never let me go out with girls like you—beautiful girls who aren't afraid to show off their bodies.'"

Are Richard Gere and Cindy Crawford Gay?
Their $30,000 *London Times* ad:

A Personal Statement by
Richard Gere and Cindy Crawford

For some reason unknown to us, there has been an enormous amount of speculation in Europe lately concerning the state of our marriage. This all stems from a very crude, ignorant and libelous "article" in a French tabloid. We both feel quite foolish responding to such nonsense, but since it seems to have reached some sort of critical mass, here's our statement to correct the falsehoods and rumors and hope it will alleviate the concerns of our friends and fans.

We got married because we love each other and we decided to make a life together. We are heterosexual and monogamous and take our commitment to each other very seriously. There is not and never has been a pre-nuptial agreement of any kind. Reports of a divorce are totally false. There are no plans, nor have there ever been any plans for divorce. We remain very married. We both look forward to having a family. Richard is not abandoning his career. He is starting a film in July with others planned to follow.

We will continue to support "difficult" causes such as AIDS research and treatment, Tibetan independence, cultural and tribal survival, international Human Rights, Gay and Lesbian Rights, ecology, leukemia research and treatment, democracy movements, disarmament, nonviolence and anything else we wish to support, irrespective of what the tabloids try to imply.

Now, that said, we do feel we have a basic right to privacy and deserve to have that respected like everyone else. Marriage is hard enough without all this negative speculation. Thoughts and words are very powerful, so please be responsible, truthful and kind. (The glam duo have since split.)

TWO-RING CIRCUS

Once a week is quite enough to propose to
anyone, and it should always be done in a
manner that attracts some attention.
—Oscar Wilde, *An Ideal Husband*

Since Hollywoodites are such sensitive souls, they're less likely to get hitched at a simple civil ceremony than to make a grandiose gesture meant to show the world just how deep and meaningful their love truly is. **Patricia Arquette** proposed to **Nicolas Cage**: "When she showed up at my house dressed head to toe in black vinyl, carrying a big purple wedding cake, I knew I was with the right woman," he gushed. Romantics **Richard Gere** and **Cindy Crawford** exchanged twisted tin-foil rings at Las Vegas's Little Church of the West, and **Bruce Willis** and **Demi Moore** were married by **Little Richard** in 1987. **Drew Barrymore** decided on the spur of the moment to marry bar owner **Jeremy Thomas**, and they were hitched the same night by a female "psychic priest" they'd found by dialing 800-I-MARRY-YOU. The happy couple split up just a few weeks later (and Thomas subsequently sold his story to the tabloids). **Jon Bon Jovi** married his childhood sweetheart at Las Vegas's Graceland Wedding Chapel. Attire? Black leather for both bride and groom (hey, it's *rock 'n' roll*, man). Then there's the sentimental saga of "actress" **Pamela Anderson** and Mötley Crüe skins-smasher **Tommy Lee** (previously married to *Melrose Place* savior **Heather Locklear**). "I met him last New Year's Eve," Anderson burbled in 1995. "He sat with me, and he kept licking my face. When I left, he was begging for my phone number. I said no way. But then I gave him my number because he was interesting. I was definitely attracted." How . . . romantic. After a five-day, hooch-soaked courtship in Cancún, the couple tied the knot on a sunny beach, wearing only the briefest of bathing suits. The devoted duo spent their honeymoon shooting stills and videotape for *Playboy*'s "Best of Pamela Anderson" release.

WEDDING DRESS

At the wedding [Pamela Anderson] wore a white thong bikini. Now, call me old-fashioned, but your wedding day is supposed to be special—you shouldn't be wearing your work clothes.

—Jay Leno

LICKETY-SPLIT

Getting married is just the first step
toward getting divorced.
—Zsa Zsa Gabor, who oughta know

All good things must come to an end, as they say. Some of the
shortest showbiz marriages on record:

6 hours: **Rudolph Valentino**
and **Jean Acker**
1 day: **Jean Arthur** and
photographer **Julian Anker**
5 days: **Cher** and **Gregg Allman**
1 week: **Robert Walker**
and **Barbara** (daughter
of director John) **Ford**
8 days: **Dennis Hopper** and **Michelle Phillips**
13 days: **Patty Duke** and rock promoter **Michael Tell**
3 weeks: **Wallace Beery** and **Gloria Swanson**
35 days: **George Brent** and actress **Constance Worth**
38 days: **Ernest Borgnine** and **Ethel Merman**
8 weeks (separated after 5): **Drew Barrymore**
and bar owner **Jeremy Thomas**
11 weeks: **Porfirio Rubirosa** and **Barbara Hutton**
4 months: **James Woods** and horse trainer **Sarah Owen**
Henry Fonda and **Margaret Sullavan**
5 months: **Eddie Fisher** and beauty queen **Terry Richard**
Ashley Hamilton and **Shannen Doherty** (Hamilton was a rebound
relationship for Doherty after **Judd Nelson** dumped her)
Natasha (*Species*) **Henstridge** and **Damian** (*Bound by Honor*) **Chapa**
almost 6 months: **Charlie Sheen** and
model **Donna Peele**
7 months: **Artie Shaw** and **Ava Gardner**
Erik Estrada and **Joyce Miller**
8 months: **Liz Taylor** and **Richard Burton**
(the second time around)
9 months: **Joe DiMaggio**
and **Marilyn Monroe**
11 months: **Paul Simon** and **Carrie Fisher**
exactly 1 year: **George Brent**
and **Ann Sheridan**
(divorce became final on
their first anniversary)

EEK A SPOUSE!

Why do Hollywood divorces cost so much?
Because they're worth it.
−Johnny Carson

...no wonder prenups are so popular!

Tom Arnold, before metamorphosing into the internationally acclaimed movie idol he is today, was a lousy actor and failed stand-up comic who demanded $100,000 per month from wife **Roseanne** upon their bitter breakup, because of the "extremely rich, opulent lifestyle" to which she'd foolishly accustomed him. Not one to take this lying down, rancorous Rosie canceled his credit cards. "You cannot do that!" the hag-ridden Arnold furiously fumed. "I am a fucking millionaire!" This wasn't the first battle caused by the bitter bust-up—right after they decided to split, the war of words began. "Tom Arnold's penis is three inches long," sniped Roseanne. "Okay, I'll say four 'cause we're trying to settle." Stung, Tommy boy retorted, "When we were married, she used to talk about how big it was . . . And like I say, even a 747 looks small when it lands in the Grand Canyon." As always, Roseanne got the last word: "I'm not upset about my divorce. I'm only upset I'm not a widow."

He loved Lucy . . . and lots of other women too. One of Tinseltown's most spiteful splits was between small-screen sweethearts **Lucille Ball** and **Desi Arnaz**. "You bastard! You cheat! You drunken bum!" she once railed at the Cuban heel. "I got enough on you to hang you. By the time I get through with you you'll be as broke as when you got here. You goddamn spic . . . you . . . you wetback!"

Cra-a-a-azy man **Jim Carrey** began an affair with his *Dumb and Dumber* co-star (**Lauren Holly**, not **Jeff Daniels**) while he was still married. He told wife **Melissa** (who'd helped him out careerwise in many ways, including administering massages to movie execs in a position to help hubby's chances in Hollywood) that in the battle of temptation, "lust won." Acrimonious accusations flew back and forth

(Melissa on Jim: "partying and lying about it"; Jim on Melissa: "paranoid and insecure") before the divorce became final in 1995.

Cher charged **Sonny** in court with putting her into "involuntary servitude" during their marriage. "He was dictatorial, unfaithful, demanding," she said. "If I'd stayed with Sonny I wouldn't be an actress, I wouldn't be a woman. God, I'd be dead."

Joan Collins rues the day she met rock star manqué/gigolo wannabe **Peter Holm**. After thirteen whole months of wedded bliss, Collins decided they were irreconcilably different (due in large part to the Holmboy's affair with **Romina** "Passion Flower" **Daniels**, the sordid details of which became public in the vicious Collins-Holm divorce brawl). Holm, of course, mightily disagreed, finding common ground in their love of the good life. He was completely broke (despite having received more than $2 million during the brief marriage), he whined, and demanded $80,000 per month to help cover the following basic expenditures:

$16,500 for rent

On July 16, 1987, Holm picketed Collins's home with a sign reading, "Joan, you have our $2.5M 13,000 sq. ft. home which we bought for CASH during our marriage. I am now homeless. HELP!"

$12,000 for clothing
$8,000 for pocket money
$7,000 for servants' salaries
$6,000 for entertainment
$4,000 for travel expenses
$1,900 for groceries
$1,300 for telephone charges
$500 for limousines
$200 for personal grooming

"I wear $2,000 leather jackets, $400 crocodile shoes and tens of thousands of dollars worth of jewelry," the humbled Holm explained. Further, "While our income and expenses may seem extraordinary to the average person, it is our normal way of life and is typical of those depicted in the television series *Lifestyles of the Rich and Famous*, on which we have been featured several times." Sadly, Holm ended up with less than $200,000 for his trouble.

G😊😊D REAS😊N

😊NE Julia Roberts and Lyle Lovett broke up this week. Roberts says that for her, the marriage was over when she realized, "I'm Julia Roberts, and he's Lyle Lovett."
                                          —Norm MacDonald, *Saturday Night Live*

Limpet-lipped loverboy **Harry Hamlin** decided to leave old blond bimbo **Laura Johnson** for new blond bimbo **Nicollette Sheridan**. According to Johnson, they continued to cohabit, but he made life hell, harassing her and calling her names like asshole, slut, and whore. She got the last laugh, however, when Sheridan dropped Hamlin like a hot potato, kissing off the entire relationship with this pithy pronouncement: "You're boring, stupid, and I don't have any fun with you. Good-bye."

Chowderhead chatterbox **Larry King** sued former galpal **Rama Fox** after she told the press she'd broken off their relationship. The world needed to know, according to King's attorney, that *"Larry terminated the relationship."*

Madonna first filed for divorce from **Sean Penn** in December of 1986, after an ugly incident in which the jealous actor slugged a friend of hers in a restaurant. (The quarrelsome couple were so renowned for their constant quibbling that they were known as the "Poison Penns.") The troubled relationship finally came to a bitter end after Madonna was reportedly tied up, beaten, and abused for hours by her horrible hubby on New Year's Eve, 1988. Waxing sentimental about the finis of a great love, Penn said, "It was all rumor. I never met the woman."

Supermodel **Stephanie Seymour** calls ex-lover **Warren Beatty** "an old man who loves to live vicariously through young people and suck up all their life because he has none of his own."

Sharon Stone has certainly had her share (and more) of men—and isn't shy about expressing her opinions of them. The actress likened onetime datemate **Dwight Yoakam** to a "dirt sandwich" (on the other hand, former flame **Hart Bochner** calls Stone "the Antichrist"). And before they moved in together the tough cookie forced producer **Bill MacDonald** to sign a cohabitation agreement that included a confidentiality clause; after the breakup, Stone was free to trash MacDonald publicly with impunity, while he was forbidden to say word one about her. BUMMER.

BREAKING UP IS EASY

Phil Collins split with his wife of ten years via fax ("I am so sick and tired of your attitude I will not be coming back"); Sylvester Stallone broke up with longtime girlfriend Jennifer Flavin via Federal Express. One year after "Flavin of the Month" was dumped, she accepted Sly's marriage proposal.

Well, surprise, surprise. The May–late December romance of blue-collar boytoy **Larry Fortensky** and increasingly enfeebled **Liz Taylor** didn't last a lifetime. In divorce papers filed in 1996, the burly one detailed the "opulent lifestyle" the two led, and called his $5,000-per-month post-split allowance "minuscule."

Point: "Elizabeth and I traveled often and, as one might expect, we only traveled first class, taking large suites in virtually every hotel that we stayed at."

Point: "Our wardrobe was only the finest . . . I shopped at Versace and other fine stores. The suits that I own cost several thousand dollars each. The Valentino sweaters I own, many of which were handmade, also cost several thousand dollars each."

Point (coup de grâce): "[Since the breakup] I have been required to live in an environment in which Elizabeth would never reside."

Husbanding their RESOURCES

Kim Basinger: $700,000 house and more than $60,000 to first husband Ron Britton, a makeup artist
Joan Collins: $1 million to record exec Ron Kass
Jane Fonda: at least $10 million to Tom Hayden
Goldie Hawn: $75,000 settlement to husband Gus Trikonis
Joan Lunden: $18,000 monthly alimony to Michael Krauss
Jane Seymour: $10,000 monthly alimony
Lana Turner: $35,000 settlement for a six-week marriage

Women who've paid the men in their lives to go away

Why the courts don't tell a husband who has been living off his wife to go out and get a job is beyond my comprehension.
—Joan Lunden

HOT DISH
PART II

(See also page 53)

Messrs. X, Y, and Z happily trot out the wife and kiddies whenever a public appearance is called for, but live separate lives—of wild, same-sex trysts—otherwise!

This heartthrob's record shows a drunk-driving arrest, which in reality stemmed from the handsome one's flight from the cops after being caught dead to rights with a transvestite hooker in his parked car!

Miss Funny Leading Lady was born with both kinds of genitalia!

This recently resurrected star is well known for cruising L.A.'s mean streets with his buddies in search of hot 'n' juicy transvestites!

Mr. Funny Star's home was burgled while he was out of town, leading to police finding evidence of a more serious crime: a dresser drawer full of cocaine and drug paraphernalia!

This occasional thesp is admired in certain circles for his unique ability to auto-fellate!

A pair of young movie lovelies was spotted at L.A.'s Farmer's Market very vocally vying for the attentions of that singing beauty (also female)— who sat passively by as the battling duo hissed and spat at each other!

7 Naughty by Nature

It seems not a day goes by without some rabble-rousing star landing on *Hard Copy* for roughing up a tabloid photographer, brawling with nightclub patrons, or wrapping his car around a telephone pole in a drunken stupor. To be fair, it's hard to enjoy a quiet night out when you're famous—if the paparazzi don't get you, starstruck fans (and, nearly as often, people who want to prove they *aren't* starstruck) will. (The moral of this story: if you see stars, leave them alone. They'll only disappoint you anyway.) There are few places in the world that stars can go to be private. Embarrassing full-frontal nude shots, taken by a prying paparazzo's telephoto lens, were snapped of vacationing couple **Brad Pitt** and **Gwyneth Paltrow** (and immediately disseminated on the Internet), and Spanish sex god **Antonio Banderas** experienced the full frenzy of tabloid fever after he took up with **Melanie Griffith**. "I went on a sailboat in Málaga," he said, "and there were seven boats circling me. Finally, I made a deal with tabloid reporters: 'Can I have Tuesdays and Thursdays off?'"

Drinking and drugging are at the bottom of many embarrassing incidents—I mean, it's hard to believe **John Lennon** would wander around in public with a maxipad in place of a hat without having a little outside (i.e., chemical) help. And celebrities can't suffer their humiliations in private. There's a huge, competitive marketplace of magazines and TV shows that pay large sums for such stories, routinely bribing parking attendants, nightclub bouncers, celebrity employees, and the like to produce the next salacious scoop.

Bad behavior isn't new in Hollywood—**Errol Flynn**, for example, once attacked **Jimmy Fidler** at a nightclub after the gossip columnist printed an unflattering item about him. When Flynn knocked Fidler unconscious, Mrs. Fidler stabbed the swashbuckling star in the ear with a fork. (The moral of *this* story: payback's a bitch.) But during those days, events were routinely hushed up by studio spin doctors, who wielded power over journalists of the day, barring them access to the studio's stars if they refused to play ball. It's a whole new ball game today, though, and there are few outlets left where stars can count on getting an unfailingly fluffy, flattering reception (*Entertainment Tonight* being perhaps the best or worst example, depending on your point of view).

C'EST LA GUERRE!

HERE COMES TROUBLE

GREAT MOMENTS IN BAD BEHAVIOR

THE '60s AND '70s

March 1969: **John Lennon** is ejected from the Troubadour, a Hollywood rock 'n' roll club, after disrupting a Smothers Brothers show. The tipsy trouper, whose inspired choice of headgear that evening is a Kotex pad, swears like a sailor, shouts, "I'm John Lennon!" and scuffles with the Smothers' manager, a waitress, and a photographer outside the venue.

1971: Best buddies **Marlon Brando, James Caan**, and **Robert Duvall**, in New York filming *The Godfather*, take a limo trip through Manhattan while holding a mooning contest.

1973: **Marlon Brando**, irritated at being stalked by a particularly persistent paparazzo, breaks the man's jaw, thereby paving the way for the future escapades of **Sean Penn** and **Alec Baldwin**.

November 1978: A "semistuporous and incoherent" **Mackenzie Phillips**, 19, is found near the Hyatt on Sunset by two sheriff's deputies; though they find drug paraphernalia on her, Phillips claims to have tripped and fallen, and says she is dazed from having hit the sidewalk.

THE '80s

Early '80s: Big-time boozer **Robert Mitchum** playfully tosses a basketball at a New York party, hitting a photographer in the face. She later sues, and he's forced to ante up a settlement in excess of a quarter million bucks.

1983: Diamond-drenched **Zsa Zsa Gabor**, appearing at a Philadelphia theater in *Forty Carats*, storms off stage because she feels handicapped audience members are making too much noise.

1983: **Dennis Hopper** is arrested on a Mexican highway, where he's found wandering aimlessly—in the buff. Hopper is reportedly high on coke at the time.

May 1983: Tough love. Roguish **Ryan O'Neal** punches out son **Griffin**'s front teeth while brawling with the boy over his alleged drug abuse. "I punched him and his teeth exploded," Ryan later confesses.

December 1983: Fractious **Frank Sinatra** expresses disapproval at the way blackjack is dealt (cards faceup from a "shoe") at Las Vegas's  Golden Nugget by telling the South Korean dealer to "go back to China." When that doesn't work, the wrinkly war-bler threatens to have her fired and says he'll never sing at the casino again unless she changes her tune. Sinatra gets his way.

1984: Surly **Sean Penn** attacks paparazzo Ian Markham in Nashville. Penn gets a ninety-day sus-pended sentence and a lawsuit.

June 1985: Superchurl **Sean Penn** pelts a photographer with pebbles and then camera-whips him as adoring wife Madonna looks on.

1986: Sorehead **Sean Penn**, out on the town with Madonna, suffers a stab of jealousy after an old friend greets her with a kiss. He attacks the man with fists, feet, and one of the club's chairs.

1986: Naughty **Nicolas Cage**, in Sean Penn mode, attacks a paparazzo and smashes the man's strobe. When the photographer threatens to give him the thrashing of his life, Cage darts into a nearby restaurant while the man loudly demands $100 in compensation. The lily-livered leading man sends one of the restaurant's minions out the front door with the dough as he beats a hasty retreat out the back.

1986: On the set of *Wall Street,* **Charlie Sheen** surreptitiously sticks a note reading "I am the biggest cunt in the world" on the back of cantankerous co-star **Sean Young**.

1987: **Sean Penn** spits on a movie extra who dares take his picture; when the man spits back at the unruly actor, Penn flips out and attacks, resisting all efforts by crew members to pull him away. Penn spends thirty-three days in the slammer.

March 1987: At a Hollywood nightspot, **Mike Tyson** tries to smooch a female valet parking attendant, and clocks a male associ-ate who attempts to rescue the damsel in distress.

April 1987: Gargoylish **Judd Nelson** is arrested for public  drunkenness at a Florida nightclub. As he's hauled away in a police car, he bangs his head against a window and screams, "My face is my business and you guys are re-sponsible! I'm going to sue you!" He con-tinues this behavior in jail, smashing his jughead against the cell door.

Memorial Day 1987: **Bruce Willis** is arrested at his home in the Hollywood Hills after cops are called to break up a very loud party. "GET THE FUCK OFF MY PROPERTY!" screams Willis, and hits one of the bluesuits smack in the kisser.

1988: Bagel-baking boytoy **Rob Camiletti** is arrested after ramming a tabloid photographer with **Cher**'s Ferrari and breaking the man's camera. Camiletti is fined $1,000.

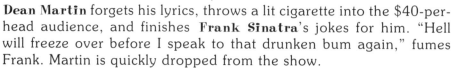

March 1988: During the opening gig of the Rat Pack's "farewell tour," drunken **Dean Martin** forgets his lyrics, throws a lit cigarette into the $40-per-head audience, and finishes **Frank Sinatra**'s jokes for him. "Hell will freeze over before I speak to that drunken bum again," fumes Frank. Martin is quickly dropped from the show.

May 1988: **Mike Tyson**, driving his Bentley with **Robin Givens** and her mother as passengers, rams a parked car. Though he claims he was attempting to avoid an animal in the road, scuttlebutt is that wifey slapped him after finding condoms in his pocket.

September 1988: After pleading with **Robin Givens** to come home (she refuses), **Mike Tyson** gets behind the wheel of her silver BMW and puts the pedal to the metal. Barreling into a tree, the car is smashed and so is Tyson—knocked cold for twenty minutes. Later that month Givens, appearing with hubby on a **Barbara Walters** special, says he is obsessive and mentally ill. Tyson sits silently while she trashes his character, but subsequently claims he was drugged. A few days later, police are called by Givens after Tyson hurls chairs and an iron grate through the window of their home. "I took it from the fireplace and threw it through the window," he snarls. "So what? I paid for it. It's my house."

1989: **John Hurt** lays siege to a cadre of reporters at London's BAFTA awards. Losing his footing, the frolicsome film star crashes into a table and is led away, sobbing, by friends.

December 1989: *Cosby* daughter **Lisa Bonet** and husband **Lenny Kravitz** go on the warpath at New York's Kennedy Airport after being approached by a female photographer and her male companion, an autograph hound. Kravitz takes on the woman as Bonet besets the man; the pugilistic pair are later sued by their victims for $24 million.

December 1989: Christian Slater is pulled over for drunk driving, but attempts a getaway in his car and crashes into a telephone pole.

THE '90s

February 1990: Former *Taxi* star/current sot **Jeff Conaway** hits a bicyclist, breaking the man's leg, with his car. Conaway's blood alcohol level is found to be nearly twice the legal limit.

1990: Roseanne spits, shrieks, and grabs her ample crotch while caterwauling the national anthem at a San Diego baseball game.

March 1991: New Kids on the Block member **Donnie Wahlberg** sloshes vodka on a hotel rug, sets it ablaze, and is arrested for arson.

1991: Ancient actress **Katharine Hepburn** is sued by a meter maid who claims the actress and her entourage slammed her hand in their car door and called her a pig.

June 1991: Ersatz angel **Whitney Houston**, along with her brother **Michael**, are arrested and charged with assault after having a fracas with two patrons in a Kentucky hotel lounge. Houston claims she and her bro were the recipients of racist remarks, but the warbler is charged with making terrorist threats after vowing to have the offenders offed.

May 1992: Problem child **Naomi Campbell** and tempestuous actress **Troy Beyer** (*Dynasty*) each think the other is paying too much attention to untalented actor **Damon Wayans** at Manhattan's Roxy disco, and get into a hair-pulling catfight out on the sidewalk.

December 1992: In response to lousy reviews of hubby **Tom Arnold**'s lousy sitcom, *The Jackie Thomas Show*, **Roseanne** fires off a vicious series of scathing faxes to the offending critics. "Roseanne read the letters to me," said Arnold proudly. "I said, 'Right on, honey!'"

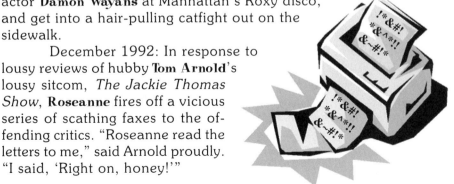

March 1993: TV star **Tom Arnold** arrives on the lot one day only to learn that someone has parked in his personal space. The deeply aggrieved "actor" quickly scrawls a note, which he leaves on the windshield of the offending vehicle: "How stupid are you? Move your fucking car, you asshole!" Unfortunately for Arnold, the car belongs to whiny *Seinfeld* star **Julia Louis-Dreyfus**, who confronts him that afternoon with the evidence. After admitting to authorship of the note, Arnold meekly says he hopes she's not mad. When she tells him she *is* mad and stomps off, Arnold runs to wife **Roseanne** and complains about the incident. At the end of the day Louis-Dreyfus returns to her car and finds soaped obscenities on her windshield, along with a Polaroid of a man's hairy butt.

May 1993: **Shannen Doherty** and dream date **Judd Nelson** go club-hopping in Dallas, stopping by the Greenville Bar & Grille, where, according to the restaurant's manager, Shannen "was drinking heavily" and "puked at her table." Apparently the Greenville welcomes patrons like these, for they are back the next night when, in response to taunts about his failing career, Nelson kicks a young woman in the nose (unintentionally, sez he, but she files assault charges anyway).

tempest in a
TEENYBOPPER

I'm a strong woman. There are still some people out there who can't deal with that.

I'm the ultimate slammer of doors. At home I busted one off the hinges—I think I got mad at my boyfriend because I thought he was flirting with somebody else. A miscommunication problem, apparently.

You don't have to be bigger than the guy to beat him up. You just attract their attention, then knee them in the balls. When they're down, knee them in the face.

I don't understand it at all . . . I'm just a nice Southern Baptist Republican girl.

[The 1994 L.A. quake] was pretty scary. You know, I woke up at 4:30 in the morning, doors slamming, dishes breaking . . . I thought, "How did Shannen Doherty get into my house?"
—Jay Leno

The oh-so-tempestuous life of drama queen Shannen Doherty

May 1993: Troubled teen **Shannen Doherty**'s onetime fiancé, **Dean Factor**, admits in a restraining order petition that he "will live in fear" after claiming the bellicose beauty tried to run him over with her car. According to Factor, the addled actress also once threw a log through a window of his house in order to get in, threatened him with a loaded pistol ("I'm going to drop you"), stole his bank records, and said she intended to "hire a few guys to beat me up and sodomize me on the front lawn."

February 1994: **Jack Nicholson** smashes the windshield of a Mercedes with a golf club after its driver cuts him off in traffic. The case is later settled out of court.

March 1994: After real actor **Gary Oldman** declines has-been **Don Johnson**'s invitation to have a drink in a hotel bar, Johnson starts an argument that ends in a shoving match.

April 1994: During a *Late Show* appearance, classy gal **Madonna** utters the word *fuck* thirteen times and demands that host **David Letterman** smell her panties. He declines.

April 1994: Two DJs accuse a rambling, slurring **Don Johnson** of being "hammered" during a radio interview in Florida. After Johnson calls them "meatheads" and threatens to "kick your ass," one of the DJs says, "You don't know how fast we would bitch-slap you, pretty boy." Replies the TV tough guy: "Hey, bubba, we'll see who gets bitch-slapped." The DJs later confess they've "never had a guest in that condition."

May 1994: Crude comedian **Bob Goldthwait** sets a chair afire during a *Tonight Show* appearance; he is forced to ante up a $2,700 fine and pay $700 to NBC for the furniture.

May 1994: **Don Johnson** has to be helped out of Planet Hollywood in Hong Kong after having a wee drop too much. (Do we sense a theme here?)

September 1994: **Johnny Depp** trashes his hotel suite—to the tune of almost $10,000—at New York's posh Mark Hotel. The thuggish thespian denies the incident took place during an argument with anorexic **Kate Moss**, explaining, "There was a bug in the place that I was trying to kill. This thing had tried to attack me and tried to suck my blood—a big cockroach. And I tried to get it, I tried to whack

it. I'd miss and I'd smash a lamp." On another occasion, Depp said, "I can only say that I'm human and I was chasing a huge rat in the hotel room and I just kept swatting at it. I couldn't catch it, and it just jumped out the window." (Ironically, **Roger Daltrey** was staying in the room next door. "On a scale of one to ten, I give him a one," said the former suite-thrashing singer. "It took him so bloody long. The Who could have done the job in one minute flat.") Bystanders allegedly reported hearing Moss remarking on Depp's "shortcoming."

November 1994: In a copycat crime, **Mickey Rourke** does $20,000 worth of damage to *his* $5,000-a-night suite at the Trump Plaza. "What's he trying to be, Johnny Depp?" wonders **Nicolas Cage**.

MOTEL HELL

Smoke can drive me mad. Otherwise, it's not getting things you've paid for. That's why we used to smash up hotels— not because we had nothing better to do, but because you're paying top money and you weren't getting any respect.
—Rod Stewart

Late 1994: At a party in England, **Richard Gere** accuses fellow guest **Sly Stallone** of getting overly chummy with Gere's estranged wife, **Cindy Crawford**. Sly ignores the belligerent Buddhist.

January 1995: Ever-charming **Courtney Love** "abuses and intimidates" (by indulging in a cussfest) the crew aboard a Qantas flight. The incident reportedly starts when a stewardess requests that Love remove her big feet from a bulkhead.

February 1995: No way to treat a lady. **Courtney Love** falls down and goes boom on an icy sidewalk in Manhattan. After being helped into the Strand bookstore, she gets on the phone, where she remains for more than twenty minutes. When the manager asks her to get off, she screams obscenities, shoves the man, and staggers out of the store.

Early 1995: Rock 'n' roll rude boy **Tommy Lee** points a loaded shotgun at a tabloid news crew stationed outside the love nest he shares with new wife **Pamela Anderson**.

March 1995: Fresh prince **Will Smith** tries to clock a paparazzo who's blocking the path to Smith's limo. The footage appears almost instantly on *Hard Copy*.

April 1995: Tattoo-festooned ex-addict **Drew Barrymore** turns her back to a *Late Show* audience and bares her breasts to a stunned **David Letterman**.

June 1995: "We're from CBS News," announce reporters at Los Angeles International Airport who've spotted **O.J.** pal **Al Cowlings**. "I don't give a fuck where you're from, CBS News," snarls the contumelious ex-athlete. This doesn't discourage the journos, however, who politely persist, whereupon Cowlings whacks one of them with his garment bag. "You shouldn't have hit me, man," the reporter whines. "No," growls Cowlings, "I should have knocked your fucking head off. That's what I should have done."

July 1995: Rock hag **Courtney Love** spots fellow Lollapalooza performer **Kathleen Hanna**, lead singer for Bikini Kill, backstage, and all hell breaks loose. In the words of Courtney itself: "There she was, sort of smirking at me. I dropped my sweater on the floor, and she sort of whispered under her breath, 'Where's the baby? In a closet with an IV?' I just snapped. My hand was filled with Skittles and a couple of Tootsie Rolls. I just threw them up in the air and went **BAAAAAAAAAAAAAAA!** And then she shoved me and I clocked her."

Love appears on stage the next day with her hand in a bandage, offering this explanation to the audience: "I punched some bitch last night. Her mouth had all these teeth that got in the way." Hanna sues, and Love gets a suspended one-year sentence plus a $285 fine. Hope she can afford it.

August 1995: **Princess Di** flirts with a married rugby player and . . . aw, who cares.

August 1995: After spying a pair of paparazzi videotaping him and his children on a Malibu beach, **Tony Danza** gives chase in his Cadillac (figures), heading them off and hitting their vehicle. The hotheaded heavyweight then kicks in their passenger-side window and grabs their camera, yelling, "I'll put you to sleep!" and "I'll kill you!" No formal charges are filed, but a lawsuit later is.

October 7 1995: At 1:30 A.M., **Robert De Niro** walks out of Manhattan's Bowery Bar, grabs a paparazzo by the hair, and demands his videotape. The photog presses assault charges, but later shoots himself in the foot by attempting extortion.

October 1995: **Alec Baldwin** punches out a reporter attempting to photograph him, wife **Kim Basinger**, and their strangely named new baby. Baldwin is placed under citizen's arrest by the man and charged with misdemeanor battery, but is later acquitted.

1996: **Cole Hauser**, one of the stars of the police drama *High Incident*, gets in trouble in a parking lot when he gives the wrong slip to the attendant. According to a lawsuit filed by Juan Carlos Evans Alarcon, Hauser posed as an LAPD officer and demanded Alarcon's green card, all the while making statements like, "You are going to jail, you fucking Mexican," "This is all you do for a living, you fucking Mexican," and "You just came across the border." Hauser is arrested by real members of the LAPD and, as he's being led away, reportedly screams, "I can't believe I am being arrested for taking ten dollars from a dirty, lousy, stinking Mexican!"

May 1996: **Martin Lawrence** is arrested after being spotted screaming at passing cars in Sherman Oaks, a suburb of L.A. Lawrence, who was also carrying a concealed weapon, "seems to be suffering from extreme exhaustion," says his publicist later. Gee, where've we heard that one before?

May 1996: **Ken Wahl** is given six months' probation after pleading no contest to a charge of disturbing the peace. Wahl was arrested in January after a neighbor called police to complain that the *Wiseguy* star was playing his music too loud.

June 1996: **John Travolta** and **Roman Polanski** have a knock-down drag-out argument (reportedly about Scientology) on the set of *The Double* in France, and Travolta walks off the picture. The producers quickly file suit for breach of contract, saying the actor's motives were somewhat less than pure—that he wanted "to conceal the fact that [he] simply changed his mind about doing the picture because his ego had been bruised by Polanski's legitimate efforts to direct [his] performance."

June/July 1996: Has-been thesp **Robert Downey Jr.** is arrested three times in thirty days, all on drug-related charges. One incident stems from Downey's drug-addled inability to recognize his own home: he is arrested after being found crashed out in a house about four blocks from his own. (Downey claimed a limo driver had deposited him at the wrong place.)

July 1996: **Demi Moore** tells paparazzi she will "get out a machine gun and shoot you" if they don't stop taking her picture.

DIRECTION-FINDER

Do you know what the hottest business on Hollywood Boulevard is? Selling Robert Downey Jr. a map to his own home.

—Jay Leno

September 1996: **Kelsey Grammer** rolls his Dodge Viper and escapes uninjured. A few days later, he checks into the Betty Ford Center (strangely, the addict-actor is not charged with driving under the influence—but is given a citation for driving with an expired license).

October 1996: **Shannen Doherty** lashes out at new neighbor **Molly Ringwald**. "I know who *you* are," screams Shannen when Ringwald introduces herself. "You don't live here, you *rent*."

October 1996: **Mick Jagger** and **Johnny Depp**'s Viper Room nightclub are sued by a paparazzo for assault and battery after an incident earlier in the month in which the photog claims he was severely beaten after snapping intimate shots of Jagger in a clinch with **Uma Thurman**.

October 1996: **Jack Nicholson** is an abusive deadbeat, according to two hookers who file suit against him for (1) refusing to pay them, and (2) roughing them up.

antisocial REGISTER

John Agar and Shirley Temple: Emil and Emma Glutz
Richard Belzer, actor, *Homicide:* Don Corleone (Brando's *Godfather* role)
Milton Berle: Elreb Notlim (try it backwards)
Marlon Brando: Lord Greystoke
Kevin Costner: Tom Feral
Johnny Depp: Mr. Donkey Penis (said he liked to hear this on his morning wake-up call), Santa Del Vecchio, Oprah Noodlemantra, and Mr. Stench
Melanie Griffith: Miss Hoover (you figure it out—she was with Antonio Banderas)
Elizabeth Hurley: Rebecca de Winter (Daphne du Maurier novel *Rebecca*)
Courtney Love: Neely O'Hara (character in *Valley of the Dolls*)
Madonna: Sugar Kane (Marilyn Monroe's role in *Some Like It Hot*)
River Phoenix: Earl Grey
Postacquittal O.J. Simpson: D.H. Lawrence

A few of the names seen on hotel registers when stars checked in

Frisky Business
Hollywood's merry prank-stars

During the filming of *Nine Months*, co-stars **Tom Arnold** and **Hugh Grant** became great friends—and practical jokers. According to Arnold, "I'd get the British tabloids, cut out any article on Hugh, and pin them to his dressing room door. To get me back he'd act out scenes from the TV movie *Roseanne and Tom*."

Marlon Brando, co-starring with **Jessica Tandy** in the theatrical run of *A Streetcar Named Desire*, ruined her big scene one evening by sticking a cigarette up his nostril—visible to the audience but not to Tandy.

Nicolas Cage once grabbed a mic aboard an airplane and startled passengers by announcing, "This is the captain speaking . . . I'm losing control of the airplane . . . Please bear with me."

Alfred Hitchcock sent **Melanie Griffith**, just a little girl at the time (believe it or not), a miniature coffin as a gift. Inside was a doll-size replica of Griffith's mother, **Tippi Hedren**. "I never played with it. I just put it away," sez Mel.

Carole Lombard secretly altered a set of contracts sent by her agent. He later signed them without reading that she was now entitled to ten percent of his income, and in fact didn't learn about it until she dropped by a few weeks later asking for her check.

Paul Newman once had director **Robert Altman**'s leather gauntlets fried in batter and served to him for lunch. The actor also had problems when he couldn't get through to director **George Roy Hill** on the phone. Solution? Newman cut Hill's desk in half with a chain saw.

On **Cary Grant**'s birthday one year, a reporter sent a telegram asking, "How old Cary Grant?" Grant's reply was sent forthwith: "Old Cary Grant fine. How you?"

"**Ray Milland** didn't want to make *Golden Earrings*. He didn't like **Marlene Dietrich**; he thought he was too young to do it so he was a real bastard at first. . . . He and Marlene fought the whole time. When we were shooting the scene where he first meets 'Gypsy' Marlene as she's eating the stew, over and over she would stick a fish head into her mouth, suck the eye out and then pull out the rest of the head. Then, after I yelled 'Cut,' she would stick her finger down her throat to make herself throw it up. This whole performance made Ray violently ill." —Director **Mitchell Liesen**

STARS 'N' BARS

Arresting developments in Hollywood (note:
rap stars not included due to space constraints).

ANTISOCIAL BEHAVIOR

Before **Roseanne** made a new man of 'im, class act **Tom Arnold** was arrested for public peeing at a McDonald's.

Former fatty **Ricki Lake** was busted for criminal mischief after taking part in an anti-fur demonstration in New York. Her biggest regret? That she missed that evening's episode of *Melrose Place*. (Hey, the girl's got her priorities straight.) Lake paid a $45 fine and performed a bit of community service. "I still stand by my convictions," she said, "but I just will not do anything to get myself arrested again."

Phil Silvers, of all people, was a gang member when he was just a lad; the hooliganism of "The Bronzes" landed him a stretch in reform school.

Motorcycle maniac **Wesley Snipes** was chased (at speeds up to 120 mph) more than thirty miles by cops in Florida after refusing to pull over. The actor pleaded no contest to reckless driving and was placed on probation, along with being ordered to perform eighty hours of community service and pay $7,300 in fines and costs.

THE HIGH AND THE MIGHTY

In 1935, **Busby Berkeley** ran head-on into an approaching car while driving drunk; all three of the other auto's occupants were killed. Berkeley was ultimately acquitted of murder charges.

Home Improvement star **Tim Allen** sold $43,000 worth of cocaine to an undercover agent in 1977, but served only twenty-eight months of an eight-year sentence after agreeing to help cops nab other dirty dealers.

Funny gal **Brett Butler** was nabbed for drunk driving in May of 1981 after taking out two trees and a mailbox with her car.

Johnny Carson was charged with DUI in February 1992 and pled no contest on the good advice of his attorney, **Robert Shapiro**.

Formerly funny **Chevy Chase** spent a night in the pokey after being stopped for drunk driving in January of 1995. He was apprehended after police spotted him straddling lanes and doing 60 in a 25-mph zone—with a blood alcohol level over twice the legal limit.

Tacky **Tony Curtis** was nailed at Heathrow after bobbies found an ounce of cannabis resin in his shaving kit. Curtis got off with a slap on the wrist—a £50 fine.

John Cusack and tubby **Tyne Daly** both have drunk-driving convictions on their records (1990 and 1992, respectively).

John Denver was "rocky mountain high" when he rammed his Porsche into a tree near his home in Aspen in 1994 (he'd also been arrested exactly one year earlier in nearly the same spot for drunk driving). But the wilderness warbler caught a break when charges were dismissed because police had failed to test his blood alcohol level within two hours of picking him up.

Amanda Donohoe had her driving license suspended in 1994 after she was convicted in England of being drunk behind the wheel.

Richard Dreyfuss was nicked for cocaine possession in 1982 after crashing into a tree with his Mercedes. It took two hours to pry him out of the car.

Cherub-faced child star **Corey Feldman** was collared in 1990 for buying heroin and cocaine.

Outspokenly anti-drug **Jodie Foster** was given a year's probation after being caught at Boston's Logan Airport with cocaine in her luggage.

Kelsey Grammer was arrested in July of 1987 for drunk driving, in April of 1988 for cocaine possession, and—during the *Cheers* 200th-episode shoot—again in 1990 for possession of coke.

Stacy Keach served three months in Reading Gaol after being busted at Heathrow in 1984 for cocaine smuggling.

Robert Mitchum spent two months behind bars in 1948 for smoking marijuana.

Gary Oldman was nabbed in 1991 for drunk driving and spent a night in jail. In the car with him when he was picked up was drinking buddy **Kiefer Sutherland**.

Anthony Perkins thought he'd subvert customs in 1989 by mailing a package of marijuana to himself at a London hotel. Unfortunately, the package arrived five days before he did, and there was another Mr. Perkins staying at the hotel. Yep, you guessed it—the wrong man opened the parcel. Perkins was arrested on arrival and fined £200.

Keanu Reeves was, like, hauled off to jail in 1993 for drunk driving and resisting arrest.

Fifty-seven-year-old former vamp **Jane Russell** spent four days in the slammer in 1978 for drunk driving.

Christian Slater has been nabbed twice for driving under the influence, and spent two days in jail in 1990.

Oliver Stone spent two weeks in stir after being busted for pot possession on the Mexican border in 1969.

Jan-Michael Vincent, after a drunk-driving conviction in 1983, served thirty days in 1986 for violating his three-year probation after being found driving under the influence—again.

Forest Whitaker was arrested in March of 1996 in Hollywood for drunk driving.

DEN OF THIEVES

Though **Farrah Fawcett** might *look* like a Goody Two-shoes, she was arrested twice for shoplifting (clothing) in 1970.

Loudmouth **Larry King** was pinched in 1971 for the theft of monies given him to be used for the New Orleans district attorney's investigation into the death of John F. Kennedy. The money went to pay the tax man after King frittered away his own funds on gambling, cars, and high living.

Sultry **Sophia Loren** spent a month in an Italian prison for tax evasion in 1982.

Roseanne was busted for shoplifting when she was not-so-sweet sixteen.

Preternaturally perky **Suzanne Somers** was picked up in the early seventies for kiting checks.

SEX FIENDS

James Farentino pleaded guilty to stalking ex-girlfriend **Tina Sinatra** and got three years' probation, along with orders to stay one hundred yards away from her and get counseling.

"Last night I did something completely insane," began a statement issued by anemic 'eartthrob **Hugh Grant** after his July 1995 arrest with a Sunset Strip streetwalker. ("There's never been a time when I've felt less inclined to get married," commented longtime girlfriend **Elizabeth Hurley**, who nevertheless continued to stand by her "man.") Meanwhile, back home in England, the actor risked the loss of his license after being caught driving under the influence and speeding one too many times.

EROTIC

I didn't get what Hugh Grant did. I've had a few sakes, driven down Sunset, had wild fantasies—but I didn't pull over and say, "Give me a blow job!"
—Pierce Brosnan

Paul Reubens (aka **Pee Wee Herman**) was taken into custody in 1991 for exposing himself in a porno theater (the flick he was watching? *Nancy Nurse Turns Up the Heat*); the onetime children's star was fined $50 plus court costs and a fifty-hour community-service stint.

Powder (1995) director **James Salva** spent time in stir after being convicted of child molestation in 1988.

"I love women," rhapsodized water buffalo look-alike **Mike Tyson**. "I like to be around as many as I possibly can." Tyson, who'd been arrested thirty-eight times as a juvenile, spent three years in prison as an adult after being convicted of the rape of eighteen-year-old beauty contestant **Desirée Washington**. She testified that she was in Tyson's limo at 2 A.M. because she thought they were going to a party, and was stunned when things turned ugly: "I kind of jumped back because I was surprised that, being who he is, he acted like that, and besides, his breath smelled kind of bad."

SLAPHAPPY

> When a man hits a woman, one of two things happens.
> Either she hauls ass in the opposite
> direction or she becomes yours.
> —Richard Pryor

According to **Roseanne** in divorce papers, **Tom Arnold** "hit me, struck me, punched me, twisted my arms and legs, cruelly squeezed me in bear hugs, has thrown objects at me, pinched me and verbally abused me. He has also slammed me against walls, thrown me down on the floor and bed, put his face inches away from mine while screaming at the top of his lungs." Later, one of her twenty-seven personalities retracted these statements.

Beauteous **Halle Berry** lost eighty percent of the hearing in her left ear after being smacked around by a onetime boyfriend she refuses to name, saying only that he is "well known in Hollywood." For the record, **Wesley Snipes**, **Eddie Murphy**, and **Spike Lee** were among her famed flames.

Humphrey Bogart and third wife **Mayo Methot** were known as the "Battling Bogarts," according to pal **Lloyd Bridges**. "I found out why. He would invite me over for dinner quite often, and nearly every time they'd have a fight. It was crazy. He'd drink a little. She'd give him more, and when he'd had enough she would say something to really provoke him. So he'd hit her. That's what she seemed to *want*. I figured she must have been a masochist. It was very embarrassing."

When **Daryl Hannah** decided to sever ties with longtime love **Jackson Browne**, she made a final trip to their home to pick up her belongings, emerging with a black eye, bruises, and a broken finger.

Drug-addled **Gary Busey**, according to fiancée Tiana Warden, would "hold me down and drag me around the house" when he was high.

The wrath of Caan: **James Caan** didn't react well at all to news that his estranged wife planned to remarry—he gave her a black eye and a cut on the forehead. The prunelike performer was also sued in 1994 for beating and strangling twenty-nine-year-old actress Leesa Anne Rowland.

"I left **Sean Connery** after he bashed my face in with his fists," recalled first wife **Diane Cilento**.

Evel Knievel inflicted injuries on the face and neck of companion Krystal Kennedy (thirty-one years younger than the doddering daredevil), but the case was dropped when she refused to press charges.

Illustrated man **Tommy Lee** was arrested in December 1994 for beating up his girlfriend, boob-job poster-child **Bobbi Brown**, who didn't press charges. Lee also reportedly beat first wife **Heather Locklear**, and brandished a gun at present popsy **Pamela Anderson Lee** (she denies, denies, denies).

Abusive actor **Sasha Mitchell** (*Step by Step*) was arrested in April of 1995 after slapping and kicking his pregnant wife, then again in August 1996 after officials learned he'd never gone to the counseling sessions the court had ordered him to attend.

Four weeks before **Dudley Moore**'s wedding to **Nicole Rothschild**, she accused him of grabbing her by the throat and beating her. They got married anyway, but separated not long afterward. In 1995, seventies supermodel **Beverly Johnson** accused ex-boyfriend **Christopher** (*Law & Order*) **Noth** of beating her, along with threatening to destroy her looks and kill her dog. Johnson was granted a restraining order in August.

Lurid rumors abounded when **Madonna** filed for divorce from **Sean Penn** after filing a police report in Santa Monica. Scuttlebutt said the ornery actor had tied his wife to a chair and beaten her, then left her alone this way for several hours.

Anthony Quinn slapped **Katherine** (daughter of Cecil) **DeMille** in the face on their wedding night after learning she wasn't a virgin.

Comedienne **Judy Carne** remembers that **Burt Reynolds** "was a very macho man, and I got the show-business break first. The more I did well, the more invalidated he felt as a man and consequently the more destructive he became. It started with pushes and slaps. As things got worse, it was very painful. I was terrified of him." This may explain why she left him—for a woman.

Eric "Julia's big brother" **Roberts** was booked for spousal abuse in February of 1995 after shoving wife Eliza into a wall.

Model/actress/whatever **Carré Otis** charged **Mickey Rourke** with spousal abuse in the summer of 1994, but when she failed to testify the suit was dropped. According to fashion industry insiders, she often showed up for

modeling assignments covered in bruises; Otis also "accidentally" shot herself in the hand on the set of one of Rourke's films.

Ah, romance: **Ava Gardner** said **George C. Scott** proposed by sitting on top of her, punching her, and threatening her face with broken glass while intoning, "I love you. Marry me."

O.J. Simpson and **Nicole Brown**: beat her severely many times, attacked her car with a baseball bat, threw her bodily out of their home . . . no wonder the jury let him go.

Dipsomaniac **David Soul**'s wife repeatedly called the cops after various violent incidents in which the sottish slugger reportedly pinned her to the wall, punched her, spat in her face, threw her across their yard, and broke bones in her hand.

Biographer José Torres once asked **Mike Tyson**, "What's the best punch you've ever thrown in your life?" Replied the boorish boxer: "Man, I'll never forget that punch. It was when I fought with [wife] **Robin [Givens]** in Steve's apartment. She really offended me and I went bam and she flew backward, hitting every fucking wall in the apartment. That was the best punch I've ever thrown in my fucking life."

Tiny terror **Hervé Villechaize**, according to normal-size wife Donna Camille, beat her, fired a gun at her, and shoved her into their fireplace. WATCH YOUR KNEES, GIRLS!

Scary-looking former heartthrob **Jan-Michael Vincent** was sued by actress Lisa Maria Chiafullo, an ex-girlfriend, who charged him with severe beatings resulting in serious injuries, including a miscarriage. In court documents, she also described prior incidents in which he'd stomped her kitten to death, forced her to have sex with his friends, and threatened to kill her. Chiafullo asked for "not less than $5 million," despite claiming, "It doesn't take much to make me happy, you know, materially."

Billy Dee Williams was freed on $50,000 bail after being arrested for knocking around an unnamed female friend in January of 1996.

Her relationship with hothead **James Woods** was no walk in the park, according to ex-wife **Sarah Owen**. Owen alleges he beat her, made her watch pornography, and forced her to have an abortion. When she finally threw him out, he pulled a shotgun on her and forced her to strip and lie on the floor while repeating, "I am a whore. I am a baby-killer."

HIT PARADE

Perennially unfaithful **Whitney Houston** spouse **Bobby Brown**'s lengthy rap sheet includes a charge of felony aggravated assault and disorderly conduct for an incident in which he and two pals attacked a man, nearly severing his ear, at Florida's Walt Disney World. Brown was arrested and thrown into a police car, where he urinated and carved "fuck" into the backseat with a sharp pen.

Johnny Depp has had a couple of run-ins with the law: for fighting with a cop over a jaywalking ticket, and for the assault of a Vancouver hotel employee.

Blowzy, bloated sugarplum **Zsa Zsa Gabor** spent three days in a Giorgio-perfume-spritzed jail cell after being convicted of slapping a Beverly Hills cop in June 1989.

Underwear model **Mark "Marky Mark" Wahlberg** was busted in 1988 for assault (he was drunk), and spent forty-five days in jail.

At age twelve, tough tamale **Rosie Perez** cut a woman's neck, and was remanded to an institution.

GREAT GUNS

James Caan was taken into custody on March 10, 1994, after waving a pistol around during a spat with a man in North Hollywood.

Retro crooner **Harry Connick Jr.** was nabbed trying to carry a gun on board a plane at JFK Airport in New York on December 27, 1992.

Martin Lawrence, soon after his arrest for screaming at hapless vehicles in Sherman Oaks, was popped again for trying to bring a gun onto a plane at the Burbank airport. At first, he claims to have no idea how it got there; days later he says he thought it was legal because he was traveling to another state.

Motley **Tommy Lee** has been arrested for possession of a semi-automatic weapon, and for trying to carry a gun aboard an aircraft. (His attorney? **Robert Shapiro**.)

Christian Slater is another who tried carrying an unregistered handgun on board an aircraft, at New York's Kennedy Airport in December 1994. The actor performed a few hours of community service as part of a plea bargain.

WELL-SUITED

Bob Barker was sued in 1995 by fellow *Price Is Right* employee **Dian Parkinson**, who claimed he forced her to engage in trysts with him over a two-year period under threat of losing her job. But according to Barker—along with numerous others who worked on the show—the relationship was nothing if not consensual. The red-faced Parkinson dropped her suit shortly thereafter, claiming "ill health." A second suit was filed in July 1996 by hostess **Holly Hallstrom**, who alleged she was fired after gaining weight due to a hormone medication she'd been taking.

FOR LOVE OR MONEY

Bob Barker may countersue Dian Parkinson, but he says he'll drop the suit if she can guess how much he would have sued her for without going over the actual retail amount.
—Bill Maher, *Politically Incorrect*

The producers of *Boxing Helena*, including **David Lynch**'s daughter **Jennifer**, won a $9 million judgment (later reduced) against actress **Kim Basinger**, who, they claimed, had given her verbal assurance she would star in their movie. Basinger immediately filed for bankruptcy protection.

Richard Pryor sued alleged deadbeat **Peter Bogdanovich** in 1995 for repayment of a $55,000 loan given him two years earlier.

Never end a sentence with a proposition: **Timothy** (*thirty-something*) **Busfield** was accused of assault in 1994 by a seventeen-year-old extra on the set of *Little Big League,* filmed in Minneapolis. The girl claimed Busfield invited her into his trailer, fondled her, and propositioned her; when she refused, he threatened her job. Though Busfield countersued, he ended up settling out of court (possibly because two more women—including **Eric Roberts**' wife—had come forward to tell *their* tales of sexual harassment at the grabby hands of the lusty lad).

X-Files creator **Chris Carter** (among others) was named in a sexual harassment suit filed by a Fox employee in September of 1996. Carter, she claimed, was always talking about sex and had porno magazines and videocassettes (with titles like *The Sex Files*) lying around the office. Carter also offered to impregnate the woman (she declined) and, at a party, "plaintiff was in a conversation with female co-workers when Carter lifted up his shirt and demanded that they pay homage to his physique."

Egocentric carrot-top **David Caruso** was sued for palimony in 1994 after he dropped longtime live-in love **Paris Papiro** like a hot potato. She'd given up her career, she said, in order to support his, and her case was bolstered by a comment made by the arrogant actor in an interview done not long before the suit: "I do the on-camera stuff, she does the off-camera. It doesn't mean the off-camera is less valuable."

Breach of contract and emotional distress were the charges leveled against **Chevy Chase** in 1995 by an employee, chauffeur Fred Moroz. Moroz had been busted in 1994 after being asked by Chase to pick up a package containing white pills (later determined to be Percocet, a prescription drug—that hadn't been prescribed for Chase). Moroz claimed Chase offered him $1 million if he'd say the package was his own.

O.J. apologist **Johnnie Cochran** was sued for palimony in 1995 by Patricia Cochran, who says she had a relationship with the loud-mouthed lawyer for thirty years (they never married). She claimed he'd stopped support payments after she appeared on *Geraldo* to tell her tale.

Ultraglam **Joan Collins** was sued by her book publisher, Random House, who said the manuscripts she turned in to fulfill her two-tome deal were so horribly written that they were simply unpublishable. Collins asserted that her contract specified only that she had to turn in two complete manuscripts—good, bad, or indifferent. And you know what? They were both right. (Collins prevailed in the suit.)

Francis Ford Coppola sued **Warner Bros.** for interfering with his wish to "bring the beloved children's story *Pinocchio* to the screen." Coppola cited the studio's "efforts . . . first to grab Coppola's film for itself at a bargain-basement price and then, when that failed, to ruin Coppola's efforts to bring his dream to life."

Best-selling novelist/screen hack **Michael Crichton** was sued for sexual discrimination when a former assistant alleged he fired her after she became pregnant and refused to have an abortion.

Tom Cruise sued a German magazine for $60 million in 1996 for purporting that an interview had taken place with the star, who supposedly revealed that he was sterile, with a sperm count of zero.

Wild child **Shannen Doherty** had her *90210* wages garnished by the California United Bank after writing nearly $32,000 worth of bad checks in 1991. "We were lucky we were first in line," said a bank spokesman. They *were* fortunate: Doherty had also skipped out on her rent (to the tune of $14,000) and had two leased Mercedes repossessed.

Hell hath no fury like . . . **Sondra Locke**. In June of 1995, the actress took former lover **Clint Eastwood** to court for fraud and breach of fiduciary duty, claiming that in 1989 he'd promised to get her a directing deal with Warner Bros. (whom she sued in 1994, but lost). He sabotaged that deal, said she, resulting in a "message to the film industry and the world at large" that Locke "was not to be taken seriously." (And I'd always thought it was lack of talent.) Eastwood responded, "I gather the people who advised her thought I would be brought to my knees by some public humiliation. Well, they misread me by thinking that making false statements would flush me into some giveaway program." However, Eastwood ultimately settled with Locke out of court.

Posing for promotional purposes on a New York City rooftop as Robin Hood in 1921, **Douglas Fairbanks** loosed an arrow from his quiver and hit a tailor across the street in the rump. The man won $5,000 from Fairbanks in court.

Melissa Gilbert sued both the *National Enquirer* and her ex-husband after the tabloid published an interview with him in which he claimed she was "a cold-blooded mother who forced our little boy to live in a car!"

Bob Hope and his wife were sued by a former butler, who says he was fired for refusing to shave his beard: "This demand . . . was in bad faith, arbitrary, and unfair, in that said defendants . . . knew at the time they hired plaintiff for the employment in question that he had for at least ten years worn a beard." **BRUTAL.**

Marc Christian sued the estate of former lover **Rock Hudson** in 1986, claiming the film star had unprotected sex with him after learning—and not telling Christian—he had AIDS. The estate countersued, claiming Christian was of low moral character (a bisexual gigolo, to be exact) and that he'd stolen many of Hudson's possessions and tried to blackmail the actor.

The exact amount of the settlement paid by **Michael Jackson** to the young boy he was accused of molesting is not public knowledge, but it did prevent formal charges being filed against the self-crowned King of Pop. However, the case is far from closed, according to Santa Barbara D.A. Tom Sneddon. Sneddon, who remains firmly convinced of Jackson's guilt, says his office will reopen the case if they can find someone to testify before the statute of limitations runs out in 1999.

Pamela Anderson Lee was sued for $5 million by the producers of *Hello, She Lied*, a film which she apparently commited to and then backed out of—just as principal photography was scheduled to begin.

Pammy and **Tommy Lee**, who'd made a home video "depicting themselves, in part, in explicit sexual and intimate relations," filed suit to enjoin *Penthouse* magazine from distributing the footage, stolen from the Lees' home by a construction worker.

"We lived together as man and wife," claimed Scott Thorson, who sued **Liberace** for $113 million in 1982. "He promised me half of almost everything he owns. He even offered to adopt me as his own son. Then, without warning, he cut me off. That's why I'm suing him. . . ." Thorson settled for $95,000 in 1987.

Sophia Loren was taken to court for libel by her father after remarking in an interview that she'd received nothing—not even so much as a pair of shoes—from him during her youth.

Madonna was sued after the release of her concert film *Truth or Dare* by three of her employees, dancers who claimed she'd invaded their privacy by using footage of them without their consent. The case was settled out of court.

Actress **Michael Michelle** (*Central Park West*) filed a multi-million-dollar suit against **Eddie Murphy** after filming *Harlem Nights* (1989), claiming she was axed from the production when she spurned his advances.

Only in Hollywood: actress **Susan Anspach**, who in the late eighties and early nineties received a series of loans from **Jack Nicholson** (Anspach's former lover, and the father of her twenty-five-year-old son), filed a nine-count breach-of-contract suit in 1995 against Nicholson, who, she claimed, was asking for repayment of the money she says she was never really expected to give back. That's why they're called *loans*, babe.

Ryan O'Neal was sued by a New York cop, Brendan Campbell, who said a bottle thrown by the antagonistic actor at someone else had hit him instead. Though he had no physical injuries, Campbell claimed "mental injury and fright." He got zip.

A judge threw out Brian Quintana's case against former employer **Stefanie Powers**, who, he alleged, had forced him to service her sexually. PUH-LEEZ.

Burt Reynolds was sued in June 1995 by the William Morris Agency for failing to make the first installment of a $140,415 commissions debt.

**Miss Pamela doesn't want the
wrong kind of attention**

Roseanne sued her former attorney for giving her bad advice about ex-hubby **Tom Arnold**—specifically, that the lawyer didn't advise her to get a prenup, and encouraged her to have Tom act as her manager. Roseanne herself is absolutely blameless, of course.

Maximilian Schell, sixty-four, was sued for sexual harassment by thirty-three-year-old Diana Botsford, a production executive, after he said she had "beautiful breasts." The action was settled in 1994, with Schell stating he "regrets that [his] remarks embarrassed her."

Blustery blockhead **Steven Seagal** was charged with sexual harassment by a film assistant in 1990, but settled out of court.

William Shatner won two suits brought against him: the first by a woman (originally hired to be Mrs. Shatner's personal assistant) who claimed Shatner initiated an affair but dropped her (and, one month later, fired her) after she was injured in a car accident; the second by an actress who said they'd had a six-year affair and wanted palimony.

Nina Huang said she gave up a promising career as a screen-writer to perform such chores as "preparing meals and cleaning residences" for former lover **Christian Slater**. According to a palimony action brought in 1995, she wants $100,000 plus assorted possessions worth about $2 million.

Busty bumpkin **Anna Nicole Smith** was sued in 1994 by the Harry Winston jewelry store after bouncing a $1 million check (unbeknownst to Smith, hubby J. Howard Marshall's son, who had control of daddy's finances, had cut off her money supply). A spat with her nanny also got Smith into a spot of trouble: after filing against Maria Cerrato for failure to repay $25,000 in loans, Cerrato counterpunched by charging that Smith had forced her into a lesbian love affair (Smith allegedly "told Ms. Cerrato that you loved her on more than one occasion," and "told Ms. Cerrato that you wanted to marry her," according to court documents). Cerrato prevailed.

Action hero **Wesley Snipes** was sued in 1996 by a Santa Monica woman who said that on a bike path near the beach he inflicted "devastating bodily harm" upon her when he "hit, slapped, punched, kicked, and choked [her], and broke her leg."

Tori Spelling sued a former assistant and the woman's attorney, who according to Tori were trying to blackmail her. They asked for $30,000, said Spelling, in exchange for not selling titillating tidbits to the tabs. Tori won.

Celebrity vs. celebrity: In 1994, **Rip Torn** sued **Dennis Hopper** after Hopper claimed on a talk-show appearance that Torn had pulled a knife on him on a movie set. Not so, said Rip: "The true facts are that it was Hopper who pulled a knife on Plaintiff and it was Plaintiff who disarmed Hopper using only one hand."

Though **Faye Dunaway** certainly looks the part of Norma Desmond, she apparently didn't have the pipes for it. "She could not satisfactorily sing the part," said **Andrew Lloyd Webber**, after abruptly closing the Los Angeles production of *Sunset Blvd.* just before it was scheduled to open. Dunaway responded in August 1994 by suing for $6 million for breach of contract, fraud, and defamation. An out-of-court settlement (reportedly $1.5 million) in Dunaway's favor was reached in January 1995.

Sharon Stone sued the **Harry Winston** jewelry store for $12 million after they demanded the return of a $400,000 necklace they say they loaned her (she claims it was *given* to her outright in exchange for publicity value).

In June of 1996, self-righteous talk-show host **Montel Williams** was sued by a couple of ex-employees, who charged sexual harassment both physical (groping) and verbal (Williams allegedly referred to women as "whores" and "bitches"). The pair also claimed Williams attended staff meetings clad only in his skivvies.

Robin Williams was sued for more than $6 million in 1986 by former lover Michelle Tisch Carter, who claimed he'd given her herpes. Williams countersued for extortion; both actions were eventually settled out of court.

money ORDERS

David Caruso
Dr. Dre
Charles (*Roc*) S. Dutton
Clint Eastwood
William Hurt
Liberace
Christopher Lloyd
Lee Marvin
Nick Nolte
William Shatner
Christian Slater
Rod Stewart
Flip Wilson

Fast fact: Attorney Marvin Mitchelson, known as "the Paladin of Palimony," has never won a palimony case!

Sued for palimony

8

Sick and Tired

OUT OF MY HEAD

There are those who would argue that *all* actors and actresses are mentally ill. Further proof—if any is needed—of Tinseltown **id**-iocy:

Well into the throes of drug addiction by the time she was thirteen, **Drew Barrymore** attempted suicide by cutting her wrists with a kitchen knife.

Rosemary Clooney was addicted to prescription drugs and, after two embattled marriages to José Ferrer, was admitted to a psych ward.

Francis Ford Coppola takes lithium.

Patty *(Call Me Anna)* **Duke** is a manic-depressive.

Frances Farmer spent much of her adult life in horrendous mental institutions (read all about it in her autobiography, entitled *Will There Really Be a Morning?*).

Peter Finch had a nervous breakdown in 1961.

In April of 1996, **Margot Kidder** was found in the backyard of an L.A.-area home. Kidder had wandered the area for days, and had hacked off her hair and knocked out her dental bridge. She was immediately carted off to a psycho ward, and later told the world about her "mood swings that could knock over a building."

Vivacious **Vivien Leigh**, according to her doctor, had a manic-depressive psychosis, resulting in alcohol abuse and "indiscriminate sexual activity." Being married to a homosexual probably didn't help either.

Kristy McNichol is a manic-depressive who claims to "have a chemical imbalance that makes you kind of incapacitated. Mentally you just aren't yourself at all. To do the everyday things that you would normally do is very difficult." Like acting.

Bette Midler had a nervous breakdown in 1985.

Marilyn Monroe spent time in mental institutions.

NAME OF THE GAME

I was very ill and afraid for my sanity, but that was before I changed my name.
—The Airhead Formerly Known as Prince

Beginning in the fifties, entertainer **Martha Raye** had periodic breakdowns, and tried suicide on more than one occasion.

After she was hit by a car in 1968, **Roseanne** drastically altered her lifestyle: living as a hippie, having an illegitimate daughter (given up for adoption), and spending several months in a psych ward (no one seems to know whether her stay was voluntary). Now it seems the fuddled fat gal has every psychiatric ailment in the book, including multiple personality disorder (twenty-seven separate personalities uncovered *so far*), obsessive-compulsive disorder (OCD), agoraphobia, and severe depression. The corpulent comedienne also says she used to be a drug abuser, self-mutilator, bulimic, and prostitute, and claims to have "recovered" re-pressed memories of childhood abuse at the hands of her parents who, she claims, nearly smothered her with a pillow (mother) and threatened her with handfuls of excrement (father). OH, GROW UP.

Mickey Rourke checked himself into a psychiatric hospital in 1994, and was admitted months later to Cedars-Sinai Hospital in Los Angeles for suicidal tendencies.

Gene Tierney (the icily perfect *Laura*), **Robert Walker**, and **Shelley Winters** all had nervous breakdowns.

Psycho-Therapy: The Beach Boys' **Brian Wilson** has a long history of mental problems, "treated" by the Svengali-like Dr. Eugene Landy. (Landy lost his license in 1989 due to ethics charges, including having sex with one of his female patients.) It seems the relationship is so symbiotic that the shrink-rapt singer has now mind-melded with the good doctor: "We've exchanged names," says Landy. "I'm 'Eugene Wilson Landy' and he's 'Brian Landy Wilson.' We've kind of merged."

Marcus Welby, M.D. star **Robert Young**, who had a history of alcoholism and depres-sion, attempted suicide at age eighty-three by running a hose from his car's exhaust pipe to its interior, but was discovered in time and rushed to the hospital.

FEAR & LOATHING

Celebrity phobias 'n' fears.

Woody Allen: showers with drains in the middle
Allen also takes his temperature every two hours.
Kirstie Alley: flying
Drew Barrymore: insomnia, claustrophobia
Kim Basinger: agoraphobia
Charles Bronson: claustrophobia
Dean (*Lois & Clark*) Cain: heights
Chevy Chase: snakes
Cher: flying
Joan Crawford: germs
Tony Curtis: flying
Johnny Depp: clowns and "little tiny babies with their little rolling heads"
Whoopi Goldberg: flying
Betty Grable: crowds
Daryl Hannah: insomnia
As a child, Hannah was diagnosed "semiautistic" by one psychiatrist.
Katharine Hepburn: fire
Alfred Hitchcock: policemen
Howard Hughes: germs
Stanley Kubrick: flying
Burt Lancaster: hydrophobia

Lyle Lovett: cows
Lorna Luft: flying
Ed McMahon: heights
Robert Mitchum: crowds, insomnia
Mitchum claimed his insomnia was cured by a sixty-day stint in jail in 1949.
Bob Newhart: flying
Peter O'Toole: insomnia
Ronald Reagan: flying, claustrophobia
Anne Rice: the dark (and, presumably, reviewers and critics)
Roseanne: flying . . . and her toes
"I can't stand nobody touching my toes. I have a real phobia about it."
Willard Scott: public speaking
Gene Shalit: flying
Carly Simon: crowds
Tom Snyder: flying
"This is it! No one will come out alive! We're all doomed!" (Snyder, to other passengers aboard a turbulent flight)
Steven Spielberg: insects
Maureen Stapleton: flying
Howard Stern: germs
Liv Ullman: flying
Natalie Wood: deep water
Joanne Woodward: flying

STAGE FRIGHT

Jim Carrey

Peed his pants during an early Arsenio Hall Show appearance.

Laurence Olivier

Cher

Chaka Khan

According to Britain's Q magazine, "Apparently, one ghastly night at a New York club gig she hit a simultaneous crescendo of emotion and emission and vomited copiously over a woman in the front row."

On a 1995 appearance: "I came out and there were all these cameras and people and I—well, I just atrophied. So I told them, 'Don't be nervous, because I'm going to calm down. After I talk for a while, I'm going to calm down.' Because I could look at the audience and they were thinking, 'What's going to happen? Is he going to just dissolve up there?'"

Al Pacino

Tim Roth

"I was so scared that I actually wet myself the first time I went out onstage—literally pissed myself."

Her decision to discontinue touring reportedly stemmed from an early incident at a free concert she gave in Central Park, where she forgot her lyrics in front of 135,000 people. Fortunately, for her recent spate of concerts she had TelePrompTers for both lyrics and snappy between-song patter.

Barbra Streisand

Jerry Seinfeld

Forgot his stand-up routine during his first appearance, fleeing the stage after mumbling, "The beach. Driving. Shopping. Parents."

YOU ARE WHAT YOU EAT

Eating Disorders

Paula Abdul (bulimia)
Karen Carpenter (anorexia)
Patty Duke (anorexia)
Sally Field (bulimia)
Jane Fonda (bulimia)
Tracey Gold (anorexia)
Elton John (bulimia)
'70s supermodel **Beverly Johnson** (anorexia and bulimia)
Gilda Radner (anorexia and bulimia)
Ally Sheedy (bulimia)

These beautiful, tall ballerinas taught me how to do it. And I remember thinking that I'd found the neatest thing. I could eat whatever I wanted and not gain weight, and it really helped me deal with my feelings and fears. Because eating disorders are about feelings as much as they're about food.
—Paula Abdul

Vegetarians

Bryan Adams
Rosanna Arquette
Alec Baldwin
Kim Basinger
Danny DeVito
Woody Harrelson
Michael Jackson
Madonna
Steve Martin
Matthew Modine
Jerry Seinfeld
Lindsay Wagner

I'm not a vegetarian because I love animals; I'm a vegetarian because I hate plants.
—*Saturday Night Live's* A. Whitney Brown

I was raised Irish Catholic, so I ate like Irish Catholics, which means every meal, meat and potatoes. Ham and potatoes. Steak and potatoes. For breakfast, eggs and fried meat. So I went to the doctor and I had my cholesterol checked and the nurse, like, offered to walk me back to my car.

—Conan O'Brien

TRAUMA IN TINSELTOWN

According to *Psychology Today*, which published the
results of a survey by Charles Figley, Ph.D.,
the top ten things that stress stars out:

The press (the tabloids in particular)* 🗣 Critics 🗣 Stalkers 🗣
Threatening communications (letters/calls) 🗣 Lack of privacy 🗣
Lack of security 🗣 Constant monitoring of their lives 🗣 Worry
about career plunges 🗣 Worries about their children's lives being
disrupted 🗣 Curious fans

*In October 1996, *ER* star **George Clooney**, incensed at footage of
himself and a new girlfriend that appeared on the TV tabloid *Hard
Copy*, wrote a scathing letter to the producers of *Entertainment
Tonight* (the same folks responsible for *Hard Copy*). In it, he reminded
them of a deal they'd struck months earlier: they'd agreed not to run
stories about him on *Hard Copy*, and in exchange he'd consented to
grant interviews to *ET*. "So now we begin," the letter says. "Officially. No interviews from this date on. Nothing from *ER*, nothing
from *One Fine Day*, nothing from *Batman and Robin*, and nothing
from Dreamworks' first film *The Peacemaker*. These interviews will
be reserved for all press but you. *Access Hollywood, E*, whoever . . .
your company and [your producer] have to be responsible for what
they say, and who they say it to. And so do I."

GLADDA MEETCHA   SOME FEARS AREN'T SO IRRATIONAL.

I met Brad Pitt at the [West Hollywood nightclub] House of Blues. He
came up to me and said, "Oh my God, it's Tom Arnold! I can't believe it!
I can't believe I'm meeting Tom Arnold! It's just great to meet you!" I
don't know what was happening. Was Brad being serious? Was he
being sarcastic or what?
—Tom Arnold

Communication Breakdown

Tongue in Cheek (s~s~stutterers)	Thay, Thailor (lispers)	A Rats Is Born (dyslexics)
	Humphrey Bogart	
James Earl Jones	Madeline Kahn	Tom Cruise (claims Scientology cured him)
Jack Paar	Charles Nelson Reilly	
Harvey Keitel	Mike Tyson	Cher
Bruce Willis	Barbara Walters	Oliver Reed

HOOKED ON A FEELING

> It's impossible to tell where the DTs end
> and Hollywood begins.
> —W.C. Fields

One way of coping with the pressures of stardom is to turn to booze or drugs. Sure, it may land them in jail and cost them a job or two, but no matter how badly celebrities may screw up or how much havoc they've wreaked, they can always count on public sympathy—after copious tear-shedding sessions and self-pitying confessions—when they decide to kick the habit.

Drugs of Choice

> Cocaine is God's way of letting you know you make too much money.
> —Robin Williams

Kirstie Alley: cocaine
Once spent $400 a day on her habit.
Gregg Allman, the Allman Brothers: heroin
*Cher broke up with him when she learned
he was addicted—three days after they'd wed.*
Ann-Margret: alcohol, pills
Tom Arnold: alcohol, cocaine
Dan Aykroyd: LSD
Tammy Faye Bakker: alcohol
*Claims she was unaware she had a
problem until one day when, flying
in an airplane, she saw cats and people on its wing.*
Diana Barrymore (actress daughter of John): alcohol
*"I lay in bed, suddenly awake, staring at it—an
enormous white crab slowly crawling across the
ceiling. I thought, this can't be the DTs. Can you
get the DTs when you're only thirty?"*

COMING CLEAN

"The fact that I'm alive, that seems to surprise people," says Keith Richards. The stoned Stones guitarist (along with other celebs like George Hamilton) has long been rumored to periodically visit expensive European clinics where his entire "tainted" blood supply is replaced with fresh over a period of several days.

Drew Barrymore: alcohol, marijuana, cocaine

Barrymore may go down as the youngest addict in history. The pint-size performer began drinking at age nine, smoking pot at ten, and snorting coke at twelve, ultimately landing in rehab at age fourteen. She admits she's drinking a little again, but explains, "Maybe I was an alcoholic a couple of years ago, but I'm not really anymore. It's not like I have to wake up every morning and go, 'OK, you're gonna get through this day and you're not gonna drink.' It's not even on my mind." Barrymore met current squeeze Eric Erlandson, a musician in Courtney Love's band, as she was throwing up outside a nightclub. "It was so, like, fate," Miss B said dreamily.

Kim Basinger: cocaine

"I hated that it made me feel so physically worn out."

Justine Bateman: cocaine

Steven (*Scarface*) Bauer: cocaine

Robert Blake: alcohol, pills, heroin

Humphrey Bogart: alcohol

The best cure for a hangover, according to Bogie, was simply to get smashed all over again. Regular drinking buddies, whom he called the "Holmby Hills Rat Pack," included David Niven, Judy Garland, Adlai Stevenson, Frank Sinatra, Peter Lorre, John O'Hara, and John Huston.

David Bowie: cocaine

Jeff Bridges: marijuana

Gary Busey: alcohol, drugs

Brett Butler: alcohol, painkillers

James Caan: cocaine

Sid Caesar: alcohol, barbiturates

Caesar refused to admit he had a problem with alcohol, even when he began vomiting on a regular basis.

Michael Caine: alcohol

Used to down three quarts of vodka per day.

Judy Carne: marijuana, cocaine, heroin

David Caruso: alcohol

DRUGS & R⊚CK 'N' R⊚LL

SEX &

I still don't understand the reason for smoking dope if you're not going to have sex. To me, drugs have no appeal other than sex.　　　　—Kurt Russell

Ray Charles: heroin
Hooked at age eighteen.
Chevy Chase: alcohol, painkillers
Jeff (*Taxi*) **Conaway**: alcohol
Joan Crawford: alcohol
Fueled by prodigious amounts of booze, Crawford once threw
Johnny Guitar co-star Mercedes McCambridge's clothing
out into the street after breaking into her hotel room.
Tony Curtis: alcohol, pills, freebasing
"I spent twenty years reaching out for a glass or pill to make me
feel good. Having a different woman all the time was part of the
same dream. If a woman wasn't available, drugs eliminated the
need for one." Daughter Jamie Lee Curtis says she and her famous
father used to freebase together.
John Cusack: alcohol
Tyne Daly: alcohol
Daniel Day-Lewis: prescription pills
Found the migraine tablets he'd been prescribed at age sixteen
"fun"; hospitalized shortly thereafter for overdose.

Shannen Doherty: alcohol, drugs
Amanda Donohoe: alcohol
Michael Douglas: alcohol, cocaine, sex
"I went into rehab to save my marriage
but I wound up saving myself."
Robert Downey Jr.: alcohol, cocaine,
opium, hallucinogenic mushrooms, heroin
Checked into rehab for the third time after having cocaine seizures
in April 1995; was once arrested after being found driving naked in
his Porsche and tossing imaginary rats out the car window.
(See also Chapter 7.)
Richard Dreyfuss: alcohol, prescription drugs, cocaine
In 1982, Dreyfuss said he was ingesting the following on a daily
basis: a bottle of cognac, Percodan, two grams of coke,
and twenty prescription painkillers.

SEX & DRUGS & ... 60 MINUTES?!?

In a new *Playboy* interview, Mike Wallace said that he smoked marijuana and that it acted as an aphrodisiac. Meanwhile, in a separate interview Morley Safer said that he'll never smoke pot with Mike Wallace again.

—Conan O'Brien

Joe Eszterhas (screenwriter, *Basic Instinct; Jade*): marijuana
Chad Everett: alcohol
Drank a quart a day before cleaning up his act.
Carrie Fisher: alcohol, marijuana, LSD, Percodan, acid, Ecstasy
Mel Gibson: alcohol
Arrested in Canada for drunk driving in 1984 after running a red light and plowing into an oncoming car.

Whoopi Goldberg: heroin
Louis Gossett Jr.: alcohol, cocaine
Kelsey Grammer: alcohol, cocaine
Melanie Griffith: alcohol, cocaine
Standing in a crosswalk, a very intoxicated Griffith was mowed down by a drunk driver. The "actress" suffered assorted fractures and had amnesia for several days.
Ashley Hamilton: heroin
Tom Hanks: marijuana, cocaine
Says he quit drugs for his children.
David Hasselhoff: alcohol
Margaux Hemingway: alcohol
Anthony Hopkins: alcohol
Dennis Hopper: the gamut
"I was doing like a half an ounce of cocaine every three days. I was drinking half a gallon of rum a day with twenty-eight beers. I never had a problem. It was other people crawling around on the floor, blithering idiots, who had the problem."
John Hurt: alcohol
William Hurt: alcohol

EVERY BREATH Y⊚U TAKE

I didn't inhale.
I didn't like it.
—Bill Clinton
"I didn't inhale" and "I didn't like it"? Of course you didn't like it! You didn't inhale!
—Bill Maher

Michael Jackson: painkillers
Checked into rehab in 1994, and collapsed during a rehearsal in December 1995.
Samuel L. Jackson: alcohol, crack
Elton John: alcohol, cocaine
". . . one line [of cocaine] every four minutes. And the alcohol used to steady me up. . . . I used to have terrible seizures and I'd still take the fucking stuff. I was blue when they found me. They were the most scary things I've ever had in my life, seizures. I felt like Linda Blair in The Exorcist, *like the top of my head was going right round. Terrifying. And yet I would have one and still ten minutes later I'd put coke up my nose. That's how bad it was. It was* not *pleasant." And, "Sometimes when I'm flying over the Alps I think, 'That's like all the cocaine I sniffed.'"*

Don Johnson: alcohol, cocaine, prescription drugs
On June 1, 1994, Johnson rolled his Jeep (son Jesse was inside the car with him) and didn't report the accident until five hours later—probably to cover up the fact that he'd been drinking.

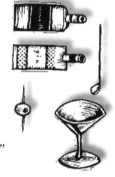

Quincy Jones: cocaine
Kris Kristofferson: alcohol, marijuana
Nathan *(The Birdcage)* **Lane**: alcohol
John Larroquette: alcohol
"I think I was born an alcoholic. The story is that I got drunk at my christening."
Traci Lords: cocaine
Overdosed several times during her career as a porno actress.
Courtney Love: heroin, prescription drugs
In August of 1995, Love instigated a suit against a therapist who, she claimed, got her hooked on muscle relaxers.
Bela Lugosi: heroin

A FAMILY AFFAIR

The Kennedy compound in Palm Beach has been sold.... The new owner said he plans to move in as soon as they clear out the empties.
—Conan O'Brien

Andie MacDowell: diet pills, cocaine
Steve McQueen: marijuana, cocaine, amyl nitrate
Liza Minnelli: alcohol, Valium
Robert Mitchum: marijuana
"I've been smoking shit for about forty years,
but it never got to be a habit with me."
Mary Tyler Moore: alcohol
Jack Nicholson: cocaine
Nick Nolte: alcohol
Once awoke in a house he had no recollection of renting, then had
sixteen tons of rock dropped onto the front lawn because he'd
always wondered what that would look like; was also in the habit
of tooling around town, dressed in surgeon's scrubs, waving a
prosthetic leg—his deceased father's!—out his convertible.
Gary Oldman: alcohol
Al Pacino: alcohol
Sean Penn: alcohol
Chynna Phillips: alcohol,
marijuana, hallucinogenic mushrooms, acid, cocaine
But only during her "high" school years, she claims.
John Phillips: heroin
Phillips says he once shot up about every fifteen minutes and
usually didn't even bother taking the needle out of his arm.
Mackenzie Phillips: alcohol, marijuana, pills, cocaine
Like father, like daughter.
River Phoenix: cocaine, heroin
Freddie (*Chico and the Man*) **Prinze**: cocaine,
Quaaludes
*Prinze had a massive habit: five grams of cocaine*
and up to a hundred Quaaludes per day.
Richard Pryor: alcohol, freebasing
Dennis Quaid: alcohol, cocaine
Robert Redford: alcohol
Redford lost his college baseball
scholarship because of alcohol abuse.
Burt Reynolds: Halcion, Valium, Percodan

LIFE
He seldom sleeps, so intense is his partying.
—Liz Smith, on Leonardo DiCaprio

Julia Roberts: cocaine
. . . to mend a broken heart
(Kiefer Sutherland).
Roseanne: marijuana
The lard-assed loudmouth also used to
smoke five packs of cigarettes a day.
Mickey Rourke: cocaine, heroin
Joel Schumacher (director,
Batman Forever): speed
Schumacher's habit nearly cost him his career:
at one time, he weighed just 130 pounds, had lost five
of his teeth, and was $50,000 in debt.
Peter Sellers: amyl nitrate "poppers"
Charlie Sheen: alcohol, heroin, cocaine
What's different about life after booze? According to
Sheen, "I don't spend the whole first half of the day
fighting a vicious hangover and convincing the direc-
tor that the character would wear sunglasses here because I can't
open my eyes. . . ."
Anna Nicole Smith: alcohol, pills
Smith was rushed from her hotel room (where she'd been staying
with an unnamed male companion—not her ancient spouse) and
hospitalized after mixing Xanax, Vicodin, and booze in 1994,
and again in 1995 after an "adverse reaction to prescription
medication" (Vicodin again), i.e., an OD.
David Soul: alcohol
Ringo Starr: alcohol
Oliver Stone: cocaine
Patrick Swayze: alcohol
Liz Taylor: alcohol, painkillers
Taylor received more than a thousand prescriptions (for
almost thirty different kinds of painkillers, tranquilizers,
and sleeping pills) in one five-year period alone.
Alan Thicke: marijuana
Spencer Tracy: alcohol
Daniel J. (*Hill Street Blues*) **Travanti**: alcohol

SHAMELESS

In 1995, Oprah Winfrey tearfully admitted to having smoked cocaine, but in the same "empowering" spirit with which she addresses her sad-sack chat-show guests, blamed it all on the Svengali-like influence of an ex-boyfriend.

Dick Van Dyke: alcohol
Drank a fifth a night.
Jan-Michael Vincent: alcohol
Broke his neck in a booze-related car accident in August 1996.
John Wayne: alcohol
Drank one quart daily for forty years!
Robin Williams: alcohol, cocaine
"Cocaine, what a wonderful drug! Anything that makes you paranoid and impotent— mmm, gimme some of that!"
"I couldn't imagine living the way I used to live. Now people come up to me from the drug days and go, 'Hi, remember me?' And I'm going, 'No, did I have sex with you? Did I take a dump in your toolbox?'"
Bruce Willis: alcohol
"I quit because I needed to quit. Having kids just kind of clinched it."
Robert Young: alcohol

a Pound of CURE

Tammy Faye Bakker
Eileen Brennan
Gary Busey
Johnny Cash
Chevy Chase
Tony Curtis
Flavor Flav
Jerry Garcia
Andy Gibb
Kelsey Grammer
Gregory Harrison
Margaux Hemingway
William Hurt
Don Johnson
Peter Lawford

Jerry Lee Lewis
Mickey Mantle
Liza Minnelli
Robert Mitchum
Mary Tyler Moore
Ozzy Osbourne
Sean Penn
Richard Pryor
Howard Rollins
Anna Nicole Smith
Elizabeth Taylor
Tanya Tucker
Alex Van Halen
Eddie Van Halen
Tammy Wynette

Betty Ford Center graduates

LOOK WHO'S STALKING

People don't come on my property because they *know.*
Two words: wood chipper.
—Dan Aykroyd

Stalkers—obsessed and often deranged fans who compulsively follow, and attempt to encounter and get close to stars—are, unfortunately, part of the price of fame. Though most are relatively harmless, we all hear about the cases—**Rebecca Schaeffer** and **John Lennon**, most notably—in which love turns to hate, ending in death. Bizarre behavior, strange "gifts" and frightening confrontations are all part of the problem, forcing many celebrities to hire expensive security specialists and turn their homes into fortresses. Nearly every star has at one time or another been stalked by a crazed fan, and some—particularly young, attractive female stars like **Pamela Anderson Lee** or **Sharon Stone**—have, at any given time, a small regiment of fanatics pursuing them.

Johnny Carson was accused by Kenneth Gause of "diverting" more than $5 million of Gause's money for personal use. Gause wrote letters (signing them "the king of goodness") to Carson for about two years demanding redress; when the chat-show host failed to respond, the loony letters became hostile and threatening. In December of 1989, Gause appeared on the *Tonight Show* lot with an unlikely weapon—a sock filled with gravel—and was arrested on the spot.

While supermodel **Cindy Crawford** was out of town, a lovesick lunatic conned a neighbor into letting him into her apartment, where he rummaged through her possessions. When she returned, he phoned to tell her what he'd done, then demanded a meeting. She agreed to see him the next day in a restaurant but sent the police in her stead, and the man, who'd previously been convicted of armed robbery, was arrested.

"It was something I needed to do," said Mark Pina, the twenty-three-year-old crazy who beset soap hunk/sometime rock singer **Michael Damian** during a concert near Boise, Idaho. Damian suffered bruised ribs, a cut knee, and whiplash.

Neil Diamond was pursued by a troubled young German woman, Suzanne Hackbarth, who sent him letters and scripts (all returned to her) via his Los Angeles representatives. In March of 1991, Hackbarth traveled to Diamond's Bel-Air home, where a live-in assistant spotted her near one of the gates. As he walked over, she held out her wrist to him. It was covered with blood, obviously from a wound inflicted by the razor clutched in her other hand. He recoiled in horror as she pleaded with him to let her see Diamond; he ran into the house, dialed 911, and paramedics bundled her off to a nearby hospital for treatment. Diamond magnanimously offered to pay for Hackbarth's court-ordered psychiatric counseling until she could return to Germany.

Brian Keith Neun was arrested by the FBI in 1992 after leaving forty-three obscene and threatening messages within a twenty-five-day period on the voice mail system at **Clint Eastwood**'s production company.

Andrea Evans, star of the soap opera *One Life to Live*, was terrorized for five years by a dangerously obsessed man. He showed up frequently at the New York City studio where the show was taped, and as the actress was coming in from lunch one day, he pounced. "There was a guard," Evans told *48 Hours*, "but this guy walked right in and went right to me and grabbed me and turned me around and started yelling at me about a dog." He was quickly removed by security, but the incident did nothing to discourage him. The very next week he slashed his wrists in front of the building, and shortly afterward started sending threatening letters.

"He asked me when, how, where I would like to die," she says. "He would put swastikas in blood all over the letters, tell me 'Death to the blond whore,' little quotes like 'Andrea, don't stay up late, you're going to die anyway.' I can't even think of how many

different ways he has said this to me. I had to have two armed guards with me everywhere I went. I was advised just to go to work and to go home, and my phones were tapped. I was fainting at work. I couldn't eat, I couldn't sleep."

Living under this intense pressure proved to be too much for Evans. "Nothing can be done until he hurts me," she says. "The scariest part to me is the way he doesn't give up. . . . In all these years, he does not give up." Evans chose to leave the city—and her high-paying role in *One Life to Live*—to escape him. She now lives far away from New York and, hopefully, her pursuer.

Laurence Fishburne had his hands full with an overweight, six-foot-tall woman who followed him around and, on Halloween night 1995, dressed up as a Playboy bunny, strutted into the Manhattan theater where the actor was performing, and threw a candy-filled plastic pumpkin at him. A few nights later she appeared at the theater again—nude save for a sandwich board reading, "Larry is a spoiled, homophobic child."

Michael J. Fox was harassed for four years by an anonymous woman who signed her letters "Your number one fan"; when she learned that Fox planned to wed actress Tracy Pollan, adoration turned into hostility. Full of hate, she began sending vituperative letters laced with obscenities, anti-Semitic statements, and venomous threats. Worse, she never revealed her name, stymieing FBI agents who were assigned to the case. Tina Marie Ledbetter was finally tracked down after she sent Fox two boxes full of rabbit droppings via UPS—the shipping labels were easily traced to the Orange County firm where she was employed as a packaging clerk. Ledbetter was arrested again in 1996 for stalking **Scott Bakula**.

In September 1988, Joni Leigh Penn appeared at the door of actress **Sharon Gless**'s Studio City house (used as an office) and told a secretary that she had a gun. This frightening statement led Gless to obtain a restraining order against Penn, requiring the disturbed woman to remain at least a thousand yards from the actress and her residences at all times. But early in 1989 Penn sent another letter to Gless, enclosing with it three bizarre and unsettling photographs. In

one, Penn held a pistol to her temple; in another she pointed the gun into her open mouth. And the third, according to the actress's brother Michael Gless, "showed a kind of a shrine she had made to Sharon, composed of publicity pictures and flowers. In the middle she had placed an attack rifle."

In late March, Penn, heavily armed, broke into the Studio City office (fortunately, Gless was not there) by shattering a window with her hand. The break-in triggered a silent alarm, and police arrived almost instantaneously. Penn, clutching an assault rifle, threatened suicide if they did not leave, and the entire neighborhood was evacuated as cops tried to talk her out of killing herself. Finally, after a tense seven-hour standoff, a female negotiator persuaded her to surrender.

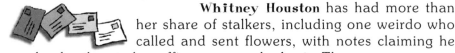 Willie James Dawson, who wrote more than two hundred letters in eight years to television personality **Mary Hart**, was imprisoned for the attempted murder of his wife, whom he stabbed twelve times with a screwdriver. Mrs. Dawson also claimed he'd been imprisoned in England after beating their seventeen-month-old child to death.

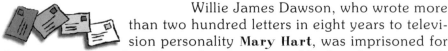 **Whitney Houston** has had more than her share of stalkers, including one weirdo who called and sent flowers, with notes claiming he was her brother, to her office on a regular basis. The man was apprehended by police in his place of residence—a truck he shared with two pit bulls and a small arsenal (guns, knives, even a crossbow).

 In 1995, a Manhattan man was arrested for stabbing and wounding a pedestrian. On his person was found a love letter, in which were written bizarre commands like "kill everyone" and "attack on sight," to **Janet Jackson**.

 Lavon Muhammad, who calls herself Billie Jean Jackson, believes herself the subject of **Michael Jackson**'s hit song "Billie Jean." Muhammad, an unemployed legal secretary, has been arrested four times for trespassing on the grounds of the singer's home in Encino, a wealthy suburb of Los Angeles. She also filed a $150 million paternity suit (later dismissed) against Jackson in Chicago.

 In 1992, a twenty-six-year-old would-be writer smashed a window of **Stephen King**'s home with a brick and crawled inside. King's wife, Tabitha, confronted the intruder, who whipped out a (phony) bomb and asked for beer and cigarettes so he could write a book of his own. The man also demanded justice for his aunt, a New Jersey woman who'd sued King, claiming she was the fan upon whom King's *Misery* was based. Mrs. King phoned 911 from a neighbor's house and the weirdo was carted off to jail.

 Longtime loser Mark David Chapman, worried that his idol **John Lennon** was somehow "selling out," shot and killed the singer in front of Lennon's New York apartment. Clutched in Chapman's hands was a copy of J.D. Salinger's *The Catcher in the Rye*: Chapman believed himself the personification of the book's protagonist, an alienated youth who doesn't want to become an adult.

 Margaret Ray is convinced she's married to **David Letterman** and that he sired her children. And while she's never been violent or even threatened him, she has exhibited some bizarre delusional behaviors. In 1988, Ray charged a number of purchases to Letterman at the NBC studios in Manhattan; later in the year she broke into his house and stole his Porsche. While attempting to drive it into New York City, she was stopped by toll-takers on a bridge when she couldn't come up with the three-dollar charge. She tried to get out of it by identifying herself as Mrs. Letterman, and her young son, whom she had brought along, as David Jr. But a quick phone call to Letterman's office brought out the truth, and Ray was taken into custody—again. "There was a time when I felt frustrated and annoyed by it," said Letterman. "But I never really felt I was the victim—this woman is the victim. She's had a very sad life. She's got like six or eight kids and is estranged from them all. We gave her many, many benefits of the doubt. Finally, she went to jail for about a year. . . ."

 **Sophia Loren** was once attacked by an ax-wielding fugitive from an asylum who claimed she was his lover. Their connection? She'd given him an autograph years before.

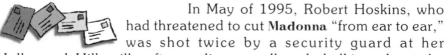
 In May of 1995, Robert Hoskins, who had threatened to cut **Madonna** "from ear to ear," was shot twice by a security guard at her Hollywood Hills villa after scaling a wall and skulking about the grounds. It wasn't the first time Hoskins had tried to get close to the material girl: he'd been apprehended on a previous occasion by Madonna's phalanx of security men, who'd handcuffed the man to a garage for forty-five minutes until police showed up.

Michael Owen Perry was fixated upon **Olivia Newton-John**, among others, and made five pilgrimages from his native Louisiana to her home in Malibu, once even setting up camp behind the singer's estate. When asked about one of his trips, Perry nonchalantly explained it away: "I caught myself in Malibu and the thought came to my mind that she lived there, so I asked a couple of people where she lived. They said, 'Oh, right next door,' so I go next door and I knock and I said, 'Hi, y'all, I'd like to speak to Olivia,' and some guy said, 'What do you want?' and I said, 'I'd like to ask her, you know, how she felt about playing a magical muse [in the 1980 film *Xanadu*]' and that was it, really."

In 1983, Perry (who had been diagnosed a paranoid schizophrenic) created a ten-person "death list" which included Newton-John and her husband, actor Matt Lattanzi, "Judge" O'Connor (Chief Justice **Sandra Day O'Connor**, whose eyes reminded Perry of Newton-John's, and whom he resented because she was doing "a man's job"), along with five members of his own family, including both his parents. Not long after, he killed those five family members, shooting out their eyes before fleeing, and was arrested fourteen days later—less than two miles from the Supreme Court building in Washington. With him in his squalid motel room were six television sets, all tuned to static and all with bizarre drawings and phrases scrawled across their screens in felt pen. Perry had told his psychiatrist that he planned to begin killing people in groups of ten, and had written to Newton-John shortly before the murders: "If you are real, please write back and say anything. If you wish to meet me, I'll try. If you're not real on TV, and only a Disneyland mirror image of all of your kind, then I'll have to take matters as such."

 **Dan Rather** was accosted on Manhattan's Park Avenue by two strange men who demanded he answer a question: "Kenneth, what is the frequency?" When Rather told them they had the wrong guy, one of them punched him in the jaw. They then chased Rather into the lobby of a building, beating and kicking the nervous newsman while repeating the question. (The bizarre incident became the subject of a song by rock band REM, "What Is the Frequency, Kenneth?")

 John Hinckley Jr. attempted the assassination of President **Ronald Reagan** to win the love of **Jodie Foster**, with whom he'd had a long-time obsession. Hinckley, like Mark David Chapman (his role model, whom he'd avidly studied), had a copy of *The Catcher in the Rye* on him at the time of his arrest.

 In the unusual gifts department, **Roseanne** was being pursued for a time by an unknown stalker who sent presents of chopped-up dolls splattered with red liquid, and **Rod Stewart** was once sent an envelope filled with razor blades.

 In 1979 in Scotland, Arthur Jackson saw a young actress named **Theresa Saldana** in *I Wanna Hold Your Hand*, a film about Beatlemania. He began writing about her in his journal, and soon journeyed to the U.S. to hunt her down. After obtaining her home address, he staked out the place, and when she emerged he attacked. Saldana suffered numerous stab wounds, and her life was saved only by the efforts of a courageous, quick-thinking deliveryman, who wrestled the psycho to the ground. Jackson ran off but was soon found and taken into custody.

Jackson's continued threats against Saldana have kept him in prison, where various doctors have reached identical conclusions. "He is what I would label a chronic paranoid schizophrenic and what most people would call crazy," said one; another called him "a very dangerous man," and a third said, "I'm uncomfortable about releasing him because he's still psychotic and still paranoid." Jackson does not believe himself ill, but rather "allergic to the world." (He once asked doctors to "go into his brain and scrape the dirt off.")

After making a number of trips to Los Angeles from his home in Phoenix to try and make contact with actress **Rebecca** (*My Sister Sam*) **Schaeffer**, Robert John Bardo finally got her address through a private detective, who simply wrote to California's Department of Motor Vehicles. "I'm obsessed with something I can't have. So I'm going to make it so that something doesn't exist anymore." The envelope was adorned with a drawing of a tombstone, inscribed with the dates "1967–1987." 1967 was the year in which Schaeffer was born. After obtaining a gun from his brother, Bardo boarded a bus for Los Angeles. He located her apartment and used an intercom system to buzz the actress, who came to the door and asked him to leave. Bardo departed, but returned a short while later. Schaeffer came to the door again, but didn't open it; as Bardo raised his pistol, he mumbled, "I forgot to give you this," and pulled the trigger. The bullet smashed through the glass, and a few seconds later the actress was dead.

James Woods claimed actress **Sean Young**, after a fizzled on-set romance, refused to let him go. According to Woods, she sent hate mail filled with gruesome pictures of dismembered animals and corpses, trampled hundreds of dollars' worth of flowers in his garden, and once left a doll—with a slashed neck and trail of iodine simulating blood—on his doorstep. He filed a $6 million harassment suit, but later recanted, blaming the entire incident on ex-wife Sarah Owen.

Stephanie Zimbalist was pursued by a lovesick man who followed her around the country, chronicling each of her performances in numerous letters sent to her. In one, he told her he'd been spying on her house (enclosing a photograph to prove it) and that he was aware she'd contacted the authorities. "I want the police to watch me," he wrote. "I want them to get used to me. I want them to get bored." In another, he warned her of his power: "In your efforts to avoid me, Miss Zimbalist, you'll win a few. You'll perform in some small town and I won't know about it. But *you* must win *every* time! I only have to win once. . . ." Fortunately, the FBI nabbed him before he was able to make good on his threats.

DEAD ENDS

They once announced on U.S. television that I was dead.
When they rang to tell my daughter, she said I couldn't be,
that she was talking to me twelve minutes ago in
Australia. They said, "No, he's dead.
It's just the time difference."
—Patrick MacNee

SUICIDES

Nick Adams, TV's *Rebel*, 1968: sedatives
Pier Angeli, fifties leading lady, 1971:
barbiturates
Don (*Red Ryder*) **Barry**, cowboy star,
1980: gunshot
Scotty Beckett, child actor, 1968:
sleeping pills
David Begelman, former Columbia
Pictures president, 1995: gunshot
Charles Boyer, 1978: Seconal
Cheyenne Brando, 1995: hanging
Dorothy Dandridge, 1965: sleeping pills
Ed (*St. Elsewhere*) **Flanders**, 1995: gunshot
Dave Garroway, 1982: gunshot
Alan Ladd, 1964: alcohol, sleeping pills
Carole Landis, 1948: pills
Marie McDonald, forties starlet known as
"the body," 1965: Percodan
Marilyn Monroe, 1962: alcohol and barbiturates
Freddie Prinze, 1977: gunshot
David (*L.A. Law*) **Rappaport**, dwarf actor, 1990: gunshot
George (*Superman*) **Reeves**, 1959: gunshot
Jean Seberg, 1979: barbiturates
Margaret Sullavan, 1960: barbiturates
Lupe Velez, 1944: drowned in her own
bathroom after taking so many barbiturates
(75 Seconals, according to one source)
that her system rejected them
Gig Young, 1978: gunshot
*Shot his bride of three weeks, then turned the
gun on himself.*

DRUG-/ALCOHOL-RELATED

John Belushi, 1982: speedball (heroin/cocaine injection)

Lenny Bruce, 1966: narcotics

Rainer Werner Fassbinder, director, 1982: heart attack brought on by a combination of cocaine, uppers, downers, and whiskey. Fassbinder was also a four-pack-a-day smoker.

Judy Garland, 1969: Nembutal

Alexander Godunov, 1995: heart failure/acute alcoholism

Margaux Hemingway, 1996: Phenobarbital

William Holden, 1981: probably fell and hit his head on a bedside table—and was too inebriated to call for help

Anissa Jones, Buffy in TV's *Family Affair*, 1976: barbiturates and alcohol

River Phoenix, 1993: collapsed after ingesting a mixture of heroin, cocaine, marijuana, and Valium; cause of death registered officially as "acute multiple-drug intoxication"

Elvis Presley, 1977: years of drug abuse and junk food took their toll on "The King," who a hospital staffer claimed had "the arteries of an eighty-year-old man." Found in his bloodstream were codeine (in an amount ten times greater than a normal fatal dosage), morphine, Quaaludes, Valium, diazepam metabolite, Valmid, Placidyl, Amytal, Nembutal, Demerol, and Sinutabs!

Natalie Wood, 1981: drowned off the California coast after falling off a yacht; autopsy revealed a high blood-alcohol level

ACCIDENTAL / MISADVENTURE

Jack Cassidy, 1977: died in a fire (probably started by his own cigarette) in his apartment

Brandon Lee, actor son of action star Bruce Lee, 1992: shot at close range with a "blank" on the set of *The Crow*

Vic Morrow and two Vietnamese children, **Renee Chen** and **My-ca Le**, 1982: during filming of **John Landis**'s *Twilight Zone—The Movie,* a helicopter crashed on top of Morrow and two children, killing them instantly. A eulogy given by Landis after the event included this self-serving statement: "Tragedy can strike in an instant, but film is immortal. Vic lives forever. Just before the last take, Vic took me aside to thank me for the opportunity to play this role." Landis was put on trial for involuntary manslaughter, but was acquitted. He then invited the twelve jurors who'd acquitted him to the premiere of his new movie, *Coming to America.*

Tennessee Williams, 1983: choked to death on a plastic bottle cap

CAR ACCIDENTS

James Dean, 1955
Janet Gaynor, 1982
Grace Kelly, 1982
Sam Kinison, 1992
Jayne Mansfield, 1967
Tom Mix, cowboy star, 1940

PLANE CRASHES

Leslie Howard, 1943
Carole Lombard, 1942
Audie Murphy, 1971
Ricky Nelson, 1986
Will Rogers, 1935
Mike Todd, 1958

MURDER, MY SWEET

Bob Crane, star of *Hogan's Heroes*, was bludgeoned to death with a "blunt linear instrument" (probably a tire iron or crowbar) in a Scottsdale motel room in June 1978. The main suspect was Crane's friend John Carpenter, a leech who tagged along with the erstwhile actor on pickup expeditions at local bars and participated with him in debauched sexual scenarios. Prior to his death, Crane had apparently grown tired of Carpenter's constant presence, and some believed that Crane's attempt to end the friendship resulted in his murder. Though Carpenter was eventually brought to trial (in 1992), he was acquitted for lack of evidence.

Poltergeist star **Dominique Dunne**, daughter of journalist/novelist Dominick Dunne, was strangled to death in 1982 by an ex-boyfriend.

Sal Mineo was stabbed to death in his apartment-house garage in 1976. His assailant remains unknown, but the murder is generally thought to have something to do with Mineo's secret life in the drug-sodden gay S&M subculture.

Director **Pier Paolo Pasolini**, who had a priapic predilection for young, itinerant boys who were part of the gay "rough trade," was beaten and run over with his own car by one of them in 1975.

Six Feet Under
What the stars were buried with

Humphrey Bogart: a small gold whistle, placed by Lauren Bacall in his coffin
Errol Flynn: six bottles of whiskey
Bela Lugosi: his Dracula cape
George (*Superman*) Reeves: the gray suit he'd worn for years on television as Clark Kent

Appendix 1 Oscarama

The Pre-Show

"It's really an honor **JUST TO BE NOMINATED.**"	(Dyan Cannon)
"**JUST TO BE NOMINATED** makes me feel like a real actress."	(Sissy Spacek)

Most Politically Incorrect Statement by a Nominee

John Malkovich, up for Best Supporting Actor for *Places in the Heart* (1984), said, "I'm up against two Orientals—one of them an amateur—a black guy, and a dead man." (For the record, the other nominees were Haing S. Ngor [the Oriental amateur] for *The Killing Fields*; Adolph Caesar [the black guy] for *A Soldier's Story*; Noriyuki "Pat" Morita [the other Oriental] for *The Karate Kid*; and Sir Ralph Richardson [the dead guy] for *Greystoke: The Legend of Tarzan, Lord of the Apes*. Solly, Cholly—Ngor won.)

Robert Duvall, nominated in 1983 for Best Actor (*Tender Mercies*), said, "I guess it's me against the limeys." (Duvall's fellow nominees were Michael Caine for *Educating Rita*, Tom Courtenay and Albert Finney for *The Dresser*, and Tom Conti for *Reuben, Reuben*. Duvall won.)

I hope my earrings
don't fall off. That's
the only thing I'm
nervous about.
—Sigourney Weaver

O
S
C
A
R
A
M
A

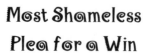

Most Shameless Plea for a Win

Margaret Avery, Best Supporting Actress nominee for *The Color Purple* in 1985, placed an ad that ran in the trades on the final day of voting: "Dear God, My name is Margaret Avery. I knows dat I been blessed by Alice Walker, Steven Spielberg and Quincy Jones, who gave me the part of Shug Avery in *The Color Purple*. Now I is up for one of the nominations fo' Best Supporting Actress alongside with some fine, talented ladies that I is proud to be in the company of. Well, God, I guess the time has come fo' the Academy's voters to decide whether I is one of the Best Supporting Actresses this year or not! Either way, thank you, Lord, for the opportunity. Your little daughter, Margaret Avery." (She lost.)

 Richard Dreyfuss, who was nominated for Best Actor in 1977, told the *New York Times*, "I was wonderful in *The Goodbye Girl*." (It worked. He won.)

Diane Ladd, Best Supporting Actress nominee for 1991's *Rambling Rose*, said, "Oscar's been courting me, flirting with me, pretending to come home to my bed, but I want him to get serious this time. Come on, man, make that commitment! Come live with me now!" Sorry, Diane—Oscar went home with Mercedes Ruehl (for *The Fisher King*) instead. HOW FICKLE!

I'll be so happy
when it's over,
no matter what
happens.
—Bette Midler

Most Extreme Love-Hate Relationship with the Oscars

John Lithgow, Best Supporting Actor nominee in 1982 for *The World According to Garp*, went from outbursts like "I'm in the lead! I stole the fucking show!" to feeling the Oscars were "brightly colored decals that we stick onto our drab and humdrum lives."

Best "I Don't Want It and You Can't Make Me Take It" Statement

Director **Luis Buñuel** (*Belle de Jour*): "Nothing would disgust me more morally than receiving an Oscar. I wouldn't have it in my home." You got it, *bambino*.

Dustin Hoffman, after being nominated (and losing) for *The Graduate* (1967), muttered, "Thank God I didn't get the Oscar. After I got the nomination I thought, 'OK, it's enough already for this one part.'" Nominated again in 1974 for *Lenny*, Dusty's comment was, "I hope to God I don't get an Oscar. It would really depress me if I did."

Andy Garcia, Best Supporting Actor nominee for his role as the young Turk in *The Godfather, Part III*, vowed that "If I win, I'll turn my Oscar over to [co-star] Al Pacino." (We'll never know, since he didn't.)

"I hope I don't win," said **Shirley MacLaine**, nominated for *Irma La Douce* in 1963, because "I don't think it was my best performance." (She didn't.)

OSCARAMA

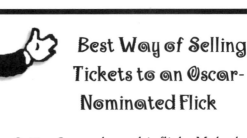

Best Way of Selling Tickets to an Oscar-Nominated Flick

Spike Lee, whose bioflick *Malcolm X* was nominated for Best Picture in 1992, exhorted members of the black community: "Don't go to work that day [the film opens]! Don't let the children go to school! Go to this movie! We have to support this film or Hollywood will have the excuse it wants!" (Apparently so—the movie lost, obviously due to the industry-wide conspiracy against Lee.)

Best Excuse for Not Attending an Oscar Ceremony

Woody Allen, who customarily tootles with his amateur jazz band on Monday nights, said he couldn't possibly attend the 1977 ceremony because "I couldn't let down the guys."

Best Manufactured Excuse for Attending an Oscar Ceremony

Jack Nicholson: "I don't like the idea of going, but I've gone out of a sense of fair play."

Sally Field, 1979: "I think it's exploitative, overcommercialized, frequently offensive, and shouldn't be televised." However, she then lamely added, "Sure I'll be there. If I said I wasn't coming, they'd still go on with the show." DARN TOOTIN'.

Best "More Than We Needed to Know" Pre-Show Confession

Sally Kirkland confessed to a reporter at the 1994 ceremony, "I don't have any underwear on tonight." Luckily, this didn't trigger the journo's gag reflex.

In 1954, Best Supporting Actress nominee **Katy Jurado** was asked about her red gown. "It's a Dior, " Jurado blurted, "and the bra and panties that came with it are flame-colored too!" **Woo-hoo!**

Best Pre-Show Disruption

Sally Kirkland (who else?) wins again. Jon Bon Jovi, nominated for Best Song in 1991, was about to be interviewed by Hollywood scribe Army Archerd when the crass chatterbox broke in for a loopy love-fest: "To all you Sally Kirkland fans out there— I love you!" (YEAH—ALL TWO OF YOU.)

I'm sixty years old.
I know how to deal with it.
I'm not expecting too much.
Enjoying the ride, that's it.
—Richard Harris

He worked the town better than
Reagan ever worked a room.
There wasn't a voter's cheek he
didn't kiss.
—Writer William Goldman,
on Richard Harris

OSCARAMA

The Main Event

"[It] feels kind of **SURREAL**, actually."	**(Bruce Springsteen)**
"This is all so surreal."	**(Christine Lahti)**
"It's very surreal, and then it's very, like, just a bunch of humans."	**(Marisa Tomei)**

Good evening, Hollywood phonies.
—Chevy Chase, 1987 host

Worst Introduction of a Presenter

Randy Thomas, the Academy's first female announcer, described **Jack Nicholson** thusly in 1992: "The man who marches to his own drummer and nominated tonight." Thomas did not, apparently, learn any kind of lesson from this initial faux pas, for in 1994 she introduced Nicholson as "Unique. Original. His nationality is Actor. Jack Nicholson." GET A GRIP, GIRL!

Best Ego Trip by a Non-Nominated Presenter

The *Herald-Examiner* reported in 1977 that "It took some doing to get a leading man whom **Farrah Fawcett**'s advisors considered of great enough stature to serve as her Oscar copresenter. Their first suggestion was **Laurence Olivier**, then **Cary Grant**. And when neither of those gentlemen were willing, Farrah finally settled on sharing the stage with **Marcello Mastroianni**."

Worst Performance by a Celebrity

In 1988, **Rob Lowe** warbled and cavorted onstage with a hideously miscast Snow White. Together they successfully embarrassed both themselves and everyone seated in the auditorium, and everyone watching at home. (Plus, Disney sued the Academy because they hadn't obtained permission to use the character!)

Madonna, with a bad case of nerves at the 1990 ceremony, shook and trembled her way through a va-va-va-vamp rendition of the Oscar-winning ditty "Sooner or Later (I Always Get My Man)" from *Dick Tracy*.

Most Obnoxious Political Manifesto

Vanessa Redgrave, the high-strung left-winger who started the lamentable trend, told 1977's audience to be proud they "have refused to be intimidated by the threats of a small bunch of Zionist hoodlums." What*ever*. (Quipped director **Paddy Chayefsky**: "I would like to say to Miss Redgrave that her winning an Academy Award is not a pivotal moment in history, does not require a proclamation, and a simple 'Thank you' would have sufficed.")

At the 1992 ceremony, **Susan Sarandon** and **Tim Robbins** decried the plight of "two hundred sixty-six Haitians . . . being held in Guantanamo Bay by the United States government. Their crime: testing positive to the HIV virus . . . we would like our governing officials . . . to admit these people into the United States. Thank you." No one was particularly interested in what they had to say, and Sarandon remains bitter about the experience: "Nominate an actress for playing an activist but ban her from being one. Wear a red ribbon but don't talk about what it means." SOUNDS GOOD, SUE.

OSCARAMA

During the same action-packed telecast, **Richard Gere** wondered "if something miraculous and really kind of movielike could happen here, where we could all kind of send love and truth and a kind of sanity to Deng Xiaoping now in Beijing that he will take his troops and take the Chinese army away from Tibet and allow these people to live as free independent people again. Send this thought out! Send this thought!" *YAWN.*

Best Veiled Threat

Paul Hogan, Australian actor/writer whose *"Crocodile" Dundee* was nominated for Best Screenplay in 1986, said, "I realize I'm not exactly the odds-on favorite, but I've traveled thirteen thousand miles to be here for this . . . if they read out someone else's name instead of mine, it's not going to be pretty." (The film lost out to *Hannah and Her Sisters*.)

Most Pertinent Question
Asked by a Heckler

Madonna, watching the 1994 broadcast from a ringside seat at Chasen's, caught producer **Steve Tisch**'s smarmy speech about *Forrest Gump*, which, he asserted, was not "about politics or conservative values—it's about humanity; it's about respect, tolerance, and unconditional love." "What about mediocrity?" cried Madonna.

I'm sweating.
—Jack Nicholson

I'm cold and nervous.
—Catherine Deneuve

Best Disruption of an Oscar Broadcast

In 1973, streaker **Robert Opal** stunned everyone with his historic starkers sprint across the stage. Quick-thinking **David Niven**, onstage at the time, had a ready comeback: "Just think—the only laugh that man will probably ever get is for stripping and showing off his shortcomings."

Most All-Encompassing Acceptance Speech

Robert De Niro, who took home the Best Actor statuette for *Raging Bull* (1980), thanked his parents "for having me, and my grandmothers and grandfathers for having them, and everyone else involved with the film, and anyone that this award means anything to, and the rest of the world. . . ."

Best Non Sequitur in a Winner's Speech

Jack Nicholson, Best Supporting Actor for 1983's *Terms of Endearment*, yelled from the podium, "All you rock people down at the Roxy and up in the Rockies, rock on!"

It's hard to enjoy it without a Valium.
—Dustin Hoffman

I've overdosed on tranquilizers,
so I think I'm all right.
—Emma Thompson

OSCARAMA

Most Repulsive Acceptance Speech

Ernest Thompson got a tad too excited when he won Best Adapted Screenplay for *On Golden Pond* (1981): "If you would all like to see me later," he gibbered, "I would love to suck face with you all." **PASS.**

1987's Best Director, **Bernardo Berto-lucci** (*The Last Emperor*), said that if New York City was the Big Apple, "then tonight Hollywood is the Big Nipple."

Stupidest Winners' Speeches

Dysphasic duo **Quentin Tarantino** and **Roger Avary**, winners of the Best Original Screenplay Oscar for *Pulp Fiction* (what else?), put the "duh" in dumb with their flimsy attempts at hip humor during the 1994 ceremony:

Tarantino: "You know what? I think this is probably the only award I'm gonna win here tonight, so I was trying to think maybe I should just say a whole lot of stuff right here right now. Just try to get it out of my system. That I thought about all year long! Everything building up and everything! And just blow it all! Just tonight! Just say everything! But I'm not. Thanks." **OH, HOW . . . HILARIOUS.**

Avary: "I want to thank my beautiful wife Gretchen, who I love more than anything in the world. And I really have to take a pee right now, so I'm gonna go. Thank you." **MMM . . . UPROARIOUS.** (Later, Avary

defended his lame try at sounding Forrest Gump-esque: "All I can tell you is at the parties after the Oscars all the **Forrest Gump** people were embracing me and telling me how funny it was and all the **Pulp Fiction** people were embracing me and telling me how sardonically funny it was…")

"I can't deny the fact that you like me!" squealed **Sally Field** in 1984. "Right now, you really like me!"

It's great to see what happened to Jughead after the Archie comic books, isn't it?
—John Larroquette, on Quentin Tarantino

Best Indian Corn at an Oscar Ceremony

Sacheen Littlefeather appeared to protest "the treatment of American Indians today by the film industry" and to refuse **Marlon Brando**'s 1972 Best Actor Oscar for *The Godfather*. (The critics' comments? Charlton Heston: "Childish." Jane Fonda: "Wonderful.") It's worth noting that in 1994 Brando asked for the Oscar back, but was turned down.

Dances with dorks: **Kevin Costner**, whose overblown Indian epic *Dances with Wolves* won Best Picture in 1990, babbled, "It's very easy for people to trivialize what we do. They say, 'If it's such a big deal, how come nobody remembers who won the Oscar last year?' But I've got a real flash for you—I will never forget what happened here tonight. My family will never forget. And my Native American brothers and sisters, especially the Lakota and Sioux, across the country will never forget."

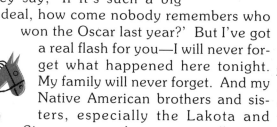

OSCARAMA

Distinguished Achievement
in Tear-Shedding

Must **Tom Hanks** cry *every time* he wins? And oh, that *lingua Hanka*:

"Man! I feel as though I'm standing on magic legs in a special process shot that is too unbelievable to imagine and far too costly to make a reality."

"Believe me, the power and pleasure and the emotion of this moment is a constant speed of light."

"I am standing here because the woman I share my life with has taught me, and demonstrates every day, just what love is."

"Here's what I know: I could not be standing here without that undying love...I have that in a lover that is so close to fine, we should all be able to experience such heaven right here on earth."

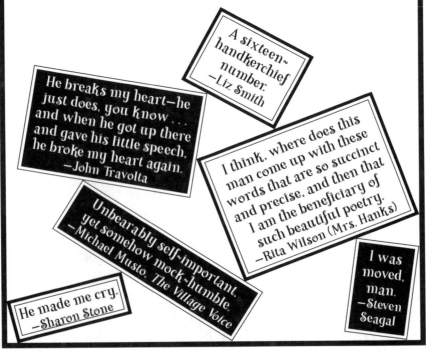

A sixteen-handkerchief number.
—Liz Smith

He breaks my heart—he just does, you know . . . and when he got up there and gave his little speech, he broke my heart again.
—John Travolta

I think, where does this man come up with these words that are so succinct and precise, and then that I am the beneficiary of such beautiful poetry.
—Rita Wilson (Mrs. Hanks)

Unbearably self-important, yet somehow mock-humble.
—Michael Musto, *The Village Voice*

He made me cry.
—Sharon Stone

I was moved, man.
—Steven Seagal

OSCARAMA

Most Interminable Acceptance Speech

When **Jonathan Demme** mounted the stage to accept his Best Director Oscar for *The Silence of the Lambs* (1991), the world was treated to, according to *Entertainment Weekly*, ninety-four utterances of the word "uh" in just three minutes and thirty-five seconds.

Best Reaction to Winning an Honorary Oscar

John Landis on **Alfred Hitchcock**: "I was there with him the day he was told he was going to receive an honorary Oscar. He said, 'Well, John, it looks like I'm going to die.'"

Sir Laurence Olivier, who won a honorary Oscar in 1978, effervesced, "In the great wealth, the great firmament of your nation's generosities, this particular choice may perhaps be found by future genera-tions to be a trifle eccentric, but the mere

fact of it—the prodigal, pure human kindness of it—must be seen as a beautiful star in that firmament which shines upon me at this moment, dazzling me a little but filling me with the warmth of the extraordinary elation, the euphoria that happens to so many of us at the first breath of the majestic glow of a new tomorrow." LIKE WOW, MAN.

I don't expect it, I don't anticipate it,
and I don't find it healthy even
to consider it or talk about it.
—Julia Roberts

Most Faux-Humble Winner's Speech

Tom Hanks, 1994: "I'm standing here in lieu of my fellow nominees, who are just as deserving—if not more so—of this moment."

Tommy Lee Jones, 1993: "I'm lucky enough to be working." I'LL SAY.

When Lou Gossett won, my mother punched the set.
—John Lithgow

I was jumping up and down so hard I broke my friend's chair. I swear to you! Then I started to cry.
—Michael Lerner

How they could not give it to me was a bit of stupidity.
—Kirk Douglas

I don't know what I said. Was I all right?
—Shirley MacLaine

I had no idea what I was saying, but I didn't want to stop.
—Laurence Olivier

[Winning an Oscar is] like chasing a beautiful woman for eighty years. Finally she relents and you say, "I'm terribly sorry—I'm tired."
—Paul Newman

The Oscars made my pits wet.
—Kevin Costner

OSCARAMA

The Finale

It's unbelievable to me, but I might really be a great actress.	(Cher)
If you think you're a great actor 'cause you've won an Oscar, you're crazy.	(Joe Pesci)

Best Self-Administered Pat on the Back by a Winner

Sylvester Stallone, who created and starred in 1976's Best Picture, *Rocky*, said the movie would be "remembered, I think, much more than any other film, ten to fifteen years from now." Of course, that was before he made *Rhinestone*.

Best Show of Greed by a Winner

Marvin Hamlisch won a 1973 Oscar for his musical contributions to *The Way We Were* and said to a reporter, "Now I want a Tony and an Emmy and a Grammy, and I won't be satisfied until I get them."

I don't even
have a mantel
to put this on.
I'll have to buy
a new home.
—Brenda Fricker

Best Excuse for Not Winning

Steven Spielberg, shut out in 1975, whined, "The same people who raved about *Jaws* began to doubt its artistic merit as soon as it began to bring in so much money."

By 1982, he'd started to take it personally. When his *E.T.: The Extra-Terrestrial* was spurned by Academy voters, he groused, "We were almost precluded from any awards because people feel we've already been amply rewarded." Hey Steve: maybe it *just wasn't the best movie*, okay?

Diana Scarwid, Best Supporting Actress nominee in 1980 for *Inside Moves*, was positive she didn't emerge victorious because she "didn't have a studio behind me."

Most Suspect Reaction to Losing

Meryl Streep expressed great relief at not winning for her performance in *The Deer Hunter* (1978). "My dress had sweat-marks under the arms," she confided to a reporter, "and I was glad I didn't have to get up to get the Oscar."

Nominated as Best Actor for his role in *Midnight Cowboy* (1969), **Jon Voight** said, "I didn't want it because I didn't really want the responsibility that year."

Lynn Redgrave, nominated for her star turn as *Georgy Girl* in 1966, expressed a strangely similar sentiment: "It really was a relief to hear them call Liz Taylor's name. At my age, while it was an honor to be nominated, the burden of winning would have been too much."

OSCARAMA

Most Ignominious Post-Victory Incident

Polish director **Zbigniew Rybcyznski**, who won Best Animated Short Subject in 1982, wandered outside for a smoke and was refused readmittance by an overzealous security guard. Frustrated, Rybcyznski kicked the man and was hauled off to the pokey.

Most Casual Treatment of an Oscar

 Meryl Streep inadvertently left her statuette in the ladies' room after winning Best Supporting Actress for *Kramer Vs. Kramer* (1978).

"I keep my Oscars right next to the bathtub so I can take a bath and look at them," says **Jodie Foster**. "What else are you going to do with them?"

It was horrible. Everybody was so embarrassed for me that nobody wanted to talk to me. They should have an anteroom for the losers.
—Sigourney Weaver

The losers make all the money.
—Jack Nicholson

Oscar Talk

The first thing I'll do to celebrate is to
take off these damn shoes.
—Whoopi Goldberg

It's a mistake to think I've been waiting for this
all my life. I've been working, not waiting.
—Olympia Dukakis

Now that I've lost, I'm going to be a rebel again.
—James Woods

[Losing] never gets easier.
—Director David Lean

I figure I made history. I'm the only nominee
who's lost twice in one night.
—Sigourney Weaver (nominated in 1988 for both
Best Actress [*Gorillas in the Mist*] and Best Supporting
Actress [*Working Girl*])

I still ride the subway and
no one recognizes me.
—F. Murray Abraham

All I got was free champagne at restaurants for
two weeks, and then that stopped.
—Dianne Wiest

I wouldn't say I didn't like it,
but it was a little long.
—Akira Kurosawa

OSCARAMA

2 A Star's Little Instruction Book

Appendix

Step One: AN ACTOR PREPARES

Attempt suicide in your teens to establish an early reputation for sensitivity.

Star in your high-school plays and believe everything your friends and family say about your performances. It's ego stroking; get used to it.

Make the decision to move to Hollywood after realizing how much better you are than everyone else in your hometown. Because you are sensitive, you've never been able to hold down a steady job, so get a loan from your parents.

Two days after arriving in Hollywood, move to another part of the city after you realize your neighbors consist mainly of addicts, winos and jumbo-size cockroaches.

Change your name. If you like your name, get creative with the spellling (i.e., SouZii).

Men: Use your college trust fund money on a good set of Rollerblades and memberships at movie-star gyms. Women: Use your college trust fund money to get breast implants and a nose job.

Emulate whoever's hot.

Learn to call movies "films."

Take Method classes and work as a waitron in an Industry hangout.

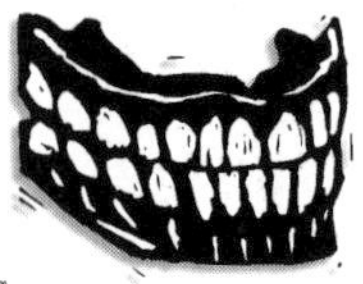

Get your teeth fixed.

Don't worry about paying your parents back. Any excess cash should be funneled into the appropriate areas: hair and makeup, clothing, head shots, tanning salons.

When you're not in acting class, beat the streets to find an agent. Plead, cry, scream, grovel—you are an actor, after all.

Wherever you are and whatever you may be doing, keep in mind that nothing impresses people as much as name-dropping.

Remember: Even the line "Yes, doctor" can be imbued with emotion.

Do a porno movie to gain valuable acting experience.

Pose nude for rent money.

Sleep with anyone, regardless of gender, who's in a position to help your career.

Skills to hone:

Air-kissing
Schmoozing
Sucking up
Critiquing the
performances of
established actors
Your
autograph

Lines to learn:

On acting: "I must practice
my craft."
On your body: "I must use
my instrument to practice
my craft."
On inspiration: "I must
nurture my little bird of
creativity."

Step Two: RISE AND SHINE

Drop all your bumpkin friends and have that inconvenient marriage to your high school sweetheart annulled.

Carry around an important work of classic literature (*War and Peace* or anything by Shakespeare will do nicely). You don't actually have to read it. If you must pretend you're reading, don't hold the book upside down.

Invited or not, show up at any party where there are likely to be good photo ops. Grinning widely, pose next to bigger stars than yourself.

Continue sleeping with producers, but only if they can land you a really good part.

Women: Overpluck your eyebrows and stop washing your hair. Men: Grow a goatee and stop washing.

Shop at thrift stores.

Start building up your entourage. If necessary, use family members. Teach them to fawn.

Date other celebs more famous than you. Tattoo yourself with their names. Don't get married. If you need cash, leak scandalous tidbits about them to the *Enquirer*.

Begin acting angry all the time.

Chain-smoke.

Get family members hired as production assistants on your films.

Men: Cultivate a "bad boy" image and date only models or strippers. Women: Have sex with Warren Beatty.

Get arrested for attempting to take a loaded pistol onto an airplane.

If you're playing the part of an addict, you can increase the realism of your performance by using real booze and drugs. Later, you can blame your *real* addiction on your dedication to your craft.

Make self-deprecating remarks to interviewers. Say you feel fortunate to be working in a town where most actors are unemployed.

Ugly-duckling roles require just a teensy bit less makeup than usual.

If you're ridiculed for having a bad accent in one of your roles, you can always blame your dialogue coach.

To add some spice to your life, try hanging out with gangsters once in a while.

Talk about your good friends "Bobby" De Niro, "Jimmy" Caan, "Sly" Stallone, and "Sandy" Bullock.

Say you never really wanted to be a celebrity, you just want the opportunity to practice your craft. Claim you'd act for free because it's so rewarding.

Take pride in your reputation as a hard-partying hellraiser.

Ignore critics' comments (except the very worst of them, which you secretly obsess over and which spawn your addiction to sleeping pills).

TV stars: Start thinking about moving from the small screen to the big screen. Movie stars: Start thinking about directing.

If you put on a few pounds, say you're gaining weight for an upcoming role.

Hit the talk-show circuit. Shamelessly flatter the hosts.

Begin attending A-list orgies.

Women: Pose for *Playboy.* Deny you've had breast implant surgery.

Remember: The *Entertainment Tonight* gang are your best friends—for now.

Save the rain forests and the whales, feed the homeless, build shacks in Third World countries, lobby for AIDS, and vote Democrat.

Jettison your few remaining scruples.

Skills to hone:

Crying on cue (not for your roles, silly;
for your first Barbara Walters interview)
Cellular phone etiquette
Getting in and out of limousines gracefully
Table-hopping

Lines to learn:

"(Current co-star) is one of the most brilliant people I've ever worked with."
"(Prior co-star) really has some unresolved issues. It's sad."
"I don't consider myself a star. I'm just a character actor."

Step Three: STAR POWER

Move to Malibu, Bel-Air, or Brentwood.

Never show up on time.

Pay off your ex-lover who's threatening to sell those kinky nude photos to the tabloids.

Insist on unshared over-the-title credit. You should also insist on being credited—and paid—as a producer (after all, the movie wouldn't get made without you).

And insist on having your own personal chef on-set. Eat when you want. You're the star—they'll wait.

Ignore your directors. What your acting coach says, goes.

Hire and fire personal assistants at least once a month.

You don't audition. Rehearsals are for losers.

Do a bad sequel (for a lot of dough) to your first surprise-hit movie.

Develop an ulcer.

Form a production company.

If you gain a few pounds, develop agoraphobia.

Whenever you do an interview, insist on being the cover story.

Complain about being misquoted.

Begin referring to the press as "a pack of bloodsucking vampires." Join George Clooney's boycott of the media.

If you're playing a historical figure, you need insight. Have a medium channel their spirit.

Moan about the amount of money you're forced to spend on lawyers, accountants, managers, agents, and security personnel.

Carry a tiny inbred dog with a foreign name wherever you go. (Note: If you're old, the dog must also be fat.) Hire an on-staff vet.

Decline the first table you're given in restaurants and the first room you're shown in hotels.

You don't do commercials. (Except in Japan, where it doesn't count.)

Have a nervous breakdown on a film set.

Go into therapy. Recover your repressed memories.

Wear outlandishly elaborate "disguises" so people will know someone really important is in their midst.

Fire any employee you catch reading a tabloid story about you.

Adopt a world-weary, jaded attitude.

Wear sunglasses to all your interviews (even radio).

Wear nonprescription glasses to give yourself that certain collegiate cachet.

Accept any honorary degree that's thrown your way, especially since you never finished high school.

Complain that you're hounded by the press wherever you go, and hit those who attempt to photograph you.

Remember: A little more plastic surgery never hurt anyone. Plus, it's a business expense.

Deny those persistent rumors that you're gay or that you used to be one of Heidi's gals.

Begin developing a spiritual side by dabbling in trendy religions. It's okay to interrupt filming for chats with your guru.

Give autographed photos of yourself to everyone on your Christmas list.

Take up a "serious" hobby, like painting. Since the finished works aren't good enough to be sold as anything other than celebrity curiosa, donate them to high-visibility charity auctions.

Get an injunction to halt distribution of that early film in which you appeared fully nude in embarrassing simulated sex scenes.

Begin optioning projects and directing "little" films; broaden your *oeuvre* by taking nonglamorous parts in "serious" (i.e., boring) films.

Complain bitterly about the ineptitude of your directors and producers; throw fits, get sick, or walk off the set. Repeat as needed until you get your way.

Join whatever cause your fifty closest celebrity friends are involved with, and give impassioned speeches on the subject to anyone who interviews you.

Take a much-needed vacation on a remote isle. Force the natives to wait on you hand and foot. Out of consideration for the photographers lurking offshore in speedboats, wait until mid-afternoon to begin your nude yoga exercises on the beach.

Attempt to have your tattoos removed.

Direct an episode of series TV.

Adopt a mixed-race baby and give it a snooty name.

Insist on script approval. Make them take out the hard words. Rewrite your dialogue.

Also insist on co-star approval. Make the director fire anyone who's better than you.

Cut a bad pop album. Write bad poetry. Sell a bad novel.

Buy an expensive four-wheel-drive vehicle to show how unpretentiously down-to-earth you are.

Believe your own hype.

Sue any journalist whose interview isn't a puff piece.

Begin referring to yourself in the third person.

Claim you do your own stunts. Pay crew members to tell journalists how brave you are.

Travel with a decent-size entourage: hair and makeup people, a dresser or two, a few personal assistant/lackeys, bodyguards, an acupuncturist, herbalist, nutritionist, masseuse, dermatologist, personal shopper, voice coach, photographer, doctor, chauffeur, publicist, and manager. Optional: nannies (one or two per child); personal astrologer or psychic. Make them all sign confidentiality agreements.

Fire all the money-grubbing family members on your pay roll, then reveal the terrible truth about your horrible childhood years.

Move to Montana. Buy up all the real estate surrounding your spread. Tell journalists how peaceful, how un-Hollywood, it is there. Convince your celebrity friends to move there too.

Break up with your longtime flame via overnight delivery.

Give the ax to the agents and managers who've stuck with you so far.

Turn Republican. You have assets to protect now.

Skills to hone:

Sulking
Hotel-room trashing
Tantrum-throwing
Humble-yet-
inspirational Oscar
acceptance speech

Lines to learn:

"What I'd really like to do is direct."
"This is the best work I've ever done."
"I never read reviews."
"Awards mean nothing to me."

Step Four: LIVING IN OBLIVION

Claim your continued unemployment is due to the fact that you just haven't gotten the right script yet.

Begin dating any of your exes whose career is currently hotter than yours.

Refuse all interviews, particularly if they're of the "Where are they now?" variety.

Claim to be a victim of financial misfeasance and sue your former agents and managers (yes, the ones who dropped you because you weren't making any money).

Blow the remnants of your fortune on drugs and alcohol. Get arrested for drunk driving or narcotics possession.

Call in your last remaining Industry favors to get out of jail. Immediately enter rehab and join AA; tearfully promise you've learned your lesson and will never do it again. (Repeat as necessary.)

Call reporters and let them know where you'll be performing your community service. Dress up!

Sell your story to *People* magazine.

Marry another newly-clean-and-sober celeb, preferably one who's younger, more attractive, and less talented than you. Have a baby. Sell your story to *Hello!* magazine.

Straight-to-video "erotic thrillers" and infomercials are a good way to remain in the public eye and make your rent.

Begin chasing paparazzi.

Ask your actor-children to get you parts in their movies. Show up, beaming with pride, at any function they attend.

Do a workout video and become a celebrity spokesmodel for infomercials.

Take a small part in a Quentin Tarantino film.

Run for public office.

Skills to hone:

Sincerity
Humility
Contrition

Lines to learn:

"Acting in CD~ROM games is an exciting new challenge for me."
"Hollywood isn't reality. I *like* living in the Valley. It's so much less stressful."
"My family is my first priority now."

THE

END

(almost)

Sindex

The Sinners

A

M

Sindex

Winters, Jonathan: 150
Winters, Shelley: 38, 248
Wood, Elijah: 100
Wood, Natalie: 4, 45, 182, 249, 270
Woods, James: 50, 64, 86, 115, 180, 199, 212, 237, 268, 291
Woodward, Edward: 95
Woodward, Joanne: 78, 249
Wray, Fay: 4
Wright, Robin: 182
Wyman, Bill: 199
Wyman, Jane: 168
Wynette, Tammy: 260

Y

Yanni: 187
Yoakam, Dwight: 103, 215
Yoba, Malik: 81
York, Michael: 152
York, Susannah: 153
Yothers, Tina: 35
Young, Gig: 269
Young, Loretta: 86, 87, 180
Young, Robert: 248, 260
Young, Sean: 71, 86, 133, 165, 170, 180, 221, 268

Z

Zadora, Pia: 22, 45, 143
Zanuck, Daryl: 197
Zappa, Dweezil: 187
Zappa, Frank: 103
Zeffirelli, Franco: 206
Zeman, Jackie: 31
Zimbalist, Stephanie: 268
Zimmerman, Don: 83
Zucker, Jerry: 82
Zuniga, Daphne: 49, 182

The Sins

Bad behavior: 79-83, 219-229
Bad judgment: 76-78, 88-89, 94, 102-103
Bad music: 61, 94-95, 97, 101, 103, 223, 279

Bad writing: 98, 119, 121, 126-127, 240 (and 2 through 322)
Coattail-riding: 10-11
Excessive plastic surgery: 4, 27-35
Exhibitionism: 28, 41-43, 97, 99, 118, 133, 195, 209, 277
False humility: 113, 114, 275, 287
Goofy superstitions and spirituality: 149-164
Hubris: 27, 36, 63-64, 84, 97-99, 107-113, 115, 117, 140, 142-143, 186, 240, 274, 281, 288
Lame remarks: 70, 105, 151-152, 155, 158, 197, 247, 273, 276, 279-282, 286
Lousy taste in lovers: 98, 184, 186-189, 239-242, 244-245
Mendacity: 22, 184, 202-206, 210, 225, 259, 277, 289
Mental instability: 128-130, 222, 247-252, 276, 286

Money and greed: 5, 55-62, 99, 141, 171-174, 177,l 239-245
Money-grubbing: 3, 214, 216
Really gross depravity: 192, 194
Schlocky merchandise: 90-92
Silly vendettas: 99, 123-125

Sticky fingers: 233
Stupid quirks: 175-177, 249
Stupidity: 17-18, 134-141, 149
Substance abuse and/or drug burnout: 11, 219-229, 231-233, 235, 237-238, 247-248, 253-260
Tantrum-throwing: 79-81, 83, 89, 221, 224
Treacly sentimentality: 62, 146-147, 280, 284
Trend-following: 38, 46-49
Val-speak: 67, 254
Whining: 6, 14-15, 56, 85, 87, 111, 116, 119-120, 213-214, 244, 275, 289

Gratuitous Heather Locklear shot

Also by Coral Amende

Legends in Their Own Time

If You Don't Have Anything Nice to Say . . .
Come Sit Next to Me

How far will the casting couch
take you in Hollywood?

Who's on~set love scenes continued
well after the cameras stopped rolling?

What shameful secrets lurk
behind celebrities' bedroom doors?

Which stars have been
dragged out of the closet?

Just how much money *does* it
take to keep a star happy?

Whose temper tantrums are the
stuff of Hollywood legend?

Now, Tinseltown's deepest, darkest secrets are revealed in

HOLLYWOOD
CONFIDENTIAL

It's not confidential anymore!

CORAL AMENDE is the composer/editor of the gossip-studded crossword puzzle in *Los Angeles* magazine and the author of two celebrity-related books. She leads a superficial and shallow life in L.A.